Is there life after Coffee?

EARLIER BOOKS IN THE QUINTET

I only came for the coffee
My coffee cup is empty
Bitter are the coffee grounds
The Cappuccino years

These are available through Somerset Libraries
Or from Elizabeth (01460 53364)

Is there life after Coffee?

Elizabeth Beattie

T

Troubador Publishing Ltd
Unit E2 Airfield Business Park,
Harrison Road, Market Harborough,
Leicestershire LE16 7UL
Tel: 0116 279 2299
Email: books@troubador.co.uk
Web: www.troubador.co.uk

ISBN 978 1 80514 139 6

Cover illustrations by Chris Loughran

British Library Cataloguing in Publication Data.
A catalogue record for this book is available from the British Library.

Printed and bound in Great Britain by 4edge Limited
Typeset in 11.5pt Garamond Pro by Troubador Publishing Ltd, Leicester, UK

One

Is there life after Coffee?

I have picked this sprig of heather.
The autumn is dead
Remember,
We will not meet again on this earth.
The smell of the weather,
This sprig of heather…
And I wait for you
Remember.

As Antonia read the familiar words from L'Adieu by Guillame Apollinaire, her tears splashed onto the page. Grief overwhelmed her. She would never see James again, never be held in his arms. The one man who had ever truly loved her was gone… and perhaps it was her fault…if she had agreed to marry him, perhaps the heart attack might not have happened…but she had not known…had not understood how much he loved her. There had been too many men who had used her. She had not known what it was to be loved. Children need to be loved, hope to be loved, grow up emotionally stunted if they are not loved.

"Why did you even have me?" she had once asked her mother, who shrugged and said vaguely:

"It was the thing to do."

"You didn't really want me."

"Not particularly."

That had been the end of the conversation. Antonia knew in some indefinable way that she was not entitled to love. She did not look for love in her relationships and did not expect to be loved…

So she had not recognized love when belatedly it came her way. And now it was too late.

She had sat dry-eyed through the funeral service, detached, as though it was a stranger they were mourning. Jake pointedly ignored her, surrounded as he was by the extended family. Only Michael spoke toher …briefly… in passing. She did not attend the lavish refreshments afterwards.

In the weeks that followed she shut herself away and concentrated feverishly on her translation work. Sleep deserted her. She could not eat. The phone rang unanswered. Mail lay unopened on the floor.

"I cannot bear to live, I dare not die." She swallowed her coffee black, unable to face going out to the shop for milk. Always fastidious, she no longer showered or changed her clothes.

"Don't think!" she admonished herself, "Just work. Shut everything else out."

But Apollinaire's poem undid her resolve: the heather ...the soft, springy heather crushed underfoot...and James reaching for her hand, happy, laughing, carefree. Days spent tramping the moors in the fresh damp air... Never again. Never, never again! Antonia collapsed onto her unmade bed and sobbed herself into exhaustion. She slept. She dreamed. She dreamed that James was holding her.

As she stirred into wakefulness in the half light of early morning, the sensation of being held was still with her. She turned onto her back, unwilling to let the dream go. The pillow beside her was dented as if someone had lain beside her. Almost she thought she could catch a faint tang of James's aftershave.

"Coffee?" enquired a familiar voice. "Only you'll have to drink it black! You seem to be out of milk. Well, pretty much out of everything as far as I can see!"

"Don't wake up!" Antonia whispered to herself. "Don't spoil this dream! I don't want this dream to end...ever."

"Antoni-ni, time to wake up. I'm putting your coffee on the bedside table."

Cautiously Antonia opened one eye. Clearly she was still dreaming: James stood there beside her bed, placing a coffee mug within her reach. He smiled down at her.

"And you need a bath, my girl!" Hesitantly Antonia reached out a hand towards him, felt it grasped and held. His hand was warm, strong, familiar. Tears ran down her face: grief mingled with disbelief. James sat down on the bed and gathered her into his arms, rocking her while she wept uncontrollably, sobbing his name over and over again. He waited until her sobs had subsided and handed her the rapidly cooling coffee.

"Are you real?"

"Yes, quite real!" He leaned forward and kissed her wet face.

"I don't understand!"

"You don't need to understand."

"But how…?"

"Never mind the *how*! Isn't it enough that I'm here?"

"Oh James! James! I don't believe it! You seem so real!"

"I am real, darling!" He caressed her face. "You've got so thin! Have you stopped eating altogether? My Antoni-ni, you'll have to put on some weight if we're to go tramping the Yorkshire moors again."

"Please stay! Please stay for ever and always!" She searched his face, hungry for his every expression. And then a thought struck her. "Does Jake know you're back?"

"Jake has moved on. He's part of Tom's family now. I am no longer part of his life."

"But…?"

"I'm here for you, my Antoni-ni, because you wanted me so badly, and are so, so lost…" He reached out and took the empty mug from her.

"James, other people lose the person they love most in all the world…but *they* don't get them back…?"

"I have my grandmother's witch-genes. I can move between two worlds. Now, no more talking! I'm going to take you home."

"But isn't it Jake's house now, under the terms of your will?"

"Not *that* house. My grandparents' cottage. We'll feed you up and get your health and strength back."

"We?"

"You"ll get to meet Granny."

"I think I'm still dreaming!"

"I'm turning on the shower, and while you're freshening up, I'll change these sheets and…"

"Is that a polite way of saying I stink to high heaven?"

"That sounds more like the Antonia I know! Come on, up you get!"

She stood under the shower letting the water cascade over her – never had a shower felt so good, so refreshing. She massaged shampoo into her scalp and watched the soiled water pooling at her feet. At last, she emerged, a towelling gown tied firmly at her waist, rubbing her hair dry. James came and stood behind her, vigorously towelling her hair…and then he turned her around, unfastened the knot she'd tied and let her gown fall open.

* * *

Antonia awoke in a strange bedroom. Daylight seeped in through partly drawn curtains. The pillow beside her was hollowed and carried a suggestion of James's aftershave. She sat up and looked about her. A cotton dressing gown was draped across an ottoman that stood at the foot of the bed, but there was no obvious sign of her clothes… and she was naked! Throwing aside the bedclothes she picked up the dressing gown. It had an art deco design. She wondered briefly whose it was. Was this what it felt like to be kidnapped and held a prisoner – but the pillow reassured her that James must have brought her here.

She ventured out onto a landing: to her left was a child's bedroom. She was relieved to find the bathroom further along to her right on the other side of the landing. Antonia stood at the head of the stairs, uncertain whether to venture down. Below, lay a large friendly kitchen. Hesitantly, she made her way down. An old woman stood at the range stirring something in a saucepan. Antonia watched her from the bottom stair.

"Are you James's Granny?"

"I might be," returned the Witch without turning round.

"I'm Antonia."

"Yes," said the Witch tersely. "I know exactly who you are."

"What time is it? My watch seems to have stopped."

"Watches do that."

Antonia waited.

"Is James about?"

The kitchen door that led out into the courtyard creaked open and James appeared. He smiled at her.

"Good morning, Antoni-ni. Did you sleep well?" He picked up a mug of coffee from the kitchen table.

"That's Antonia's coffee!" snapped the Witch, pouring the contents of her pan into a china bowl. "Come and eat your porrage," she addressed Antonia.

"I don't…" began Antonia.

"Highly nutritious. Flavoured with seaweed. Put some flesh on your bones."

"It is rather nice, actually," James encouraged her. "Try a spoonful."

Obediently, Antonia, who never ate porrage, sat down, tasted a reluctant spoonful and found it surprisingly appetising. The seaweed gave it a salty taste, enhancing a nutty flavour. James watched her over the mug of coffee he had appropriated.

"I didn't see my clothes?" Antonia looked questioningly at him.

"We'll sort you out as soon as you've finished breakfast. Would you like a coffee seeing as I've purloined yours?"

The Witch banged another mug down on the table so hard that coffee splashed over.

"I'm so sorry!" apologised Antonia, thinking it was somehow her fault.

"You'll need to find her some shoes," remarked the Witch sourly. "The floor's cold."

"But your porrage was really nice! And I enjoyed it."

"Well, there's a thing!" observed the Witch, secretly pleased.

"I don't remember coming here," Antonia mentioned as she followed James upstairs in search of some clothes. "And my watch has stopped."

"It's the effect of coming through the pentagram. You were far too tired to drive here – it's a long way. It was simpler to bring you with me. We can go back the same way later and bring whatever you need. But first we have to find you some clothes." So saying, he turned her around and gathered her into his arms. "You look very beautiful, my Antoni-ni. Your dressing gown is very chic!"

"It was just there…on the ottoman… waiting for me." Slowly James unfastened the gown…the lack of clothes was no longer important.

***

Much later, wearing unfamiliar clothes which nevertheless fitted her perfectly, Antonia followed James downstairs to the kitchen which was now bathed in sunshine. Of the Witch there was no sign.

"Coffee?" enquired the Range, welcoming them.

"That would be nice."

Antonia stared at him:

"Do you *talk* to your kitchen appliances?"

"I'd have expected you to be more surprised that they talk to us."

"Well, that too."

"You'll get used to it."

"I'm not sure I want to get used to it!"

"Coffee's up!" announced the Range. "Sugar's on the table. Help yourself to a biscuit, if there's any."

"I don't believe it!"

"The coffee's real enough. For the moment, just accept that things are different. Don't try and fight it or question too much." He touched a gentle hand to her cheek. "Is that too much to ask?"

Antonia sighed. The world seemed to have slipped askew…but James was here.

"Are there any biscuits?" she enquired.

James picked up a battered biscuit tin which had not been there a moment ago. He shook it gently. It sounded remarkably empty.

"What sort of biscuit would you like?"

"How about those malted biscuits with an elephant on them?"

She had not expected anything so precise and was almost discomforted when James offered her exactly what she'd requested.

"You were going to show me round," she mentioned, when they'd drunk their coffee.

"Yes, of course."

James led her through the kitchen into a room which had clearly been unused for many years. Dust lay thickly on every surface. In the hearth a dead bird lay in the ashes of a long-ago fire. A substantial desk stood in the bay window whose glass was so grimy the outdoor light barely filtered through. A sofa and a deep armchair sat in front of the fire.

"A room fit for Miss Haversham!" murmured Antonia. James smiled. He moved across to the desk and picked up a pile of papers, disturbing a large black spider and cascading dust over himself.

"It just needs a good spring clean! This was my grandfather's study. Some of these papers would be fifty years old…"

"Do the windows actually open?"

James leaned over the desk and attempted to unfasten the window catch. Clouds of dust arose. The window catch remained resolutely closed. James turned back to Antonia, covered in dust and coughing.

"Not today!" he said when he'd recovered. "We'd have to move the desk. I don't suppose it's been moved since Grandad came to live here …before I was born."

"Oh, ancient history then!"

James grinned at this spark of the old Antonia.

"I lived here when the boys were small, before we went to live with Caroo – Phil, to you. It was a really cosy room once upon a time – and can be again. We could start on it tomorrow, if you're up for it?"

"Do I have a choice?"

James looked at her, seeming to see into her very soul.

"There is always a choice," he said softly, and led the way out of the room into a narrow hall whose front door had stood immovably shut for many years. To the left an open door gave onto a small lounge devoid of furniture.

"The boys used to watch television in here when they were little."

"So only a matter of twenty-five years ago?" There was a note of asperity in her voice which James ignored.

"It might make a decent study for you if we emptied the desk and moved it across," he suggested.

"You mean, throw away all your Grandad's ancient papers!"

James grinned. She was sounding more like herself. He turned and appeared to walk *through* the back wall. Antonia stared after him. He was not there. Gone. Really gone!

"James!" Scared, she rushed at the wall, desperately

trying to find some handle or secret panel to push. "James!" Frightened now, her voice rising in panic.

An unseen door opened. James stood there, reaching out a hand to her.

"You scared me!"

He gathered her against him and held her "This is my studio," he said, indicating the room behind him. "It's where I paint. We'll block the door open when I'm in here so you can always find me."

Releasing her, he drew her into the spacious, airy studio. Two easels stood side by side with half completed, complementary scenes of a bay, viewed from the east and from the west.

As Antonia studied them, it seemed to her that she could faintly hear the waves washing onto the beach… and glimpse the movement of the sea as it susurrated over the shingle. Sunlight danced on the crest of each wave… as if the paintings had come to life.

"I love this bay," James murmured. "I'll take you there and we can dance barefoot on the sea shore."

"By the light of the silvery moon?"

"If you want. But I usually dance by daylight." There was about him a glimpse of the carefree happiness she had seen in him on their holiday tramping the Yorkshire moors. She wanted to ask if it would always be like this – the love, the sense of freedom? Was it a dream? Would she wake up and find it was all…fantasy? Or had she stepped into another sphere of living…was the cost simply a willing suspension of belief?

There were many canvasses stacked against the wall.

One by one he showed her his landscapes. They took her breath away.

"You could have been a professional artist!"

"Grandad painted. He sold his paintings through a London Gallery. They were kind enough to take some of mine too."

"If you wanted to sell some of these…?"

"If the Gallery is still there, yes. It would pay the bills. Not that there's many bills: from outside the cottage appears derelict."

"You mean you're using utilities illegally?"

"We don't exist in their world." He smiled at her. "It will take a bit of getting used to."

"Just a bit!" Antonia echoed.

***

Through another door that wasn't there, and back into the kitchen where the Witch was serving lunch. At the far end of the kitchen table sat old Dr Mikilari patiently waiting to be served. The Witch set down a bowl of brown soup in front of him.

"Brown soup?" he said plaintively. "It was brown soup yesterday."

"And there's hungry people who would be grateful for a bowl of brown soup, old man!" retorted the Witch sharply.

Dr Milkilari sighed and began spooning his soup in a martyred fashion.

"Highland broth." The Witch set a bowl before Antonia as she took her place.

It tasted of venison, warming but slightly pungent. James offered her a wooden platter with chunks of grey bread. The soup and bread tasted surprisingly good, once you had got past the pungent flavour. Dr Mikilari set down his spoon and wrinkled his nose. He did not care for venison. For a moment he thought about emptying his bowl over the Witch's head…but thought better of it.

"I'll deal with you later!" The Witch's look was calculating. She was well able to read his mind. "Another bowlful?" she asked Antonia who was surprised to find she had finished her soup.

***

"What would you like to do this afternoon, Antoni-ni?" Antonia considered. She carefully wiped a piece of bread round her bowl, mopping up the last traces of soup.

"We could make a start on clearing the desk, or…you could take me to see the bay you painted so beautifully?"

"Let's leave the spring-cleaning till tomorrow and enjoy today!"

"Only my car's still in the garage at home."

"We don't need a car."

"Oh? Is it in walking distance then?"

"In a manner of speaking." James gave her an enigmatic smile. He stood up, offering her his hand and led her back into his studio where they stood contemplating his painting.

Antonia glanced around her. The studio had melted away. She could feel the sea breeze on her face, her hair lifting in the off-shore wind. All around her was space, distance, shingle and sand stretching away …and the waves plashing gently on the shore line. Behind them weathered cliffs rose, rocky and silent. Gorse clung where it could gain a foothold. Antonia lifted her face to the sun. She could hear faint music. Beside her, James kicked off his shoes. She watched his bare feet leaving imprints in the damp sand, the waves inviting him in, teasing him.

"Isn't the water cold?" she called.

He stopped, turned his head and then held out his hand. She kicked off her own shoes and ran down to him. Together they stood at the water's edge as the little waves splashed over their bare feet. Antonia shrieked. James laughed and caught her hand in his. The water was icy cold, but exhilarating. The waves retreated, and then chased them. They walked hand in hand along the shore, their feet sinking in the wet sand.

"I love this place," James said. He was happy, at peace with himself.

"It's just as you painted it!"

They strolled along the deserted beach, enjoying the warmth of the sun on their faces. James stooped and picked up a small flat pebble shaped like a heart. After examining it for a moment he turned to her.

"Antoni-ni, may I offer you my heart?"

She shook her head, overcome, unable to respond. And then, as she took the pebble from him, a tear slid down her cheek and plopped onto the pebble's smooth surface.

"Are you asking me to marry you?" she whispered,

remembering how she had turned him down so firmly when he had proposed that last day of their holiday on the Yorkshire moors.

"Officially, I no longer exist." A shadow crossed his face. It was the same for Grandad. He would have loved to marry Granny, but no one could prove she actually existed."

"She seems pretty real to me!"

"Oh, she's a redoubtable old lady. She was there all the years of my childhood. And she made Grandad very happy… he adores her!"

"One could be forgiven for thinking the adoration is one sided!"

"Granny doesn't wear her heart on her sleeve."

"Not like you, then!"

James laughed and caught her to him. She lifted her face to his, burrowing her hands under his fisherman's jersey. She wanted to tell him that she loved him, but the words wouldn't come…had never come. They stood for a long time in an embrace from which neither was willing to break away.

A seagull swooped down from the cliff behind them, narrowly missing them.

"Bit close for comfort!"

James frowned at the lone bird as it flew out to sea, emitting its plaintive cry. They walked on.

"I can imagine you with a dog," Antonia remarked. "A dog would love racing over the beach and charging into the waves!"

"There was a dog. Tom desperately wanted a dog.

I remember he wanted to clean Dad's car for extra pocket money – saving up for a dog. Our other Grandad – Gramps – bought one for Tom and the twins, They called him Puddles. I don't think he was house-trained! The twins went to live with Gramps and GiGi after Mum…well, after Mum died. She never got over losing Baby Margot."

"Yes, you told me. It must have been devastating for your Dad."

James sighed. It had been devastating for them all. After a short silence he said:

"But he's very happy now with Debs. He met her on a cruise. He'd planned a cruise for when he retired – after the twins were finally off his hands. And he came back with Debs in tow. She has a heart of gold."

"Whereas I have a heart of stone?"

"I didn't say that!"

"I thought that was why you presented me with this!"…Antonia took the pebble from her pocket.

"That wasn't what I meant at all!" And then he saw that she was teasing him. She danced away from him, her face alight with mischief. He chased her, sensing that she wanted to be caught, and wrestled her down onto the sandy beach…

***

The kitchen was warm and welcoming, its light casting a friendly glow as they arrived back, shedding sand on the newly washed floor.

"You were gone a long time. It's quite dark outside!" remarked Dr Mikilari from his seat at the kitchen table.

"We went to the beach – the one James painted. It was lovely!"

"Roast pheasant," stated the Witch. "Found him in the woods. Pity to waste him."

They sat down. Antonia discovered she was really hungry. The sea air had given her an appetite.

"We're going to spring-clean the living room tomorrow," she announced. "We thought we might move the desk into the small room across the hall."

"It will make a study for Antonia to do her translation work."

"You're staying, then?" enquired the Witch, passing a plate of roast pheasant to her. "Help yourself to vegetables."

"Yes, Antonia's staying," said James. He exchanged a long look with his Grandmother.

Dr Mikilari reached for the vegetable dish and piled up his plate.

"That's nice!" he said – though whether he was referring to the meal or to Antonia's intentions, was not clear.

Two

Spring-Cleaning

Antonia awoke as James set down a mug of coffee beside her.

"This is very civilised!"

James smiled at her and sat down on the edge of the bed, cradling his own mug.

"We have work to do today," he reminded her.

Antonia stretched. She would have liked a lazy morning in bed. She drank her coffee in silence, glancing at James to see whether this might be negotiated. But he had already put down his mug and was beginning to get dressed. She watched him: his body firm and lithe... the body of a man younger than his forty odd years. She wanted to invite him back to bed. As if he had read her thoughts, he came back and sat briefly on the edge of the bed, drawing her into his arms. She responded eagerly, expecting that he would make love to her...but he only removed her nightie, kissed her briefly and stood up, taking the bedclothes with him.

"Up!" he said succinctly.

Reluctantly Antonia began to dress, then a thought struck her:

"James, where do your grandparents sleep?"

"In the back garden."

"What, in a summer-house?"

"No, just a hammock in the orchard."

"A hammock? In this weather! But, James, it's winter!"

"Not in the back garden. You'll see, later on."

"But, why don't they sleep indoors? There's room. And isn't it uncomfortable with two in a hammock... you'd just roll into each other all the time!"

James grinned: "I think that's part of the attraction!"

"I'd have thought they were past all that."

"I have a very sexy Grandmother."

"And I suppose you inherited her genes?"

Antonia pretended disinterest.

A moment later James had divested her of her underwear and pushed her gently back into the bed she'd just vacated.

"So, this is how we do the spring-cleaning, is it?"

The seductive smell of frying bacon wafted up the stairs.

"Granny's cooking breakfast," said James unnecessarily. "Shall we get dressed and go down."

Antonia stretched pleasurably and purred. She was in no hurry.

"You're already dressed," she pointed out. "Why don't you go on."

"Because you'll just curl up and go back to sleep!"

Antonia sighed and slid out of bed. She made for the bathroom. He waited while she dressed and followed her downstairs.

"All loved up!" remarked the Witch with some amusement.

She piled a plate with crispy bacon and set it by Antonia's place. Dr Mikilari reached out and surreptitiously took a rasher.

"You can't have that!" screeched the Witch, snatching it from him.

"Why can't he?" asked Antonia.

"He's Jewish. He's not allowed bacon."

The Witch moved the plate out of his reach.

"That's rather hard when he was going to enjoy it!"

"They're his rules!" snapped the Witch. "Do you want a fried mouse with your bacon?"

"Is that an invitation or a threat, Granny?" enquired James, taking his place and helping himself to a crisp rasher. "Is there any fried bread? Or hash brownies?"

"There might be, if you ask nicely!"

James smiled at her beguilingly. He munched a second rasher.

"I suppose I'll settle for toast and marmalade," Dr Mikilari said sadly.

"You'll get what you're given, old man!"

"Why are you so unkind to him?" asked Antonia, treading on dangerous ground.

"Because I choose to be! Not that it's any of your business!"

James shot Antonia a warning look. He offered her the bacon platter. The Witch banged down a second platter with fried bread, fried tomatoes, fried potatoes… She was clearly cross.

"This is a wonderful breakfast!" Antonia helped herself. "I haven't had such a splendid breakfast in… I don't know how long!" She glanced at the Witch. "It's just a pity that Dr Mikilari can't enjoy it with us."

She glanced down at her plate giving an involuntary squeal. On her plate lay a crisply fried mouse.

James reached over and removed it.

"Not nice, Granny!"

"So, you want one that runs around the table?"

"Granny," James said sternly, "I know that mouse is not real. You know that mouse is not real. But Antonia doesn't. If you can't behave I'll have to take Antonia away."

"Pshaw!" muttered the Witch.

Antonia pushed her plate away.

"I don't think I can face this."

"I could!" murmured Dr Mikilari. "Pity to waste it!"

"I thought you weren't allowed…?"

Dr Mikilari gave her a small sad smile, but reached for her plate anyway and began tucking in with evident enjoyment. James drained his coffee mug and got up from the table. He held out his hand to Antonia:

"Let's survey the scene and plan our campaign."

"I thought I'd start on the windows in the room that's going to be my study – before we move the desk in."

"Okay. There's a bucket under the sink…cloths and things…"

"I'll find what I need."

Antonia found the bucket and filled it with hot water, squirting in *Fairy* liquid. On the opposite side of the kitchen a tall cupboard nestled under the stairs. She pulled it open.

"Walkies?" enquired the Witch's Broom, dancing on its twig-ends with excitement.

Antonia shrieked and slammed the door shut. The Broom howled as the door slammed on its emerging twig-ends.

"What is it?" James reappeared, concern written all over his face.

"It's… It's alive!" Antonia pointed to the cupboard, even as James gathered her into his arms.

"It's only Granny's Broomstick. It's alright. It won't hurt you."

From the cupboard the Broom gave a plaintive howl. James released Antonia and pulled open the door.

"Squashed twig-ends!" whimpered the Broom.

James lifted the Broom out and gently shook it. A handful of broken twigs dropped off along with a couple of spiders.

"Alright now?" James soothed the Broom and replaced it in the cupboard.

"I don't believe it…" whispered Antonia, who was still considerably shaken. Inanimate objects aren't supposed to talk!"

"I know!" James picked up her bucket. "What were you looking for?"

"I just wanted some cloths.

He found her some cloths and carried her bucket through to the small lounge. The windows had not been cleaned for years. Antonia washed and rubbed, changing her water three or four times. She carried a small step-ladder outside and washed the exterior glass until that too sparkled. Her arms ached. Her back ached. She threw the last of her water away and went to see what James was doing.

"Emptying the desk," he said as she came to look for him.

There were piles of papers everywhere.

"What are you going to do with all… this?"

"Burn it."

"Bonfire?"

"No need. We'll feed it to the Range."

"Have you looked through it…in case there's anything you need to keep?"

James picked up a pile and handed it to her.

"Just go and stuff it into the Range."

Antonia carried the pile through to the kitchen. She raised the lid of the Range and shoved in a wodge of papers. The Range coughed.

"Suffocating!" he protested, coughing some more.

"Sorry!" apologised Antonia. My goodness, she thought! Here I am talking to the Range as if it's a sentient being!

She wandered back into the chaos of the other room and watched James emptying yet another drawer.

"Oh dear! All this because I wanted to open the window!"

James turned and grinned at her:

"That's okay, it needed doing!" He emptied the last drawer and straightened up. "We can dust it now…well, actually I'd better wash my hands – I'm pretty filthy!"

"How about we wash the desk and when it's dry, I'll, polish it. Have we got any furniture polish?"

"I doubt it. Granny wasn't into polishing, and Grandad never noticed dust."

"Well, let's take all this rubbish out, and then you can wash your hands and I'll start washing the desk and drawers …and while it all dries, we can walk down to the village and buy some polish. Yes?"

"Yes, ma'am!" James straightened up and smartly saluted. "What're you laughing at?" he demanded.

"You! You're absolutely filthy!"

"I expect I am! Look, I'll take all this rubbish out or you'll get filthy too! You can start washing the drawers."

Some time later they returned from the village with an assortment of furniture polish and impregnated cloths.

"Coffee, I think," said James judiciously. "Before we begin the elbow grease!"

"Coffee?" enquired the Range cheerfully. "Would you fancy hot buttered crumpets?"

"Oh wow! Haven't had hot buttered crumpets in years!" Opening the oven door, James extracted a plate with three crumpets all oozing butter. "Three?" he queried.

"One for herself," mentioned the Range.

Butter dripped off their fingers and chins and daubed their coffee mugs. James laughed delightedly.

"Better put Granny's back to keep warm…before I eat it myself!"

Even without the drawers, the carcass of the desk was heavier than they'd expected. It was not easy to manhandle it through the doorway and was almost impossible to turn into the narrow hall.

"It came in," panted James. "It hasn't got bigger…It just feels like it!" Slowly they edged it along the hall into the doorway of the small front room.

"Oh! Oh! Oh, James!"

"What?"

"Look! The carpet!"

James, who was backing into the room, put down his end of the desk and turned round. The old threadbare carpet had gone, replaced by a new carpet in a shade of burnt orange.

"Granny!" he breathed.

"She's organised this?"

"I'd say so!"

"Just while we were out shopping?"

"Just while you were shopping," said a familiar voice, "Did you want a hand with that desk?"

"It's beautiful, the carpet! Such a warm colour! The room feels furnished already!"

The Witch acknowledged Antonia's pleasure.

The desk suddenly felt lighter. They positioned it in the window.

"Facing in or facing out?" enquired the Witch.

Antonia looked puzzled.

"She means, are you going to sit facing the window, or with your back to the window?"

"Facing the window, please. But leave me room to get to the windows."

"I fed the curtains to the Range," mentioned the Witch. "They just fell to pieces as I took them down. I thought Antonia and I might have a little trip to that nice shop where I bought the curtains for the first bedroom I shared with Milkil…they were very expensive! But they were…delicious!"

"You've already been so generous!" murmured Antonia.

"Speaking of carpets," reminisced the Witch, "Did I ever tell you about the carpet Milkil purloined for me out of a skip? The psychiatrist with the rakish air…He was much more fun in those days. That carpet was burnt orange too! My favourite colour…"

"There's a hot buttered crumpet in the oven for you, Granny."

"I know," said the Witch. "I put it there."

"They were exceedingly yummy!"

"Yes, well you've some polishing to do," said the Witch dismissively. She took herself back to the kitchen.

"That was amazingly kind of her!"

"M'm… she's taken a liking to you!" James smiled at her. "You'll enjoy choosing new curtains!"

"Yes," Antonia sighed. "And, as she said: we've got some polishing to do!"

Three

Brascombe Woods

"We should fetch your stuff from the flat," suggested James. "Unless you were planning to work from there?" He studied her profile. "Maybe bring the car back so you can go places…?" He paused. "Remember I can only go where I've been before, which means there will be places you might want to visit where I can't come with you."

Antonia glanced at him. She said nothing.

"Where might I want to go?" she enquired.

"Well, for example, when you go to see your publishers. I've never been to Munich."

"Michael has. That's where I came across him. Only I didn't know he was your brother then…He…he was the only one who spoke to me at your funeral"

James caught her to him and held her for a long moment.

"Let's go."

Antonia blinked, and stared at the familiar walls of her flat.

A moment ago they had been standing in the cottage. James released her.

"Okay, let's gather all the stuff you want and then we'll put it in the car."

The flat was cold and uninviting. Antonia gathered her work, her laptop, various dictionaries and notebooks, her address book and mobile phone. In her bedroom she piled up clothing and shoes…toiletries from the bathroom and extra towels.

"Can I make you a black coffee?" enquired James.

"M'm! It fees awfully cold in here!"

"The Range certainly keeps the cottage warm."

"And offers us coffee and friendly chat!"

"So, you think you might stay with me for a bit?"

"How long is a bit?"

James wrapped her in an embrace and kissed her lingeringly.

"To have and to hold from this time forth…to cherish."

"As in marriage?"

"We can't do that, Antoni-ni. Officially I no longer exist."

"You seem pretty real to me!"

"I should hope so! Now, are you nearly ready?"

Antonia fetched her car from the underground garage and brought it round to the flat. They loaded the boot and the back seats, took a last look round and locked up.

"Do you need to let anyone know where you are?"

"No one will be looking for me, if that's what you mean." James settled himself in the passenger seat. Antonia got in beside him and inserted her key in the ignition.

"It seems funny," she said, "driving you – when we went anywhere before, you always drove."

"My licence expired." James placed a hand on hers. "And people might think a ghost was driving the car."

***

Breakfast the next morning passed without incident. Antonia spent a happy morning arranging her things in the newly polished desk. An aroma of lavender polish lingered in the room. Someone had arranged a vase of fresh flowers on the window sill. When she wandered through to the kitchen for a mug of coffee, she found Dr Mikilari drowsing contentedly in the rocking chair by the Range. The Witch had taken herself off and there was no sign of James. Antonia took the mug of coffee back to her study, wrapping her hands around its warmth. She wondered if James was in his studio – he'd promised to prop open the door between their rooms. There was no door visible. Antonia tapped on the wall, but there was no response. She returned to her work with a lightness of spirit she had not felt since the news of James's fatal accident had reached her.

A bell rang, alerting her to the dinner hour. Shuffling footsteps entered from the hall. Dr Mikilari put his head around the open door.

"Lunch," he murmured. "Is on the table."

Antonia pushed back her chair and stood up. She smiled warmly at the old man.

"I hope it's not brown soup!" she said conspiratorially.

"I hope not, too!"

She took his elbow and steered him towards the kitchen.

"Roast partridge," mentioned the Witch, serving generous portions. Setting a jug of gravy on the table, she indicated a steaming bowl of root vegetables.

"They've made a nice job of that little front lounge," observed Dr Mikilari, to no one in particular.

"And someone put fresh flowers for me!" Antonia looked questioningly at the Witch.

"Well, there's a thing!" muttered the Witch crossly.

"Where's James?" Antonia looked round the kitchen as if he might materialise from the broom cupboard.

"Perhaps he's in the studio," suggested Dr Mikilari, spilling gravy down his knitted waistcoat. "I didn't look. Was I supposed to?"

"He'll come when he's hungry," scolded the Witch. She served herself and sat down to enjoy the meal.

"Is there a butcher in the village?" enquired Antonia. "This meat is so tender!"

"Can't say I've noticed," returned the Witch. "This here is road-kill."

Antonia was piling their empty plates into the sink when James appeared.

"Sorry!" he said, sounding remarkably unrepentant. "Lost track of time!"

"Your dinner's in the oven," remarked the Witch shortly.

"Thanks, Granny!"

Antonia observed James as he retrieved his meal and began wolfing it down. He looked younger, carefree, boyish. Sensing her scrutiny, he smiled at her.

"Had a good morning?" he asked.

"Yes. What have you been doing? I looked for you earlier."

"Preparing a surprise!"

"Pshaw!" spat the Witch.

"Is there something tasty for 'Afters'?" enquired Dr Mikilari, polishing his spoon hopefully.

"There might be jam roly-poly and custard." The Witch observed the gravy stain on his waistcoat. "But you don't deserve any."

"Let him have mine!" protested Antonia.

James threw her a warning look.

"I'll just have to eat Antonia's flowers," murmured Dr Mikilari sadly.

"Why don't you stand up to her!"

Dr Mikilari looked at Antonia, mildly surprised that she was aroused on his behalf.

"Gone are the days…" He began.

"Yes?"

"When my heart was young and gay…"

"Pshaw!" muttered the Witch, remembering such days… "The psychiatrist with the rakish air!"

"I see we have a burnt-orange carpet!" mentioned Dr Mikilari. "In the study."

"And flowers!" added Antonia. "Were the flowers from you, James?"

"I wonder?" James smiled enigmatically and exchanged a look with the Witch. "About the jam roly-poly, Granny?"

***

"Can I wash up?" offered Antonia. "I'm sure James will help me." The Witch took off her apron and threw it at James.

"Know your place, my boy!" murmured Dr Mikilari settling himself in the rocking chair.

James rinsed off the dinner plates and filled the sink with hot soapy water. He offered Antonia a tea towel. A black cat wound its way around her legs, purring loudly. Antonia took a handful of washed cutlery and began wiping it dry.

"I think it's sad that your Grandmother couldn't be bothered to give the cat a name!"

"She won't mind if you want to choose a name for him."

"No! Down, Cat!" Antonia shooed the cat who had jumped up on the table and was eagerly devouring the remaining partridge. The cat fixed one eye on Antonia and dragged the remains of the joint off the serving dish. Antonia lunged for the plate…too late. Cat and joint poured themselves over the edge of the table. "No! Bad Cat!"

The cat yowled angrily and dragged the battered joint, now liberally coated in fluff, under a built in cupboard.

"Don't worry!" murmured James over his shoulder.

"But the cat shouldn't be allowed to do that!"

"You didn't exactly *allow* him!"

"What *will* your Grandmother think!"

"She probably won't notice."

"What d'you mean 'she won't notice'! She'll wonder whatever happened to the rest of the joint."

"You don't know Granny!"

They finished the washing up in silence. Antonia wiped the table. She noticed that Dr Mikilari had vacated his rocking chair which he had left rocking, invitingly. The cat emerged from under the cupboard, leapt lightly into the rocking chair and curled up, purring loudly.

"What would you like to do this afternoon?" enquired James.

"Perhaps we could go for a drive somewhere?"

"Why don't I show you Brascombe Woods – where I grew up. I could show you the family house and the woods. I loved those woods!"

"Do your parents still live there?"

"No, they've moved into a Retirement complex. I can't take you there, but Michael might, if you wanted to meet them."

"So, where is Brascombe?"

"About a forty minute drive. Shall we go?"

A wide, gravelled drive swept up to the house. Antonia looked up at the generously proportioned family home.

"Big," she commented.

"Four double bedrooms and a single; a really big lounge taking up half the ground floor, then a dining room the other side, which sat the whole family comfortably, with French windows out into the garden. It was a lovely garden with this huge weeping willow tree at the bottom. Gran had a beautiful display of flowers and shrubs… It got so neglected after Mum died."

"How many of you were there?"

"Mum and Dad, Gran; Lim, my older sister, us four boys and then Baby Margot."

"She died, didn't she?"

"Yes. Mum never recovered."

"I'm sorry."

"M'm… It's a lovely house for whoever lives there now…and lots of memories…"

"I'm sure." She slipped her hand into his.

"Let's go and explore the woods."

The path into the woods was muddy after recent rain. The trees dripped gently overhead; wet, shiny bark; branches that had mostly shed their leaves, leaf mould underfoot muffling their footsteps. A squirrel scampered high in the tree tops, dislodging a shower of raindrops. Somewhere unseen a bird sang a sweet sharp note. The woods which had given James so much solace as a boy, seemed to have shrunk …yet they still spoke to him. He stopped and rested his hand against a familiar tree.

"I loved this tree!"

Antonia watched him communing with this tree and then another. To her, a tree was just a tree, but she could see that to James each tree embodied something real and precious. He took her hand and together they wandered through the woods…James noticing and pointing out a clump of toadstools, a late butterfly, a tiny mouse scampering among the tree roots… naming birds by their call… Indeed a special place.

Four

The Back Garden

Antonia sighed and stretched, noting the page number
of the novel she was translating. She closed her laptop,
turned off the bright desk lamp and pushed back her
chair, glancing at her watch. She had put in three hours
work and needed a break…maybe a mug of coffee. She
wondered what James was doing. He was not in his studio.
She wandered through to the living room which wore an
air of comfortable disarray and recent occupancy…but no
James. As she entered the kitchen the Range brightened:

"Coffee?" he enquired.

"That would be nice." Antonia glanced around:
"James about?"

The Range blew out a wisp of smoke.

"No one else for coffee," he mentioned. "But I could
offer you a Welsh cake."

Antonia accepted the coffee, absent-mindedly stirred in a spoonful of sugar and reached into the warming oven for a Welsh cake. She settled herself in the rocking chair (that wasn't there) and sipped her coffee, mildly surprised at its unaccustomed sweetness. Was James upstairs? Rinsing her empty mug at the sink, she went to investigate. In their room the bed was neatly made and the window opened to air the room. She closed the window and pushed the wardrobe door shut. It promptly reopened. The second bedroom, which was wallpapered with a child in mind, was minimally furnished and failed to convey charm or welcome – not that she envisaged they would have any guests.

In the bathroom the bath bore a faint tide-mark and could do with cleaning. There was no sign of James. Antonia tackled the bath – and while she was at it, scrubbed the basin and lavatory, polishing taps and handles. Immaculate bathrooms and an almost obsessive standard of personal hygiene had balanced her innate distaste for the clients who had been willing to pay extraordinary amounts for the privilege of using her body. What was it Phil had said to her once? She had been explaining to him that in a sense her body was like a suit of clothes she wore and could discard, but no one could touch her soul or her feelings.

"My dear," Mr Carew Robinson had said to her over their restaurant table, "I want you to listen to me: divorcing body and soul is crippling you emotionally. This is your God-given body. Do not disdain it. You are beautiful, Antonia. Allow yourself to enjoy your body.

You dress with care. You carry yourself with grace. You are highly intelligent, but you are not happy. I enjoy your company. I enjoy taking you to the theatre, the opera… dining with you, dancing. You are a highly desirable companion – and that is what I would like you to be: a lovely girl whom I can take out with pride. But I want your exclusive company. No other clients."

"They pay the mortgage," Antonia pointed out.

"Then I will pay off the mortgage. Is that a deal?"

"Why? Why would you do that for me – I'm nothing to you."

"On the contrary, you are an exceptional girl and I want to see you realise your potential. One day someone will come along with whom you feel a deep connection – I know that seems impossible right now – but it would be a tragedy to throw away your life in order to punish the men whom you accept as clients."

"Punish?"

"My dear, that is what you are doing, consciously or not. So are we agreed? I will settle your mortgage and from today we will have an exclusive relationship."

"I am not going to live with you!"

"Nor would I want you to. Now, would you care to peruse the dessert menu?"

***

And James had changed all that. Antonia sat on the edge of the pristine bath and reflected. Like Phil, James knew exactly what she had been, and yet loved her. She did not deserve him. She had tried telling him so, but love is not about deserving, was his reply. Last August, when he had asked her to marry him, she had rejected him. She had not wanted to let him into her life, to share her life with him. No man was going to take her over, possess her… but she needed James! She could not live without him! Where *was* he? She ran downstairs. He must be outside! She flung open the kitchen door into the little walled courtyard and shouted desperately for him.

Where he came from she could not say, he just appeared, and swept her into his arms.

"My Antoni-ni, what is it?"

"I didn't know where you were!" she sobbed, beating clenched fists against his chest.

"I'm here. Did you think I'd left you? I was in the Back Garden. Come, it's time I took you through."

She saw now that there was a green gate set into the far wall of the courtyard – a gate with no latch, no handle. James opened the gate and led her through. A lawn stretched away leading into an apple orchard. The sun felt warm on her back. The trees were in leaf although it was winter…in fact, it clearly was not winter in this garden. She could hear birdsong…and something else…as if the wind was whispering to itself. She looked about her. There was a swing dangling invitingly from an apple bough, underneath which two prams stood companionably. The sweet notes of a flute reached Antonia…and then, dancing across the lawn came a little girl about seven years old, flute in hand. The child stopped and stared at Antonia.

"Who are you? She asked.

"This is Antonia," said James. "I've brought her to see the garden."

"And what's your name?" enquired Antonia of the child.

"Mlilka." The child smiled at her and danced off. The music drifted back.

"What a sweet little girl! Tell me about her?"

"She was Grandad's daughter – my mother. She lives in the Garden as a seven year old because that was the age at which she and Grandad were happiest."

"I see," said Antonia, thoroughly confused. "Does she know she's your mother?"

"No. She will always be seven."

They walked towards the stationary prams. Antonia looked at the sleeping face of a baby who was perhaps six months old.

"And who is this?"

"This is my daughter, Persephone. She was a springtime baby. She died in the first winter of her life."

He reached over and tucked her blanket more securely around her. There was sadness in his face.

"I'm sorry," said Antonia inadequately.

They moved to the second pram. A chubby little girl gurgled happily, waving tiny fists, inviting someone to pick her up.

"This is my baby sister, Margot… She drowned. Mum never got over it."

"How?" whispered Antonia, appalled.

"The twins were playing Moses in the bulrushes.

They'd put her in a cardboard box and pushed it out into the pond… she sank."

"That's horrible! No wonder your mother…"

Antonia watched as James gently picked up the baby and held her in his arms, talking to her as if she could understand. He sat down on the swing and gently rocked back and forth.

"They will never grow up, but they are safe and loved, here in the garden." He glanced up at her. "Everyone has a Back Garden where they can visit the people they've loved and lost, but very few know how to access it."

He stood up and returned the baby to her pram.

"Do they cry?" asked Antonia.

"No. They cannot experience pain or unhappiness, or anxiety – but they can know they are loved."

"And they stay out here all the time?"

"Yes." He offered the baby a woolly toy, watching her fingers close around it. "Come and say hello to Grandad."

Dr Mikilari sat on an old, weathered garden bench, drowsing over an ancient newspaper. He roused as they approached and regarded Antonia with pleasure.

"Hello, my dear! How nice to see you!" He patted the seat beside him. "What have you been doing?"

Antonia sat. She took the wrinkled old hand in hers and smiled at him.

"I was translating a Russian novel this morning. And then I cleaned the bathroom…and came to look for James."

"My grandparents came over from Russia," Dr Mikilari mentioned, patting the hand that held his. "They were Jewish. I always hoped I could take my Snaggletooth there one day."

James smiled at the old nickname.

"I don't suppose the village where they lived is still there."

"War is a terrible thing...six million Jews..."

"But not your grandparents. And you were able to grow up here and become a deeply respected doctor...and enjoy your grandchildren. And Granny!" James added as an afterthought.

"And my little daughter!" His face lit up.

As if he had called her, Mlilka danced across the lawn and scrambled into his lap.

"This lady is called Antonia," she informed him.

Somewhere a bell rang. Dr Mikilari pricked up his ears:

"I do believe it's dinner time!"

"Hopefully not brown soup!" whispered Antonia mischievously. She stood up and walked hand in hand with James across the lawn and through the green gate with no latch. Following them slowly came Dr Mikilari, alone.

"What about Milka?" asked Antonia.

"*Mlilka*," James corrected her. "She doesn't join us for meals."

"Why not?"

"She just doesn't," James said firmly.

"I'm sure she'd like to!"

"Granny and Mlilka do not interact."

"Why not?"

There was a touch of exasperation in James's voice: "Granny disappeared when Mlilka was three. She doesn't connect in Mlilka's childhood. They don't recognize each other." And over his shoulder: "Come on, Grandad!"

"Lentil cutlets with bacon," announced the Witch.

"Is Grandad allowed bacon today?" enquired Antonia provocatively.

The Witch threw her a complicit smile.

"Today is Tuesday. He's allowed bacon on Tuesdays." It was not, in fact, Tuesday; but seeing the old man's evident pleasure in his meal, Antonia let it pass.

***

"You may wash up," said the Witch as if conferring a great honour on Antonia.

There seemed a great many dishes and containers in the sink, some of which looked as if food had been burnt to their surfaces. The washing up took her a long time – and James had taken himself off somewhere instead of staying to help. Antonia's temper was beginning to fray by the time she finished. She hung up the wet tea-towels and walked across to the sitting room. There was nobody there. Across the hall the door to her study stood open. She stood a moment, irresolute…and then she saw the two completed paintings of the bay: dawn and sunset, framed and hung on the wall, facing her. James had given her the paintings of his special place …and as she stood there the pictures came to life:

A little breeze chased the waves towards her; sunlight

danced and reflected on the water… A bird gave a single, lonely cry and moved on silent wings across the bay.

Antonia stood transfixed. James stood behind her, his hands on her shoulders.

"Oh James!" she breathed, "I don't know what to say! They're beautiful! Thank you so much!"

"I thought you'd like them."

"Oh yes!"

"And they look good in here."

"They look wonderful!" She leaned back against him. "And perhaps a potted plant, a Cyclamen or something, on the window sill, d'you think?"

"And curtains!" said the Witch, appearing in the room.

"I shall take Antonia off to choose new curtains…in here, in the living room and your bedroom, I think. We might go tomorrow."

"I could drive," offered Antonia.

"Pshaw!" spat the Witch, rejecting her offer.

***

They were gathered in the kitchen enjoying toasted tea cakes and coffee when the front door bell jangled.

"I didn't know the door bell worked!" observed Dr Mikilari, helping himself to another tea cake.

"Fell off years ago," remarked the Witch, observing him.

"Aren't you going to answer it?" asked Antonia.

"If it's Michael, he'll come in anyway," said James.

"And no one else has any business here."

"Don't you answer the door to the postman?"

"No."

The front door protested and grumbled and grudgingly scraped open an inch or so. Footsteps came along the hall. Michael stood in the kitchen doorway. He dropped his holdall on the floor and came over to envelop James in a long hug.

"Good to see you!"

Over James's shoulder Michael glanced across at his grandfather munching tea cakes. As James released him, he went over and dropped a kiss on the old man's cheek.

"Ah Michael! Good to see you, lad!"

"And you, Grandad!"

Dr Mikilari considered the remaining tea cake and after considerable thought, offered it to Michael.

"No, you enjoy it, Grandad."

He walked over to the range and hugged his grandmother.

"Pshaw!" she muttered, secretly pleased as she pushed him away.

Antonia had stood up to greet Michael. She waited, watching, silent.

"Antonia!" Michael held her by the shoulders, his smile warm and welcoming. "I have tried and tried to make contact. Your phone just rang out every time. I tried your publisher, but they said you were out of contact – they couldn't reach you either. I didn't know you were here."

"Yes." Antonia found herself suddenly shy and tongue tied.

"I've been so worried about you! But you're looking well!"

"Yes."

His eyes smiled into hers with kindness and deep affection. Finally, he turned his head and addressed James.

"When I've played in Munich, Antonia is usually in the audience. I look forward to taking her out to dinner. She comes over to see her publisher…"

"She's spoken for," murmured the Witch distinctly.

"James came and rescued me," whispered Antonia.

"That's great!" Michael beamed at her, and turning to James: "You look good!"

"You don't look so bad yourself, Mikey!"

"Coffee?" The Witch dumped a mug of coffee in front of him.

"Thanks, Granny!"

"Will you stay over? Antonia will get your room ready."

"Yes. That'd be great."

Antonia excused herself and went to prepare the guest room which, she discovered, was at the far end of the landing. She had thought the landing ended in a blank wall. The guest room was Spartan, but adequate. She made up the bed and put clean towels out. When she came downstairs the family had moved into the sitting room. James lit the fire and brought an armful of logs in from the courtyard. Michael glanced around:

"It seems so much bigger without Grandad's desk!"

"It's Antonia's desk now. We've turned the small front room into a study for her."

"And Granny provided a beautiful new carpet!" said Antonia. "D'you want to see?"

Michael followed her across the hall.

"I'm impressed!" He looked around. "James?" he asked, indicating the pictures.

"They're wonderful, aren't they!" Antonia's eyes were shining. "He took me to see the bay – it's one of his special places – It was such a special afternoon… magical!"

"Except it's not a real place," said Michael quietly.

"Yes! We went there! He took me!"

"Antonia," Michael spoke seriously. "Before James came for you, had you tried to kill yourself?"

"I wasn't far off. I knew I couldn't live without him… to never see him again… never be held by him… I'd never imagined such grief. Perhaps I would have died if he hadn't come."

"I just needed to know. You see, I can visit because, like James, I inherited this gift enabling me to pass between worlds. But you do understand that everyone here has passed from life as you and I experience it. They exist in a different time frame. To put it bluntly you are living in a houseful of ghosts."

"But…" Antonia floundered…"How can James be so real if he's a ghost?"

"For you, he is real… But you mustn't lose your hold on the real world out there."

He moved to comfort her as her breath caught in her chest and tears slid silently down her face.

"I've been so happy!" she whispered. "James loves me… He…"

And James was suddenly there, gathering her into his arms, holding her.

"I want you to be real! I don't want you to be a ghost!"

"Do you doubt it, my Antoni-ni?" He kissed her, a long lingering kiss. "Granny thought you might like to help her prepare the evening meal." And to Michael: "Road-kill alright with you?"

The Witch was hunched over the Range. She did not turn as Antonia came into the kitchen.

"You mustn't mind him!" she said briskly. "He lives out there in the real world and just visits from time to time. We have our own reality; and James loves you… He cherishes you… He will never leave or forsake you. Now, will you set the table."

"Am I a ghost?"

The Witch turned round and gave her an appraising look:

"If I prick you with a pin, will it hurt?"

"Yes."

"Will you bleed?"

"Yes."

"If you touch the Range, will you suffer a burn?"

"Yes."

"Do you feel the cold?"

"Yes."

"If you fall down the stairs, do you bruise?"

"Yes."

"And when James makes love to you, is it real?"

"Oh yes!"

The Witch smiled at her, a warmly affectionate smile:

"Now, set the table and then you can peel some *real* potatoes!"

***

James and Michael sat up late talking, over the log fire, drinking copious amounts of coffee and catching up on family news. Antonia, unaccountably exhausted, had a long hot soak in the bath and went to bed. She was sleeping soundly when James slid in beside her and wrapped himself around her.

***

It was still dark when she awoke, thirsty. The roast whatever-it-was had been spiced and over salted – just short of pungent. James was still deeply asleep. Antonia padded barefoot to the top of the stairs and crept down to the kitchen. She filled a glass with cold water and drank it slowly.

"Coffee?" enquired the Range, waking up.

Antonia thought about it. She was wide awake now, perhaps she would sip a mug of coffee in the sitting room by the remains of last night's fire. To her surprise, someone was already there, dozing on the sofa. Had Michael not gone to bed? The fire was still smouldering. She bent down and gently added another log. The figure on the sofa rolled over and smiled at her.

"Good morning!" He unwound his blanket, pushed pyjama'd legs over the side and sat up. "Is the coffee for me?"

"I already started this one. Hold on and I'll fetch you one."

She returned, handed him his mug and sat down opposite him.

"That bedroom is freezing! I was shivering too much to sleep! James doesn't feel the cold." He sipped his coffee gratefully. "Sorry I upset you yesterday." He looked at her keenly. "But it is important to keep some contact out there. Do you have friends you could see from time to time?"

"I pretty much kept to myself."

"Family? Parents? Acquaintances in the village?"

"One or two – just to exchange the time of day." Antonia felt an urge to confide in him: "I had to ask Granny if I was a ghost myself."

"No, you're not a ghost… though you might have become one if James hadn't come for you." He stretched out his legs. "Tell me about you and James."

There was no need for Michael to know how they had met or the basis on which he had first come to her.

"Phil, Mr Carew, introduced us. We began seeing quite a lot of each other…we went on holiday together up on the Yorkshire moors. James asked me to marry him, but I…

I wanted to keep my independence. I didn't want to be owned. I didn't do 'committed' relationships… .And then James had that heart attack…I felt it was my fault. I hadn't understood about love. I hadn't understood he loved me. It was my fault."

"James had a dodgy heart. Grandad did too. It would probably have happened anyway… James knew about his heart, but he didn't do anything about it. Life hasn't been very kind to him, one way and another. He made work his focus because he was unhappy. He had to take on too much responsibility too young. He felt driven…and he was losing Jake."

"Was that my fault? Jake resented me."

"Jake wanted family. Tom offered him a warm, friendly family and cousins. They've scooped him up and made him feel wanted and appreciated. And they're very proud of him. He graduates next summer."

There was a short silence while they drank their coffee.

"The babies in the back garden…?"

"They've always been important to James. It's the way he taught us to deal with loss… But the rest of us have moved on." He yawned. "Yes, I drop by to see Granny and Grandad, occasionally; but I see the rest of my family too. You need to be part of the family. I could take you to meet Dad and Debs – they're out of James's range."

"James took me to see the house where you all grew up – but he said they'd moved."

"They live in a rather swish Retirement facility. I'll take you."

"Where will you take her?" asked a tousle-headed James, joining them. He had a glass of water in his hand. "Bit strong that meat last night!" He came and sat down beside Antonia, on the second sofa, slipping an arm around her. "Alright?"

She reached up a hand to touch his face. His eyes held hers. She snuggled against him.

"Poor Michael found the spare bedroom too cold. He came down and slept on the sofa."

"Which room did you put him in?"

"The one along the landing at the far end. I thought that was the guest room."

"I expect it *was* cold! You should have used the small bedroom just across from us."

"I didn't know. I'm sorry."

"No need to be sorry! I was lovely and snug down here. The fire stayed in all night."

"Pyjama party?" enquired the Witch, putting her head around the door.

"Good morning, Granny! Yes, we need to get dressed. What's for breakfast?"

"I suppose you're all after a big fried breakfast?"

"But no fried mice for me, thank you!"

The Witch concealed a smile and went to speak with the Range.

"Pushing your luck?" James squeezed Antonia affectionately. "Granny wouldn't let Grandad have any bacon," he said to Michael. "And Antonia didn't think that was fair, so Granny served up a fried mouse."

"That sounds like Granny!"

"D'you want to use the bathroom first?" Antonia suggested, smiling at Michael.

Michael folded his blanket over his arm, drained his mug and crossed the kitchen to the stairs. James pulled Antonia onto his lap and nibbled her ear. His hands caressed her. Antonia was torn between arousal and propriety, aware of the Witch in the kitchen.

"Michael takes ages," murmured James, kissing her neck. "He's a fastidious dresser."

"I'm not sure this is the time or place!" whispered Antonia, thoroughly aroused and wanting him.

"Love you!" James took her face between his hands. "Only you!" He slid her off the sofa onto the hearth rug, removing her pyjama trousers…

"All loved up!" murmured the Witch approvingly to the Range. "Reminds me of the days when himself was a little more active… chasing me round the kitchen, pocketing my knickers…I only wore knickers for him because he so enjoyed ripping them off! Such a staid, respectable, inhibited man he was! It was sheer wickedness to seduce him!"

The Range coughed politely.

"You don't know the half of it!" murmured the Witch.

Michael came downstairs on quiet feet. He was wearing a green sweater that had once belonged to his grandfather. He came over and hugged the Witch.

"Sit!" said the Witch, pushing him into the rocking chair (that wasn't there). She thrust another mug of coffee at him. "*They* are not quite ready for breakfast… but you know nothing about that, do you!" She gave him a penetrating look from under her snaggled eyebrows. "How come you haven't fallen in love yourself, Michael?"

"Would I confide in you?" He grinned at her. "I have my music, Granny. Anyone else would just get in the way."

"Fiddlesticks!"

"Well said! When is a fiddle not a fiddle? When it's a Stradivarius!"

Looking decidedly rumpled and not a little embarrassed, James and Antonia crept across the kitchen to the stairs. The Witch followed them with her eyes. She turned back to Michael:

"Of course, you might be gay like your brother."

"I might," said Michael equably. "But not."

"It's unnatural," chided the Witch. "A man of your age. I thought you might have fancied Suki?"

"She's too wrapped up in that daughter of hers. In any case, she's James's wife. She may have discarded him but she wouldn't agree to a divorce."

"I think you'll find the marriage was dissolved despite her reluctance. In any case, she's a respectable widow these days. So, my boy, you want to be celibate all your life?"

"I didn't say that, Granny. You're hassling me. How I choose to live my life is none of your business."

His voice was pleasant but carried a slight edge.

"You don't fancy Antonia, then?" asked the Witch provocatively.

Michael stood up irritatedly and walked around the table. The Witch smiled to herself.

"Three fried mice! Three fried mice!" she sang. She picked up a carving knife and carried it purposefully to the table.

"Is Grandad joining us for breakfast?"

The Witch shrugged eloquently.

"Did someone say Breakfast?" Dr Mikilari shuffled into the room. "Good morning, light of my life!"

"Pshaw!"

"Good morning, Michael... Do I sense a little tension?"

"Not if you want a rasher of bacon, you don't!"

Dr Mikilari regarded the Witch's back which unaccountably emanated hostility.

"Dear me!" he muttered.

"It's me she's cross with, Grandad. She wants me to take a paramour."

"Does she indeed! Whatever will she think of next!"

He sat down and waited for his porrage. Michael sat down beside him. James and Antonia came scuttling down to join them, looking for all the world like children in disgrace.

Five

Meeting the parents

As Michael had promised, the next time he visited, he drove Antonia to the Retirement Facility where Gavin and Debs now lived. Parking in the wide sweep of the drive. He ushered Antonia into a spacious foyer with deep couches, exotic indoor plants and an air of quiet luxury.

"It must be quite expensive!" commented Antonia.

"I believe so," Michael agreed. "But there's a wealth of facilities: library, games room, bar, swimming pool, lounges, a restaurant, and a golf course in the grounds. I think there's a cinema as well." He guided Antonia towards a lift. "They know we're coming and they've booked us in for lunch – the food is wonderful! I've told them you're a special friend of James's, but they don't acknowledge his continuing existence. To them, James died. Full stop."

"Have I not to mention him?"

"It's you they want to meet. Just be yourself."

The lift delivered them smoothly to the fourth floor. Michael led her along a wide carpeted walkway furnished with arm chairs, bookcases and framed landscapes. He stopped outside a door numbered '425: Dr and Mrs Gavin Gregory', and rang the bell.

"Michael!" Gavin opened the door wide. "We've been expecting you. And this is Antonia? Come in, my dear! Come in! Welcome!"

Antonia found herself drawn into a spacious sitting room whose huge windows looked out over parkland. An older lady, white haired and motherly, came forward to greet her.

"I'm Debs. I'm sure Michael has told you? Come and sit down. Michael, take her jacket. Can I get you both a coffee?"

"That would be lovely." Antonia slipped off her jacket and settled into a comfortable armchair. "Have you lived here long?"

"About nine months," Gavin told her.

He ushered Michael toward another arm chair and turning back to Antonia, invited her to tell them about herself. It was Michael who replied.

"Antonia translates Russian novels. She works for a publisher in Munich which is where I met her. She came to a concert of mine and I took her to dinner. But she's based in England. She was a very special friend of James's, which was why I knew you'd want to meet her."

"You already told us that," said Debs quietly. She handed Antonia a cup of coffee. "What would *you* like to tell us?"

"I loved James…"

"I'm sure you did! He was very special." Debs smiled warmly at her.

"He took me to see the house where you all lived… and the woods. He loved those woods.

"He used to take us on expeditions when we were small," put in Michael. "We used to come home all muddy! He was a wonderful big brother!"

Gavin sat quietly watching Antonia, assessing her, wondering whether Michael had taken her on out of sense of indebtedness to his beloved brother – much as James had taken in Suki after Tom had discarded her. Perhaps this son of his was finally forming a close relationship with someone other than his violin? Without probing he gradually elicited snippets of information about her background and interests. They talked about James and exchanged family news.

"Jake graduates next summer," Michael mentioned.

"I expect you've met Jake?" Debs asked.

"I seemed to get off on the wrong foot with him," Antonia admitted.

Debs got out photograph albums and introduced Antonia to Gavin's children and grandchildren. Seeing James as a little boy brought tears to Antonia's eyes. Debs resolved to get some prints made for her.

Finally, Gavin rose to his feet:

"The restaurant is serving lunch if you'd care to join us? And then we'll take you on a tour of the Facility and grounds."

The food, as Michael had promised, was delicious.

They lingered over coffee and then Gavin showed them round, introducing them to various residents on the way. Having spent her teenage years in the embassies to which her father was posted, Antonia carried herself with an assurance and quiet dignity which was not lost on Gavin. He wondered why James had never brought her over to meet them. He had met Mr Carew Robinson only once... It seemed that Antonia had been a protégée of his. Debs noticed that Michael placed a hand loosely on Antonia's shoulder as they sauntered to the golf course – Gavin had taken up golf since they had come to live here. She watched Michael talking to his father, while keeping an arm around Antonia...she was obviously at ease with him. Debs hoped that Michael was finally making a relationship.

They left at three-thirty and drove back to the cottage, neither saying much.

"Might it be possible to renew some sort of contact with your parents?" Michael asked.

Antonia glanced across at him.

"Why?"

"Parents are important. Whatever caused the estrangement, I'm sure they have often wondered about you: how you are, whether you're happy...if you're married."

He turned his head to look at her. "Whether perhaps they have grandchildren?"

"It must be sixteen years..."

"And what happened during all those years?"

"I was briefly married and divorced. I began working

as a translator …I was befriended by Phil – Mr Carew Robinson …I met you…"

"How did you meet Caroo?"

Antonia hesitated. These were dangerous waters.

James might know something of her history, but Michael most definitely did not.

"Much the same way I met you, at some concert – only, of course, *he* wasn't the principal violinist!"

"I just think…" Michael began. "I'm sure your parents would be so glad if you could bring yourself to get in touch."

"I don't even know where they are. My father was posted to the States. I've no idea whether they stayed there. I've no address. As I said, there's been no contact for years."

"I'm sure you could find them if you put your mind to it."

"Possibly. Tell me, Michael, apart from gladdening their hearts, why this sudden concern?"

"You need to maintain relationships in the real world."

"That again!"

"Cocooning yourself with James has given you security and a real sense of being loved – I can see that! But five, ten years down the line, it may not be enough." He glanced at her again. "I care about you. You're a different girl since James came back for you. You've blossomed. You've come alive in a whole new way. It's wonderful to see you happy."

"Thank you."

"Please try and make contact. If it doesn't work out, you don't have to maintain it."

It was not difficult. Antonia wrote to the British Embassy enquiring if they could put her in touch with her father. They did not have a current address but informed her that he had returned to the U.K. on retirement. The Foreign office would not divulge an address but would forward a letter. She used the flat's contact details and waited a couple of weeks before driving to her flat. There was a hand-written envelope awaiting her. She procrastinated: phoning her publisher, running the hoover round the flat, making herself several cups of coffee, opening accumulated mail which comprised bank statements, council tax, utility bills…and finally her father's letter:

Dear Antonia,

What a wonderful surprise after so long! I only wish your mother had been able to share my pleasure in hearing from you. I am sorry to tell you she died three years ago. Since then I have returned to England. I am in good health and have settled down to a reasonably comfortable lifestyle. I miss your mother, but one gets used to it.

I hope very much that you would like to meet me. Perhaps you would telephone? We could meet at the Regent Palace Hotel, which is fairly central and I will offer you lunch.

I look forward to seeing you again, more than I can say.

Regards, your father.

It was signed with his unmistakable flourish. Antonia sat for a long time with the letter in her hands. Years ago he had betrayed her and she wasn't sure she had forgiven him for that. They had abandoned her to boarding school and neglected her in the holidays. After she had graduated from the Sorbonne, she had quietly dropped out of view… but they had made no real effort to find her. They didn't deserve her. Whether they had loved each other she had no idea – they were not demonstrative – and they hadn't shown much love to her. She was quite glad that her mother was dead.

"Good riddance!" she muttered to herself. But her father, despite his unforgivable betrayal, was certainly the nicer of the two. She had liked her father. Perhaps it would be interesting to renew some sort of acquaintance. She could simply disappear if it didn't work. No one would find her at James's cottage. To a casual observer it was derelict…and yet there were people in the village who were friendly, who remembered that there had been a family living there ten or so years ago… who remembered Dr James Gregory and his little boy.

***

Elegant and poised, Antonia nursed a glass of white wine and waited for her father. Would she recognize him? Would he recognize her?

They had arranged to meet at midday. At exactly five to twelve her father appeared – older certainly, but undeniably handsome. A distinguished looking man in a tailored suit, he carried himself with assurance. He glanced around the hotel foyer, his eyes briefly resting on her and then he approached her.

"Antonia?" She inclined her head and smiled at him.

"I wouldn't have recognized you... It's been, what, nearly twenty years?"

"Something like that."

He scrutinized her for a long moment.

"A daughter to be proud of!"

She acknowledged the compliment and waited for him to offer her a second glass of wine. They moved to a secluded seating area. A waiter brought drinks to their table.

"So, was the States your last posting?"

"It was. Your mother was very settled in Washington, and we decided to stay out there when I retired. We moved to a retirement complex in Florida. One can have a good life..."

"So, what brought you back?"

"After your mother died, everything seemed to lose its appeal. I felt a change of scene might help. I have friends here in London. And I suppose I hoped you might make contact." He smiled at her. "I'm so glad you did!"

Antonia sipped her wine and regarded him.

"So, tell me about yourself," he invited.

"After the Sorbonne I spent a year at a Russian University studying literature, and then looked for a job as a translator. Basically that's what I've been doing ever since – translating Russian novels...occasionally I might translate some German and French – being fluent in five languages opened many doors."

"You're not married?" He glanced at her left hand for confirmation.

"Briefly. Marriage didn't suit."

"I'm sorry."

"No need. I was glad to be shot of him."

Over lunch Antonia found herself talking about James, despite her resolve not to divulge their relationship.

"When might I get to meet him?"

"James… is something of a recluse."

Adroitly, Antonia changed the subject.

The food was delicious. The wind flowed freely. Antonia floated.

"I wondered whether you might join me for Christmas?" Her father studied her unguarded expression.

"I already have plans for Christmas."

"Plans that include your James?"

"M'm."

Clearly she was not going to invite him to share their Christmas. He repressed a sigh. Antonia saw that she had disappointed him.

"Will you have friends? Go to friends?"

"Yes indeed. I have a standing invitation for the festivities. Perhaps we can meet again in the New Year?" He left the suggestion dangling.

"Shall we order coffee?" Antonia felt in need of strong black coffee. She had drunk more wine than she'd intended. "What had you planned for this afternoon?"

"Would you care for a walk? A Gallery? A trip down the Thames to Greenwich?"

"There's an exhibition on at the Tate."

"Let's do that."

Antonia excused herself while they waited for coffee. She splashed cold water on her face in the Ladies, in an effort to dispel her dizziness. It was a long time since she'd drunk so much wine. She returned to find coffee had been served.

***

It was late by the time Antonia had driven home. She had left the car at her flat to save parking charges in central London. The village was in darkness. She turned into the drive that wasn't there, cheered to see lights in the cottage.

An old fashioned carriage lamp (which she didn't remember noticing before) threw its light across the front garden, welcoming her. She gathered herself together and considered the fact that she had no front door key. It hadn't been a problem if she was out with James – he could simply walk through doors. Then she saw that the front door was ajar, waiting for her. She pushed it open. The door protested, screeching on the hall floor. Antonia leaned against it to shut it. Down the hall, pausing at the living room door, glancing in. Soft music was playing. A fire danced in the hearth. James rose from his chair to greet her.

"I'm back."

"So I see!" He smiled at her. "Have you had a good day? Did it go well?"

Antonia frowned. Something was different. Something had changed. There was a different ambience. James remained standing, looking at her questioningly.

"Yes. Yes, I had a good day. Better than I expected. It was nice to see him…"

"Coffee?"

"Please."

Why hadn't he swept her into his arms? Kissed her?" She followed him into the kitchen. James filled the kettle and set it on the range. Antonia glanced at the unusually silent range. She noticed that blinds had been pulled down over the windows – a cheerful pattern of orange and yellow sunflowers. She didn't remember noticing the blinds before.

"Are you hungry? Would you like something to eat?"

"I had a good lunch."

"I'm sure you did." James smiled. "I expect it was a long time ago. I thought you might like a hot egg sandwich?"

"What is a hot egg sandwich, exactly?"

"Two slices of thickly buttered bread with a fried egg slapped between them. Jake's favourite."

He placed a frying pan on the range, dropping a knob of butter into it. She watched him slicing a loaf, buttering the bread and then dropping an egg into the frying pan where it sizzled seductively. Within moments she was presented with a hot egg sandwich. He turned back to make one for himself. Antonia ate hers standing up, watching James – he seemed very domesticated. The egg was surprisingly good. She licked her fingers and reached for her coffee. They migrated into the living room and sat either side of the fire. James added another log.

"So, what did you do today?" Antonia asked.

"This and that. I changed the bed and washed the sheets. It was a good drying day."

"Shouldn't I be doing that?"

"Be my guest!" His eyes smiled at her.

Why had he chosen to sit apart? Why had he not gathered her into his arms? What had changed? She wanted to ask whether he was glad to see her back, but he had turned his attention back to the fire.

"You... didn't mind me going?" She could hear the diffidence in her voice.

"Not at all."

"He wanted me to do Christmas with him..."

"By all means. Yes, why don't you?"

"I thought... I thought you would want... well, I would like...I ...Don't you want to spend Christmas with me...?"

She had his attention.

"What's wrong?"

"That's what I wanted to ask *you*! It's different somehow. You're different. You're treating me like a stranger..."

"Am I?" James shrugged. "Perhaps you're tired. It's been a long day, and maybe something of an unknown quantity, meeting your father after all these years. Shall we go up?" Without waiting for a reply, he arranged the fireguard in place, straightened up and smiled at her. "Coming?"

She followed him upstairs. Curtains billowed at the window. He crossed to close it. She saw their bed was made up with fresh linen. A clean nightgown was folded on her pillow.

In a strange way it felt as though he had erased the Antonia she had been yesterday. She had become a stranger.

"Would you like to use the bathroom first," he invited her. "There's clean towels."

Antonia gave a small sigh: was nothing the same? Is there anything that smells of me? She shut the bathroom door behind her and raised the lid of the linen basket. It was empty. Their underwear, their pyjamas, their towels had all been laundered. Obscurely Antonia felt a frisson of fear. She ran a bath. The hot water was comforting. Perhaps James was right and she was just overtired. Presently, she pulled out the plug and while the water gurgled away, towelled herself. The art nouveau dressing gown was not on the back of the door – had that been laundered too? She found a white towelling dressing gown which she slipped on, tying the cord around her waist. Would James actually be there when she returned? Or would he have dissolved into the ether?

He was there. Sitting on the edge of the bed in his pyjamas, glancing at a magazine while he waited for her. She walked around the bed and slipped into her nightgown, keeping her back to him, obscurely shy. The bed had been turned down. She slid between the sheets. The bed was cold. She shivered. An electric blanket would not come amiss! Picking up her hairbrush from the bedside table – at least that was still the same! – she brushed her hair. There had been a book on the table. It had gone. The bed bounced slightly as James got up. She heard the toilet flushing. James would be cleaning his teeth. He came back and slid into bed. What was it Michael had said? 'James doesn't feel the cold.'

"Do you want to read?" he asked.

"You've taken my book."

"Have I? It won't be far. We'll look in the morning."

"We? I was beginning to feel we weren't a '*we*' anymore!" James turned his head, frowning.

"What's got into you? H'm? Perhaps next time you see your father, you might want to stay overnight at the flat." Although his voice was gentle, she felt rebuffed. Tears slid down her face. Turning her back on him she slithered down the chilly bed.

"Antoni-ni?" James gathered her against him. He held her while she cried…and long after she had stopped crying and fallen into an exhausted sleep. In the morning he let her sleep on.

***

She woke to sunshine peeping around the curtains. James's pyjamas were neatly folded on his pillow. She rolled over and buried her face in his familiar smell. Presently she sat up and threw back the bedclothes. As she opened the bedroom door the aroma of frying bacon wafted up to her. The world was back on its axis. Everything would be alright. She must have left her clothes in the bathroom last night… but she had dressed up for her father and she didn't feel like wearing what she had worn yesterday. She pulled on slacks and a comfortable sweater, and then she hurried down the stairs, wanting to be greeted by the

Range, expecting to see the Witch peering into her frying pan… The Witch was not there. James, an apron tied around his waist, looked up and smiled at her: "Good morning, Antoni-ni! Ready for breakfast?"

She hesitated on the bottom step.

"Where's Granny?"

"I think she's leaving it to us. Two rashers or three?"

"Was she offended because you did the laundry?"

"Not in the least. Fried bread?"

"James…?"

"M'm?" He looked up. "It's just about ready…and no fried mice!"

"And Grandad?"

James pretended to look under the table.

"Can't see him!"

Antonia came across and sat down at the table. James placed a heaped plate in front of her:

"Two of everything! But leave anything you don't want." He brought his own plate to the table and fetched two mugs of coffee. "Sleep well?"

Suddenly Antonia didn't feel hungry. She pushed her plate aside.

"Why are you being so breezy and efficient? I liked you better the way you were! Look at me when I'm talking to you!" She raised her voice. "Something's different! Have you had a quarrel with your grandparents? Have you decided you don't want me here anymore? James, yesterday you loved me! What's changed?"

James shrugged. He turned his attention back to his breakfast and began eating ravenously.

"The real world intruded yesterday and altered the dynamics of how we are," he said quietly.

He continued eating. Antonia watched him.

"Michael said it was important to maintain contact with the world out there. It's why he took me to meet your parents and encouraged me to contact my father."

"It is important." James wiped up spilled egg with his fried bread. "It's important because one day you may want to return to the real world on a permanent basis."

Antonia digested this. She picked up a piece of crispy bacon and chewed it thoughtfully.

"You mean, without you?"

"M'h'm."

"Because you don't want me?"

"No, Anton-ni. Not because I don't want you. But one day you might meet someone out there in the real world and fall in love. You may want to marry …to have children…to pursue your career. You are beautiful, you are accomplished. You could make a better life for yourself in the real world… And I want you to be free to do that."

"You want me to go?"

"That isn't what I said. I want you to know that you are free to go whenever you may want to…without feeling tied to …all of this."

"Why didn't you want to make love to me last night?"

"Goodness! Well, you fell asleep."

"No, I wasn't! I was crying and you were holding me… but you didn't…and I wanted you to…I thought you loved me!"

"You *are* a bundle of insecurity! Let's go down to the

beach and smell the sea air, feel the wind fresh on our faces …and let the waves wash away all this misery."

"The beach that isn't really there? That only exists in your imagination?"

James pushed back his chair decisively. He held out his hand and pulled her to her feet.

"I am inviting you to share my world, my love, my home…my everything." He drew her into his arms. "All I'm saying is that if there comes a time when my everything isn't enough, I won't stand in your way if you want to go." He kissed her very gently. Antonia clung to him fiercely, emanating a mixture of distress and aggression. "Tell me what you're feeling?"

"If I had teeth big enough I would tear you apart! Never mind breakfast!"

"My tigress!"

A sudden breeze enveloped them as if a door had opened. Antonia blinked: the kitchen had gone. They stood on the beach facing the sea. An off-shore breeze lifted her hair, billowed her skirt – and she was sure she had put on slacks this morning! A gull called plaintively from the cliffs above. James stooped and gathered a handful of sand, letting it trickle through his fingers. He smiled at her.

"Yes!" whispered Antonia. "Oh yes!"

"What?"

"You're back!"

"I hadn't been away."

"But it felt as if you had! It felt as if we'd suddenly become strangers! Everything seemed different and…scary!

I thought perhaps you'd murdered your Granny or something!" James grinned. "I thought perhaps you were…I thought I might wake up dead!"

"Antoni-ni!" The grin vanished. James was horrified. He shook his head and pushed her face into his chest, holding her tightly. After several minutes' thought he said: "But you didn't feel like this after Michael took you to meet Dad and Debs?"

"I know."

"Perhaps you need Michael to accompany you on your forays into the real world."

"They thought I was his girlfriend, without quite liking to ask."

"Mikey doesn't do girlfriends."

"Well, if ever I tire of you!" She released herself and danced away from him, mischief lighting her face.

He chased after her and they fell into a laughing, sprawling heap on the shingle…

***

"How do you normally spend Christmas? Antonia asked, as she washed up their supper dishes.

"When we were growing up Gramps and Gigi– that's my father's parents – would come and stay. They made it very special for all of us. Everybody came. The house was full: log fires, wonderful meals, a splendid Christmas tree… And everyone was happy. I think Tom and Trisha try to recreate that sort of Christmas for their tribe. Well, it's more like a house-party: Steve and Charlie, Mike…I went for one day last year… and, of course, Jake regards himself as one of their family now."

"Don't you have any contact with him since…?"

"Since I died? No. He just wants to be part of Tom's family. Perhaps at some level he's aware of me, but he chooses not to acknowledge me."

"Will you go over this Christmas?"

"No." He picked up a handful of cutlery, dried it and sorted it into the cutlery drawer. "How about you – what's your Christmas like?"

"I usually went out with friends on Christmas Eve and largely ignored Christmas Day: slept till midday… buried myself in a book …listened to music."

"Do you want to see your friends?"

"Not particularly. I'd rather be with you."

"You see, I'd wondered…"

"Yes?"

"Whether we might spend Christmas to New Year in Yorkshire – at the guest house we stayed at last summer?"

He dried a saucepan carefully and hung it up. "They do open over Christmas, I checked." He studied her back as she stood at the sink, emptying the washing-up bowl. "I can come with you because it's somewhere I've been before. What d'you think?"

"Will they be able to see you?"

"They will, because they'll believe in my reality. No one will have told them that officially I'm dead. Whereas my Dad knew I was dead and he never believed in an existence beyond death."

"You'll need me to book it, won't you? The bank isn't going to honour any cheque you write!"

"Actually, I asked Mike to book it for me."

"So, you were presuming I'd say yes!" Antonia turned round confrontationally. "Isn't that a bit high handed?"

"It was going to be a surprise. But then I wondered if you were planning to do whatever you'd usually do…or even if you wanted to spend the holiday with your father."

Antonia stepped forward and touched her hand to his cheek. She smiled at him.

"I think it's a lovely idea! And this time it won't end in tears!"

***

Antonia drove. They stopped at a service station for lunch, and continued on. As James had predicted the couple who ran the guest house welcomed them, said how pleased they were to see them again, and showed them to the room they'd had before.

"Just the two of you?" confirmed the landlady, and without waiting for an answer: "Tea and hot mince-pies in the lounge downstairs… When you're ready."

Antonia shut the door carefully and chuckled:

"She thought I was suffering from morning sickness when we were here before! She was hoping for the patter of tiny feet!"

James paused in his unpacking and pulled her into his arms.

"I wouldn't mind!"

"Get off!"

"You don't fancy the pattering?"

"No Way!" Antonia pushed him away. "Even if we wanted to… it wouldn't be possible, would it?"

"Highly unlikely."

"I don't need to go back on the pill, do I?"

"When did you stop?

"Well, obviously, after your heart attack."

"There you are, then. The likelihood – the possibility is so remote, it's not worth another thought. He smiled at her boyishly. "Can I have that kiss now?"

***

There were no other guests. After the landlady had washed up the plates from their evening meal, she and her husband joined their guests by the fire and chatted.

"You'll be wanting to spend Christmas Eve in York," suggested the landlord. "There's a lot going on." He threw another log on the fire. "There's another couple joining us for New Year. You just make yourselves at home."

Christmas Day dawned wet, and progressively worsened. The rain was torrential – the wettest Christmas on record. James and Antonia enjoyed the cosiness of the lounge and its blazing log fire. They made jigsaws. They played Scrabble which Antonia won hands down. They played chess, at which they were evenly matched. They watched television with their hosts, munching nuts, crystallised fruits and chocolates. James wore the beautiful lambs-wool sweater Antonia had given him. Her own present concealed in yards of tissue paper was the most exquisite nightgown she had ever seen.

"Where did you get it?" she breathed.

"Switzerland. I asked Michael to look for the most beautiful one he could find."

"It's amazing! Look! It's all hand-embroidered! I've never seen anything so...so...!"

"Well, it makes a change from your pyjamas!" James grinned.

Six

Windover Ridge

Early evening. James was playing a game of chess with his grandfather at the kitchen table. Antonia was wrapped in the comfort of the rocking chair (that wasn't there) reading. She looked up suddenly, aware of the presence of someone who hadn't been there a moment ago.

"Michael!" she exclaimed.

James and Dr Mikilari looked up:

"Hi, Mikey! Good to see you! Can you stay over?"

"It's Half Term, so I have the week off. Thought I'd spend the weekend with you, then drive up to see Steve and Charlie…and down to Tom's."

"Quite the gad-about!"

"Coffee?" enquired the Range hospitably.

Michael strolled over to the Range, accepted a mug and then pulled up a chair to the table, watching the game for a moment.

"Any news of Jake?" James enquired.

"He'll be at Tom's. You know he graduates this summer?"

"He still won't acknowledge me."

Michael wondered whether to divulge that Jake occasionally took himself through the pentagram to visit Caroo. He refrained, knowing how hurt James would be. He turned to Antonia:

"I've a concert coming up in Munich in March. Might see you if you're over to visit your publisher?"

"That would be nice!" Antonia seemed to light up.

"Have you eaten, Mike?" James asked.

"Had a bite before I came. Had stuff to finish up."

"As in finishing up work or finishing left-over food?"

"Well, both!" Michael grinned.

He was visibly relaxing. Dr Mikilari glanced across at Antonia:

"You two seem to know each other," he observed, removing James's red bishop.

"Ouch!" James considered the board and made his move. "Check!"

Dr Mikilari positioned a knight to deflect the attack.

"Yes," said Michael. "I met Antonia out in Munich. She came to one of my concerts. I thought you knew that?"

"Did I?" Dr Mikilari gave a small deprecating smile. "Anno Domini!"

The evening passed pleasantly and Just after nine-thirty Dr Mikilari rose, thanked James for the game and indicated that he was ready for his bed. He patted

Antonia's arm affectionately on his way out.

"I'll just make sure your room is ready," Antonia addressed Michael as she headed upstairs.

Originally the landing had only extended as far as the bathroom, ending in a blank wall. But since Michael had started visiting, the Witch had flung a single bedroom at the end of the landing. Antonia remembered how cold Michael had found it! The room was still cold. Although the bed was made up, ready, she would have preferred to have aired it. Perhaps a hot water bottle would warm it through…if there was such a thing in the cottage?

Downstairs the brothers were chatting:

"She should get out more in the real world, James."

"She seems happy enough. You took her to meet Dad and Debs. She went up to see her father. We go for walks. We swim. She has acquaintances in the village. Occasionally Granny whisks her off for a shopping expedition."

"But no friends?"

"I don't see the problem. I don't stop her doing anything… and she has her flat." He saw Antonia hovering at the foot of the stairs. "Come and join us!"

"Actually, I wondered if you had such a thing as a hot water bottle?"

***

Antonia woke early. James was still asleep, his breathing deep and regular. Antonia slipped out of bed and padded downstairs.

"Good morning!" The Range greeted her, "Coffee?"

Antonia wrapped her hands around the mug, appreciative of its warmth. "And will you have one for the gentleman in the sitting room?"

"What?"

Antonia was confused. Had Dr Mikilari sought refuge from his hammock in the garden? She picked up the proffered mug, pushed open the sitting room door, adjusting her eyes to the darkness. In the light from the kitchen she could make out someone asleep on the sofa.

"Good morning, Antonia!" Michael sat up. "I hope you don't mind my decamping down here. It's so infernally cold in that bedroom!"

"I'm so sorry! I hoped the hot water bottle would make a difference."

He reached for the mug of coffee.

"This is good!"

"James is still asleep…" Antonia was acutely aware that she was still in her nightdress – but Michael appeared oblivious. "I'll ask him to do something about your room. Did you sleep in little boy's room before?"

"Complete with the train wallpaper Jake chose!"

"I'm afraid he blames me for stealing his Dad."

"He enjoys being with his cousins. Says it's like a proper family. And Trish *is* his Mum." He sighed with pleasure over his coffee. "Jake doesn't believe in life after death. He no longer believes in the Back Garden. As far as he's concerned his Dad died. Full stop."

Antonia finished her coffee.

"I'm going to take a coffee up to James. See you at breakfast."

***

Michael tossed aside the newspaper he had been perusing.

"Why don't we go out somewhere?" he suggested. "Weather's brightened up. Fresh air'd do us good. How about it?"

Antonia looked across at James.

"What d'you think?"

"Anywhere in mind?" he asked.

"Actually, I thought Antonia might like Windover Ridge. Dad used to take Steve and me up there. We always fancied camping overnight but he would never let us." He turned to Antonia. "Spectacular views from the top."

"Well, why don't you take Antonia – obviously I can't come with you. Just have a nice day out."

"Why can't you come?"

"I can only go where I've been before. I've never been to Windy Ridge."

"Windover Ridge. How come you never went?"

"Maybe I'd left home by then."

"Would you rather we went somewhere else, James?" Antonia searched his face.

"No, you two go. Enjoy a day out. Have lunch at a country pub. I'll see you when you get back. I'll probably do some painting. I don't suppose you'd take a consignment up to the Gallery for me, Mike?"

"Could do, on the way to Steve's perhaps."

"I'd better put on some walking shoes." Antonia excused herself.

"Right!" Michael stood up. "Okay if I take some chocolate and apples?" he asked, helping himself.

"Fine. Do Antonia good to get out… keep her in the *real* world!" There was a wry note in his voice. He picked up the discarded newspaper and glanced at it. "Same old news," he remarked. "Nothing much changes."

Antonia reappeared. She came over and hugged James.

"Sure you don't mind?"

He smiled at her affectionately:

"Have a great time!"

***

In the car Michael showed her the route they would take.

"There's a really nice country pub, just here!" He pointed. "And here's Windover Ridge. The view from the top is amazing! Well worth the climb." He smiled at her, relaxed and happy.

He drove towards Brascombe and then veered off to the right along narrow country lanes, bounded by hedges which presently gave way to woodland – the road took them through a forest. The pub where they stopped for lunch seemed to be in the middle of nowhere, but the food was excellent. They lingered over coffee, chatting. Michael was good company. Finally, he pushed back his chair:

"Better be on our way! We've some way to drive and

we want to be down before dark…before the goblins appear!"

"Goblins?"

"Dad always warned us the goblins would chase us if we weren't out of the woods before dark!"

"And you believed him?"

"I expect it was a ploy to get us down. Steve and I liked to run off and explore. There's a ruined chapel up there – great place to make a camp!"

"D'you see much of Steve?"

"Now and again. Not as much as I'd like, but we lead very different lives."

They drove along narrow lanes whose hedgerows were studded with spring flowers…snowdrops, crocuses, wild violets, primroses, celandine. Antonia gazed at the passing scenery. It was a long time since they had left the last small village behind. She checked she had her phone with her and was reassured.

"Not far now. Bit in the middle of nowhere!" observed Michael, turning his head to smile at her.

Eventually, he pulled off the road and parked in a small clearing which boasted a picnic table and bench… and a rusty litter bin bearing a tattered injunction to take your litter home. Antonia laughed.

"Put your handbag in the glove compartment. It'll be safer there." He patted the pocket of his anorak. "I've got some chocolate and apples for when we get to the top."

They set off along a broad track which shortly began to climb up between the trees. Birds sang. Small animals scuttled among the brushwood. Higher up a young fawn leaped across their path. Sunlight filtered through the canopy overhead.

"Considering how much it rained yesterday, the path's surprisingly dry." Antonia observed.

"It drains well. Sandy subsoil. And it's sheltered. Quite a steep climb! I'd forgotten how steep it is!"

"When were you last here?"

"I suppose Steve and I would have been eleven or twelve."

"Long enough to have forgotten it's a bit of a challenge!"

The path was narrower now and they climbed in single file. The trees were closer together, the path riddled with their exposed roots. A squirrel scampered overhead, sending a shower of raindrops on the walkers.

"It's surprisingly steep!" Antonia paused to draw breath.

"But worth it for the view at the top!"

"I believe you!"

Michael paused to ease his back.

"There's a lake somewhere down on the right," he remembered. "And a spooky place over there!" He pointed. "It was such an exciting place to explore."

They continued up. Although Antonia was fit, she was finding herself out of breath. She observed that Michael was noticeably limping. It had better be worth it, she thought!

And then, suddenly, there was light ahead! Flagging steps revived.

Despite his limp Michael forged ahead, stopping at

the summit to breathe deeply as he drank in the breath-taking view. They emerged into bright sunshine. Before them the land fell away in meadowland and scrub. The view, as Michael had promised was spectacular. He indicated a weathered bench where they could sit and enjoy the view. Peace enfolded them.

"What an amazing place!"

"Yes, isn't it! You see why I wanted to bring you here!" He reached into his pocket for the chocolate and apples. They sat munching the apples in a companionable silence. "You can see for miles and miles! Steve and I used to roll down the meadow and come back covered in sticky burrs and twigs!"

The vale fell away before them to a winding river, and beyond lay hedged fields and sprawling woodland. They sat watching the sunlight caressing the scene below.

"Sun's beginning to go down," observed Antonia. "D'you think we should make a move? We don't want to be chased by your mythical goblins!"

Michael sighed. He got reluctantly to his feet.

"Well, at least it's downhill all the way!"

"Shouldn't take us so long then."

They set off. After the sunshine and open vista, the woods already seemed dark. The birds were no longer singing. It felt chilly under the overhanging trees. It was very quiet.

"Watch your footing! The path's a bit slippery," warned Michael.

A branch cracked underfoot, startling Antonia. The path which had seemed so smooth as they climbed, spread exposed roots across their way – visible and avoidable on their ascent, but in the gathering darkness liable to trip them.

"Ouch!" Michael caught his foot in just such a root and fell heavily.

"Are you okay?" Antonia squatted down to help him up.

"No! My ankle! Ohhh!"

Michael struggled to sit up. His face was white. He was clearly in intense pain.

Antonia regarded him anxiously, aware that her phone was securely locked in his glove compartment.

"I don't suppose you've got your phone on you?"

"Wouldn't be any use up here. There's no signal."

"Well, I could have climbed back up to the summit. There'd be a signal up there."

"And what? Ask the ambulance men to bring a stretcher and torches to find us *somewhere* on Windover Ridge?"

"It's the main path up, isn't it?"

Michael thought for a moment.

"Actually there's loads of paths branching off. You just don't notice them on the way up. Anyway the answer is no, I don't have my phone."

"What are we going to do? Spend the night with the goblins?"

Michael bit his lip against the pain. He had fallen awkwardly on his bad leg, but the injury was to his other ankle. There was no way he could walk.

"Look, Toni, if you can find a stick and draw a pentagram around us, we can be back with James."

Antonia glanced at him sharply. He'd never called her Toni before. She looked about her: roots everywhere, leaf mould, tiny twigs… She needed a bigger stick, stronger. She crawled under low, overhanging branches and searched, eventually finding a suitable stick. It was now dark, and somehow the trees did not feel so friendly. She brushed the thought aside, impatiently, and began drawing the pentagram.

"Make sure you stand inside it," instructed Michael. "You don't want to be left behind."

"What about the car?"

"Sod the car!"

"Isn't it more sensible if I go back to the car and drive it home. You'll need it to go back to Morton's."

"You'll get lost. Windover Ridge is in the middle of nowhere. And I don't have a satnav."

"There's a map in the car and I'll have my phone. I can drive to the nearest town and get directions. Just give me the keys."

"Come with me!" Michael urged.

The rest of what he was saying was lost as Antonia completed the pentagram… and suddenly she was on her own. She stared at the space where he had been…and then reached out and picked up his car keys.

It was, of course, downhill on the path by which they'd ascended, but it was now dark. If only she had a torch! She would just have to be careful not to fall. Shortly the path would widen out and then the going would be easier… and once she got back to the car she could phone James. It would be wonderful just to hear his voice! It was not as if there were any wild animals in the woods – or indeed, goblins! It was going to be alright! She made her way carefully, anxious not to trip. The wood was ominously quiet. Nothing stirred in the undergrowth. Her foot slipped and she sprawled in an ungainly heap. At least she hadn't twisted her ankle! She seemed to have fallen into a soft bed of pine needles… Was this where she lost the car keys? Where was the path? She picked herself up, recovering the path and walked gingerly on. It was more difficult than she had supposed. Ahead of her the path forked. She did not remember the path dividing…What was it Michael had said: there are lots of paths branching off, you just don't notice them on the way up.

Left or right? Right or left? The carpark below must be to the right. She took the right path and continued downhill. However, this path seemed much less well defined. Antonia hesitated. At least it was going downhill, but it soon deteriorated into an animal track rather than a proper path. She retraced her steps to the fork and took the left. This was definitely wider. She heaved a sigh of relief. The path levelled out – was she nearly there? But then it began climbing up, and turned a corner. Where was it going? The trees began opening out into a clearing. There was just enough light to make it out.

Ahead of her was what looked like an old headstone. She stared at it. Definitely a headstone – once white, but now covered in lichen and moss. What was a grave doing up here? Michael had said something about an old ruined chapel off in the woods…a place where he and Steve had explored and played. *It must be where the goblins lived*, they'd decided. And begged to be allowed to camp overnight. No wonder their father had refused to let them camp overnight in a graveyard! She was obviously on the wrong path. She would have to go back to the fork and take the narrow path to the right. She took what she thought was the path by which she'd entered the clearing. It started to go downhill, which was a good sign. She tripped over a protruding root and fell. As she picked herself up, she felt in her pocket for the keys. Her pocket was empty. She felt around her on the ground. Nothing. Perhaps she had lost them on her earlier fall? Well, she'd just have to deal with that once she got back to the car. If necessary, she could smash a window and at least retrieve her phone.

Ouch! She had trodden in a puddle! There had been no puddles on the way up. In fact, she had commented on the dryness of the path. In the dark the path tilted to the left unbalancing her. She slid into a ditch full of leaf-mould and water. Scrambling out of the ditch, feeling for firm ground… Yes, path…going downhill. Not so steep now. Soon be out onto the broad path and the carpark. Her feet squelched in her wet shoes. Was the path becoming slightly boggy? Michael had mentioned a lake. Perhaps she was on the edge of this lake? Well, at least she must be at ground level. Each step seemed to suck her deeper. She had to get out of this! She tried to go back, but the bog was sucking her in, swallowing her. She floundered, reaching for something – anything – to grasp. She was frightened.

She was up to her knees in this filthy sucking swamp.

"James!" she shrieked. "Help me! Help!"

***

Michael had been made comfortable on the sitting room sofa. His ankle, which James thought was sprained rather than broken, was strapped up. Strong analgesics were making Michael drowsy. James watched over him. He did not expect Antonia back for quite a while. Windover Ridge was a good two-hour drive in daylight. It was now dark and she was unfamiliar with the road. Fortunately, Michael always carried a map. James was not worried. Antonia was a very competent driver. He did wonder why she had not phoned to tell him she was safe and on her way home. Perhaps the phone signal was inadequate. Well, she would phone at some point. He turned the light low, leaving Michael to rest.

In the kitchen he sat with the Witch, drinking coffee and enjoying a hot egg sandwich. They had been chatting. An hour passed.

"Something's wrong!" James looked at his grandmother. "Antonia's in trouble!"

"Yes!" The Witch was alert. "Deep trouble!" She flung her cloak, over her shoulder and opened the broom cupboard.

"Walkies?" enquired the Broom, dancing ecstatically on his twig ends.

"Rescue mission," said the Witch tartly. "And be quick about it before the girl drowns!"

She grabbed the nameless cat and tucked him under her arm. A moment later the kitchen was empty. A few displaced spiders scuttled back into the cupboard. James sighed and went back to watch Michael sleeping. There was nothing he could do, except hold Antonia in his love, and will her to hold on.

The Witch circled Windover Ridge. Darkness and night were no problem to her. The problem would be the spirits abroad in the wood. Without a torch, Antonia had likely tripped, been lured off the path and enticed into the swamp. Malevolent spirits! Antonia had no idea! The Witch headed the broom into the woods.

"Swamp!" directed the Witch.

The cat's fur rose along his back He hissed, sensing the spirits. He spat. Coiled, tense and angry, giving a low growl deep in his throat. Something shadowy moved. The cat snarled. *Getting warm*, reckoned the Witch!

Floundering, struggling, terrified, Antonia gave a faint desperate dry. The swamp was constricting her chest. She could hardly breathe. She was going to drown out here in this evil swamp!

"Hold on, Antonia!" growled the Witch, hovering over the swamp. assessing the situation. She could not land the broom in the swamp. She would have to drain it.

There was a sudden flurry as Antonia was sucked under the surface. A shriek as the cat sank teeth and claws into an insubstantial spirit and a revolting gurgling as the murky waters of the swamp oozed away. The Witch waited until she could step into the drained swamp. She wafted her broom over the area where Antonia lay collapsed, unconscious, covered in the vile black slime which had so nearly drowned her. The Witch uttered an ancient Phoenician curse holding the swamp at bay before it could start oozing back. Crouching over Antonia's inert body, the Witch traced a pentagram in the slime. No matter that the swamp immediately oozed into the outline she'd imprinted, the evil which had drawn Antonia to the swamp to drown her, was no match for the Witch.

Leaving the Broomstick in the courtyard to be hosed down in the morning, the Witch hosed Antonia's unconscious body, removing her filthy clothes. James ran a hot bath and carried her up to the bathroom where he gently lowered her into the warm water. She smelled appalling. James's eyes watered. He retched. The Witch sat on the bath stool and watched him.

"I remember my first bath," she said. "Milkil had a ground floor bathroom. The bath was so filthy, I doubt it ever recovered! Now, do we cut her hair off or try shampooing it?"

"You can't cut her hair off! She'll be distraught!"

"And you'll be distraught trying to sleep next to her while she stinks like a pigpen!" James swallowed. "The stench will last for days! You'd better give me the scissors."

Reluctantly, James handed over the scissors. He lifted Antonia out of the bath and laid her on a towel. The bath was filthy. Black slime coated its surface. He swilled the bath and then refilled it, while the Witch cut Antonia's hair. It fell in filthy matted clumps onto the towel. The Witch stepped back to survey her shearing. Then she picked Antonia up as if she was feather-light and lowered her into clean water. Vigorously shampooing Antonia's scalp, she observed the bruises from a number of falls –

heritage of Windover Ridge. Then, supporting her head as if she were a baby, she dowsed her scalp in clean water. A third bath later, Antonia, less offensive and clean, was dried and carried to bed.

"She'll sleep, now," said the Witch. "I'll take the towel with her hair and burn it. You can scrub the bath, I suggest you have a bath, yourself. You smell pretty rank!"

"Yaugh!" protested the Range. "What's this obnoxious filth you're feeding me!"

"Best you don't know!" the Witch told him.

She stood up and considered herself: wet through, dirty, smelly, utterly vile! "And don't think you can get away with tepid water!" she scolded the Range. "I want a nice hot green bubble bath."

That had been her illicit delight, a deep green bubble bath in the bathroom that Milkil shared with that pesky wife of his…his long-since dead wife. She discarded her clothes and fed them to the Range, accepting a mug of coffee while she waited for James. Presently she wafted upstairs in a veil of invisibility, so as not to discomfort her grandson with her ancient nakedness.

"Go down and check on Michael. Make yourself a mug of coffee. And throw your stinking clothes into the Range!"

The Witch climbed into her scented green-bubble-bath and slid down so that only her nose was visible.

She lay and soaked. Scented warmth seeped into her old bones. She smiled…

James looked in at Michael, peacefully sleeping. He walked out to the kitchen. The Range eyed him balefully.

No coffee was on offer. Reluctantly, James filled the kettle and made his own coffee.

"Not a patch on your brew!" he told the Range.

"There's no hot water left," the Range mentioned, somewhat mollified by James's compliment. "Five baths in less than two hours! Not to mention the obnoxious rubbish you've been feeding me!"

"You've done a sterling job! At least you can rest now."

"Good night!" The Range clamped his lid shut and prepared to drowse.

Presently James put his head around the bathroom door. He was in pyjamas, having washed his hair and splashed on cologne.

"I just wanted to say thank you, Granny."

"You *just* did, did you!" The Witch snorted. "Well, you've got her back! Now, leave me in peace!"

James padded along to his bedroom. At least the worst of the pervasive stench had abated. He slid into bed beside Antonia. She was breathing normally, but still unconscious…unaware of his presence.

***

Antonia awoke to daylight. The curtains were open. She was at home in bed. She felt confused, disorientated. Memory seemed to elude her. She reached for James, but his bed-space was empty. His pillow smelled of cologne. She tried to remember… she had been struggling in a swamp, drowning. Was she alive…or? … Had she, in fact, drowned? Was she a ghost? Was she now like James…

existing in a houseful of ghosts? Was it only Michael, who passed between the world of past and present, fully alive? What had happened to Michael?

He'd fallen and hurt himself. Where was he? Where, for that matter, was James?

She was clean, no longer covered in putrid mud and slime. She was dressed in a nightgown, Did that make her *real*? Or was this her new ghostly body?

"Would you like some coffee?"

Relief surged through her. She sat up, reaching up to where her hair had been... running her hand over the short stubble covering her scalp.

"My hair! James, what's happened to my hair!"

"Hush! It's alright! Well, it's not alright: we had to cut your hair because everything was covered in that horrible, putrid slime. You smelt as if you'd fallen into a slurry pit!"

"What?"

"You stumbled into the swamp at Windover Ridge. Granny came to rescue you. You don't remember?"

"I lost Michael's keys! The car's still out there!"

"I expect he's got a spare set."

"He fell. He couldn't get up...I had to draw a pentagram around him."

"That's right. He sprained his ankle. He's downstairs in the sitting room, all bandaged up."

"He wanted me to come back with him, but I thought I ought to drive his car back..."

"Granny will see to that. She came and rescued you. We had to bath you three times over and cut your hair, just to get rid of the stench of the swamp."

Antonia swallowed a mouthful of coffee.

"James! I'm going to be sick!"

He had brought up the washing-up bowl against this eventuality. He offered it to Antonia. She retched and vomited a flood of putrid, black, slimy liquid. The room was filled with its stinking odour.

"I'll get you some water."

James took the bowl and emptied it down the lavatory. He filled a glass with cold water from the tap.

"Salt," said a voice at his shoulder. "Salt water. She needs an emetic to get all that poison out of her system."

James took the swilled bowl and the glass of salt water to Antonia. She swallowed a mouthful of water and was violently sick. It seemed there was no end to the amount of filth she'd swallowed, and now brought back. James was almost sick, himself. Eventually, Antonia lay back, utterly exhausted. James sponged her face and hands. The Witch appeared, cast a glance at his white, drawn face and remarked:

"Better out than in!" She offered Antonia a glass of herbal tea, laced with a soporific. "Drink this," she said briskly. "This will just help you relax." She stood back and observed Antonia. "Michael's awake," she mentioned. "You'd best attend to him. I'll stay with Antonia."

She crossed to the window and flung it wide open. Fresh air lightened the atmosphere. The curtains billowed. An envelope blew to the floor. The Witch stooped and picked it up. It was addressed to her. She opened it and saw that James had written her a thank you note expressing his deep gratitude.

Michael was in pain. He accepted a mug of coffee gratefully and swallowed the pills James offered him. He had been aware of ongoing disturbance throughout the night, but no one had come to see him as far as he was aware.

"Antonia get back alright?" he enquired.

James's hands were gentle, expert, always a doctor first, but his face was drawn. He did not shout. He did not reproach.

"You should have insisted she came back with you," he said quietly. "I don't think you had any idea what an evil place it can be after dark."

"*Evil?*" Michael sipped his coffee and stared at James. "Antonia didn't really believe in the goblins, did she?"

"Whether Dad knew the history of that place, I don't know, but he knew enough to keep you boys safe."

"What happened?"

"Antonia was lured off the path, terrified and caught in the swamp. She nearly drowned. She's lucky to be alive."

"But she only had to follow the path we'd come up by. It was straight down. She should have made it within twenty minutes. I just assumed she got lost driving back."

"*I* nearly lost her."

"What can I say!"

"You could try saying sorry."

"James," Michael bit his lip. "I am so, so sorry! I had no idea! D'you want me to go?"

He winced as James unwound the bandages. James's hands were gentle but sure.

"Where were you thinking of going?" James smiled. "You won't get far on that ankle. You're going to need crutches for a while."

"I thought you might want me out of your hair?"

"Speaking of hair: we had to cut Antonia's hair – it was so matted and slimy. I just mention it in case you're shocked when you see her."

"Right."

"It will grow again, but she looks a bit like a scarecrow at the moment." He smiled ruefully at his brother. "Would you like some breakfast?"

When he returned with a breakfast tray he saw at once that something was wrong.

"Pain, Mikey? Aren't the pills helping?"

Michael shook his head. He was clearly distressed. James put down the tray and squatted down in front of the sofa.

"What is it, Mikey?"

Michael took a deep shuddering sigh.

"First I drown Margot and now I almost drown Antonia!"

"You were five. You were too small to understand what you were doing. If anything it was my fault. If I'd been there, it would never have happened. I was on a school, trip. Mum blamed *me*."

"Do you still have Margot out in her pram…in the back garden?"

"Indeed I do. When you can manage your crutches, you can come out and see her, pick her up and cuddle her."

"I feel like a murderer!"

"You're not. I guess you never had the chance to talk about it. Bring it out in the open. You and Steve were whisked off to Gramps and Gigi. I'm sure they loved you both, but nobody discussed what had happened. We'll talk about it later, if that would help. But, for now, eat your breakfast while it's still edible."

James left him and accepted a mug of coffee from the Range. He couldn't face breakfast, himself. He sat in the rocking chair, reflecting on his brother's anxiety. How different he was from Steve who never brooded, as long as there was a football to kick!

"Granny," he said when she reappeared. "What are we going to do with Mikey? He can't manage the stairs but he'll need the bathroom."

"He's got a perfectly good bathroom in his bungalow at Morton's," remarked the Witch unfeelingly.

"It's half term. Everyone will be away. I don't think he could manage on his own."

"Ship him over to Tom's?" The Witch gave James a penetrating look, assessing his concern. "Very well, I'll create a small ensuite in the broom cupboard."

"Thanks, Granny! You're a star!"

***

Antonia awoke to daylight. The curtains had been drawn back. The windows were slightly open allowing the morning air to freshen the room. She was at home. In bed. Safe. Alive…or was she? Had she, in fact, drowned in that bog? Was she herself a ghost? Like James … existing in a houseful of ghosts? What was real? She longed for a mug of coffee. Did longing for coffee make her real? Where was James? Why didn't he come? Antonia flung back the covers and reached bare feet to the floor.

She was wearing the nightdress which James had given her for Christmas – which Michael had bought in Switzerland.

She stumbled out of the bedroom on wobbly legs – they'd kept her in bed for two days…or was it three? At the head of the stairs the friendly warmth of the kitchen rose up and wrapped her in comfort.

"Coffee?" sang the Range. "Hot buttered toast? Bacon Buttie?"

Antonia felt an overpowering sense of gratitude for the Range. She came downstairs and settled herself in the rocking chair (that wasn't there) gratefully sipping her coffee.

James strolled into the kitchen from the courtyard, hands in pockets.

"Antoni-ni!"

"James!" Antonia leapt out of the chair, spilling her coffee and hurled herself into his arms, sobbing with relief. He held her for a long time.

"James, did I drown? Am I a ghost like you, now?"

James chuckled.

"No. Antoni-ni, my precious, wonderful Antoni-ni, you're absolutely real! You've just had a couple of days in bed, recovering. Michael should never have left you!"

"I was worried about the car."

James shook his head gently. His eyes were kindness.

His sensitive fingers stroked her cheek.

"Granny will recover the car in her own inimitable way. Everything's as it should be…apart from Mikey's sprained ankle."

"Is he…will he…?"

"He'll survive."

"I seem to have spilt coffee all down myself…"

"Well, you weren't going to say hello to Mike in your nightgown, were you! Let's go upstairs and get you dressed," he guided her to the stairs. "Then, when you're in your right clothes and your right mind, you can come down and give him a piece of your mind!"

"I'm just grateful to be here!"

"M'm, I'm pretty grateful too!"

"I just needed to know I was real."

"Will you feel more real if I kiss you?"

He picked her up and carried her back to their bedroom. It was as long time before they came downstairs.

***

Antonia, looking frail and tired, sat by the fire in the sitting room, keeping Michael company. Although forewarned, Michael was shocked by her appearance. Normally her face was softly framed by her long dark hair, but the shearing starkly emphasised her features. He couldn't take his eyes off her.

"It will grow again," James said quietly.

"By the time your ankle's healed, I'll have a new head of hair," said Antonia bravely.

"That's good." Michael swallowed. "I owe you an apology, Antonia. I should never have let you try to make your own way back."

"It very nearly cost Antonia her life."

Michael observed his brother. Did he need to rub it in at every turn!

"I've said I'm sorry!"

Betraying a hint of impatience, James got up and left the room. After a moment, Antonia stumbled after him, needing the reassurance of his presence.

Dr Mikilari shuffled in from the kitchen and glanced with pleasure at the blazing fire.

"Ragwort sent me to keep you company," he said to Michael.

"Come on in and make yourself comfortable, Grandad."

"Did I ever tell you about the time Ragwort fell off her broomstick into the pond in St James Park? Sprained her ankle. She said the broomstick was unbalanced by her increased weight – she was pregnant at the time."

Michael looked up with interest.

"I thought she'd done it deliberately," said his Grandfather "so that I'd let her stay!"

"Didn't she live with you? I mean if she was pregnant?"

"Ah well, I wasn't responsible for that! And I already had a resident wife…" He paused reminiscently. "Ragwort set herself up in my basement…turned it into what you'd call a bedsit."

"I'm not sure I remember. Gran must have found that difficult…"

"A menage à trois…"

"One could feel some sympathy for Gran."

"I don't think sympathy was what she particularly wanted." Dr Mikilari took out his handkerchief and wiped his nose. "But she adored Ragwort's baby!"

"Couldn't Gran have babies of her own?"

"Apparently not. But Ragwort gave me Mlilka – your mother, Michael."

"Actually I don't remember Mum very much, either."

"No? Well, you were only five when the other grandparents took you and Steve…"

The Witch was drowsing in her rocking chair. James strolled in from the courtyard – where Antonia had followed him. He had calmed down and had come in for some coffee. He looked at his grandmother questioningly.

"Grandad?" he enquired.

"He's reminiscing about the old days. Got himself a captive audience! Remembered the time I fell off my broom. He'd forbidden me to go riding while I was pregnant – it upset the ergodynamics of the broom! Course, the broom's homeless since I converted the cupboard into an ensuite for your useless brother. Poor old Broom, out in the rain." She smiled deviously to herself. "I fancied him rotten!!" she admitted.

"Who, the Broom or Grandad?"

The Witch chuckled.

"Grandad adores you."

"Yes, he does." The Witch's eyes softened. She gently rocked herself. Her eyes had a faraway look.

"Excuse me!" The Range interrupted the reverie. "How many coffees?"

***

The nameless cat walked with a distinct lurch. It seemed dazed and bedraggled. Not itself at all. Antonia sat with the cat on her lap, stroking and soothing it. The fire leapt in the hearth, logs smouldering. Across the room Michael sat with his bandaged ankle supported on a stool. He seemed quiet and subdued. The Witch brought in supper on a tray. She was solicitous of Antonia, but clearly unsympathetic towards her 'errant' grandson. James sat with his arm around Antonia, watching the dancing firelight.

"How's Grandad?" asked Antonia after a long silence.

"As ever." The Witch shrugged.

"Wouldn't he like to join us?"

The Witch exchanged a smile with James.

"Prams in the hall before you know it!"

They ate supper on their laps. Antonia shared hers with the cat, hand-feeding him.

"I need to get back to Morton's." Michael caught James's attention. "When d'you think? I can manage pretty well on my crutches now, and classes will start on Monday. I'll have to let Steve know I can't see him ...and I'm afraid I won't be able to take your paintings to the Gallery."

"No, you won't be able to weight-bear for a bit – nor drive. I'll see you back to Morton's, make sure you're okay. You'll be able to take your classes." He paused significantly.

"But I shan't trust you gallivanting off with Antonia in a hurry!"

***

The nightmares continued relentlessly. James would be woken by Antonia's screams as she lashed out, hitting him, flailing as she relived the trauma.

"Wake, up, Antoni-ni! Wake up! You're safe! I'm here!" James pinioned her arms, holding her securely while she writhed and struggled. She was still held by the nightmare, convulsing as she fought against his restraining arms.

He continued talking to her, trying to comfort her. Finally, he reached out and switched on the light. The enveloping darkness retreated to the far corners of the room. Antonia sat up, disorientated, frightened. Gradually, she came back to herself. Her heart was beating alarmingly fast. She shivered, whimpering:

"I thought my chest was going to explode! I couldn't breathe! I thought I was drowning!"

"You're safe! You're alright! Let's go down to the kitchen: warmth, coffee, familiar things. Come on, let's get a warm dressing gown around you."

He helped her out of bed, put his thick winter dressing gown around her shoulders and, taking her by the hand, led her downstairs. The Witch was drowsing in the rocking chair (that wasn't there). She opened her eyes and assessed Antonia from under her snaggled brows.

"Coffee!" she said decisively.

The Range sat in somnolent mood.

"Bestir yourself!" scolded the Witch. The Range yawned, and puffed a wisp of smoke at the Witch. "Coffee!" demanded the Witch, "And be quick about it!"

"We'll be in the living room," James mentioned. "I'll stir up the embers."

He tucked Antonia up on the second sofa, wrapping a blanket around her, while he knelt down and coaxed the fire back to life. Hesitant flames licked at his handful of sticks. By the time the Witch joined them with a tray of coffee, the fire was burning nicely. James added a log. Antonia watched the dancing firelight. She watched James's hands tending the hearth. Accepting a mug of coffee she wrapped her hands around its comforting warmth. On his sofa, Michael stirred, turned over and pulled his blanket over his head.

"What time is it?" he muttered from under his blanket.

"Middle of the night!" said the Witch tartly, "If it's any concern of yours, which it isn't!"

Michael sat up and looked at her. He yawned.

"Why…?" he began.

"Antonia had a nightmare," James answered him. "Granny did you make a coffee for Mikey?"

"Does it look as if I did!"

"Here, have mine. I'll get myself another one." James stood up, handing his mug to Michael.

"Thanks!"

Antonia smiled up at James as he passed. He laid a hand on her shoulder.

"Beginning to feel better?"

"Yes."

"That's good. I'll be back in a moment."

The Witch settled herself in an armchair. There was a protesting yowl from the cat. The Witch scooped up the offending creature from underneath her and threw him across the room.

"Granny!"

The Witch glared at Antonia.

"(a) I didn't know he was there. (b) he bit me!"

"Poor Cat! He's been through quite enough without being thrown across the room!"

The cat retreated under the sofa, glaring balefully at the Witch. James returned with his coffee and perched on the arm of Antonia's sofa, slipping an arm around her shoulders. Michael put down his empty mug and yawned.

"I would really like to go back to sleep," he protested. "Or are you planning a midnight breakfast?"

"Three fried mice!" sang the Witch. "Three fried mice!"

"Granny, why don't you go back to your rocking chair," suggested James diplomatically. "We'll let Mikey go back to sleep, and Antonia and I will just sit here quietly until…"

He glanced at her. "D'you feel ready to go back to bed?"

"I'd rather stay here."

He dropped a kiss on the top of her shaven head.

"You stretch out. I'll make myself comfortable in the chair that Granny's kindly vacating for me."

"Am I?" The Witch pursed her mouth sulkily. "*He's* the fly in the ointment!"

"Leave it, Granny! We're all tired. It's three o'clock in the morning!"

"Pshaw!" spat the Witch…and was gone.

Silence. Firelight threw shadows on the ceiling. The log shifted and settled. Michael drowsed. James sank into the vacated armchair, his head resting against its cushion. He watched over Antonia who was resisting sleep despite eyes drooping with weariness,

***

"I should be getting back to Morton's." Michael munched a plateful of toast. "Granny's made it clear that I'm surplus to requirements."

Antonia, toying with one slice of uneaten toast, said nothing. She looked exhausted.

"I'll take you back through the pentagram," James offered. "With your crutches. See you settled. We'll need to organize some food."

"What about his car? My handbag and phone are still in his glove compartment… there's things I need."

"Granny will sort all that, in her own good time."

"Where *is* Granny?"

"Expect she's skulking in the orchard," muttered Michael through a mouthful of toast. "I'm certainly persona non grata in her books!" He reached for another slice of toast and smiled at Antonia: "Sorry about your nightmare." He paused, his toast halfway to his mouth: "That's a corker of a black eye, James! Who hit you?"

"Antonia hit out in her sleep." He reached across and squeezed her hand.

"Oh James, I'm sorry!"

"Separate beds tonight?" Michael attempted a joke.

James frowned at him and shook his head. There were dark circles under his eyes. He had not slept much for the last four nights and he was tired beyond belief.

Michael had returned to Morton's and appeared to be coping. Always popular with his students, some of whom wanted to mother him, there was no shortage of help. But terrified, distraught and violent, Antonia's nightmares continued. Each night James brought her down to the warmth of the living room, to soft lamplight, friendly firelight, and the suggestion of Mozart's music. After another five nights of broken sleep and nightmares, James took matters into his own hands. He prepared the living room as for their night sojourn: firelight, soft music and two chairs facing each other.

"We're going to try a therapeutic procedure," he explained. "For brief moments I will take you back into what happened, and then bring you back here into this room and re-orientate you into the present moment. I will not let you get trapped in the Fear. I will be here with you for as long as it takes. Do you trust me?"

"Yes."

"Think back to that afternoon, climbing up Windover Ridge with Michael. Tell me one thing you see?"

"Sunshine."

"Good. Now come back into this room and tell me one thing you see."

"Log burning on the fire."

"Good. Okay, back to Windover Ridge. What do you see?"

"Trees."

"Right. Now, come back to me: what do you see?" Antonia hesitated and looked at him.

"I see you."

"O.K." he smiled at her. "Now, back to those woods. What do you see?"

"There was an amazing view from the top…we sat for ages…then the sun was beginning to go down…"

"Good. Come back to this room. What do you see?"

"The curtains."

"O.K. Now, the sun is going down over Windover Ridge …what do you see?"

"The light is going. It's getting dark under the trees… It's getting chilly…the trees seem to be closing in…" Gradually, painfully slowly, James took her step by step down the path under the faintly hostile trees, recounting Michael's fall, their debate whether she should return with him via the pentagram… And then her growing discomfort in the gathering darkness, her uneasiness as she sensed the trees' hostility. She recounted her falls, losing her way in the dark…the clearing with the gravestone. And at each point James drew her back into the familiar living room and the security of his presence. Then, inch by terrifying inch to the swamp. Caught in her living nightmare…but brought sharply back to the present moment. The horror of the bog sucking her down, the impossibility of escape…the constriction of her chest…unable to breathe…knowing she was going to drown in the foul putrid slime. Back and forth, back and forth…until suddenly Antonia stopped and looked directly at him, no longer terrified:

"It's gone! It's…I can't explain, but it's…gone!"

"Yes." James smiled at her. His eyes caressed her. "It's gone."

"I don't understand."

"You don't need to understand. It was terrifying. It was horrible. But it's in the past. It no longer has the power to hold you. Well done, my Antoni-ni. You were very brave. I'm proud of you!" He eased his stiff back and stood up. "We need some coffee."

He felt utterly drained.

In the kitchen the Range greeted him pleasantly:

"Hot buttered buns with your coffee?"

"That sounds nice!" He returned to the living room and set down the tray. "How do you feel?" he asked.

"Exhilarated! Free! Wonderful! Isn't that amazing!"

"Yes, it's how I hoped you would feel." He sat down and reached for a hot buttered bun.

"That eye looks really painful!"

"It's just bruising. It isn't hurting now."

"I didn't mean…"

"I know you didn't."

***

Antonia sat on the toilet while James cleaned his teeth. He swilled the basin and sat on the edge of the bath, regaling her with the Witch's account of her first bath.

"She saved my life," said Antonia soberly.

"Yes, she did."

"You know, I used to think she was rather…I thought

she didn't like me very much…I thought she…"

"Was an interfering old baggage?" The Witch put her head round the bathroom door. "Your breakfast's ready."

"Oh!" Antonia was embarrassed.

"Thank you, Granny. We'll be down in five!"

James ran a basin of hot water for Antonia to wash. She caught sight of her reflection and stared appalled at the sight of her shorn head.

"It will grow back, darling." He drew her into his arms for a moment and then released her, a mischievous grin on his face. "At least ghosts don't have to shave!"

Seven

Early morning Tennis and Shaz

Antonia awoke after a long dreamless sleep. For a second night there had been no nightmares. She stretched and opened her eyes. Morning light filtered through the curtains.

It was a new day… A good day…a day when good things might happen. She sat up. James opened one eye and squinted at her.

"Good night?"

"Yes."

"Splendid! Then you can fetch me a coffee!" He grinned at her and closed his eyes.

Antonia slid out of bed and padded downstairs. The kitchen was quiet.

"Good morning!" The Range gave a little sigh. "Coffee?"

"Yes, please."

"There's biscuits in the tin," said the Range pleasantly. Antonia picked up the biscuit tin and shook it. There were indeed biscuits. She removed the lid. She would need a tray to carry both coffee and biscuits upstairs. She cast about for a tray.

"Use the lid of the biscuit tin," suggested the Range. Then, "Full English breakfast?"

"I don't think James has any plans to get up just yet."

"Perhaps he has a little ravishing in mind?"

Antonia nearly dropped the coffee. She didn't believe her ears! Blushing, she balanced the mugs and some biscuits in the lid of the biscuit tin and beat a hasty retreat. James was propped up on an elbow. He smiled at her as she set down the improvised tray.

"You wouldn't believe what the Range just said!"

"Wouldn't I?"

"He offered us a full English breakfast, and when I said I didn't think you wanted to get up just yet, he said: '*Perhaps he has a little ravishing in mind!*'"

James spluttered into his coffee, coughed, chuckled and grinned at her.

"That's not such a bad idea!"

***

Over breakfast, the Witch sat watching them with intent. Finally, James gave her a long scrutinizing look:

"What?"

"From tomorrow, the two of you will play tennis for an hour before breakfast. Exercise and fresh air…do you good."

"It's years since I played!" Antonia said.

"But you were rather good!" the Witch mentioned.

James considered Antonia with interest.

"And I probably haven't played since I left school," he remarked.

"So, you'll have to work at it!" The Witch sounded decisive.

"Neither of us has a racquet…"

"Since when was that a problem? Racquets and balls will be waiting for you tomorrow."

"Granny has spoken!"

The Witch glared at James, assessing whether he was making fun of her. Antonia took a deep breath:

"I don't suppose you could recover my handbag and phone while you're accessing the racquets?"

"What am I – a magic genie?" snapped the Witch. "Haven't noticed you needing your phone these last several days!"

"Were you thinking you might call your father?" James asked.

"No, it's just… Well I hoped I could get it back. Even if I drive all the way out there, I won't be able to get into Michael's car. I lost the keys."

"Careless, girl!" The Witch was clearly displeased.

Antonia flinched. She stood, gathering their breakfast things. and carried them over to the sink.

James looked at her hunched shoulders. He picked up a tea towel and began to dry up for her.

"And don't cry into the washing up!" snapped the Witch.

***

It was barely daylight the next morning when the Witch breezed into their bedroom, set down a tray of tea beside James and walked purposefully across to the window, pulling back the curtains and flinging the windows wide.

"Up!" she commanded. "Tennis. Drink your tea. Get dressed. And be downstairs!"

"Tea?" queried James.

"You'll get what your given!" said the Witch tartly. "I'll expect you down in ten minutes."

Antonia sat up and shivered:

"James, shut the windows!" And when he made no move: "James! Doesn't anyone ever stand up to her?"

"What do you think?"

"I think I'm going to shut the windows and get back into bed!"

James drank his tea thoughtfully.

"I think this is fall-out from what you've both been through. She didn't just rescue you, she had to battle with Evil out there,"

"I never believed in Evil."

"Well, now you know. You've experienced it. Even the cat didn't escape unscathed."

Antonia shut the windows and climbed back into bed. James handed her a mug of tea.

"Why are we having tea this morning?"

"Who knows! Perhaps the Range is on strike. Actually, this tea is rather refreshing!"

"Do I hear you getting up?" asked a disembodied voice.

"Yes, Granny!" James threw back the bedclothes, discarded his pyjamas trousers and pulled on his clothes.

He sat down on the edge of the bed to tie his laces.

"If it's good enough for the Range to go on strike, it's good enough for me!" Antonia scowled. She drank her tea nevertheless. It was surprisingly refreshing. "What happens if I want a morning in bed?"

"I won't answer for the consequences! She might lock you in the broom cupboard! D'you want to be locked in the broom cupboard?"

"I'd hope that you'd come and rescue me!"

"She'll have thrown away the key!"

"I don't want to play tennis!"

"We'll give it a go, Ni-ni. Come on, now. Rise and shine!"

"Rise and sulk, more like!" But she began to get dressed.

***

At this early hour, the tennis court was deserted. It was cold. They had walked briskly up the lane, but it was not a temperature for hanging about. James adjusted the net, bounced a couple of balls and looked across at Antonia.

"Ready?"

He served. Antonia returned it. They hit the ball to

each other for a while and then she slammed hard at him, taking him by surprise.

"If we're going to do this, we may as well put some drive into it!"

She sent another fast ball streaking past him.

"Granny said you were good!" he said ruefully.

"She also said we were evenly matched. You'll just have to work harder at it."

James hadn't remembered anything about an even match.

He wasn't as lithe, and his reactions were not as sharp. And Antonia was younger than him! They returned with huge appetites and devoured a cooked breakfast.

***

Over the next week James's tennis improved. They became fitter, healthier, energy levels increased. Antonia slept soundly.

She enjoyed her food. She enjoyed the challenge of their play. She felt fit and happy. After their breakfast, she spent the rest of the morning in her study, working, while James painted. The connecting door stood open.

One morning a small girl appeared outside the tennis court and watched them. She was there again the next day but had scampered off while they wound down the net and gathered their things. On the third day she unlatched the gate and stood inside, watching them.

"Hello. What's your name?" James paused between games, and smiled at her.

"Shaz."

"That's an unusual name."

"Yeah, well I'm quite unusual too!"

James grinned at her – feisty little girl! The child scuffed the toe of her shoe in the fine gravel at the edge of the court.

"I could be your ball-boy," she suggested.

"Okay!"

The child made herself useful, chasing stray balls, scampering across the net line to retrieve missed serves. James was impressed.

"Thank you," he said at the end of their match. "You're pretty good!"

"Yeah, I know! I watch how they do it at Wimbledon. I gotta go now. See you tomorrow!"

"How old d'you suppose she is?" Antonia asked. She hadn't spoken to the child, James noticed.

"Oh, seven or eight?"

"Shouldn't she be at school?"

"It must be the school holidays. She said she'd be here tomorrow."

"I wonder if her parents know where she is?"

James slipped an arm around her shoulders,

"You worry too much! She's just a kid at a loose end."

They strolled back down the lane, looking forward to a cooked breakfast.

The child was waiting at the court for them the next day. James greeted her warmly as he slid back the latch on the gate. Winding up the net, he heard her asking their names. He turned his head:

"I'm James. And this is Antonia."

"Okay." The child looked at Antonia: "You serving first?" She did not scamper off at the end of the hour but hung around while they shrugged into their anoraks, gathered their racquets.

"My Dad's getting me a racquet for my birthday," she announced. "Then you can teach me to play."

"And when is your birthday?" Antonia asked.

"First of July. And I'll be eight." She did a little dance. "See ya!" She scampered off.

The following day she waited for them and walked beside them as they strolled back down the lane.

"Does your Mum know you come and watch us play?" Antonia enquired.

"I don't *watch* you. I ball-boy."

"You do a great job! I was asking if your Mum knows you come here every day?"

"My Mum don't live with us."

"So who looks after you? Your Dad?"

"You sure ask a lot of questions! So, you two, you got children?"

"I have a son called Jake. He's away at college." James told her. The child digested this information.

"You was married before?"

"You're a smart cookie!"

"That's what my Dad says." She grinned at James.

"Well, you tell your Dad that we're happy for you to be our ball-boy so long as he knows where you are and who you're with. Will you do that?"

The child gave Antonia a long look, then turning to James she said:

"Your Antony's a bit of a fusspot, in't she!"

"Antonia," corrected Antonia.

"Yeah! Antony, s'what I said."

***

"Hello, Antony!" Antonia felt her sleeve tugged. The child smiled at her, pleased to see her. "You shopping?"

"That's right. What are you doing?"

"Choosing my lunch. What are you buying for lunch?"

"Salad. D'you like salad?"

"Not much. Salad's for rabbits."

"Have you told your Dad about the tennis, like I asked you?"

"Maybe."

"Where's your Dad now? Is he at home?"

"Course not! He's at work. That's what Dads do."

"So who looks after you while he's at work?"

"I look after myself. I'm very sensible."

"I'm sure you are, but…" Antonia made one last try.

"Is there a neighbour who keeps an eye on you?"

The child sighed deeply.

"I don't do neighbours. They fuss!"

Antonia had reached the head of the check-out queue.

"Good morning!" The check-out girl smiled pleasantly and passed her purchases through. Antonia transferred her shopping into her basket and paid. The check-out girl turned her attention to the next customer: "Hello, Shaz"

"This is my friend, Antony!"

"Antonia," corrected Antonia."

"She's going to teach me to play tennis. My Dad's giving me a tennis racquet for my birthday! How much is this, please?" She dug in the pocket of her shorts and counted out the money. "Bye, Antony! See you tomorrow!"

***

The half-term holiday ended but Shaz continued arriving at the tennis court every morning to ball-boy for them.

"Shouldn't you be at school?" Antonia asked. "You'll be late!"

"So what if I am!" The child shrugged.

"Don't you like school?"

"Not much!"

A few days later Antonia saw Shaz disappearing out of the doors as she approached the check-out. There was no queue today, so she stopped to chat to the check-out woman.

"That little girl, Shaz? Do you know her?"

"Everyone knows Shaz."

"She doesn't seem to spend much time at school!"

"I don't think she likes school!"

"She told me her Dad's at work all day – doesn't she have anyone looking after her?"

The check-out woman packed her basket for her.

"She has her Gran." The woman shook her head. "I reckon she's something of a pain as far as her Gran's concerned. Runs a bit wild, does Shaz."

***

"Ought we to check with the Authorities?" Antonia asked James as she unpacked her shopping.

"She's not your responsibility," he returned gently.

"Well, her Gran doesn't seem to take much responsibility for her. They said at the supermarket that she runs wild. She's in there buying stuff when she should be at school."

"As I see it, she has a home; she's not neglected; she's healthy and she's fed..."

"I think she shoplifts in the supermarket."

"A lot of children pilfer confectionary. If the supermarket turns a blind eye, I don't think it behoves you to stir up a hornet's nest."

"But she should be in school! They could hold her father responsible. He could be prosecuted. He's probably no idea she's truanting."

"Antonia, she is not your responsibility."

The way he spoke her name told her that she had irritated him with her persistence.

Sunday morning. They did not play tennis on Sundays. Antonia had elected to sleep late. James was already downstairs chatting to Michael who had joined him for one of the Witch's big breakfasts. Eventually Antonia awoke. She had been dreaming. Wisps of the dream dispersed as she got out of bed. She showered. Opening the wardrobe she saw a dress she had not worn for years – had forgotten about. She did not remember it even being in her flat… She took it off its hanger and held it against her. It was a very sexy dress. She remembered buying it for an evening at the opera with Phil. It was very revealing, very much a statement dress. She'd hoped it would shock him a little! It was certainly eye-catching and jazzy. She tried it on. She remembered now that the dress was worn without any underwear! She had worn a G-string under it – an item that could easily be pulled undone. She no longer owned a G-string, but she could wear the dress now to surprise James. She anticipated his reaction. It was a very sexy dress!

She took some time applying make–up and then, choosing stilettos to accentuate her long legs, left the bedroom and stepped carefully down the stairs. Michael looked up and stared, shocked, embarrassed, appalled. James, who was sitting with his back to the stairs, stared for a moment at his brother's face, then swivelled round. He had never seen Antonia dressed like this!

"Good morning, James." She had not expected Michael to be there and was amused by his evident discomfort.

"I don't think I've seen that dress before! It's rather provocative!" James's voice was measured, neither shocked nor angry.

"Yes, it is a bit!" Antonia reached the bottom step and approached the table, the epitome of a seductress.

"Antonia, I don't think this is an appropriate dress for breakfast."

"I can let it slip down altogether but I must warn you I have nothing underneath." There was a strangled gulp from Michael. Antonia held his eye. "Bit out of your comfort zone, Michael?" she asked remorselessly.

"Antonia!" James was out of his chair. He came across and took her by the shoulders. "Take off those stupid shoes before you twist your ankle!" And as she discarded her stilettos, "Get back upstairs and get that dress off! Now!"

He gave her a push.

"My bedroom is just up here!" she said flirtatiously. "I can offer you a good time!"

"Shut up!" He was propelling her up the stairs. "I don't know what's got into you!"

"You know you fancy me!" Antonia murmured. "You can't wait to get your hands all over me!"

They reached the stair head. He pushed her into their bedroom and shut the door decisively behind her. She heard his footsteps going back down to the kitchen.

"I'm so sorry, Mike. I don't know what's got into her this morning! Let's walk in the garden. Let the sea breeze blow it all away."

Antonia waited for James to return. Half an hour passed. Perhaps he wasn't coming back? She took off her dress and regarded her naked reflection, remembering the evening she'd worn the dress for Phil. She was to meet him in one of the exclusive restaurants he favoured. Heads had turned as she'd entered. Conversations had stopped.

Mr Carew Robinson half rose from his seat and stared at her, horrified. Then he was ushering her out of the restaurant.

"I'm taking you back to your flat!" His voice had been icy. "You will take off that dress – if you can call it a dress

– and put on something decent. I am not taking you to the opera in that!"

He had hailed a taxi and thrust her inside. He was clearly very angry, in a very calm controlled way. He did not ask the taxi to wait.

He came up to the flat with her and waited while she slowly and sensuously slid the dress down, watching his reaction.

"If you behave like a slut, I should treat you like one," he said. There was nothing but cold contempt in his voice.

He had never been angry with her before. Now, he pushed her back on her bed and took her. It was the only time he was rough with her.

"Now," he said coldly. "Get dressed. We are going to the opera and you will behave impeccably!"

They did not return to the restaurant. He bought her a drink in the foyer. She sat through the overture in disgrace. During the first act he began to relax. She observed him covertly, seeing him caught up in the music the drama, the exquisite voices. In the interval he had thawed enough to take her out to the bar – although he would only allow her fruit juice.

"I expect we are both hungry," he acknowledged. "We'll dine later."

Over the late meal, he was his usual considerate self. companionable, talking as if nothing amiss had occurred. She was quiet. She listened attentively. She sipped the wine he now allowed her. But she had no spark, no repartee. While they waited for the plates to be removed and the dessert menu offered, he spoke. His voice changed. He waited until he had her complete attention.

"I do not intend apologising," he said. "I never want to see you dressed like that again. You disgraced yourself and embarrassed me. We will draw a line under this evening."

She had not seen him again for weeks.

***

When she eventually went down to the kitchen, it was deserted. She made herself a sandwich and shut herself in her study. She did not hear James come in. Perhaps he came through from his studio. His hand rested on her shoulder. She reached up and caught his fingers.

"Are you okay?" he asked – and his voice was as kind as always.

She nodded. Was he waiting for an apology?

"I didn't know Michael was here"

"Obviously." He dropped kiss on the crown of her head – a kiss among the stubble.

"I wouldn't have…if I'd known… It was for you!"

"It was certainly a very dramatic entrance!"

"You don't sound angry? I thought you'd be angry with me! I thought…"

"My Antoni-ni! In retrospect it might even have been funny if it hadn't been so shocking!"

"If Michael hadn't been here…would you have reacted differently?"

"Quite possibly!" James grinned.

"I only ever wore it once…Phil was taking me out to dinner. He was horrified!"

"I bet he was!" James chuckled. "I expect he left you in no doubt that you had incurred his grave displeasure. And that can be a very uncomfortable place to be!"

Antonia pulled herself upright and turned into James's arms, wanting to be held.

"Missed you! It's been a lonely day!"

"I'm here now." He kissed her. "Not today, but sometime in the future, when it's just the two of us, you might wear that dress again, and let me seduce you!"

Eight

Intruders in the sitting room

At Michael's suggestion, James had gone to Morton's to sit in on Jake's performance of Schumann's second piano concerto.

"Your Dad would be so proud of you." Michael had observed to Jake. "Why don't I bring him to listen."

"He's dead." Jake shrugged. "I've moved on with my life."

But Michael had brought James irrespective of his son's lack of interest. Sadly, there was no connection. Was Jake even faintly aware of his father's presence? He walked past him without apparently seeing him. He turned a deaf ear to James's greeting, and when James laid a gentle hand on Jake's arm, there was the faintest shrug as if to dislodge a small insect. It was disappointing.

At the end of the afternoon James spent some time

with Michael in his staff bungalow, reminiscing over coffee.

Antonia had elected to stay at home. She had translation work to do. She needed time to catch up. She would be fine. She hoped his day would go well. James was looking forward to returning home to Antonia... to sitting in front of a blazing log fire with coffee...just being with her. As he arrived in the hall he could hear voices. He pushed open the sitting room door to find Antonia crouched on the hearth rug in front of an unlit fire absorbed in a game of chess with the seven year old Mlilka.

"You're really quite good." The child said. "But not as good as me!"

"What d'you think you're doing!" stormed James, unaccountably angry. "That child doesn't come in here!"

Antonia looked up.

"Hello, James, we've had a lovely afternoon! We made scones and had tea. And we've been playing chess..."

"So I see," said James icily. "Get out!" he addressed the child. "Now!"

Mlilka shrank into herself, looking doubtfully at James and then uncertainly at Antonia.

"How dare you!" Antonia shouted. "You waltz off to Morton's and then come back and tell me I can't invite Mlilka in for the afternoon! Who do you think you are!"

"She does not come into the house," said James with quiet fury."

"Why not? Why can't she come in and spend time with me like a normal human being?"

"Because she isn't. She isn't a normal…human… being. Now, get her out of here!"

"No!"

Mlilka scrambled to her feet, knocking over the chessmen. Addressing Antonia, she said:

"Thank you for a lovely afternoon. I want Daddy now. Goodbye."

The space where she had stood was empty. The child was gone. Antonia glared at James.

"How could you! You spoiled the happiest afternoon I've had in a long time. She's a delightful child. She'll probably never come back after the way you shouted at her! You're a monster! If that's how you were with Jake…"

"Yes?" There was a note of menace in his voice. "What were you about to say?"

"It doesn't matter." Antonia backed down.

"I think it does!"

Antonia faced him.

"Why don't you just go back to Morton's!"

The room suddenly felt chilled. James no longer stood facing her. Only the iciness in his voice lingered. Antonia caught her breath. How had it come to this that she was quarrelling with James! But why was he so heavy-handed with the child? Why wasn't Mlilka allowed in the house? James's Grandfather came in and was clearly part of the family set-up.

Was James's antagonism because His mother had taken her own life? But how could you reconcile this innocent child with whom she became in her adult life? Had he never forgiven her? They would have to talk about it…But, clearly, she wasn't going to tolerate being dictated to like that! Antonia strolled out to the kitchen, in need of a strong coffee. She looked at the Range. The Range said nothing.

"Someone else not speaking to me?"

Antonia picked up the kettle, shook it and moved across to the sink to fill it. Placing it on the hot plate, she found herself a mug and the coffee jar. It seemed odd to be making herself a mug of coffee in the normal way!

"Am I persona non grata?" she asked the Range.

The Range said nothing.

Antonia shrugged, made her coffee and took it through to her study. She drew the curtains, noticing that the connecting door to the studio remained ominously shut. Not that she really wanted to speak to him after the way he'd behaved.

She was too wound up to settle to her translating. What she needed was to lose herself in a good novel… where were her books? Why had she not brought a box-load of books from her flat? She had always surrounded herself with books until…well, until James had brought her here. She wandered back to the living room, irresolute, uncertain what to do. She wondered if she was hungry? Had James had a meal? Was he expecting one? Should she start meal preparations? Where was Granny? She hadn't seen Granny since… Had Granny even been around at breakfast? The big table in the kitchen stood empty and impersonal. She opened the door to the courtyard and stepped out, staring up at the night sky, remembering standing with her father as a small child, her hand in his, watching as he pointed out the constellations.

A precious memory because he had not often had time for her. She thought about her father. Perhaps she would contact him tomorrow… drive up to see him. He would be pleased. After all, she did not have to ask James's permission!

The light from the kitchen cast a friendly glow, but most of the courtyard was in darkness.

"Granny?" she said softly.

There was no answer. She waited.

Presently, aware that she was cold, she turned and went back indoors. The hearth was empty apart from long dead ash. It felt unnaturally quiet. Although she and James often sat for hours without talking, theirs had been a companionable silence. Perhaps she would play her clarinet. It was a long time since she had played…in fact, she wasn't sure she'd brought it over from the flat. She unearthed it from a drawer in her desk, assembled it and began to play. Once she had been quite good – not the high standard Michael and Jake attained – but today she had no audience.

James did not reappear all evening. Antonia made herself a sandwich. Finally, she switched off the lights and took herself upstairs for a long leisurely bath…and bed. A bed that seemed too large and too empty. She discovered that the book she had been reading had now reappeared on her bedside table. She read for an hour and then curled up under the covers and waited for sleep, wondering if James would be beside her when she woke up.

"Coffee?" said a familiar voice.

Antonia stirred and opened her eyes. James was already dressed – which might mean that he had never come to bed, or alternatively, that he had been up long before she'd wakened. She glanced blearily at the bedside clock, realising that she had slept more soundly than usual. James had already placed her mug beside her. Now, he sat down on the edge of the bed, facing her and smiled:

"Good morning, I trust you slept well?"

Antonia glanced across at his side of the bed. His pillow was undented. He had spent the night downstairs. She felt a flicker of resentment – he hadn't wanted to share her bed…perhaps he was still angry?

"How was Jake?" she thought to ask. "Did his recital go well?"

"He wouldn't acknowledge me."

"I'm sorry. That must have been so hurtful!"

"It was disappointing."

"No wonder you came home and bawled me out!"

"Did I?" He smiled at her as if it was all past and forgotten.

She sat up and drank her coffee. Today was obviously a new day.

"What are you doing today?" she asked.

"I thought you might like to see your father, spend some time with him?"

"You want me out of your hair?"

"I think it's important to maintain your real-life

relationships. And he'll be delighted that you've made contact."

"How would you know!"

"Because I'm a father too."

Antonia reached for his hand and squeezed it.

"I'd say come with me, but of course, you can't."

"He wouldn't know I was there."

"I suppose not…" Antonia frowned. "Then how was it that the Guest House people were able to see you and talk to you?"

"Because they didn't know I was dead. I was real to them because they believed I was real. It wouldn't have made sense to them if you were talking to me and clearly being with someone who wasn't there. They saw what they believed."

"Well, my father doesn't know you're dead. I just told him you were something of a recluse. He's said several times how much he'd like to meet you."

"Remember, I can only go where I've been before, in real life."

"Like my flat."

"That sort of thing."

"I haven't actually invited him to the flat. It would be awkward if he just turned up and I wasn't there. I'm not there very often."

"Have you told him you commute to Munich?"

"Hardly 'commute', but yes, I told him I travel to see my agent and the publishers."

"Think about it." James drank his coffee thoughtfully. Antonia almost said 'Funny you should mention it – I was only thinking about going up to see him…' But James probably knew that!

"We might go down to the beach and commune with the waves," James suggested.

"That would be nice."

He picked up their coffee mugs. He was polite and considerate. There were little gestures of kindness and affection, and yet underlying that, it seemed to Antonia that something was broken.

The sea soothed them. The breeze ruffled his hair and caressed her shaven scalp. The sun was warm on their backs. But he did not pick up pebbles. He did not reach for her hand. He did not enfold her in his arms. He was quiet.

They strolled further along the beach than they'd ever been and bought shrimp rolls from a little take-away bar that wasn't there, munching them as they strolled back. James stood taking deep lungfuls of sea air. Presently he turned to her:

"What would you like to do now?" he asked.

"Actually, I'd quite like to spend a little time at the flat. I'd like to bring back some books, so it makes sense to go in the car. Shall you come with me?"

***

She felt a huge sense of relief as they drew up outside her flat. She'd enjoyed the drive there in the sunshine. All her things were there, exactly as she'd left them… familiar…hers.

She inserted a C.D. into the player and the flat was filled with rich, deep cello music.

"Haydn's cello concerto!" James said with pleasure.

"Did you never learn to play?"

"Too busy studying."

He might have added that much of his time had been taken up with the twins…hurrying home from school, unable to take part in after-school activities because they were waiting for him to read to them, bath them, give them the caring and affection that their mother seemed increasingly unable to offer.

In the kitchen Antonia made coffee which they drank black because there was no milk. James browsed through her books. He seemed very much at home. Antonia wondered whether to suggest they stay the night.

"What I would miss here," remarked James thoughtfully, "Is an open fire. I do enjoy sitting in front of our log fire – there's something so welcoming and comfortable, sitting in the firelight…"

"Then we'll go home and light one," said Antonia, savouring '*our*' log fire.

"We'll come again soon. Have you got the books you wanted?"

Antonia finished packing her box and closed the lid. Resting on the top was her mobile phone. She picked it up, turning it over and over.

"My phone!" she exclaimed.

"I told you Granny would sort it out in her own good time."

"What about my handbag?"

James smiled at her.

"I expect you'll find it in the glove compartment of your car." He picked up the box of books. "I think you've enjoyed this afternoon."

"Yes, I have!" She hovered, hoping for a hug, an embrace...

He put the box down and held out his arms:

"Oh, come here!" He pulled her against him, kissing the tip of her nose. "You've been in a odd mood all day!"

"I thought that was you!"

"What was me?"

"You were the one who was being standoffish."

"Pshaw!" He gave a fair imitation of the Witch.

Antonia laughed. The long drive home was companionable.

***

Antonia woke first. She leaned up on an elbow and studied James's sleeping face. He was her soul mate, her friend, her lover... She wanted him to open his eyes and smile at her. There was so much affection and love in his smile. Reaching out she traced a gentle finger across his cheek. James opened his eyes.

"Coffee or...?"

"Both!" he said, grinning.

Antonia slid out of bed and padded across to the head of the stairs. James loved her. She was happy. All was right with the world. She skipped lightly down the stairs. Humming. The Witch turned from the Range and regarded her with interest.

"Good Morning, Antonia."

Suddenly aware that she was wearing an almost diaphanous nightdress, Antonia faltered, acutely embarrassed.

"Don't mind me!" The Witch turned back to the Range. "Many's the day I danced in the kitchen in nothing but a nightie! In fact, sometimes I danced barefoot in the park in my nightie – at night, you understand."

"Ill met by moonlight?"

The Witch chuckled. She stirred whatever she was heating in her saucepan.

"*He* danced with me, of course. But he never remembered in the morning and was perplexed why his pyjama trousers were wet-bottomed Silly man!" it was said with great affection. "We lived in London then, almost opposite the Park." She was in a forthcoming mood. Antonia perched on a stool, listening. "I suppose you came down for some coffee?" remarked the Witch, breaking into her reverie. She glanced at Antonia. "Is he awake?"

"He was when I left him." Antonia took a deep breath – perhaps this was foolhardy – "Why was he so angry that I'd brought the little girl into the house? We had such a happy afternoon …and then he came home. and shouted at me and threw her out. He was *so* angry! And he didn't even come to bed that night. I don't understand why it was such a…" she trailed off.

"You know that Mlilka is Daffyn's mother?"

"Well, yes…when she grew up… but…"

The Witch regarded Antonia from under snaggled eyebrows.

"The child does not belong in his time-frame."

"I don't understand."

"He doesn't exist in her childhood. For that matter, neither do I."

"But you're her mother...aren't you?"

"She was a very pesky three year old, and one day I'd just had enough. Toddlers can be particularly trying – and I'm not good with small children. So I took myself off for the afternoon, but unfortunately I strayed into another century and it took the devil of a time to get back! I didn't manage to return until Mlilka was fifteen and already pregnant. Silly girl!"

"Pregnant with James?"

"No. He came later... after she'd married Gavin... Where was I? Ah yes! So, I was explaining: I wasn't around in Mlilka's childhood. I didn't exist in her seven year old context." She gave Antonia a penetrating look. "And she cannot exist for Daffyn as a seven year old. She doesn't know she's meant to be his mother!"

"It's so complicated!" Antonia frowned. "But she interacts with Michael! They make music together."

"Well, Michael doesn't remember his mother. He was only five or so, when she killed herself... and his grandparents took the twins and brought them up. Daffyn had to hold the family together: comforting Tom, supporting his father who was as much use as a fish out of water! Daffyn had to cope with everything, He was...twelve."

"That must have been a huge burden!"

"And he's gone on comforting and supporting everybody ever since!" The Witch sniffed disparagingly. "Putting himself at everyone's beck and call, except himself. Thinking he had to care for every troubled soul that washed up at his hospital. Letting himself be dragged into one disastrous marriage after another!"

"Am I another disaster?" whispered Antonia. The Witch regarded her thoughtfully.

"Leave the child in the Back Garden where she belongs, and take Daffyn his coffee!"

Antonia accepted two mugs of coffee. She felt somehow chastened.

"Biscuit?" offered the Witch in a conciliatory manner.

"Just the coffee," murmured Antonia. "Thank you."

She climbed the stairs, careful not to spill any coffee. As she set one mug down beside James, he opened his eyes and smiled at her.

"You were a long time!"

"I was having a philosophical discussion with your Granny."

"Were you indeed! What was that about?"

"Well, she began by regaling me with tales of dancing barefoot in the Park in her nightie…and your Grandad being surprised to find his pyjama trousers wet when he didn't remember getting up in the night to dance with her!" Antonia sat down on the edge of the bed and sipped her coffee.

"Come back to bed," James pulled aside the duvet, invitingly. "You're chilled! Snuggle down and let me warm you up!"

***

Antonia had been working on her current translation all morning. She closed down her laptop, stretched, and pushed back her chair. Glancing at her watch, she frowned – it was well past lunch-time.

She walked through to the kitchen which was singularly empty and regarded the Range which was in a somnolent mood.

"Where is everyone?"

"Out," said the Range shortly, and went back to sleep. Antonia made herself a sandwich and stepped down into the little walled courtyard. On the far side, the green gate which led into the Back Garden stood invitingly ajar. Perhaps James had deliberately left it open so she could follow him? Carefully she pushed the gate and stepped through. The Garden was pleasantly warm. The sun shone through the orchard trees and a friendly little breeze set the leaves dancing. The old swing moved gently as if just vacated. Antonia glanced about. It seemed that she had the Garden to herself. After a while she noticed Dr Mikilari on his accustomed bench, absorbed in one of his ancient newspapers. She started towards him, trying to picture him dancing in the Park in his pyjamas…

"I've been waiting ages for you!" complained Mlilka. Startled, Antonia looked about her. "I'm here! I've been waiting for you to come and finish our game!"

Now, Antonia could see the little girl sitting cross-legged on the grass, a chess board set out in front of her. She sat down on the warm, dry grass and studied the board.

"Who's move is it?"

"Yours, if you like. Doesn't much matter. I'm going to win anyway!"

They finished the game and began another. The sun was warm on Antonia's back. Mlilka won both games. She looked at Antonia expectantly.

"Can you play scrabble?" enquired Antonia.

"Oh yes!" Mlilka beamed. "I might even let you win – though I'm pretty good at that too!"

"Do you have a set out here?"

"Absolutely!" As if it had been there all the time, she reached for it and they began unpacking the game. "Daddy's rules!" announced Mlilka.

"You'll have to explain."

"You take seven letters and whoever can make the longest word gets to start…and no slang!"

Utterly absorbed in the game, Antonia was unaware of James approaching. He stood silently observing her. Mlilka ignored him. Dr Mikilari put down his newspaper:

"Ah, James!"

"Grandad?" James strolled over to his grandfather and sat down beside him.

Antonia looked up, startled, But James seemed to have eyes only for his grandfather.

"It's your turn!" Mlilka prompted. "I've got my word ready if you don't spoil it." Antonia looked down at her letters. "You could turn *sand* into *sandwich*," suggested Mlika helpfully.

"How do you know what letters I've got!"

"I just do!"

"Well, I'm not going to make *sandwich*. I'm going to make *wardrobe*. And I get the triple word!"

"That's why I wanted you to make *sandwich*, so I could get the triple word!"

"Bad luck!"

"Daddy would have let me have the triple!"

"I'm not Daddy!"

Mlilka wrinkled her nose and gave Antonia a long look. She took a considerable time finding her next word. Antonia observed James while she waited. The game began to drag. After a few more words, desultorily played, Mlilka began to lose interest.

"Sometimes Daddy helps me," she pointed out. There was a long silence. "I don't want to play anymore." She pushed her letters across the board. "You can pack it up."

She jumped up and ran across to her father who lifted her onto his knee, but continued talking to James. Antonia collected the letter-squares and slid them into their bag. She packed up the box, wondering whether to join James. He said something to his grandfather and stood up, coming over and offering her his hand to help her to her feet.

"Did you get a good morning's work done?"

"It was way past lunch-time and there was no one in the kitchen. The Range didn't even offer me a coffee!"

"Poor Ni-ni!" James pulled her into his arms and ran his hand over the stubble on her scalp. "Soon be able to brush your hair."

"I made myself a sandwich." It sounded like a reproach.

"Granny was going down to the village. There might be the makings of dinner when she gets back."

"Or Brown Soup!"

James grinned. Antonia released herself from his embrace. He must have seen that she was playing with Mlilka. Was he not going to comment? James strolled across to where the two prams stood under their shady tree. Picking up his baby daughter, he dropped a kiss on the little fair head, murmuring to her, rocking her in his arms. His expression was very tender. After a few moments he gently laid her back in her pram and stood there, watching her, loving her. Tiny fingers held his middle finger. Persephone, the baby who had not survived her first winter. Antonia stood watching him, wondering…

The Witch appeared through the Garden Gate. She took in the scene.

"Lunch," she said shortly, turned on her heel and disappeared.

"Lunch." James smiled at Antonia. "Coming?"

Across the grass Dr Mikilari shuffled slowly, in happy anticipation of a meal…hoping it would not be Brown Soup.

"Lentil cutlets and cabbage," announced the Witch, serving generous helpings. As she gathered up their empty plates, she remarked: "They were suggesting in the village that Antonia might like to join the W.I."

James looked questioningly at Antonia.

"Not really my thing."

"Might meet some interesting people? Make friends? Learn to make jam?" Antonia threw him a look.

"I'll take that as a No, then? Perhaps, if Granny had suggested a chess club there might have been more enthusiasm?"

"Chess?" Dr Mikilari perked up. "Does Antonia play chess? Do you, my dear?"

"Even Granny plays chess!" offered James provocatively.

"*Even* Granny? I invented the game!"

"I beg to differ, my dear," put in Dr Mikilari gently. The Witch threw a tea-cosy at him. She served chocolate brownies covered in chocolate sauce.

"See what this will do for your cholesterol!" She said unkindly.

"Oh yes!" Dr Mikilari polished his plateful off with almost indecent haste. He looked hopefully at the Witch. "Seconds?"

The Witch raised an eyebrow. She gave James an insouciant smile.

"Sleep like babies this afternoon!" she murmured, replenishing his plate.

James exchanged an amused smile with her.

"We could have a chess tournament this afternoon!" suggested Dr Mikilari enthusiastically. "Each of us play the others…" He cleared his plate. His head drooped.

Antonia began to feel unaccountably sleepy. She was having trouble focusing. James removed her plate and handed it to his grandmother.

"Naughty Granny!" he chided, giving her a hug.

"Pshaw!" returned the Witch, batting him away.

***

It was dusk before Antonia awoke. She found herself slumped over the kitchen table. Straightening up, she noticed that Dr Mikilari was sitting at his end of the table. He smiled at her.

"Hello, my dear. You've had a little sleep! Too much sun in the garden? We were thinking of playing a game of chess, you and I."

"I feel a bit muzzy," confessed Antonia.

"Coffee?" enquired the Range helpfully.

"Just the ticket!" Dr Mikilari beamed.

"Where's everyone?" Antonia looked round. She rubbed her neck. "Got a crick in my neck! Was I asleep long?"

"I expect James is in his studio…and Ragwort…who knows where Ragwort might be!"

"Ragwort? Is that her name?"

"One of her names." Dr Mikilari sighed. "Time was…" he began.

Antonia slid off her chair and fetched the two mugs of coffee which the Range had thoughtfully provided. She thanked him.

"Quite alright!" The Range gave a little cough and blew a wisp of smoke towards Dr Mikilari. "I believe Herself may have gone for a little ride," he observed.

Antonia glanced at the broom cupboard from which the Broom had been summarily ejected to make way for Michael's ensuite.

"She does that," Dr Mikilari conceded. "Takes off when the mood takes her. I prefer to stay grounded myself."

"Me too!" agreed Antonia.

"Broke a few bones, falling off that damn thing at Beachy Head, once…"

"Does *she* never fall off?"

"I don't think her bones break," observed Dr Mikilari thoughtfully. "She did sprain her ankle once, falling into the Pond – I had my suspicions that it was deliberate. I'd told her not to fly while she was pregnant. Did she listen! A good ruse, if you ask me! She knew I wouldn't turn her away when she appeared, wet and dripping on my doorstep."

He reached into his pocket for a handkerchief. "I took her in…and the rest, as they say, is history."

"She's quite a character!"

"And she usually knows exactly what she wants!"

"Coffee?" asked James, appearing in the doorway. "Hello, Antoni-ni, have you woken up?"

"I'd have thought that was obvious! Did Granny put something in the Brownies?"

"Funny you should ask that!"

James strolled over to the Range and waited while the Range served up a mug of freshly brewed coffee.

"Not funny! Underhand!" Antonia glared at James who seemed remarkably unconcerned. "Why didn't it affect you?"

"It just doesn't," said James shortly.

"They were very tasty!" Dr Mikilari licked his lips reminiscently.

"James, why is there no television here?"

James regarded her with mild surprise.

"Is this something you need?"

"Well, if nothing else, it would keep me focused on the *real* world, as you're so keen to urge me! There's one in my flat. We could bring it over."

"If it's important to you," said James patiently. "But we have music. Would you like some music?"

"Books, music, chess, conversation, but somehow the outside world never intrudes…"

"Perhaps it's time you went to visit your publisher in Munich."

Antonia studied him for a long moment.

"And would it matter to you if I didn't come back?"

"I've told you before: I would never stand in your way."

"That's not the right answer! I want it to matter to you! I want you to say it would break your heart if I disappeared! Don't you care? I thought you loved me! I thought we belonged together! I thought…"

"Oh Antoni-ni!" James scooped her into his arms.

He kissed her for a long time until her resentment and anger dissipated.

***

The days went by. They played a hard game of tennis each morning before breakfast and then Antonia spent a long morning translating while James painted. Sometimes the Witch scooped Antonia up and took her off to choose outrageously expensive curtains or wallpaper.

They would then take tea and cakes in elegant surroundings.

It was clear to James that his grandmother had taken a liking to Antonia and, for whatever devious reasons of her own, wanted Antonia to feel at home. In fact, the Witch was often fun to be with… outrageous, extravagant, funny. Antonia would return home exhilarated, alive, eager to tell James about the latest excursion.

Sometimes James would take her off into the countryside where they would go for long walks returning home tired and muddy. It was after one such afternoon when they had walked rather further than they'd planned, that they awoke stiff and aching…and by mutual consent eschewed tennis and stayed in bed. James lay nuzzling her breasts with great contentment, stirring an unexpected response from Antonia who had never felt proprietorial toward her breasts…and had never, until that morning, wondered what it would be like to breastfeed a baby – a baby that would be hers and James's…except, of course, that conceiving his baby was beyond the bounds of possibility – hadn't he said as much – which left her free to fantasize pleasurably, guilt free… though why she should feel guilty she had no idea.

Much later, after they had made love and were lying relaxed in an intimate post-coital sprawl, she remarked on his prolonged nuzzling.

"One of my earliest memories," said James, raising himself on an elbow. "Was watching my mother breastfeeding Tom. I'd have been three. I remember standing close to her knee, watching, yearning, hungry for what he had… Waiting patiently for her to finish feeding him, winding him and putting him down. And then I'd ask: 'Me? Now me?' But she'd shake her head and say: 'No, dear. That's for Tom. You're a big boy. You can help me look after Tom.' – And that was my assigned role, looking after the younger ones…when I so wanted to be lifted into her knee and be cuddled."

Antonia reached out and touched his cheek.

"Didn't anyone cuddle you? What about your Dad?"

"He was a busy G.P. We'd be asleep in bed before he came home after Evening Surgery – they weren't group practices then, like they are now. It was one doctor looking after all his patients, delivering babies, up in the night for urgent calls…even on Sundays! And, as you'll have noticed, Granny doesn't do cuddling."

"Every time my father had a new posting, it was a new country and a new Nanny. My mother would tell her 'Antonia is not a very affectionate child, I'm afraid'. I expect I was quite hostile! It didn't seem worth making friends with someone who'd disappear with the next move. Still, it was good training for dealing with the clients, later."

James winced. It was the part of Antonia's past that he found hardest to accept.

She sensed his slight withdrawal…and, recognizing her hurt, he gathered her to him in a long comforting embrace.

"Shall we go down and ask the Range for a full English Breakfast?"

"He'll probably tell us that Breakfast finished two hours ago!"

"Or, as we didn't get up early to play tennis, we don't deserve it!" James sat up and swung his legs over the side of the bed. "I need the bathroom and coffee, in that order!"

"What shall we do today?"

"Would you like to drive over to your flat? We could even watch television, if you want!"

Antonia picked up her pillow and threw it at him.

Nobody had wanted to nuzzle her breasts before. It evoked a strange hunger in her. At the same time, she felt very protective of James – of the little three year old boy who'd had to bury his feelings of rejection because he was expected to be the care-giver looking after his younger brothers. She ached for him, yearned to comfort the little boy he'd been. Increasingly she found herself spending time in the Back Garden with the baby, Persephone... lifting her out of her pram.

Cradling her as she sat on the swing. If no one was about she sometimes sang to her. Spring had clothed the garden in colour and birdsong and, in Antonia's mind, the baby seemed more alert. She found herself wondering what it would be like to hold the baby to her breast.

"Getting broody, that one!" remarked the Witch to Dr Mikilari.

"Is that so?" he commented in the irritating manner of psychiatrists. The Witch threw a cushion at him.

***

James was going up to London with Michael to take a consignment of paintings to the Gallery which had marketed his grandfather's paintings for many years.

James invited Antonia, thinking that it would make an interesting day for her.

"No, you enjoy your day with Michael. I'll be here when you get back…and you'll have room for more paintings if I'm not occupying the back seat."

"This is true," observed Michael who had been loading the bubble-wrapped canvasses into his car. He would do the driving and present the paintings. He had opened a new bank account so that the Gallery could deposit the money directly.

"I'm afraid I have an evening rehearsal at Morton's," he said. "So I won't be able to do more than drop you back late afternoon…but we'll grab lunch somewhere."

Antonia worked on her translation for the morning and, finding the green gate ajar, wandered into the Back Garden, after finding and devouring a slice of quiche.

In her pram Persephone wriggled pleasurably at Antonia's approach. There was no sign of Mlilka. Dr Mikilari was dozing in his garden seat. Antonia lifted the baby out and sat cradling her on the swing. No one would know if she brought the baby into the house, just for the afternoon… She could pretend this was her baby – hers and James's…in the seclusion of the sitting room she could offer the baby her breast and experience what it would feel like.

Carefully she carried the baby through the Back Garden gate, across the courtyard and into the house. She laid her down while she lit the fire which James had thoughtfully laid before he'd set off. And then she sat before the fire, rocking the baby and singing to her.

Persephone gazed wide-eyed up into her face. Antonia pulled up her sweater, unfastened her bra and, holding her breath, offered the baby her breast, feeling the little mouth fasten on her nipple.

This, then, is what it is like to breastfeed your baby, thought Antonia, feeling a new, almost sexual fulfilment. After a while she eased her nipple from the baby's mouth, experiencing a little tug as the baby let go. Moving the baby to her other breast, she felt a surge of sheer joy as the little mouth fastened onto her.

Perhaps they could keep the baby – make her part of the household? She was James's child, after all. Surely he would not mind! She could understand, in a way, that Mlilka did not belong in their present life together, but Persephone belonged in a very special way. Tomorrow they would go down to the village for nappies and baby powder and a cot... Antonia was lost in a happy reverie in which she introduced Persephone to her father – the grandchild he'd never expected! I am so happy, she thought! I never guessed that a baby could make me feel so complete, so wonderfully happy!

***

James returned home. He took the unsold canvasses through to his studio and, (through the door that wasn't there) went directly into the kitchen. He chatted to the Range as he helped himself to a mug of coffee. He was humming as he entered the sitting room.

Oblivious to the sound of Michael's car drawing up

outside, Antonia was still blissfully nursing the baby when James walked in. He stood absolutely still and stared, horrified, at her.

"What do you think you're doing!"

Antonia looked up. She held the baby protectively to her.

"Give her to me!" James voice was cold as he reached to take the baby.

"No! Let her stay! Let her be our baby! Oh James, you've no idea how happy…how wonderfully happy I've been just holding her!"

"*Just* holding her?" he looked at her exposed breasts. "What d'you think you were doing!"

"I wanted to know what it would be like!" protested Antonia, tears running down her face as James put down his coffee and tried to remove the baby from her.

"Persephone does not belong in here."

"But why, James? She's your *daughter*, for heaven's sake!"

"I'm well aware of that!" James glared at her. "She belongs in the Back Garden. *Not* in here."

"But I want her! I want to keep her here and love her! Please let me keep her!"

"Antonia, give her to me." He spoke in the firm reasonable voice he used with difficult patients. "Antonia, give her to me."

Antonia turned away, shielding the baby with her body, Tears saturating the baby's shawl.

"Persephone is dead," said James quietly. "You cannot spend your life nurturing a dead baby. She needs to be back in her pram. I shall have to lock the Back Garden gate, if you carry on like this."

"Let me keep her just for tonight! We'll put her back in the morning. Please!"

James bit his lip. After a long moment he turned away and went back to the kitchen. He made himself a hot egg sandwich and another mug of coffee and went through to his studio, leaving Antonia cradling the baby, rocking her, whispering words of love to her.

It was approaching midnight when James appeared in the doorway.

"Come to bed," he said, not unkindly.

Antonia had already fallen asleep. She wanted to stay down here on the sofa, cradling the baby all night – the only night she was allowed!

"You're tired," James said reasonably. "Come to bed now. Tuck Seph up on the sofa."

He coaxed her to her feet. Antonia was tired. She let herself be gently propelled up the stairs. He helped her undress and eased her into bed. She fell asleep almost immediately. She would get up at dawn and run down to her baby.

***

Antonia awoke the next morning in a bedroom that felt cold and unwelcoming. When she eventually sat up, she was chilled through. James had not come near her. He had not come to bed last night. She remembered her baby waiting for her downstairs! Because it was so early, no one would be about yet, and perhaps she could slip down and cuddle Persephone before James took her away. She hoped he would have had a change of heart and allow her to keep Persephone. Although he'd threatened to lock the gate into the Back Garden, she didn't think he really would. She crept downstairs, not bothering to get dressed.

The baby had gone! Where was her baby? She had been tucked up so securely on the sofa in a nest of cushions… now the sofa was as it always was. Frantically, Antonia hurried through to the kitchen.

"Good Morning," said the Range politely. "Coffee?"

"Where's my baby?"

"I should know?" enquired the Range.

"Do you know? Has James taken her?"

"Perhaps he has…" mentioned the Range thoughtfully.

After he had seen her to bed, James had come back downstairs, picked up his daughter, and placing the baby against his shoulder, for a brief moment rested his face against the little fair head.

"Back to your pram where you belong," he said to his daughter. His voice was strangely muffled. He carried his child out through the kitchen. Only the Range observed the tears that slid down his face.

***

Antonia hurried out of the kitchen. Barefoot across the courtyard to the gate. The gate was locked. Antonia hammered her fists against it. She begged, she pleaded, she shouted at it.

"James ! James! Open the gate! Let me in!"

The gate did not yield. In despair she retreated to the end of the courtyard where the garden table and chairs sat waiting. Antonia gave way to grief. Not since James had died, had she wept like this. Her arms were as empty as if her baby had died and been lost to her. She had wanted that baby so much! She sobbed her heart out, crying until there were no tears left to cry. Only then did she become aware of James sitting at the table beside her. She raised her swollen, tear-wet face and stared hopelessly at him, beyond reproach, beyond words. He said nothing. He just went on sitting beside her – as if his very presence might comfort her.

Eventually they went in. The Witch was serving breakfast.

"I don't want anything," said Antonia, accepting a cup of tea. She toyed with a slice of toast, not really wanting it.

The Witch gave her a long considered look.

"I would be glad if you would go down to the village and get some fresh salad and a loaf of bread," she remarked. "Better get some clothes on first, or you might raise a few eyebrows!"

Antonia looked at James. He hadn't eaten any breakfast either. And he still hadn't spoken to her. He looked incredibly tired and strained. He deserves to! Antonia thought resentfully. I'm the one who's upset! What's he got to be upset about! Resentment would fuel her. She pushed back her chair and went upstairs to dress. When she came back to the kitchen, James had gone.

The Witch handed her a basket and a purse that Antonia didn't remember seeing before.

"Off you go," said the Witch, not unkindly.

Antonia walked in the opposite direction to the shops. She sat for a long time in the park beyond the tennis courts, watching toddlers digging in the sand pit, clambering on the climbing frame, shooting down the slide. She was never going to be a mother. There would never be a toddler to bring to the park. It had never mattered before. She had never wanted a baby. If only James had let her have Persephone…she could have wheeled the baby up here and sat with her. So, Persephone would never become a toddler, but it didn't matter. I would love her just as she is!

It was as long time before Antonia retraced her steps and walked down to the village. The Witch accepted the loaf of bread and the basket of salad. Antonia handed back the purse.

"How am I meant to access the Back Garden?" she asked forlornly.

"You're not!" said the Witch shortly. "You may set the table for lunch. Make yourself useful."

"How many for lunch?"

"Four, of course."

Resignedly, Antonia set the table. Presently voices, as James and Dr Mikilari crossed the courtyard and entered the kitchen.

"Hello, my dear! A pleasure, as always, to see you," Dr Mikilari greeted Antonia – as though he had not already seen her at breakfast. Antonia glanced at James who was stooped solicitously over his grandfather, helping him into his chair.

"I see it's Brown Soup again," observed Dr Mikilari sadly.

"But treacle sponge and custard for Afters," mentioned the Witch.

Dr Mikilari brightened considerably.

"When you get to my age," he said reflectively. "Food is one of the few things left to look forward to."

"Rubbish!" snapped the Witch, passing him his soup.

"I saw Shaz in the supermarket," said Antonia, to no one in particular.

"That's the little girl who watches us play tennis," James explained to his grandfather.

"Her parents are separated and no one seems responsible for her while her father's at work," Antonia elaborated.

"Corn bread?" Ignoring her, the Witch passed the bread board down the table.

"Thanks, Granny." James helped himself and passed the board to Dr Mikilari.

The Witch, having served the menfolk, passed a bowl of soup to Antonia, who, having set places for herself and James, side by side, found that the table had been rearranged so that she was estranged from him on the far side of the table.

"Antonia bought the cheese and salad in the village," mentioned the Witch.

"And the corn bread," added Antonia. "And I saw Shaz in the supermarket."

"You already told us that."

"Apple blossom's coming along," said Dr Mikilari into the silence.

"Might be a good crop," James smiled at him. "This is jolly good bread, Granny! Did you bake it?"

"*I* bought it! In the village." Antonia half expected the Witch to say 'You already told us that'. She waited. Silence…

"Isn't anyone speaking to me? She demanded.

"What would you like us to say?" James looked up from buttering his bread.

"You could at least comment on Shaz's neglect – she should have been in school! And you can explain why I've been excluded from the Back Garden!"

She realized she was shouting.

"We thought it was for the best," James said gently. "We need to keep you focused on the real world."

"While you hide yourself away out of reach!"

"Children! Children!" remonstrated Dr Mikilari.

"Why don't we talk about this after lunch," said James smoothly.

He reached a hand across the table to her in a gesture of reconciliation. Antonia snatched her hand away and swore at him. She restrained herself from throwing her soup at him and hid her shaking hands in her lap.

"She feels she's being treated like a child!" observed the Witch, placing the cheese board and the salad on the table and removing empty soup bowls.

Antonia pushed back her chair and stormed out of the kitchen, taking refuge in her study. As she opened the door her senses were wrapped in the perfume of sandalwood, herbs, freshly mown grass...her study was filled with flowers. A card on her desk read: *To my Antonini, love of my life... Know that I love you with all my heart...James.*

Nine

Dead man's shoes

For a moment Antonia thought of seizing the flowers and
hurling them across the room. When had James written
that card? Nothing felt normal anymore. Was it just two
days ago they'd scrambled downstairs for an early coffee
and then walked briskly in the chilly morning to the
tennis court which they'd had to themselves – no Shaz. An
exhilarating three set match, stretching and challenging
them, which she'd narrowly won.

"I won! I won!" she'd exulted, racing to the net and
hurdling over it, to tumble into his arms.

"Steady on! You could have caught your foot…
sprained your ankle!"

He'd pulled her into a hard embrace and a long kiss.
They'd been fizzing with happiness as they dawdled home
to be greeted by the Range and offered a full cooked

breakfast. There had been no whiff of exclusion. He seemed to have forgiven her for bringing Mlilka into the house. They'd been happy...she'd been in no doubt how much he loved her... How could everything have gone so wrong!

She didn't hear him come in. He put his arms round her, startling her. Not wanting to be held, she struggled angrily against him as his arms tightened about her.

"Get off!" she hissed, surprised at his strength. He pulled her head round and kissed her hard. "I hate you!"

"No, you don't. You're just very angry...and outraged."

"Hate you!" Antonia wanted to batter him, kick him, scream at him. "You didn't have to take my baby! You didn't have to lock me out of the Back Garden! And you think putting flowers in my study will make everything alright! I am so, so angry!"

"I know. Antoni-ni, I know."

"And you pretend you love me!"

"Yes."

He was still holding her. Now he gently stroked her face. She jerked her head away. His hand rested on her head, stroking the fine soft hair which was replacing the stubble. Her hair was growing back. It was baby-soft. As fine and soft as Persephone's hair. He laid his face against it. Antonia couldn't see his expression and yet know something had changed. She stopped fighting.

"My Antoni-ni!" he murmured, gently kissing her hair, turning her head to kiss her forehead, her face, and finally gaining a response.

"I wanted her so much!"

"I know you did! But Ni-ni, think for a moment: if your toddler's in danger, you can pick him up, remove him from the danger – but when your back's turned he'll probably head right back, enticed by the danger. So then you have to remove the danger from him."

"Are you calling me a toddler?"

"The Back Garden represents too great a risk. You'll find the courtyard's been enlarged and includes all the beauty and loveliness of the Back Garden…"

"Except…"

James shook his head. There was an expression of such sadness in his eyes.

"Except the prams." He touched his finger tips to the tears that were sliding down her face. "I cannot promise you a baby, Ni-ni. You know that. And perhaps one day you will leave me in order to have a baby with some other man…"

"I don't want some other man! I want you!"

She suddenly looked up at him: "Why were you so horrible to me at lunch?"

"You mean because I gave Grandad more attention than you?"

"You ignored me! You all just ignored me!"

"Am I ignoring you now?"

"I was so happy…and now you've ruined everything! You're…"

She felt a great shudder pass through her, a moment when she was enveloped in a huge sneeze…and found herself standing in the cove, James's special place. A tangy, salt-laden breeze caressed her. Overhead a lone seagull cried plaintively. She could feel pebbles underfoot. Any moment James would stoop down and choose a pebble for her. She breathed in great lungfuls of fresh, almost damp air. This was their place. No one intruded. Nothing spoiled the peace…she felt calm. She turned her face and saw the love, the kindness, the understanding in his eyes.

"I was so angry with you! But it's alright now."

"That's what this place is about… There have been times when *I've* felt so hurt, so betrayed… If I hadn't been able to come here, I couldn't have coped…"

"Thank you for sharing this place with me."

"Shall we walk a little?" He tucked her under his arm. They strolled along the beach, saying nothing because there was no need for words.

***

They found the Witch and Dr Mikilari already at the breakfast table when they came down next morning. Dr Mikilari was spreading honey on his toast.

"My honey-bee!" he murmured.

"Pshaw!" retorted the Witch.

"Beloved!" The Witch sniffed disparagingly.

"Heart of my own heart, I *cherish* you!"

"That's more like it!" The Witch slid into his lap, took the honeyed toast from his hand and bit into it.

"That was my toast!"

"Really? And very nice toast it is, too!"

"Are you going to make me another one?"

"Shouldn't think so!"

James, his arm around Antonia, smiled, and drew her out into the courtyard. Antonia stared about her. The courtyard was so much bigger! Spacious enough to hold a full-grown tree, which was providing shade for the garden table and chairs.

Sturdy pots of shrubs and flowers welcomed happy bees – orange bottoms buzzing in the foxgloves (although it was only March!) A fountain splashed musically into a small brick pool. The scent of new-mown grass wafted towards them. From nowhere the nameless black cat appeared and wound sinuously round Antonia's legs, purring rustily. It was all very beautiful. Finally, Antonia glanced across to where the green gate led into the Back Garden. There was no green gate. The walled courtyard stood, as it had always stood. There was no trace of any break in its stonework.

"Now, breakfast." James drew her back to the kitchen.

"Good morning!" The Range greeted Antonia. "I hope you slept well?"

"Are we interrupting?" whispered Antonia, glancing across at James's grandparents.

"Good morning, Grandad!" James accepted a mug of coffee from the Range and strolled over to join him.

"She stole my toast!" said Dr Mikilari plaintively.

"There's plenty more!" Antonia took a plate from the Range and placed it within his reach.

"Would you like me to butter it for you?" James offered. "Since you seem to have your hands full with Granny!"

"James, do you want porrage?" asked Antonia, sipping her coffee. "Are we playing tennis this morning?"

"Antonia and I are taking a shopping trip to town," announced the Witch unexpectedly.

"Anything in particular?" James handed a slice of toast to his grandfather and buttered one for himself.

"Possibly." The Witch gave him an enigmatic smile. "Come and sit down," she invited Antonia. "Have some scrambled egg."

"You didn't offer me any scrambled egg!" protested Dr Mikilari.

"You're scrambled enough as it is!"

James stood up and fetched two plates of scrambled egg from the Range. He placed one in front of Antonia.

The other he devoured himself…watched hungrily by his grandfather.

***

"You may drive," said the Witch, getting into Antonia's car. I never learned to drive. We're going into town."

Antonia inserted her key in the ignition. "You may park outside the Town Hall. I wish to apply for a bus pass."

"Goodness!" Antonia stole a quick look at her.

"He doesn't care for riding pillion on the broomstick," observed the Witch.

"I don't think I would, either."

"No sense of adventure!"

Antonia wondered if the rebuke was aimed at her or at Dr Mikilari. It was a forty minute drive into town. She turned into the car park. Cars could be parked free for half an hour. She didn't think it would take that long to complete their fruitless errand.

"Do you want me to come in with you?"

"Possibly."

"Um, don't you need to bring your paperwork – birth certificate …stuff like that?"

"They didn't issue birth certificates in the Eleventh Century!" said the Witch tartly.

"But they will expect proof of your age. I don't suppose you have a passport?"

"Hah!" The Witch walked smartly up to the Enquiry desk and made her mission known.

"Do you have your documents?"

"You can see I'm an old lady. A very old lady! Isn't that good enough for you?"

"I'm afraid we will need some documented proof of your age and a current utility bill."

"Balderdash!" muttered the Witch. "Tell her, Antonia. Tell her I want a bus pass!"

"I'm sorry, Granny. These are their rules: no birth certificate, no bus pass."

"And a current utility bill," added the desk clerk. "Where is it you live?"

The Witch told her. "But that's… That cottage has been derelict for years! No one lives there!"

"I do," Antonia mentioned.

"This is my daughter-in-law," said the Witch, introducing her. "She translates books from the Russian."

"If you live there, you should be paying Council Tax

and Water rates," said the clerk severely. "We understood the cottage was derelict."

"It was Dr Mikilari's cottage," replied the Witch. "He died thirty five years ago. And I, myself, belong in the Eleventh Century. They didn't issue birth certificates back then. We're as derelict as the cottage!"

The clerk looked distinctly uncomfortable. She turned her attention to Antonia:

"And you said you are living there, yourself?"

"She lives with my grandson who died last September …or was it October?"

The Witch was enjoying the clerk's discomfort. Antonia began to feel sorry for the clerk, who was clearly out of her depth. Suddenly the clerk brightened:

"Shall I put you down as Squatting?"

It seemed an eminently sensible arrangement. Antonia steered the Witch out of the Council Offices.

"Tea, Granny?" she suggested.

They were served tea and hot buttered tea-cakes in a small friendly café with a view of the High Street.

"Where would you like to go, now?" Antonia enquired. The Witch did not seem to have a particular shop in mind. They strolled along the High Street, glancing in shop windows…and there was the one shop which Antonia could not resist. She stopped and gazed longingly at prams and teddy bears, maternity wear and baby equipment. The Witch observed her for a few minutes and then walked resolutely into the store. Diffidently Antonia followed.

"Can I help you?" An eager shop assistant approached.

"Not today," answered the Witch. "Today we are just looking. After all, one doesn't want to clutter up the hall with a pram for eight months before it's needed!"

"Quite!" The assistant glanced furtively at Antonia's flat stomach. "We can, of course, place items on a deferred order …you pay at today's prices. Would you like a catalogue?"

"Thank you," Antonia accepted the proffered catalogue.

"But we would like to look round," insisted the Witch.

"If that's quite alright with you!"

Antonia followed her round, touching, feeling, coveting… overwhelmed with longing.

"James said he didn't think it was possible…" she confided in the Witch as they walked back to the car. They had well overstayed their half hour, but no one seemed to have noticed.

"You may call him Luca," said the Witch, "If you should find yourself pregnant…which is unlikely. But you should always believe in the impossible." She settled herself in the car for their return journey. "Study your catalogue: choose your pram, your baby clothes, and all the other items. Study them every day. Decide where you will place them. Decorate the nursery. Hang curtains. Visualise. Spend time in the nursery, visualising. The power of visualising is not to be sneezed at."

"I would have settled for Persephone."

"She belongs in the past. In James's past. You are his present and his future. Take him forward. Love him. Cherish him…" The Witch fell silent for a moment.

"Cherish…" she murmured to herself, remembering her daughter's wedding vows…and the wonderful new all-encompassing word of love…cherish!

***

As they got ready for bed. James picked up the catalogue and glanced at it. He said nothing. Defensively, Antonia repeated the Witch's adjuration to visualise. He took her in his arms and held her for a long time, remembering Suki's desperate longing for a baby, and her grief with each month's disappointment.

"I cannot promise, Ni-ni. You do understand that!"

"But I can visualise! I can start decorating the nursery! I can…"

James shook his head. It had been unlikely then, but not impossible. But he was not who he had been, then. Ahead he saw only disappointment and betrayed hope… and the possibility that she would leave him for a more virile man.

The moon shone through their bedroom window, caressing Antonia. James raised himself on his elbow and studied her sleeping face. Presently he slid silently out of bed, moving barefoot to the top of the stairs. Antonia did not stir. In the kitchen the Range drowsed contentedly. The back door stood open. James walked across the courtyard and through the green gate into the Back Garden. The grass felt warm beneath his feet. Apples hung on the trees in the orchard. The garden, lit by moonlight was in summer mode. The Witch was dancing. She wore a diaphanous gown which flowed about her as she moved. She reached out to Dr Mikilari as he stepped within the circle of her arms.

"Ragwort! My Snag-rag!" he murmured. "My adored Snag-rag, I cherish you!"

Their bodies melded in sinuous movements, graceful and suggestive. And then the Witch leaned back within his arms and began to sing. James thought he had never heard such a beautiful melody. She sang in a language he had never heard, and her voice filled the garden with such sweetness, he could feel it pulsing through his body. He stayed watching them until the moon began to wane, then he turned and slipped away as noiselessly as he had come.

Antonia stirred as he slid into bed. He gathered her in his arms.

"You're cold!" she muttered sleepily.

"Soon warm up!"

"You were gone a long time!"

"I was watching Granny dancing in the Garden."

"What?" Fully awake, Antonia frowned. "Why?"

"When she's not observed, she is so beautiful! Age falls away. I've never seen two people dance so exquisitely… and she sang as if…as if…"

"As if?"

"Beyond words…"

"Maybe I'd have liked to have seen that too…if I wasn't excluded from the Garden!"

"Oh, Ni-ni! My beautiful, beloved Ni-ni… Heart of my own heart!" His fingers caressed her cheek. He placed a lingering kiss on her lips and made love to her with great tenderness.

***

Following the Witch's suggestion, Antonia set to work on the little bedroom which had once housed Hugo and Jake. There was still Jake's small bed and chest of drawers. Antonia wondered how Michael, with his long legs, had managed to sleep in Jake's bed. The room had stood unused and unloved for too many years. Antonia stripped wallpaper, scrubbed and visualised. She walked down to the village to buy paint, but the small hardware shop did not have the nursery rhyme paper she'd envisaged – that would be a trip to Town. She scrubbed out and repainted the small chest of drawers and considered what she might choose for the flooring.

"You've been very busy!" James remarked as they sat down for lunch. He smiled at her warmly. "Your hair's beginning to look very pretty!"

"Roast pheasant! exclaimed Dr Mikilari. "What a treat!"

"Not for the pheasant!" muttered the Witch.

"So what have you been doing this morning?" enquired Dr Mikilari, helping himself to roast potatoes and cabbage.

"Antonia's ben decorating the small bedroom," observed the Witch.

"I was hoping to find some attractive wallpaper in the village, but they only seem to stock utilitarian woodchip." Antonia served herself with vegetables and passed the tureen. "I wondered whether we could dispose of the small bed? It's quite rickety and the mattress is badly stained."

"It'll chop up nicely for firewood," suggested Dr Mikilari, balancing too much on his fork and losing a potato. He smiled at Antonia.

***

"James, I didn't have a period in over two months. D'you think…?" James shook his head,

"I expect it's the trauma you suffered on Windover Ridge. Shock, stress. All sorts of things can have that sort of impact. Don't worry. It'll right itself soon enough."

"It would be so amazing if…"

"Amazing is about right," he gave a wry smile. "I want to say, don't get your hopes too high, darling. It's so unlikely."

"Granny…"

"I know. But Granny's not infallible." He came across to her, drawing her into his arms, resting his head against her soft new hair. "I wish it were possible, Ni-ni. But, sometimes the things we want so badly, are not… there are some things I cannot give you, however much I'd like to."

"I could make do with Persephone, if you'd let me back into the Garden. Why not, James? I know she can never grow up, but I'd have a baby – your baby! I could wheel her up to the park each day, make friends with the mums there. I would feel authentic! She could sleep in the nursery that I've got ready! Please, James!"

"Antonia, we've been there before. I've explained why that's not possible. You know very well that you cannot have Persephone. Please don't start all this up again!"

A blazing row followed. Antonia shouted. She threw things at him. She hurled accusations at him.

"You're just a bloody hypocrite!" she yelled. "You can go into the Back Garden and cuddle Persephone whenever you like, but you're too mean to let me love her! I hate you!"

James retreated to the bathroom. Antonia took the opportunity to lock him out. He could sleep in that cold, spare bedroom!

He was *supposed* to love her! But he wouldn't allow her even one night with the baby! One measly night!

Gradually a plan began to form. She would pack some clothes, toiletries, her computer and translation work, and drive to her flat early in the morning. And she wasn't coming back in a hurry either! She would spend a day with her father who would be pleased to see her. She might even invite him to the flat for a meal. She could fly out to see her publisher…where James could not follow her! There was a flicker of spiteful pleasure in that thought. James could keep his Back Garden and his dead babies. Perhaps she could adopt a real baby. That would serve him right! She heard him try the bedroom door. Heard him knock. Heard him turn away and go to sleep elsewhere – without his pyjamas – she hoped the spare room was really chilly!

Early the next morning Antonia dressed, picked up

the suitcase she'd already packed overnight, and crept silently downstairs.

"Coffee?" asked the Range, waking up.

"Thank you." Antonia felt the need to inform the Range of her departure.

"Sorry to see you go," observed the Range. "Of course, trying to bring past life out of the Back Garden where it belongs, is counter productive at the best of times." He blew a wisp of smoke at her. "Persephone belongs in the past. You've been privileged to visit her in the Back Garden, but you can no more spend the rest of your life in the Back Garden, than you can attempt to bring the Back Garden into the present. Either way is venturing into the realms of madness."

"You sententious old… As if I don't get enough of this from James!"

Antonia banged her empty mug down on the table, picked up her suitcase and made her way to the study to collect her laptop, dictionaries and paraphernalia. She carried it all to the front door which was reluctant to open. She put everything down, tugged at the door, kicked it, swore at it… stood back.

"If you don't bloody open, I'll have to climb out through the window. But I *am* leaving!" She gave a final tug at the door. "You F…!"

"Outside my experience," observed the Front Door loftily.

"Look…please will you open and let me out!"

"Certainly!" responded the Front Door. "You only had to ask."

Antonia loaded her belongings into the car, inserted

her key in the ignition, and without a backward glance, drove off. Had she looked back, she might have seen James standing at the bedroom window watching her departure. She had left their bedroom door open and he had come to ask if he could bring her a coffee.

Down through the village, out into the countryside as the early morning light dispersed the darkness, chasing away the shadows, dripping wetly from twig and branch. Lawns were silvered with frost. Fragile sheets of ice had formed on the puddles and potholes. Sleepy birds began twittering. A lone fox trotted across the road. Antonia switched on the car radio and listened to an early news broadcast. The real world. She would be back at her flat by eight-thirty. Mentally she ran over her to-do list: switch on the heating, clean sheets on the bed, coffee, stock up the fridge, check mail, phone her father and arrange to meet.

The flat was cold, cheerless and wore an uninhabited air. Antonia set-to purposefully: heating on, music on – she chose Scott Joplin. Kettle on for coffee. Strip the bed, bedding and towels into the washing machine. Make up the bed with fresh sheets. Make coffee. Drink it black. Air the fridge and write a shopping list. Add flowers and a bottle of wine! She gathered up the mail, discarding advertising and junk mail. Down to the shops, coming back to stock the fridge and cupboards. More coffee, this time with milk. She arranged the flowers, noticing the layer of dust covering all the surfaces. Perhaps she would give the flat a thorough clean.

She began to feel more cheerful, in control of her life

…positive. After all, she had lived on her own all her adult life – she didn't need James. It was a pity it hadn't worked out because they'd been happy together, most of the time. And he had loved her…but on his own terms. No, she was better off without him. She phoned her father and arranged to meet.

***

At least *he* hadn't changed. He was still the handsome, silver-haired, older man with impeccable manners. He rose to greet her as she entered the foyer.

"It's wonderful to see you! You're looking well!"

Actually, he thought, she looked strained.

Someone took their coats and they were shown to a table. Her father requested wine and they studied the menu.

"Perhaps, one of these days, I might get to meet your boyfriend?" Antonia glanced at her father but he appeared to be concentrating on the menu.

"We've broken up," she said shortly.

"I'm sorry to hear that." Covertly he studied her. She was more brittle, less animated than when he'd last seen her. "I thought we might go to the theatre, if there's a show you'd fancy?"

Antonia brightened.

"That might be nice." She smiled. They placed their order. "How are you?" she asked.

"Life's treating me pretty well. I keep active. See friends …miss your mother, of course."

"At least you can choose where you live."

"There's that. Yes, I have a lot of choices open to me."
He smiled at her gently.

She decided to give him the address of her flat. She would invite him for a meal. Seeing more of him would cushion the absence of James while she readjusted to her solitary life.

***

A week passed. The flat was pristine, tidy, familiar. She worked hard at her translation. Her father came for a meal.

His visit was pleasant, undemanding. They went to the theatre. She took in a couple of films. She kept busy. But her bed felt empty and she constantly dreamed of James, waking to find her pillow wet. It's going to take time, she told herself. For years she had lived alone, self-sufficient, purposeful. She thought about Phil – he had been a good friend to her…and a father figure to James. She had loved James…better not go there!

She felt reproachful that he had not tried to contact her. If he had *really* loved her, surely he would have phoned or sent a letter…or just turned up? She imagined how it would be if he unexpectedly rang her door bell – would she be pleased to see him? How would she feel if he put his arms around her, and she felt his warmth, his strength…and the way he ran his fingers through her hair… touched his finger tips to her cheek …or… She missed him! On the other hand, he had repeatedly said that he would never stand in her way if she wanted to leave. If he loved her, wouldn't he at least have begged her to stay, to reconsider? He was the nicest, kindest, most considerate man she had ever known. He was so gentle… their bodies fitted together so beautifully…and he had begun letting her into the vulnerable places in his life – she recalled the image of his three-year-old wistfulness.

***

Three weeks on, she found herself constantly distracted from her translation work, unable to enjoy its challenge. It was difficult to sustain concentration. She was aware of feeling lonely, however much she tried to shut her feelings down. Even her father irritated her. She slept badly. Her body ached, hungered for James…only James. She found herself crying for no reason, at odd times of the day. But she was resolved. She wasn't going back! No way was she going back! She rehearsed her grievances. She even missed the chatty Range! How stupid was that!

The flat was silent. Her C.D. had played out. The flat shrieked with emptiness. She threw her magazine across the room.

She didn't want to read. There was nothing she wanted to do… Somehow she had lost the art of living alone, self-sufficient. Somehow, living with James and being loved by him had spoiled her from returning to her previous life. There was no way back. The future stretched ahead lonely, unbearable. She needed James. She needed him and she had thrown him away! Once before, he had come to her when she had been so distraught after his... but she couldn't expect him to come now...not after the way she'd treated him. Antonia gave herself up remorse, anguish...grief. She wept. Without James there was nothing to live for.

***

She was lying on the carpet when she awoke, stiff and chilled. Daylight crept around the drawn curtains. There was a noise from the kitchen a chinking of china, as if a small rodent had found its way in. That was all she needed! Antonia curled herself into a ball, partly to ease her back, and partly to shut out the realisation of another day to face... another twenty-four hours of despair.

"Antoni-ni?" said a familiar voice. "Would you like a coffee? It even has milk! Sit up and get some hot coffee down." Blearily Antonia uncurled herself and sat up. Was she dreaming? Was that...could it be, James? She saw that he was handing her a mug. Her hands shook as she reached for it, spilling coffee over the carpet. She began to cry.

"It's only coffee! Not the end of the world!"

It was James's voice, familiar and so, so comforting. She crawled towards him and found herself gathered into his arms. She wanted to tell him how much she needed him, how much she wanted him...to tell him she was sorry...but she was sobbing so much she was incoherent. All she wanted was for him to hold her.

Much later, when she had calmed down, there was

fresh coffee, and there was James holding her, stroking her hair, touching gentle fingertips to her face, wordlessly comforting her, as only he could.

"I wanted a baby," she whispered.

"I know."

"I wanted Persephone."

"No. You have to live in the real world."

"Are you part of my real world?"

"Always."

"You said…"

"I said I would never stand in your way if you wanted to leave, but I don't think leaving measured up in the long term?"

"No."

"So, we'll have to do something about a baby."

"I thought you said it was impossible?"

"I said *unlikely*, not impossible. I don't know if it's possible, I really don't."

"I didn't know how much I wanted a baby, until…"

"I know. You were so sure you never wanted a baby."

"I didn't want to put a child through the sort of childhood I had."

"It wouldn't have to be like that, Antoni-ni."

"How wouldn't it?"

"When there is love, love for each other, a child born out of that love…"

"A baby we created together? A real baby?"

"I don't have a wonderful track record: Seph died… …Delfina's quality of life is severely compromised…even Jake has defected. I can't even promise that I can father a child. But I will love you with all my heart and soul. I will cherish you."

"Will, you stay with me?"

"Yes."

"Here?"

"If that's what you want."

"I don't think I can cope with going back."

"I know."

He cradled her against him. Of course he would stay with her, comfort and reassure her. He would stay for as long as it took until she was happy again.

And when she was ready, they would go home... however long it took. He kissed her.

"And we will see what faith can do, when love is making all things new..."

***

Two days later her father arrived unexpectedly, without prior warning.

"Oh!" exclaimed Antonia, "I've got James here."

"I've been looking forward to meeting him!"

Her father would not be sent away. Reluctantly, Antonia showed him in. James rose courteously to greet him. They shook hands. Antonia stared in disbelief – how come her father could *see* James?

"Antoni-ni, I expect your father would like some coffee." She retreated to the kitchen, returning with a tray of coffee and biscuits. She half expected that James would have vanished, and only her father be sitting there.

But the two men sat chatting, obviously at ease with each other. When at last her father rose to go, she belatedly invited him to lunch.

"No, it's time you young people were thinking about lunch. And I have to be elsewhere. James, it's been such a pleasure to meet you at last. I look forward to inviting you both to a meal. Give me a call, Antonia." As she showed him out, he smiled at her: "What a very nice chap! I'm so glad you made it up!"

"What a very nice man your father is!" James reached out a hand to her.

"How come he could see you and talk to you?"

"Because he believed what was in front of him. You had told him I was here. He had no reason to doubt it."

"He liked you." Antonia sat down beside him. James put an arm around her. "Is he lonely, d'you think?"

"I expect he is." James snuggled her against him. "I'm glad you see each other."

"I wasn't sure about giving him my address."

"I think he might have wondered why you were withholding it."

"James?"

"M'hm?"

"Do you get bored when I'm translating… now you don't have your studio?"

"Boredom is a very human trait."

"I'd have thought anger is a human trait!"

He nibbled her ear.

"So, I might get angry, but no, I don't get bored."

"You were horrible!"

"Was I?"

"I hated you!"

James regarded her appraisingly: she had probably never had a sustained relationship that lasted long enough, or deeply enough, to warrant such an explosion of emotion. Antonia had been a very self-contained, isolated, singleton. Perhaps it was only now that she felt secure enough within their relationship to express negative feelings. He kissed the top of her head.

"Don't you care that I hated you?" she asked suspiciously.

"As long as it's past tense!" He ran his fingers through her hair – it was just long enough to do this. "You may hate me yesterday...but I hope you won't hate me tomorrow."

"And if... if..." she dared not express that wild hope.

"I can't promise. You know that." James knew exactly what she was thinking. "But I do promise to love and cherish you for ever and always."

There was sadness in his smile. Regret might be a human trait but he deeply regretted that he could not share fully in her life.

***

The phone rang, interrupting her work. Antonia marked her place before answering.

"Antonia?" It was her father.

"Yes, hello?"

"I was wondering if you'd care to come and have

lunch with me at the Club. There's something we need to discuss."

"Thursday?"

"Fine."

"Usual time?"

"I'll look forward to it."

Antonia put the phone down and pondered. Given her father's age, perhaps he wanted her to witness documents…discuss his will?

"I didn't actually ask him if he was expecting both of us?" she said to James.

"I wouldn't be able to go. He said *his Club* – I've never been there. And wanting to 'discuss something', sounds more like a private meeting."

Two days later she joined her father for lunch in the discreet ambiance of his Club. It was not until they were drinking coffee in the lounge after the meal, that her father cleared his throat.

"Antonia, my dear, there's something I need to clarify." Antonia waited. "Tell me how you came to meet James?"

"Oh… through a mutual friend, someone I've known for years."

"I see… You said James is a doctor – a psychiatrist, I believe you said?" He waited for her assent. "Only, it has come to my attention that a Dr James Gregory died last autumn."

He waited for her to react. Antonia sat very still, watching her father's face.

"Well, you've met James. You liked him."

"I have met someone calling himself James Gregory." He paused. "Well?"

"What d'you want me to say?"

"What do you really know about him?"

"I've met his parents...his brother. He is who he says he is. He's also a highly respected artist. I can take you to the Gallery which exhibits and sells his work. Would that interest you?"

Her father extracted a newspaper cutting from his wallet.

Beneath a photograph of the late Dr James Gregory, Consultant Psychiatrist, there was lengthy obituary... He handed the cutting to Antonia.

"The photograph is very much like your James, but I fear he is an imposter. He has stepped into a dead man's shoes. I advise you to have nothing more to do with him."

A smile crossed Antonia's face as she envisaged recounting to James that he walked in a dead man's shoes.

"Antonia!" Her father's voice was suddenly sharp.

"I love him."

"I dare say you do, but he is trouble. You mark my words, girl!"

"I appreciate your concern. It's been an unexpected pleasure renewing our relationship. Thank you for lunch – I hope we will stay in touch. If you are asking me to make a choice between you and James, I choose James...dead or alive!"

She rose, said goodbye to her father and went to collect her coat.

James was sitting reading a magazine when she returned to the flat. He enfolded her in a welcoming hug.

"That was unfortunate!" he observed.

"How would you know!"

"I know." He helped her off with her coat. "Thank you for choosing me!" He smiled at her with a depth of affection. "Could you use a coffee?"

"He wouldn't even come to see your work in the Gallery!"

"No matter." He held her close for a moment, and then chuckled. "I liked that comment *walking in a dead man's shoes*!"

"I do love you, James!"

"Antoni-ni, you are my sunshine! Where you walk, flowers spring up! When you enter a room, I hear music! When I paint, your spirit inhabits my studio! The cottage comes alive when you grace it with your presence…"

"Rubbish!" whispered Antonia, lifting her face for a kiss.

It was a long time since he'd had a studio to paint in, she reflected while he made their coffee. She studied his face as he set down their mugs.

"Do you miss the cottage?"

"I miss the cottage, and the cottage misses us."

"That's a bit far-fetched…anthropomorphic, even!"

"You add life and character to the cottage!"

"And the small matter of a quarrel!"

Ten

If only dreams came true

A car drew up. Antonia glanced out of the window. As they never had visitors at the cottage, she wondered who this could be. She had been working at her desk. A bee buzzed in through the open windows which were letting in the welcome sunshine. She stood up to encourage it to find its way out and saw the visitor getting out of his car and approaching the cottage. The young man smiled at her as he reached the front door and rang the bell. Antonia stepped back involuntarily. The bell rang twice. Would James answer the door? The bell rang again. Antonia pulled herself together and stepped into the hall.

"Good Morning," said the stranger. "I'm Hugo. I wondered if Mike was here?"

"I'm afraid not," Antonia breathed a sigh of relief. Now this young man would go away.

"Hugo?" James had come through from his studio.

"Daddy One? Is that really you?"

"Hugo!" James reached out his hands in welcome and found them grasped. "Hugo! Hugo Bear!"

Antonia watched in amazement. They were utterly oblivious of her. "Well, don't stand there on the door step, come in!" James registered her presence. "Hugo, this is Antonia. I don't think you've met. Antonia, this is Hugo, Jake's older brother."

"I know who Hugo is. Why don't you go through and I'll bring some coffee."

"This is such an unexpected pleasure, Hugo! What brings you here?"

"I thought Uncle Mike was spending this weekend here?"

"He does come quite often, but not this weekend. Will I do?"

"More than!" Hugo shook his head in wonder. He had to keep touching James to make certain he was real.

"So, how are you? How's work? Tell me about yourself."

"Work's fine. I have a career ladder. Job pays a decent salary. I have my own flat which I share with Eleanor – met her at Oxford. Andy and Stephen are still at school. Andy goes up to Oxford in October. Mum and Dad are fine. It's their silver wedding anniversary next month – big shindig! All the family invited. Shall you come?"

"Probably not. They won't recognize me. Not even Jake!"

"Jake likes everything cut and dried. I'm more open minded."

"Which is why you can see me."

"Oh, it's just great to see you!" Hugo beamed. "Are you and Antonia married?"

"As good as!"

"Jake graduates this summer."

"I know. I'm so proud of him – even though he won't acknowledge me."

"Did you know Margaret's married? She threw over college, couldn't wait to get hitched! Philip's a pilot. Nice chap. Think that brings you up to date…" Hugo drank his coffee. "How did you meet Antonia?"

"Do you remember coming over to spend time with Jake when we lived with Carew Robinson?"

"Sure! Caroo! I really liked him. He taught Jake to play, didn't he."

"Antonia was a friend of Caroo's."

"Right." Hugo considered the contents of his mug. He had heard Jake's version, which painted Antonia in a most unfavourable light. He assumed Jake's nose had been put out of joint by competition for his father's affection.

He was prevailed upon to stay for lunch. It was neither Brown Soup nor road kill. He did not remember his great grandfather – nor did Dr Mikilari have any idea who he was.

After the meal, Antonia brought coffee out to the courtyard.

Hugo and James were already seated at the table, chatting.

"Antonia translates Russian novels," James mentioned.

"Really? You speak Russian?"

"Antonia speaks five or six languages fluently," said James proudly.

"My father was a diplomat. We moved every five years. So I learned a new language with each new country."

"How come you chose Russian, particularly?"

"There wasn't much to do in the long summer holidays in Moscow, except read! I wasn't allowed to fraternise. It was frowned upon. I just got into Russian literature. You might say, it got under my skin!"

They chatted easily. Hugo liked Antonia. He discounted Jake's opinions. On the whole Jake had led a rather cloistered life.

"Do come again," Antonia urged him with real warmth, as he made his move.

"Perhaps I could bring Eleanor next time?"

***

James was dreaming. He was watching his grandmother dancing in the Back Garden, graceful, almost disembodied… and then it wasn't his grandmother, it was Antonia dancing in a long floating nightgown – not in the Back Garden, but beside a lake, beneath the trees… the park where, as a medical student he'd come early on Sunday mornings to jog. He'd shared a small fourth floor flat with Sam. It was really a one bedroom flat, but Sam's Dad had partitioned a slice of the living room to create a tiny bedroom for James. It was stuffy at the best of times, but in summer, it could be unbearable – hence the early morning jog in the fresh air. And then one morning there had been this young girl dancing under the trees, so graceful and vibrant, totally unselfconscious. He'd stopped to watch her. She was unaware of him. It was like watching an impromptu ballet. At the last minute, he must have made some random movement startling her. She stared at him and gave him a little wave as she scampered off. There was something about her. He thought of her as his woodland sprite.

But although he looked for her Sunday after Sunday, he never saw her again…

James realised he awake. He had been dreaming, certainly, but he had also been remembering. He turned his head and looked at Antonia.

"Are you awake, Ni-ni?" She looked at him. "I just wondered if you might have been in Hyde Park one Sunday morning when you'd have been about fourteen?"

Antonia regarded him thoughtfully. Where had they been living when she was fourteen? Not in London. None of her father's postings had been London. She was about to tell James this, when she remembered there had been an occasion when he'd been summoned to some high level meeting in London…and her mother had seen this as an opportunity for a shopping trip…and a chance to show Antonia London. As she remembered it, Antonia had found most of it painfully boring. She wasn't interested in shopping, in clothes, in the things that interested her mother. The Tower of London was most memorable for the lengthy time-wasting queues. She'd asked to go to the zoo, but her mother complained that her feet hurt. However, there had been one day when she'd escaped, very early, just after sunrise. Their hotel overlooked the park and she'd revelled in the space, the freedom to dance, to be herself. Yes, she had been in Hyde Park early one Sunday morning when she was fourteen.

"You danced with such unconscious grace," said James. "I could have watched you for hours, but I startled you and you ran off." His voice was wistful. "I searched and searched for you, but I never saw you again!"

"We were only there for a week."

"I had this fantasy that one day I would find you again!"

"I guess you have!" A self-deprecating expression crossed Antonia's face. "But I'm not that graceful fourteen year old!"

"To me, you will, always be that vision of grace and innocence." He touched gentle fingers to her cheek.

"Tonight, if it's a moonlit night, I shall take you to dance barefoot in the Back Garden with me!"

Antonia wondered whether to remind him that she wasn't allowed in the Back Garden, but she didn't want to spoil the magic of this moment.

***

"That boy worships the ground she walks on!" The Witch muttered.

"Is that so?" Dr Mikilari murmured, irritating her so much that she tipped him out of their hammock.

***

Antonia roused. Daylight filtered around the curtains. She glanced at her watch. It was later than she'd expected. There was a curious tingling sensation in her breasts. She pulled herself upright, hearing footfalls on the stairs. Expecting James, she was surprised when it was the Witch who pushed open the door and entered, bearing a breakfast tray.

"Breakfast!" she said unnecessarily, setting the tray on Antonia's lap, and crossing to the window to draw back the curtains. "Nice spring morning!" She flung open the windows.

"It's a bit cold!" protested Antonia.

"Invigorating!" corrected the Witch. "Enjoy your breakfast!"

"This is really very kind of you... going to all this trouble! Is it a special day today?"

"Possibly." The Witch shrugged.

A moment later she was gone. Antonia surveyed her breakfast tray: a glass of freshly squeezed orange juice; an egg boiled just the way she liked it, the white firmly set, the yolk runny. Buttered fingers of toast with a small dish of marmalade which tasted delicious – almost certainly the Witch's own recipe: sweet, but not too sweet, tangy, exotic... and tea! Antonia had become so used to the Range's ever present offer of coffee, she'd forgotten that she had always preferred tea at breakfast, strong and black because throughout her student days at the Sorbonne, none of them had milk to spare.

As she pulled on her slacks she noticed that she was struggling to fasten the zip – she'd been putting on weight!

The bedroom was chilly with the windows open. She shivered and pulled a thick white sweater over her head. It was almost certainly one of James's sweaters! She ran a brush through her hair – at least she had hair to brush, now! Pulling back the bedding to air, she picked up the tray and carried it to the stair head. Below, James was sitting at the kitchen table in earnest conversation with his grandfather.

"Good Morning, Antonia. I hope you slept well?" the Range greeted her. "Coffee?"

"Yes please!"

James had not seen her come in. He half turned and held out his empty mug.

"What about you, Grandad?"

Dr Mikilari gazed in surprise into the depths of his mug.

"I don't even remember drinking it!"

Antonia set down her tray on the draining board and collected fresh mugs of coffee from the ever obliging Range.

"Granny brought me breakfast in bed," she mentioned.

"Did she now! I don't remember her ever bringing *me* breakfast in bed!"

"You don't remember zilch, old man!" scolded the Witch, appearing through the back door. "What about those endless months when you were in a wheelchair!"

"I seem to remember you tipped me out, and told me to stand on my own two feet!"

"And did you?" asked Antonia.

"Not him! An annoying crowd of well-wishers

converged to pick him up. So embarrassing!"

"I find it hard to imagine you being embarrassed, Granny!"

"Well, Daffyn…" The Witch threw him an enigmatic look and busied herself at the Range.

***

"James?" Antonia was undressing. The bedroom windows were firmly closed, the curtains drawn. She fiddled with the waistband of her slacks. "James, I've had this funny tingling in my breasts. What d'you suppose it is?"

"Anything else you've noticed?"

"Only that my slacks are too tight. I seem to have put on weight. We haven't been playing enough tennis."

"And you still haven't had a period in how long… three months?" Tenderness and amusement chased across his face, as he came around the bed to gather her in his arms. "I'd say you're a good three months pregnant, Ni-ni! Didn't you guess?"

"Was that why Granny brought me breakfast in bed?"

"Quite likely."

"She said it was a special day, but she didn't tell me why!"

"Antoni-ni! My wonderful, precious Antoni-ni! We're going to have a baby! It's what you wanted so badly, darling."

She had schooled herself to believe that it was so unlikely, that she hardly dared believe what he was telling her. And then she was laughing and crying, astonished, delighted.

"Did you know?"

"I had a pretty fair idea." His eyes danced with amusement.

"Oh James! Now I can buy all the things in the catalogue, and fill the nursery. And… I can buy the pram!"

"Hey! Not so fast! You'll be tripping over the pram for months before you need it."

"No, I shan't. It'll have pride of place in my study. I can visualise our baby lying in it, kicking his little legs and waving his arms. I can talk to him each day!"

"Are we expecting a little boy, then?"

"Luca. Granny told me his name is Luca."

"Did she now? She does like choosing everybody's names, irrespective of what we might prefer."

"As in Daffyn?"

Eleven

Margaret et al...

"Congratulations!" said Michael, when they told him. "You must be delighted."

"Just a bit!"

"D'you want to see the nursery?"

Michael looked at Antonia's excited face.

"Isn't one nursery much like another?" He glanced at James:

"Perhaps Mike will look in on his way up to bed, darling."

"I don't suppose you'd heard that Tom's Margaret is expecting, too?"

"She didn't waste any time!"

"She wants a big family!" Michael looked across at Antonia. "Would you like to meet Margaret? It's her first baby too."

"That sounds lovely! Shall you bring her down?"

"Or I could drive you up there?"

"Where does she live?"

"Quite close to Heathrow. Philip's a pilot. "You'll like Philip."

"Can I phone her?"

"Sounds like a good idea."

Armed with Margaret's phone number, Antonia went off to make contact. James and Michael fell into easy conversation.

***

Morning. A chill breeze sneaked in through the window which had not been properly fastened. Antonia shivered and pulled the duvet up to her ears. James was already out of bed, pulling on his boxer shorts. She watched him. He had the most perfect legs, long and lightly tanned. She had always noticed men's legs…long tanned legs in shorts, dressed for tennis, or jogging, or just strolling along the beach. Men went for breasts and bottoms and a cheeky smile, but for her it was always legs.

She adored James's legs… well, she adored pretty much everything about him! She loved his gentle hands and the way his finger traced her face. And she was going to have his baby! She wished she could erase the memory of the men who had used her, paid for an hour or two taking their pleasure with her body. Although, at the time, she had schooled herself to feel nothing, regarding her body as no more than a suit of clothes, there was this miasma of unwanted feelings: leaving her feeling besmirched, soiled…

James came around to her side of the bed and held out his hands to her:

"Up you get! Tennis calls us! Let it blow away all these negative feelings!" How well he understood her! "D'you want to wear my white sweater again?"

"Do you mind?"

"Of course, not! It looks better on you!"

He held her close against him, his hands cupping her buttocks. She wanted him, wanted him to fall back into bed with her.

"Later, Ni-ni!" he murmured, dropping a kiss on the tip of her nose. "I'll leave you to get dressed."

He released her and swiftly pulled on his tennis shorts, before disappearing to the bathroom. Reluctantly, Antonia pulled on her pants and James's white sweater. She loved wearing his clothes which were always impregnated with a sense of him – his aftershave, a faint suggestion of sweat. She caught sight of herself in the mirror: long legs under the sweater which came down over her bottom. She rather liked her reflection, and without stopping to think, she skipped down to the kitchen as she was.

Dr Mikilari paused, his spoon half way to his mouth. He stared at this vision of Antonia, half-dressed and rather delicious! Then, in case the Witch might notice, he averted his eyes and continued eating his porrage. James also feasted his eyes upon her:

"The new tennis outfit?" he enquired, his eyes dancing with amusement.

The Witch gave Antonia a swift covert glance. She said nothing. Dr Mikilari caught her eye and looked at her hungrily, seeing her as the vision of beauty who had danced suggestively in his kitchen, in the park by moonlight, in the Back Garden... remembering the things of long ago.

"Good Morning, Antonia," the Range greeted her. "Were you disturbed in your dressing?"

"Good morning!" Antonia danced across to the Range. "I'm going have a baby! We're going to have a baby! A baby boy! I'm so excited!"

James came across and gathered her into his arms. He felt so proud of her, so overwhelmed with love for her...

"Ahem!" The Range gave a little cough and blew an embarrassed wisp of smoke. "We don't do that there 'ere!"

***

It was Philip's rest day. Margaret had invited Antonia to come and meet them. Michael would drive her up, so that she would know her way for next time. They were late setting off. Michael had a puncture.

"No matter!" said Margaret cheerfully. "We'll be here. We're not going anywhere. Tell Uncle Mike to drive carefully!" It was not a part of London Antonia knew: built up, crowded, depressing. The noise and smell of constantly moving traffic, the continuous thud of heavy lorries. The roar of planes taking off.

"I'm glad I don't have to live here!" said Antonia with feeling.

"I agree."

"I suppose they have to live within reach of the airport."

"I expect they'll look to move. Their flat's going to feel much smaller once their baby arrives."

The flat was well insulated against the constant roar of planes taking off, and coming in to land. It was warm, pleasantly decorated and comfortable. Philip rose to welcome them. Michael was clearly a regular visitor.

Antonia studied Margaret's husband: he was considerably older that Margaret who looked about nineteen. She was plumply pretty and excited to show off her new maternity smock, and engage Antonia in talk of babies. She brought in a tray of coffee and slices of Victoria sponge.

"The coffee pot was a wedding present!" she gushed. "Antique Silver! You don't see many coffee pots like this!" She poured the coffee into pretty cups which, Antonia guessed, had also featured on the wedding present list. "They told me I should cut down on sugar during the pregnancy," she mentioned, stirring two heaped spoonfuls into her cup. "I hope you like the sponge. I made it this morning."

The sponge was light and delicious. Margaret had completed a Cordon Bleu course between school and college. She'd been offered a place at a Teacher Training College, but had left after her first term, having met Philip and fallen in love – though she still described herself as a teacher. Michael and Philip sat together, chatting easily. Margaret was eager to show Antonia the small second bedroom which had been commandeered as the baby's nursery, and already boasted an impressive array of baby equipment. Antonia was amused to discover that Margaret was barely one month pregnant. They compared due dates and maternity plans. Margaret had researched everything from layettes to nursery places in great detail.

"You're quite old to be having a first baby," she observed with disarming candour.

"I had a career first. I wasn't planning to get married and have a family. In fact, I've only known James about eighteen months."

"They tell you to really get to know your man before you commit yourself to marriage, but I decided I could get to know Philip better by living with him, than by having a long engagement." She offered Antonia another coffee. "I want a really big family! How many are you going to have?"

Antonia sipped her coffee.

"I thought we'd start with one and see how that goes."

"Right. Oh, I'm so excited to have you as a friend! We can compare notes all the way through our pregnancies! Of course my Mum and Dad are so excited for me too! Did Uncle Mike tell you that it's their silver wedding anniversary soon? Everyone's invited! Huge party! You must come too. You know, it's funny, but we all thought Uncle James was dead. We all came to his funeral, for heaven's sake! But Hugo said he'd been to visit and Uncle James is alive! Well, he'd have to be to get you pregnant!" She gave a little laugh.

Across the room Philip gave her a small frown. "Oh!

He thinks I'm being a bit cheeky! But you don't mind, do you!" She chattered on artlessly.

Margaret had obviously taken a great deal of trouble preparing their lunch.

"She's a wonderful cook!" said Philip proudly. "It's why I married her!"

"And I'm pretty good in bed!"

Michael cleared his throat, embarrassed. But the meal was undeniably good. Antonia gave Philip a small smile:

"I expect you'll have to settled for less magnificent meals once your baby's arrived."

"Yes, probably have to exist on corned beef sandwiches!"

"Grounds for divorce, I wouldn't wonder!"

***

"She's very immature," Antonia commented to James.

"I'm afraid she's been rather spoiled – the only girl among four brothers. Trisha's father spoiled her rotten, brought her up to believe she could have whatever she wanted. Margaret's his only granddaughter."

"I liked Philip, but I did wonder if they'll last. He's quite a bit older than her."

"And I'm quite a bit older than you, but that doesn't seem to be a problem."

Antonia ignored that remark.

"She's quite excited about coming down to see you – Hugo told her you're not as dead as they all thought!"

"Well, there's a character reference!" He ruffled her hair. "Have you told your father yet?"

"No. We didn't part on especially good terms."

"Give him a call, Ni-ni. He's going to be a grandfather!"

***

Cyril Fortesque Frogmorton was delighted to hear he was going to be a grandfather. Whatever reservations he harboured, he was prepared to put them aside. He would be pleased to drive down to see them. The Witch had prepared a lavish high tea ready to carry out to the courtyard. The table and five chairs sat under the shady tree which now graced the far end of the courtyard garden. Mr Frogmorton parked alongside Antonia's car in the driveway (that wasn't there) He rang the front door bell and waited while the Bell decided whether to respond. James answered the door, extending his hand to the impeccably dressed older man. They shook hands formally. This was clearly a man who valued formality. James brought him through to the courtyard. Antonia stood up to welcome him.

"Hello, my dear. I gather congratulations are in order." James noticed that Antonia's father made no attempt to touch her, hug her, or even place a kiss on her cheek. Here was another child who had grown up without affectionate cuddles.

"Are you ready for a cup of tea?" enquired the Witch.

"Quite a long journey – and not the easiest place to find!"

"Did someone mention tea?" enquired Dr Mikilari, shuffling across from the direction of the Back Garden.

"This is my grandfather, Dr Mikilari," James introduced him to Antonia's father.

"Another doctor!" Antonia's father glanced at Antonia.

"Oh, yes! James's father was a doctor too!"

James looked up sharply, aware that his grandfather had used the past tense.

"Was his name James?" enquired Antonia's father, thinking this might be the answer to the dilemma of the deceased Dr James Gregory.

"I think his name was Gavin?" replied Dr Mikilari uncertainly.

The two men began chatting. The Witch poured tea and handed it round.

"James, I need a hand in the kitchen." The Witch had prepared a rather special tea, with sandwiches, scones and cakes.

James followed her in.

"I hope you haven't prepared any of your special Brownies, Granny!"

"Would I do that?" The Witch was all injured innocence. "The poor man has to drive back to London. We don't want him falling asleep at the wheel!"

James carried out the tray while the Witch replenished the teapot. Dr Mikilari's eyes lit up at the sight of such a splendid repast. The Witch refilled everyone's cups.

"Tell me," she said, smiling wickedly at their guest. "With a name like Frogmorton, were you called 'Froggy' at school?"

"Indeed I was!" Mr Frogmorton gave an embarrassed laugh.

James grinned at Antonia. Dr Mikilari was too busy scoffing sandwiches to notice.

"So, Froggy, may I offer you another sandwich before his nibs eats them all."

The plate of sandwiches rapidly diminished. James helped himself to a scone piled with cream and fresh strawberries.

"These are delicious!"

He passed the plate to Dr Mikilari, who took two.

"James's niece is expecting a baby too," Antonia told her father. "I went up to meet her. They live near Heathrow. Her husband's a pilot."

"So, not another doctor!"

Antonia was not comfortable with her father' edgy banter. She relapsed into silence. James reached for her hand under the table and squeezed it.

"Do have another scone, Froggy!"

James realised that his grandmother was flirting with Antonia's father. He watched her pour another cup of tea and pass it to him, looking so deeply into his eyes that he was distracted and stirred a spoonful of sugar into his tea. Antonia stared at her father. He never took sugar in his tea – he had emphatically held that the downtrodden Third World peasants who grew the sugar beet were unfairly remunerated. Antonia had never quite appreciated how her father's sugar ban made any difference to the Third World. After all, there was any amount of sugar in the cakes and pastries her mother enjoyed.

The Witch was enjoying teasing Mr Frogmorton, drawing him out of himself.

"Well," she said, surveying the depleted plates. "We made short shrift of that!" Seeing Dr Mikilari reaching for the last scone, she handed the plate to Antonia's father. "Do have the last one, Froggy!"

"Perhaps someone else would like it? They're delicious, but I am really quite replete."

Dr Mikilari looked hopefully at the Witch.

"You've had more than enough!" she chided. "I shall give it to Antonia, seeing as she's now eating for two!"

***

James and Antonia washed up.

"Would you like a walk?" he asked, when they'd finished.

Taking her hand, he led her across the courtyard, where Dr Mikilari drowsed contentedly at the table, and through the green gate into the Back Garden.

"James, are you sure?"

He smiled at her, tucking her under his arm, as they crossed the lawn. The swing still hung under the old apple tree, but of the two prams there was no sign. She caught her breath.

"We'll bring Luca out here," he said easily. "You'll sit on the swing and nurse him…and sing to him!"

She had thought herself unobserved when she had sung to Persephone, but James had known. They strolled through the orchard and down to the beach, walking along the shingle, hand in hand, watching the sun sink, crimson, into the sea.

***

Antonia had not been sure she really wanted to pursue a friendship with Margaret, but before Michael had brought her home, Margaret had brought out her diary and made an afternoon date for their next meeting. And, despite *her* reluctance, James clearly wanted the afternoon to take place. Philip was flying to Singapore, which required a stop-over. He wouldn't be back until Tuesday.

"She's looking forward to seeing you," James said encouragingly. "And I'm sure you'll enjoy showing her the nursery."

***

"Hugo drove me down," burbled Margaret excitedly. "He said it wasn't an easy place to find the first time! I can see what he means!"

"Come on in!" James welcomed them, delighted to see Hugo. He took him off to the studio while Antonia took Margaret up to the nursery.

"You still paint, then?" Hugo smiled. "I was never allowed in here. I remember Jake used to find a door, but I was always left outside! I'm afraid I used to beat him up over it!"

"He survived"

"And now you're going to have a little one to share your studio." Hugo began examining the canvasses. "I don't suppose you'd sell me one?"

"I'd be delighted to *give* you one!"

"That's incredibly generous!"

"It's my pleasure."

Hugo chose a painting of the sun setting into the sea, leaving a golden wake spreading across the waves. James bubble-wrapped it for the journey home.

"May I bring Eleanor next time. She'd love to see your paintings. And I'd so much like you to meet her."

"By all means!"

They left the studio and walked out to the courtyard where they sat and chatted.

Upstairs, Margaret was entranced with the wallpaper that Antonia had finally tracked down. The nursery was ready and waiting, the cot already made up, and home to a brand new teddy bear. The pram, which Antonia had insisted she wanted right away, was parked in her study. Downstairs in the sitting room they pored over the Mothercare catalogue. Margaret had begun furnishing the room that would be her baby's nursery, but saw more things she coveted.

"Are you hoping for a boy or a girl?" she asked.

"We having a little boy."

"Oh, you've had your scan? I've told Philip it really doesn't matter which we have first because I want a really big family!"

"You'll need a bigger flat!"

"I know! I've told Philip we have to buy a house by the time number two is on the way."

"Houses are expensive."

"Grandad will help. He can afford it! He has pots of money! It's going to be such fun house hunting!"

"How did you and Philip meet?"

"He was up at Oxford with Hugo. Grandad said that was the best reason for going to Oxbridge, finding a husband! But I wasn't bothered about a degree. I mean I went to Teacher Training college, but a degree would have been a waste when I just wanted to be married and have a family."

Antonia doubted whether Margaret had the capacity for a degree.

The Witch had thoughtfully left their tea on the kitchen table, ready to be taken out to the courtyard. Antonia made the tea.

"Not a silver teapot, I'm afraid!"

"But it's pretty china. Was it a wedding present?" Antonia shook her head. She showed Margaret out to the courtyard and asked James to help her carry through the tea. Margaret congratulated her on the sandwiches and scones assuming that she had made them. Antonia did not correct the impression.

"Well, Maggles, my girl, I think we should be making tracks. The light's going and I'd like to get you home safe and sound."

"I'll just run up, and use the bathroom. Us, pregnant ladies, have to watch our bladders!"

James showed Hugo to the broom- cupboard ensuite. They waited for Margaret to reappear.

"You've actually got three bedrooms!" she said, joning them. "I had a snoop round. I knew you wouldn't mind!"

***

James and Antonia cleared away the tea things and washed up.

"I'm exhausted!" complained Antonia. "She never stops talking!"

"I think she regards you as the older sister she never had." James considered her. "You do look tired! Would you like a walk, or just sit?"

"Sit."

"Hugo asked for one of my paintings. I felt quite proud."

Twelve

Betrayal

"It might be nice for Antonia to meet the family before the hordes descend for the Anniversary Do," suggested Michael. "I'm going for the weekend and could drive her over. She already knows Margaret and Hugo. I don't think Philip will be there, but Stephen and Andy probably will. Margaret's been chattering about you – her new best friend! so Trisha and Tom are looking forward to meeting you."

"Jake?"

"No. He'll be there for the Anniversary, but not this weekend."

Antonia did not look pregnant. She had been amused by Margaret's ostentatious maternity smocks. She agreed, after a little persuasion, to allow Michael to introduce her to the family, but she insisted she would only go for the

Saturday. Michael agreed to pop her back through the pentagram before the evening meal.

"I'd hoped you could meet Steve and Charlie," Michael said as he drove her through the countryside. "Perhaps you might like to come to the Anniversary Do?"

"I don't think so. There'll be far too many people there. And, anyway, James won't come."

"It's a bit difficult for him."

"So, remind me exactly whom I'm going to meet."

"Tom and Trisha, Trisha's parents. Tom and Trisha have four youngsters: Hugo, Margaret, Andy and Stephen. They regard Jake as one of theirs now – but he won't be there. Philip's in Singapore. Oh, Eleanor will be there with Hugo. That's about it. Not too terrifying! Oh, and they have an enormous dog. Are you alright with dogs?"

It had, initially, been a very large house from which a generous extension had been flung out to accommodate Trisha's parents after her father had made over the main house to Tom.

A wide driveway led up to extensive grounds, including a tennis court. The property backed onto a golf course. As they stepped out of the car, Trisha's parents were waiting to welcome them. They greeted Antonia courteously; Michael, was obviously a frequent visitor.

"Mike!" Tom hurried across the lawn to greet his brother, slapping him on the back. "Good to see you!" He glanced at Antonia, "And this is Antonia?"

He stared at her rather rudely.

"Hello, Mike! Hello, you must be Antonia?" Trisha

joined them. "Margaret never stops talking about you! She's so excited about being pregnant – we never hear the end of it! By the time she's on to number four, she won't be quite so excited, I think!" Antonia glanced about her, wondering if Margaret was about. "No, she's not here yet. Any time soon!"

"Hugo?"

"Hugo isn't able to come. He's had to take Eleanor to hospital. She fell and hurt her knee."

Antonia was disappointed. She liked Hugo and had been looking forward to seeing him. The two brothers had drifted off, deep in conversation.

"Let me show you round," offered Trisha hospitably.

She took her through French windows into a huge banqueting hall, laid out with a buffet lunch. A covered veranda shaded a ground-floor guest suite, and beyond that was an extensive music room with a grand piano. There were more French windows opening out onto a different aspect of the house.

"We've put the guest suite at your disposal."

"But I'm not staying the night! Didn't Michael make that clear?"

"We thought you might like a little rest after lunch. Margaret insists on having a rest now she's pregnant! We humour her! There won't be much rest once baby's here! She might rethink 'large family' when she realises how much work is involved!"

She put Antonia at ease. This had been James's first wife. Privately Antonia envisaged her in James's arms, in James's bed, felt a flicker of jealousy… though it had been twenty years since Trisha had left James. She wished James was here with her.

"Ah, here's Margaret, now!"

Trisha led her towards the lawn. Margaret hugged Antonia effusively, pleased to see her. She'd driven herself over as Hugo had some problem and couldn't come…which was such a shame! She chattered on, sixteen to the dozen, greeted her mother and ran off to find her grandfather. Antonia looked round for Michael…for Trisha…for anyone. She decided to explore the grounds. The lawns were immaculate. They probably employed a gardener. She wandered through a well-kept shrubbery beyond which lay extensive kitchen gardens and greenhouses. There was a secluded seating area tucked in behind the parents' wing. The property even had its own arboretum… Antonia could envisage children climbing these trees. It must have been a wonderful place to grow up! She made her way back to the front lawn. There was still nobody about.

"Antonia!" Margaret stood in the entrance of the banqueting hall. "Lunch! Come and get it!"

Antonia joined her, relieved to have someone to talk to.

"What a magnificent hall!"

"We have dances in here too."

They loaded plates with slices of quiche, chicken legs, fresh salad, asparagus, coleslaw…Not since her days at Embassy functions had Antonia seen so much food.

"Did your mother prepare all this?" Antonia asked in amazement.

"Don't be silly! We have caterers in. They do it all.

And then they clear it all away. All we have to do, is eat! There'll be a strawberry cream tea later."

They sat down at a small table already laid with cutlery and serviettes. At another table Michael sat with Tom and Trisha.

"Were you expecting a lot more people?"

"Well, Hugo and Eleanor should have been here. I think Steve and Charlie were expected. Have you met them?" Margaret lowered her voice: "Steve is gay."

"So I gather."

"I think Andy and Stephen might be here tomorrow. They eat like horses – so you don't need to worry about lots of foods going to waste! Anyway, you'll see them tomorrow."

"I'm not staying for the weekend. I just came today so I could meet you all – well, some of you!"

"That's a shame! I was looking forward to having you to myself! Well, never mind, we can be girls together this afternoon, after our rest."

Antonia was shown to the guest suite after the meal. She didn't need a post-prandial rest. She wished she had brought a book to read, Anxious not to crease her dress – it was newly bought to accommodate her increasing waistline – she slipped it off and loosened her bra (which was beginning to feel too tight). She lay back on the bed, which, she conceded, was extremely comfortable. She dozed.

The door opened and shut very quietly. A key turned in the lock. Tom flung himself down on top of her, his face close to hers.

"So, Antonia, this is the new respectable Antonia, is it? No need to pretend! I know all about you! You're just a common slag! Thought you could fool us all? No such luck, my girl! Now are you going to give me what I want or do you want to play rough?"

"No," whispered Antonia, too scared to scream for help. Tom gave a harsh laugh, as if he had read her mind.

"Don't even think about it. No one would hear you. They're all too far away."

He ripped her delicate slip – she liked the exquisite underwear James bought her – and grabbed her breasts, squeezing painfully. She winced.

"Like that, do you?" He made her cry out.

"Please don't! Please, no! Please don't hurt my baby!"

"Scum like you don't deserve a baby!" He bit her breast hard, making her whimper.

Ripping her pants as if they were as insubstantial as tissue paper, he began mauling her, observing her distress as if he were a small boy pulling the wings off a captured fly. It was useless to plead with him. She clenched her teeth against the agony he was causing her. He was rough. He was brutal. She was terrified she would lose her precious baby. Just let it be over! Please just let it be over! She felt the stream of hot semen flood into her.

"Scumbag!" he hissed at her as he rolled off her, wiping himself on her torn pants. "You got what you deserve!"

He had gone. He had gone. She lay, shaking uncontrollably, whimpering like a small animal in pain. Unable to think coherently. Unable to move…feeling as if she had been hammered into the very fabric of the bed.

Terrified he might return.

"James!" she whispered, "Oh James!"

When she heard the door creak open, she tried with all her being to scream. The scream died stillborn in her throat. She squeezed her eyes shut, unable to bear to look at her assailant.

"Antoni-ni, what's happened to you!"

James's voice choked. He could see all too clearly what had happened to her. He gathered her up in his arms and carried her out of the room… Back through the pentagram.

At some level she knew it was James. At some level she recognized his arms holding her. But she was unable to acknowledge him, unable to respond…unable even to cry. She felt his tears on her face, as though he was weeping the tears she could not shed. She heard the little wild animal in her whimpering in pain.

There was a sharp prick in her arm making her cry out…and then for a long time there was nothing…

***

Trisha had taken Michael off for a walk around the golf course. Her parents had retreated to their own quarters. Eventually Margaret emerged from her room – the room which had been hers ever since she was a toddler. She came downstairs and finding no one about, took herself into the music room and began playing. She had had piano lessons, but lacked the passion and skill…and perseverance, to achieve Jake's accomplished performance.

She wondered if Antonia was still sleeping, or if she'd taken herself into the garden…

Eventually Trisha and Michael returned. Trisha busied herself with tea which they were would enjoy in the lavish new summerhouse. She sent Michael to gather the troops. He returned with Margaret who chattered busily to him about the music she was attempting to play. Tom appeared belatedly, seeming preoccupied.

"Granny and Grandad?" enquired Margaret.

"No, they said they wouldn't join us for tea. They'll be with us for dinner." Trisha looked round "Where's Antonia?"

"I knocked on her door, but she didn't answer. I don't suppose she's fallen asleep?" Michael got to his feet.

"I'll come!" Margaret jumped up. "She might be embarrassed if you barge in!" She hurried after him.

The bed was rumpled. Antonia's dress was still neatly folded over a chair. Margaret went to check the bathroom. Michael saw what remained of Antonia's knickers, tossed on the floor by the bed. Quickly, he kicked them under the bed so that Margaret would not see.

"I can't understand it! She's not here, but her dress is! She can't have forgotten to put it on! Where can she have got to?"

"I think your Dad…" Michael shook his head. "Give your mother my apologies. I want to make sure she's safe."

"Shall I come with you?"

"Not this time."

He suddenly wasn't there. He had been standing right beside her and now he simply wasn't there! She returned to the summerhouse and described what they'd found.

"He's gone to look for her," she said. "He said to give you his apologies. I think he meant: don't wait tea."

"Tom?" Trisha looked hard at her husband.; "Do you know something you're not telling me?"

He shrugged. She decided to leave the inquisition until after Margaret was out of the way.

She found Antonia's knickers when she went to 'refresh' the room next day.

Michael let himself into the cottage and called upstairs to James. A moment later James came half way down the stairs. He was shaking. He stared at his brother with haunted eyes.

"How could you let this happen!" he demanded. "You were supposed to be *with* her!"

"She went to rest after lunch. Trish and I went for a walk. I never dreamt that…that Tom…"

"Well, now you know!" James voice was cold. Almost to himself he murmured: "First he stole Trisha, now he destroys my Ni-ni!"

He made no attempt to check his tears.

"What can I do?"

James stared at his brother with a hostility Michael had never seen before:

"What can you do? You can go! I should never have trusted you with her! Just go!"

He turned back up the stairs and shut the bedroom door.

Returning through the pentagram, Michael hurriedly threw his things into his overnight bag, collected

Antonia's dress – though she would probably never wear it again – and drove back to Morton's. He could not bring himself to speak to Trisha. He would not be attending the Anniversary Party.

Thirteen

Aftermath

"Did you do what I think you did?" asked Trisha as they got ready for bed.

"Possibly." Tom did not meet her eyes.

He turned his back while he unfastened his jeans. Trisha observed his non-committal back.

"Aren't you ashamed of yourself?" she reproved him lightly.

Tom turned round and scrutinised her. He had expected a fight, shouting, recriminations.

"She had it coming!" he said cruelly. "All that pretending to be translating Russian books – it was just a cover for prostitution. She's nothing but a slag!" He frowned. He was not getting the reaction he'd anticipated. "Did you know?"

"Daddy hinted at something. Only he called her a

high class prostitute… He did some research. He always checks out Margaret's friends. Well, young people sow wild oats. You did!"

"Was I 'checked out'?"

"I already had Hugo by then!" Trisha gave him a seductive smile. "He liked you better than James! Said you had more gumption!"

"Why didn't you tell me – about Antonia?"

"I know you, Tom! I knew you'd never keep your hands off her, if you knew."

"Well she can't continue her so-called friendship with our daughter. That's obvious!"

"Margaret is quite smitten with her. Talks about her all the time. She'll be very disappointed."

"I don't care! I'm not having my daughter hooked up with a prostitute!"

"Hooked up with a hooker?" Trisha giggled.

"Not funny! Now, am I going to tell Margaret or will you?"

"By the way, Tom, you did know Antonia's pregnant?"

"Suppose so," he said crossly.

"Margaret says it's James's, which can't be right, can it."

"Who does she say it is?"

"Well, you know, Michael drove her over, and he also took her to meet your Dad and Debs… Could it be Michael's?"

Tom turned the idea over in his mind. But Mike didn't do girl friends…

"Actually I don't care whose it is. She's just a slut! And

I don't want our Margaret having anything more to do with her!"

***

James took the call in Antonia's study.

"Uncle James? It's Margaret!"

"Yes, Margaret?"

"It's just that…Mum and Dad don't want me to see Antonia any more. I mean, I really liked her…but on account of her… *colourful* past, shall we say, they'd prefer I drop her. I mean, I still like her and I think it's so exciting, the secret life she led! – I didn't have time for a *colourful* past, getting married straight from college! But Philip agrees: we don't want her coming here anymore…and… Hello? Are you still there?… Hello?"

It seemed he had put the phone down on her.

For a long moment James stood, seething with rage against his brother. Tom could be sent down for several years for this if… But there was no way he could subject Antonia to court proceedings. And, knowing how fickle a jury could be, and the field day the Defence would have at her expense… No. Absolutely not!

And then, unbidden, he saw the eight year old Tom, crying because his bed was wet – as it was every night since their mother had… He remembered coming in from school, and finding Tom sitting on the stairs waiting for him…

'I can't wake Mummy'…

And he'd run upstairs…seeing the empty pill bottles… knowing she was dead before he even felt for a pulse…

And every night after that he'd be wakened by a tearful Tom. Helping him into clean pyjamas, stripping off the wet sheets, taking him into his bed. And then, early in the morning piling the urine soaked sheets and pyjamas into the washing machine. And (what was her name?) the girl who came in to sort out the house while he and Tom were at school and Dad was at the surgery. She'd hang the washing out on the line and it would be dry – and clean sheets on Tom's bed – by the time they came home. What was her name? She'd just completed her degree and was taking time out at home before looking for a job… Nice girl…Why couldn't he remember her name?

He'd been looking after Antonia since that afternoon… she didn't speak…wouldn't eat… flinched if he touched her…

It was going to take a long time. He'd helped her into the shower and been appalled at the purple bruising and bite marks on her breasts. She'd been unsteady on her feet and he'd carried her back to bed. And there she lay, curled up like a foetus, shutting out the world. He was sure that at some level she knew he was there. Just occasionally she would let him hold her hand. She slept. Sometimes she whimpered in her sleep like a little animal in pain. He brought cassettes up to the bedroom and played her favourite music…he talked softly to her. He lay beside her at night, not touching because she could not bear it, holding her in his heart, his love.

There were flowers. A bouquet of beautiful flowers,

from Hugo and Eleanor. He took them up and offered them to Antonia who seemed to be awake. She reached out and took a rose, holding it to her nose, examining its petals. Her lips formed the word *rose*, but she did not speak aloud.

"From Hugo and Eleanor," he told her.

There had been a call from Hugo, who had heard from Mike, and been equally devastated and horrified.

"When Antonia's ready for visitors, we'll come," Hugo promised. Michael also phoned:

"I guess you don't want to speak to me?" he asked awkwardly.

"Not really."

James still blamed him for allowing it to happen – even though he knew this was illogical. Even though he knew Michael had only gone for a walk with Trisha because he understood Antonia was resting and should have been safe.

***

Antonia awoke to bird song. She opened her eyes to sunshine streaming in at the window – the windows were wide open, but it did not feel cold. She heard footsteps on the stairs, the Witch came in carrying a breakfast tray. She looked at Antonia.

"You're feeling better today."

It was a statement, not a question. As it was not a question, Antonia did not answer. She sat up. The tray was placed on her lap. It looked inviting. A grapefruit cut into segments, two slivers of toast. Yes, she could manage this. The Witch stalked around to her side of the bed and placed a cup of tea beside her.

"You may get up today," she said decisively.

Antonia ate her breakfast, drank her tea and considered. She wasn't sure how many days she'd been in bed, but it was probably time she made an effort to resume normal life. She did not want to think about what had happened...but she couldn't spend the rest of her life hiding in bed. Throwing back the bedclothes, she had a shower, noticing that the bruises on her breasts were beginning to fade. Her tummy was now quite rounded. She placed her hand over the mound...and remembered James's hand... He had laid his hand gently on her tummy and talked to Luca – even though he knew she didn't like to be touched any more. Luca...

She had been so frightened that Tom's assault on her might cause a miscarriage. But it seemed Luca was safe! She dressed and made her way downstairs – forgetting her breakfast tray.

"Antoni-ni! Darling!"

James was on his feet, wanting to sweep her into his arms, and realising even as he reached for her, that she was not yet ready to be held. He stepped back. There was an awkward silence.

"Good Morning, Antonia," remarked the Range. "Coffee?"

Antonia smiled at James.

"Would you like a little walk around the Back Garden?" Antonia thought about it. She smiled at James again and nodded. They sauntered across the courtyard, slowly, because Antonia did not seem to have her sea legs yet. The green gate stood invitingly open. They walked through. Sunshine. Birdsong. Apple trees in full blossom. Dr Mikilari dozing on his accustomed bench.

"How are you feeling?" James asked.

This was a question requiring an answer. Granny has said that she was feeling better. She was up and dressed, but she didn't know the answer to James's question. He turned his head and looked at her with concern.

"Perhaps you're not feeling very 'How'?"

She shook her head. She didn't feel like talking. Not yet. Perhaps not ever. They walked to the end of the orchard and turned back. She wanted to sit down. Lying curled up in bed for…how many days, had weakened her legs.

"Hugo and Eleanor sent you flowers," James mentioned as they sat, not touching, on another garden bench (which Antonia did not remember seeing before).

She remembered the flowers. Roses. She had held one rose and stroked its petals.

"They would like to come and see us, when you're ready."

Antonia thought about seeing Hugo and Eleanor. She liked them. She thought about Margaret. She didn't want to see Margaret. The girl was too immature, too bouncy and effusive… and she never stopped talking. Michael was alright. She liked Michael. Perhaps Michael would come?

***

Sunday. Hugo and Eleanor drove down. Hugo brought an enormous bouquet of flowers for Antonia. Eleanor brought a big, furry teddy bear. She offered it to Antonia who cuddled it close to her, pressing her face into the soft brown fur. They had been warned that Antonia wasn't speaking yet, and chatted quietly to James. Antonia was absorbed in her bear, and appeared to pay them no attention.

The Witch brought in tea and cakes to the sitting room. After tea, James expressed a desire to stretch his legs and invited Hugo to take a turn round the garden with him. Eleanor talked quietly to Antonia without asking her any questions. The Witch came in with the flowers arranged in three tall vases. She collected the tea tray.

"More tea?" she enquired.

Eleanor glanced at Antonia who was not paying any attention.

"Thank you, I think we would like more tea…if it's not too much trouble?" She smiled at Antonia. "We've been looking forward to seeing you. I'm so glad we could come today." There was a muffled sound as if Antonia was saying something. "I'm sorry, I didn't quite catch that?"

"Michael?" Antonia raised her face fractionally from the bear.

"You want to see Michael?"

Antonia nodded. She buried her face in the bear again.

James had hoped that Antonia might respond to Eleanor, but it looked as though she hadn't stirred.

"I think we should be making tracks," Hugo suggested.

"It's been lovely to see you both!" James offered Eleanor a hand to help her up.

"Antonia said she'd like to see Michael."

"She *said* that!" James looked from Eleanor to Antonia in amazement.

After he had seen them off, he came back into the sitting room and knelt down in front of Antonia.

"You'd like to see Mikey?"

She nodded.

Sunday evening. Mike should be home. From the study James phoned his brother.

"James? Hello?" Michael hoped this was not bad news.

"Antonia is asking to see you."

"Really?"

"Yes. Really. When can you come?"

"I could pop straight over…or is that too soon?"

"I guess it's either tonight or not till next Friday."

"How is she?"

"Traumatised. She still isn't talking. But Hugo and Eleanor came to visit this afternoon…and while I took Hugo for a stroll round the garden, she said she'd like to see you. I mean, she actually *spoke!*"

"Have I to come now?"

"Please."

Within five minutes Michael stepped into the kitchen from the courtyard. James ushered him into the sitting room. To their surprise Antonia put down her bear, lurched to her feet and appeared to fall into Michael's arms. She began to cry, great heaving sobs, as if floodgates had finally been pushed open. Utterly out of his depth, embarrassed, confused, Michael held her, not knowing what else to do. He had no idea what to say. He held her for what seemed a painfully long time until finally her outpouring of grief subsided.

"Would you like to sit down?" he asked diffidently. "James will get you a glass of water."

Antonia sat down. She seemed to want to hold Michael's hand. James fetched coffee for himself and Michael. He offered Antonia a glass of water. She would not take it.

Michael held the glass for her and she drank. She looked at him. Made eye contact with him. Seemed to want to say something... James watched, puzzled. He had been so angry with Michael who should have protected Antonia, but Antonia did not seem to see it that way. She seemed to be looking for comfort from Michael in a way that she was unable to accept from him. She continued holding his hand while he drank his coffee. He was thinking about suggesting it was time he went home, when Antonia managed one word.

"Goblins!" she whispered.

Windover Ridge. The day he had left her to face the evil of that place alone. It had nearly cost her life. James had been so angry with him then, but now, it seemed, Antonia was acknowledging that he had not only left her alone to face the demons of that place – but had also (unintentionally) left her to face what might well have cost her baby's life... And there was no reproach... It was almost as if she was forgiving him! James watched, his coffee forgotten, his emotions in turmoil.

"I'm sorry, Mike!" James clasped his brother's shoulder

as they said goodbye. "I shouldn't have blamed you. I apologise."

Michael nodded, not trusting himself to speak.

Antonia let James hold her that night, let him rest his hand gently on the bump that housed their baby... let his fingers gently wipe the tears from her cheek and leave kisses on her shoulder. He loved her and that was all that mattered.

***

Antonia was sitting in the Back Garden keeping Dr Mikilari company. She felt very safe with him. He talked endlessly about the small Russian village his great grandparents had left behind, describing their cottage, the Synagogue, the culture... wedding celebrations, the school – it was as if he could picture it all in his mind, although he had never set foot in Russia. Antonia had lived in Moscow, studied at the university... and devoured Russian literature. She was fond of the old man.

Sometimes the seven year old Mlilka scampered out of the shrubbery and danced for them. Sometimes she played her flute, haunting melodies and Russian folk songs. When Michael came over, as he often did on Sundays, he and Mlilka would play together.

"Why don't you play too?" Mlilka asked. "On your clarinet!"

Antonia wasn't aware she had mentioned her clarinet to Mlilka. She had certainly not told Michael she played – he was a professional! And she had never aspired to play at that standard. She was about to decline when she saw that her clarinet was lying beside her on the garden seat. She picked it up, assembling it and played a quick scale. Michael smiled at her, raised his bow and played the introduction to Mozart's clarinet concerto. They played, the three of them, in harmony.

"I didn't know you could play so well!" James said admiringly.

"She does everything well!" retorted Mlilka. "But not as well as me!"

"Cheeky!" Michael reproved her.

Mlilka laughed and danced away. The Witch appeared and summoned them to lunch. They went in.

"Venison!" exclaimed Michael. "You have gone to town, Granny."

"Road kill," muttered James.

"We have so much 'road kill'. D'you suppose Granny goes out scouring the countryside for dead animals?"

"Someone's getting a bit above themselves!" The Witch looked meaningfully at Antonia. "I'll have you know it's fresh!"

"I remember it was a bit 'high' not that long ago – I was up and down all night drinking water!"

"Yeah! I remember that!" Michael exchanged a rueful smile with his brother.

"Hugo and Eleanor are joining us this afternoon," mentioned the Witch. "I invited them."

"Shall we put on an impromptu concert," asked James.

"Oh yes? And what instrument will your goodself be playing?"

"I could contribute," offered Dr Mikilari unexpectedly. "I used to play the violin…a Stradivarius, as I remember."

"You did indeed, Grandad! You gave it to me when I was ten."

"You started him on his career," James added.

"Until he carelessly fell out of his plane," put in the Witch. "That scuppered him for a bit!"

"If Mlilka had stayed with the flute instead of being enticed into ballet by that wife of mine…" began Dr Mikilari.

"That pesky piece of interference!" snapped the Witch.

"Let's not go there." James cleared his plate and put his cutlery down decisively.

"What's for Afters?" asked Dr Miklari hopefully.

"Cold Rice Pudding," said the Witch.

***

They had resumed their early morning tennis. Antonia's shorts no longer did up and she wore a comfortable pair of joggers.

"Hey! It's you!" exclaimed a familiar voice. "Where's you been? You haven't forgotten you're going to teach me to play!"

"Hello, Shaz! I think we agreed you were expecting a tennis racquet for your birthday? And that's July. And you'll be eight."

The little girl looked at Antonia with respect.

"Antonia's expecting a baby!" James told her.

"Yeah!" said Shaz staring at Antonia's bump disdainfully. "Any fool can see that!"

"So much for 'congratulations'!" murmured Antonia.

"So, what you calling it?"

"Not *it*! We're having a little boy. We're going to call him Luca."

"Girls are better. Why don't you have a girl?"

"Perhaps we'll have a girl next time." Suggested James.

"You'll be lucky!" muttered Antonia under her breath. "I was brought up with *Boys* are better!" Antonia mentioned as they strolled home. "I remember my mother saying that she didn't particularly want me – a boy would have been better."

"Think of all we'd have missed if you'd been a boy!"

"We'd never have met."

"And there would be no Luca!" He placed his hand proprietorially over her bump.

"I am so glad we did meet!"

"So am I, my Antoni-ni! So am I!"

***

Trisha's parents sent a hand-embossed invitation to Tom and Trisha's Silver Wedding Anniversary. James tore it into shreds. His face set and angry.

"How dare they!" he raged.

"I don't think they can have taken it very seriously," Michael commented. "I certainly shan't be going."

Hugo phoned.

"I feel sorry for Mum," he said. "But I simply can't

bring myself to face Dad after what he did. It was reprehensible! I thought about pretending one of us was ill, but then I thought I have to be upfront over this. I've told them exactly why Eleanor and I will not be there."

He refrained from telling James that Jake and he had exchanged heated words on the issue, Jake still bore Antonia a grudge and had expressed the view that it served her right. He was, as Michael was very much aware, a very angry young man.

Fourteen

Jake's Graduation

The whole family had been invited. Margaret had volunteered to collect Gavin and Debs, and drive them down. Hugo came separately. Andrew (senior) and Trisha's Mum would make their own way, as Tom was collecting his younger sons from school for the occasion. Steve and Charlie sent Jake a Congratulations card but would not be attending – neither of them was into music.

Morton's had laid on an extensive buffet in the college's refectory. Additional parking was available in the field opposite the grounds. The concert hall was set out with row upon row of chairs. Michael stood with Jake in the reception area, waiting to welcome family members. James waited with them, briefly acknowledged by Michael, ignored by Jake. Trisha's parents were the first to arrive and were greeted enthusiastically by Jake. Andrew (senior) was not happy at being asked to move his expensive car to the adjoining field. Despite the considerable detour to collect Stephen and Andy, Tom and Trisha arrived shortly after. Gravel flew in all directions. The boys climbed out, hugged Jake and their grandmother and looked round for their grandfather who was just returning from his errand.

"Tom drove like a madman!" Trisha complained. "Doesn't he always!" She hugged Jake. "Hello Mike! Sorry you couldn't make our Anniversary."

"I'm afraid I must ask you to move your car. There's parking in the field opposite."

Unlike his father in law, Tom did not demur.

"Margaret's bringing the grandparents," Trisha mentioned. "So they'll be a while yet."

"Jake will take you into the Refectory," Michael suggested. I'll wait here for Margaret."

Next to arrive was Hugo. He followed the signs to the field and walked across.

"The others have all gone through to the Refectory. I'm just waiting for Margaret." Michael indicated the way. While he waited for Margaret, he chatted to James. "After everyone's gone, come and spend some time at my quarters."

Other guests arrived and were ushered through. The Refectory was filling up. The noise level rose. Michael glanced at the Reception Clock. Margaret should have been here by now. He frowned.

"I think we should grab a bite while we can. The students are putting on a Recital before the prize-giving. You won't want to miss that."

There was now no room to sit. Michael piled a plate conservatively and strolled over to join the family. James watched them, chatting, laughing, clearly in good spirits. He had hoped for a sign of recognition from his son…but Jake stared straight through him.

An announcement requested all guests to take their seats in the Hall. And still Margaret had not arrived. Michael went backstage to check on the orchestra. There were always last minute nerves. The graduates were ushered on stage to loud applause. They had just started the opening chords when there was a disturbance at the doors: Margaret had arrived. She looked round, waved to her family and found seats for her grandparents at the back. The concert proceeded.

There were some prestigious awards. Some coveted top places were announced: recommendations for the most significant progress… Finally, Jake walked up to the stage, shook hands with the Principal and received his certificate. He had been expected to do so much better. He had been a high flyer with enormous potential. It was almost as if he was about to throw away the glittering career which should have been his. He stepped back and glanced at his family. His eyes raked the audience, searching for Margaret. For a brief moment his eyes met James's – but without recognition.

"Champagne, tea and sandwiches in the Refectory."

There was a general scraping back of chairs, and excited chatter as everyone converged on the exit.

"I need the loo! Excuse me! I'm pregnant, will you let me through!"

That could only be Margaret, James reflected. He stood aside while the hordes pushed past him. Michael had gone to rescue his father who looked utterly bewildered.

"We weren't in time for lunch," Debs murmured. "Margaret got lost."

Michael found them some sandwiches and a cup of tea. He caught a fleeting glance of Charlotte, one of his erstwhile protégées. She had come to see Jake graduate. He moved to speak to her, but she had been swallowed up by the crowd – and it was Jake she'd come to see, not him.

Hugo waited for Margaret to reappear.

"Absolutely horrendous queue for the ladies!" she complained. "Is there any food left? I'm starving!"

"I'll see what I can do, Maggles. You find a seat and I'll be back." He elbowed his way through the crowd and managed to secure her a plate of sandwiches.

"Couldn't risk the tea!" He apologised. "It would have been all down my suit!" He watched her devouring the sandwiches hungrily. "I understand you got a bit lost on the way down. Why don't you drive yourself home and I'll take Grandad and Debs back."

"Would you! You're a star!"

"We have to take care of you now you're going to be a Mum! When's it due?"

"October."

Gradually the crowd thinned out. Jake elected to go back with his grandparents. Tom was returning his boys to their school. Hugo gathered up the other grandparents and set off for their Retirement complex.

"Did you go over for the Silver Wedding Anniversary?" Hugo asked.

"We were invited," Debs replied, "But it's a long way –Someone would have had to take us. And there would have been a huge crowd there. Gavin gets tired..." She smiled at her husband and patted his knee. "We don't drive anymore," she added unnecessarily.

"Didn't see James there," Gavin mentioned. "Thought he'd have been there to see his son graduating. Wish he'd come over and see us."

"I brought some photos for Antonia," said Debs brightly, refraining from reminding Gavin that his eldest son had died. "I had some reprints done of James as a little boy. I was going to give them to Michael. He sees quite a lot of her, I think. Will *you* be seeing Antonia at all?"

Hugo said he would be pleased to pass them on.

"She was very fond of James," Debs continued. "I'm glad Michael takes such an interest in her now."

***

Antonia welcomed James home.

"How did it go?" she asked. He looked tired, she thought.

"All the family there, making a big fuss of Jake. Nobody spoke to me apart from Mike. He invited me to go up to his bungalow afterwards, but he was so caught up with everybody, I just came home. Anyway, Jake's got his certificate. He could have done so much better, but

I think either he's lost heart, or he's bored. I don't know what his plans are. He went off with Trish's parents."

He sounded depressed.

"Why don't we go out and sit in the garden for a bit."

"That's a nice idea. Been stuck indoors since late morning – be nice to have some fresh air."

The Back Garden was in spring mode, a great spread of snowdrops under the trees, shy little violets peeping through the green leaves of cyclamen… cheerful yellow crocuses.

"The mice eat the purple ones," James mentioned as they sat down on Dr Mikilari's bench.

"They must taste different from the yellow ones!"

Antonia lifted her face to the sunshine. "It feels like spring here, in the garden."

"The Back Garden doesn't always reflect what's going on in the world."

They were silent for a while, a companionable silence. A gentle breeze wafted across the garden. A solitary grey feather drifted down. James leaned down to pick it up.

"May I offer you a little grey feather," he said, smiling at Antonia.

Accepting the feather, she sat silently stroking it between her fingers.

"You're so much kinder now," she said, without looking at him.

"Am I?" There was a hint of amusement in his eyes.

"Well, it wasn't that you were unkind before, but…"

"But?"

"But you're just so much kinder now!"

"Well, I'm really glad you recognize that!" he said teasing her.

She leaned against him. He kissed her forehead and laid his face against her silky new hair. They sat for a long time, together, thinking their own thoughts, while the sun slowly slipped down behind the trees.

Fifteen

Luca

"As it's your first baby, it would be sensible to be in hospital."

"Will you be with me?"

"No, darling. I've never been to the new Maternity hospital. It wasn't there…before."

"Well, you're a doctor. Can't you deliver him?"

"If you were a healthy nineteen year old, like Margaret, I might. But sometimes there are complications and it's not as though the hospital is on our doorstep."

Antonia noticed gratefully that he didn't call her an elderly prima gravida.

"I'd still rather be at home!"

James suggested that possibly Eleanor could be with her.

He envisaged that Antonia might make heavy weather

of childbirth. Despite his misgivings, he finally relented in the face of her persistent entreaties.

Luca was due in early September, but Antonia went into labour late August. In the event it was a very quick birth. Antonia shrieked like a banshee.

"Make the pain stop, James! I can't do this! I don't want a baby!"

"Breathe, Ni-ni! Like I taught you. You're wearing yourself out!"

Antonia screamed.

"Hold it! Don't push Don't push! His head's crowning! He's almost here!... Now one huge push, darling!"

And suddenly he was there. Luca. A tiny yowling baby. James wrapped him, in a towel and handed him to Antonia.

"Antoni-ni, meet your son!"

"Is he all here?"

"You can count his fingers and toes later." James smiled at her. Antonia gazed at her baby in wonder – this tiny scrap of humanity that she had grown in her tummy.

This little creature who had kicked inside her unremittingly when she tried to sleep. This tiny precious treasure that James had given her – that they had created together.

"You did it! You gave me a baby!"

The Witch glanced curiously at the little bundle. She didn't do small babies. She had forgotten her euphoria when Dr Mikilari had first put Mlilka into her arms. She filled the baby bath with warm water while James waited for the afterbirth.

"Messy old business!" she observed.

"Thank you for your help, Granny."

James gave her a tired smile. In some ways it was easier delivering other people's babies. Antonia's screams still rang in his ears.

Antonia allowed the Witch to sponge her down and help her into a clean nightie. James carried her along the landing to their own room. It was already made up with clean sheets. He brought her Luca, newly bathed and nappied.

"Offer him your breast, my Ni-ni."

He watched as Luca's tiny mouth fastened onto his mother's nipple. His heart surged with love for them both. Despite all the odds, they had created this tiny life…their Luca.

"I'll bring you up some tea," The Witch announced. "And then I'll clean up the spare room. Michael would have a fit if he knew Antonia gave birth in his bed!"

***

Having her baby nuzzling at her breast seemed to Antonia the happiest moment of her life – and not just a moment! Luca was content to nuzzle for twenty – sometimes twenty-five minutes – with the little tug and pull of concentrated suckling until his mouth would slacken and he would let go of her nipple and fall asleep. She had thought he would sleep in his new cot in the nursery she had so lovingly prepared, but she could not bear to have him out of her sight! James brought the cot into their room and placed it beside Antonia. He changed Luca's nappy and let Antonia sleep.

"Am I allowed to get up?" she asked the next morning.

"You can do whatever you like," James said indulgently. "You can get dressed and come downstairs and take Luca for a walk in the garden in his new pram. How about that?"

Antonia got gingerly out of bed and dressed carefully. She was very sore.

"I think you'd better carry Luca downstairs," she said anxiously. She held onto the bannister…glad to sit down once she reached the kitchen.

"Good Morning!" The Range greeted her cheerfully. "Coffee?"

The Witch was busy with her frying pan. She glanced at Antonia over her shoulder.

"Good to see you up and about. After breakfast you can take a walk round the garden and acquaint Luca with his great-grandfather."

"You already brought me breakfast in bed,"

"Did I? Perhaps I did," murmured the Witch vaguely. She considered the baby in James's arms and gave him a long look.

"I know you don't really care for small babies, Granny, but we think he's very special!"

The Witch gave a disdainful sniff. She placed a cooked breakfast in front of James, who gently placed Luca in Antonia's arms as the rocking chair cradled her.

Dr Mikilari watched the pram being wheeled towards him. He put down his newspaper. It dated from the

Sixties and was yellowed with age. Like me, he thought wryly. Antonia proudly pushed the pram over the grass and sat down carefully on the bench beside him.

James lifted Luca out of the pram, offering him to his great-grandfather.

"This is Luca, Grandad!"

"So I see!"

With practised ease Dr Mikilari cradled the tiny scrap. His face creased into a smile, he murmured to the baby. After a moment he began to sing one of his old Russian lullabies.

He had sung these first to Mlilka and then to his grandchildren. Luca opened his eyes and stared up into the kindly face.

"Would you like a coffee, Grandad?"

"Very much! Nobody thinks to bring me a coffee out here!"

James smiled at Antonia and started across the lawn, returning with a tray of coffee.

***

"It's bath-time!" James told her the next morning. "I'll show you how to bath Luca."

Antonia looked at him doubtfully.

"He's so little! Are you sure he needs a bath?"

"Baths are comforting to babies – after all, they spend nine months floating in a bath in your womb. I'll help you, and tomorrow you can bath him."

"No! I don't think so!"

Antonia was clearly alarmed at the prospect. She followed James into the bathroom, clutching Luca so tightly that he began to fuss. She sat down on the bathroom stool. James spread a towel over her lap and invited her to undress the baby. Luca began to cry, angrily, kicking tiny legs, protesting.

"See, he doesn't like it!"

James took a now naked Luca from her and gently immersed him in the baby bath. The crying stopped as if he had switched it off. James smiled at her. He gently splashed water over the baby, while supporting him with one hand.

"There! That feels good, doesn't it, my little man!"

***

Antonia was clearly terrified at the prospect of bathing Luca.

"He won't break!" James assured her. "Babies are tougher than you think."

"He's so little!" Antonia almost whimpered. "I might pull his arm off!"

James took the baby from her, immersing him in the warm water, supporting the little head with one hand, with practised ease bathing the tiny scrap of humanity that was his son.

Holding Luca against his shoulder, he patted him dry and laid him in Antonia's lap to powder and fasten his nappy.

Luca did not care for this.

"See, he doesn't like me! When you hold him he's happy, but when I try and do anything with him, he cries!"

"Talk to him, Ni-ni. Tell him what you're doing. It doesn't really matter what you say, it's the sound of your voice. Isn't it, little man!"

"You're so confident!"

"I've had a lot of practice!"

"The only thing I can really manage is feeding him."

"Well, that's a relief! That's something I really can't do!"

***

The Back Garden was bathed in sunshine. Antonia sat on the swing, cradling Luca. He lay in her lap, staring up at her.

"James, the baby book said that babies can't focus at first, but I'm sure Luca is looking at me."

"Luca has his great-grandmother's genes. He'll be able to do a lot of things that normal babies don't."

"I just wanted a normal baby!"

"He's normal in most ways: he has ten little toes, and ten fingers! He cries when he's hungry. He fills his nappy. What more d'you want?"

James took out a sketch pad and began drawing. Later he would paint. Over the days and weeks that followed, James painted Antonia cradling Luca. He painted Antonia breastfeeding. He painted Luca naked and Luca clothed. He painted Antonia looking directly at him, her happiness evident. He painted Antonia looking down at her baby while he nuzzled. Why had he not painted Hugo? Jake? Persephone? Delfina? Well, he admitted, He had been struggling with long hours at the hospital, trying to fit in hours of study at home... constantly badgered by Trisha who wanted to be the centre of his world and his attention. And then, of course, when her father bought them the London flat, there was neither study nor studio.

It had not been the happiest time of his life – nor of Trish's...

"Have you let your father know?" he asked. "He'll be delighted. We must invite him to meet his grandson."

He smiled at Antonia. "And I expect Hugo and Eleanor would love to come and see us."

Gradually, Antonia gained confidence handling her baby. The realisation that he was solely dependent on her came as a surprise. He was always there – there were no days off! Fortunately, James was always there too, to reassure her, to help and encourage her...to hold her. She relaxed in his arms... but she wasn't sure she wanted him to make love to her...not yet.

She could hear the unmistakable sound of a lawn mower, a hand-held push mower! As she wheeled Luca into the Back Garden she could see James, tee shirt hanging out of his trousers, striding out. Whirr and pause, whirr and pause. He reached the end of the orchard and turned back towards her, giving her a cheerful wave.

"I've never seen you mowing before?"

James stopped mowing and rubbed his arm across his damp forehead. He was obviously happy, glowing with health and energy.

"Isn't the scent of new-mown grass utterly delicious!" Antonia looked at him curiously.

"Why expend all that energy? Why not use an electric mower?"

"And where would I plug it in!"

"Well, there's that."

James turned and began his long walk back through the orchard. He would be wanting to resume their tennis matches soon, she reflected. He was just buzzing with energy!

When he had completed his mowing he came across and hugged her.

"You smell all sweaty!" She pushed him away.

"I expect I do! You can't make an omelette without breaking a few eggs!"

"Omelette? Did someone say omelette?" Dr Mikilari raised his head from his ancient newspaper.

"It's not lunch-time yet, Grandad."

"I used to make omelettes for Ragwort. We used to fill them with love."

"How do you do that?" asked Antonia.

"I seem to remember we dropped kisses into the mixture... "

James smiled affectionately at him. He wondered if, when he was as old as his grandfather, he might make omelettes for Antonia.

***

"Why don't we take Luca down to the village? I expect Granny would be grateful for a bit of shopping."

Antonia proudly wheeled her baby down to the village. Acquaintances smiled and peeped in the pram. They had just passed the supermarket when a voice shouted crossly after them.

"Antony! Where you bin? I bin waiting for you every day!"

"Hello, Shaz!" James greeted the child. "Antonia's had her baby. We have a little boy."

"Yeah! Luke!"

"We're calling him Luca. D'you want to peep in the pram?"

"So, when's you comin' back to play tennis?"

"When Antonia's a bit stronger."

Shaz eyed Antonia suspiciously. She looked at the little bundle under the pram blanket.

"He's a bit little!" she objected.

"He'll grow!" said James comfortably. "All babies start small. You were once that small."

"I never was!"

As they completed their shopping and turned for home, Antonia remarked:

"Her birthday was in July, wasn't it?" She frowned. "I wonder if she got her racquet?"

"That'll be why she's been looking for us – didn't you promise to teach her to play once she'd got her racquet!"

"That was you!"

"What was me?"

"It was you who promised. Not me!"

"Well, we'll have to see what we can do about it… when you're ready to start playing again."

"I really don't feel like it at present…I don't even want to make love."

"I had noticed!"

"Are you very frustrated that I don't?"

"Well, let's say that I'll be waiting eagerly when you feel ready."

***

The Witch was serving lunch. She glanced at Antonia as she sat down:

"Your father's coming for tea. I invited him. It's time he met his one and only grandchild."

"Nice man," said Dr Mikilari reflectively.

"You flirted with him!" There was amusement in the look James gave his grandmother.

"Every dog has his day," observed Dr Mikilari inconsequentially.

"No chocolate brownies, Granny!" James said severely.

"As if I would!"

In his pram Luca began to grizzle.

"He's hungry."

"I know he's hungry. He'll have to wait!"

"Antoni-ni, Luca doesn't have the concept of waiting. He just knows he's hungry."

James reached into the pram and picked up his son, holding him against his shoulder, rubbing his back.

"Milk Bar's not open yet!" muttered the Witch.

"I'm hungry too!" protested Antonia. "My dinner will be cold if I stop and feed him."

She watched James offering Luca the tip of one finger. Luca sucked. He stopped crying.

"It's lucky he has such an experienced father!"

There was a touch of bitterness in her voice.

***

Cyril Fortesque Throgmorton was indeed delighted that he had a grandson. He brought flowers for Antonia and a teddy bear whose label certified that he was safe – no loose parts – washable. The Witch showed him out into the courtyard where the five of them sat around the table under the tree. Antonia offered Luca to her father who was clearly uncomfortable holding a baby.

"He doesn't do babies!" chortled the Witch to herself. Luca began to fret. James reached across and took Luca, draping him against his shoulder.

"Alright, little man! Grandad will enjoy you when you're bigger. Take you to see the Tower of London...and the zoo."

Antonia's father looked hugely relieved.

"In my day, we didn't do hands on fatherhood," he remarked. "Antonia had a nanny."

"Antonia had a whole schmuck of nannies!"

It was said with feeling. Her father glanced at her and shook his head. It had all been a long time ago. And, if he was honest, his daughter had been something of a disappointment.

"Tea," said the Witch decisively. "Antonia, d'you want to help me carry things through."

It was not an invitation. It was a request. They carried out trays of sandwiches, scones, iced cakes…squares of something which Antonia hoped were not chocolate brownies.

The Witch poured tea. She handed a cup to their guest.

"Sugar, Froggy?" she enquired, looking deeply into his eyes.

"My father doesn't take sugar in tea," said Antonia crossly.

"Quite so." Antonia's father nevertheless took a heaped spoonful from the proffered bowl.

"Chocolate brownies!" remarked Dr Mikilari eyeing the plate with happy anticipation.

"Granny!" James's voice had a warning note.

The Witch smiled seductively and passed the plate of sandwiches. James rested his face against Luca's thistledown hair, remembering the soft regrowth of Antonia's stubble.

"Unusual name, Luca?" Antonia's father murmured.

"Granny chose it. She chooses most of our names. She called me *Daffyn*."

"We were going to call our daughter Anthony if she'd been a boy."

"Boys are best!" muttered Antonia savagely.

"No, my dear! I wouldn't have a grandson, if you'd been a boy!"

"Have another sandwich, Froggy."

"Thank you, yes!" he gave the Witch a sly smile.

Tea continued. Cups were refilled. Scones disappeared. Presently James stood up.

"Little man needs changing," he observed and headed indoors.

"He'll be wanting a feed, too." Antonia considered whether it would be too embarrassing to feed Luca in her father's presence...

When James reappeared with a sweetly smelling Luca, the Witch stood up, smiled warmly at Antonia's father and invited him to step into the Back Garden for a stroll. James gave Antonia the baby who began blindly searching for her nipple. She unbuttoned her blouse and bra and began feeding him.

Dr Mikilari looked on with approval, remembering the things of long ago.

It was after six o'clock before the Witch escorted Antonia's father back to the courtyard. He looked a little rumpled and considerably surprised.

James had carried the remains of their tea back to the kitchen and washed up, unexpectedly helped by his grandfather.

"It was a very nice tea, but not her usual chocolate brownies," he said sadly.

"Well, Grandad, we can't have him falling asleep at the wheel while he drives back to London, can we!"

He left his grandfather dozing contentedly in the rocking chair while he went to help Antonia put Luca to bed. A shared ritual she was beginning to enjoy.

***

"I thought I might walk down to the village this afternoon," Antonia suggested.

"Yes, why don't you! Take Luca with you."

"Aren't you coming too?"

"I thought I'd work on one of the paintings." James smiled at her.

He was fizzing with energy. She recognized his creative mood. She carefully wheeled Luca's pram out of the house and down the lane leading to the village. She could, of course, have left Luca in James's care... but she was still in the early stages of motherhood where pushing her baby out filled her with pride. She admitted to herself that she wanted to show him off.

She paused outside the small picture framer's, glancing at the pictures on display, wondering if James would be interested in placing any of his paintings here rather than sending them up to the London Gallery. She would ask him, but probably they fetched London prices which would be considerably more than a small country business would charge, or could afford.

"Antony!" That could only be Shaz – "Antony, wait!"

She stopped and waited for the child.

"You should be at school, Shaz. You do know the law says you have to go to school? They could take your Dad to Court if you keep bunking off!"

"Yeah. Yeah. You do fuss! Anyway, I'm lookin' after my Gran today 'cause she's not well."

Antonia wasn't sure she believed her.

"Is the doctor coming to see her?"

The child shrugged eloquently, unconcerned.

She peered in the pram.

"He smiled! He smiled at me!" She squealed.

Antonia knew that babies this small didn't really smile.

It was probably wind. Nevertheless, she had several times thought Luca smiled at her. She turned the pram to head home. Shaz accompanied her, chattering away excitedly. They reached the cottage. Antonia turned the pram into the drive. Shaz showed no sign of leaving.

"Shouldn't you go home now? See if your Gran needs anything?"

"She's alright." She smiled coyly at Antonia. "You could invite me in for tea. I mean, I don't need tea – but I could come in and you could let me hold Luca. Please? Please, Antony!"

"Well, just for a little while. Then you really must go home. They won't know where you are."

"Don't matter! Nobody's home, anyway!"

She followed Antonia into the cottage. Antonia left the pram in her study and took Shaz through to the sitting room.

"Cor! You got a real fire!" The child looked around the room. "Hey, you ain't got no telly! What you do in the evenings then?"

"Read, listen to music, talk…"

"You must be bored outa your head!"

Antonia smiled. She laid Luca carefully down on the hearth rug and let him kick. Shaz knelt down and offered him one of her fingers, beaming with pleasure as he took hold of it. She smiled happily up at Antonia.

"See! He likes me!"

The studio door opened and shut. Presently James came in, carrying a mug of coffee.

"Thought I heard you come back. Oh, hello, Shaz!"

If he was surprised to see the child, he did not appear displeased. He sat down, affectionately ruffled Antonia's hair and smiled at the little girl who was entertaining Luca. They chatted.

"I'm eight now!" Shaz informed him proudly.

She twisted round to make sure she had James's attention.

"I believe so! Is eight good?"

Shaz gave him a considering look.

"S'not much different really!"

James stood up.

"I'm going to make some tea for Antonia. Would you like some tea, Shaz?"

Luca stared up at the little girl, focused, unblinking. Antonia watched their interaction. Presently James carried through a tea tray. He had found a few scones, left over from her father's visit. There were some iced cakes which had not been such a success. He brought tea for himself and Antonia.

"What would you like to drink, Shaz?"

"Dunno. What you got? I drink tea, if you're making it."

James handed her his mug and returned to the kitchen for another. Shaz ate all the iced cakes and most of the scones. She was clearly hungry.

"One advantage of going to school," James observed dryly "Is that you get school dinners."

Shaz did not deign to reply.

At six o'clock James said it was time Shaz went home. He offered to escort her home.

"I gotta wee, first," she told him disarmingly.

She was taking advantage of the erstwhile broom cupboard when there was an officious hammering at the front door. Antonia looked at James. Sometimes he wasn't visible.

"I'd better go!" she said, scooping Luca off the floor and handing him to James.

Further hammering! A very angry man stood on the doorstep.

"Have you got my daughter?" he demanded without preamble.

"Shaz?"

"Have you got my daughter?" he was shouting now. "Someone said they'd seen you going off with my Sharon!" Shaz appeared, wiping her hands on the back of her shorts.

"Hi, Dad!" she said with mock bravado. "I came to tea with Antony," she added uncertainly.

"You get here!" Her father was furious.

"James, my husband, was just about to walk her home," Antonia offered, aware that Shaz was standing behind her – out of her father's reach. He made a grab for the child.

"How many times I tell you: you don't go off with strangers!"

Antony's not a stranger! We play tennis. I came to see her baby!" Shaz was close to tears.

James came through from the sitting room, with Luca snuggled against his shoulder.

"We're really sorry you've been so worried," he said as if he were counselling an anxious patient. "Not knowing where she might have got to! Children do wander off with no idea of the anxiety they cause. My wife and I play tennis early in the morning and Sharon volunteered to act as ball-boy – before school. She was hoping for a tennis racquet for her birthday… I'm sorry we've not had the opportunity to meet. I'm James Gregory, Dr James Gregory. And this is Antonia, my wife."

He held out his hand. While Shaz's father did not take his hand, he did appear a shade mollified. He grunted.

James placed a hand on Shaz's shoulder and gave her a little push.

"Off you go now," he said firmly. "You'd Dad's been very worried about you."

Shaz hung her head. She shuffled forward. Her father seized her wrist, gripping it tightly.

"C'mon!"

As they disappeared down the drive, her father striding out and Shaz almost running as she tried to keep up, they heard a muted "Sorry, Dad!"

Sixteen

Expecting Dominic

Antonia gradually overcame her fears that Luca would break or that she would dislocate his shoulder...or indeed, drop him. She gained confidence handling him, bathing him. She began to enjoy him and he responded to her growing confidence by accepting her ministrations without fretting and whimpering. The Range grumbled on a daily basis about the quantity of nappies he was fed. He was so out of sorts that the Witch felt sorry for him! James, however, was happier than he remembered being in a very long time. He enfolded Antonia in his love. Their love-making seemed to encompass the happiness they shared. They swam, they played tennis (without a ball-boy), and Antonia spent productive mornings in her study while Luca slept in his pram. In their bedroom, James had hung his painting of Antonia breastfeeding

Luca. He had caught her expression of wondering love as she marvelled at the tiny child she held in her arms.

Luca was a thoughtful baby, content to consider a daisy, turning it round and round in his small hand. By six months he was crawling. If Dr Mikilari was in the garden, reading his newspapers, Luca would crawl towards him and wait to be picked up to sit on the old man's knee, listening intently while Dr Mikilari read aloud from his newspaper. James had taken to bathing with Luca, sitting him securely between his outstretched legs. Luca splashed and chortled happily.

Down on the beach James took him into the sea, perched on his chest. Luca would be swimming before he could walk. Back on shore, happily naked, Luca tumbled the sand castles James built for him. Antonia watched James playing with his son. Play seemed a foreign concept to her. All summer, either on the beach or in the Back Garden, James wore little else except his boxer shorts and Luca wore nothing at all. He would be a year old in August. Already walking, if unsteadily; understanding a whole range of words, beginning to talk.

He was weaned. Antonia no longer offered him her breast.

At mealtimes, she had expected that Luca would be in a highchair, fed with a teaspoon, but James sat his son on his knee and encouraged him to use his hands to eat. She loved Luca, but James idolised him.

They were getting ready for bed one evening. James sat on the edge of the bed, taking off his socks.

"James?"

"M'm?"

"James, there's something I've been wanting to ask."

He turned his head to look at her, aware that she was concerned about something. He waited.

"I've been wondering…"

"Yes, darling?"

"Well, whether I might be starting the menopause early? I don't seem to have had a period in several months."

Amusement lit James's eyes.

"I'd say you're about three months pregnant, Ni-ni!"

"What?" Antonia looked shocked. She hadn't expected this. "I'm not sure I want another baby!"

"Haven't you loved having Luca?"

"Well, yes. But that doesn't mean I want another baby."

"Children benefit so much from having brothers and sisters. Luca will love having a little brother so close in age. He'll be eighteen months. They'll have so much fun together, get up to so much mischief. We'll be a proper family, Ni-ni!"

"You didn't tell me you wanted another baby! I don't think it's fair to spring it on me!"

"I didn't know it would be possible. It was something of a miracle that we have Luca." He stood up and came across to her, pulling her into his arms and kissing her passionately. "My Antoni-ni, I'm thrilled! I love you so much! Thank you for conceiving my child! My precious, precious Ni-ni!"

Antonia was not thrilled. Obscurely she felt that James had deceived her. While she had not wanted to be menopausal, she had not wanted to be pregnant either!

She had a shower while she thought about it. He was so happy and excited. She knew from the way his hands caressed her that he wanted to make love and she really didn't. She hoped he would desist…in the end she submitted…in the end, despite her reluctance, she could not resist…he had this effect on her.

***

The Witch was preparing breakfast. She observed Antonia as she came downstairs.

"Congratulations," she said dryly. "I see Domino is on his way!"

Antonia scowled. She resented the fact that the Witch had discerned her pregnancy before it had been announced.

"It might be a girl."

"Boys are best, don't you think!" The Witch was playing her at her own game.

James came downstairs with Luca astride his hip. He beamed at his Grandmother.

"I see Antonia's shared our news!"

"No, I didn't! She already knew!"

"Someone got out of bed the wrong side this morning!" The Witch addressed the Range.

James seated himself at the table. He sat Luca on his knee, facing him.

"You're going to have a little brother next spring, my little man. How about that!"

Luca reached up a little hand and patted his father's cheek.

"Dadadada!"

Antonia sat down opposite. She scowled at James.

"We're definitely not calling him Domino! What kind of name is that!"

James looked across at her thoughtfully.

"Would you settle for Dominic?"

"Do I have a choice?"

"Probably not!" He grinned at her. "Granny does like to choose the children's names!"

Antonia took Luca up to the little park. He crowed happily while she pushed him on the swing. She was still angry with James.

"I'm taking Luca out," she'd announced. "Since you're so thick with your Grandmother, you can spend the morning with her."

***

Over the next weeks Antonia veered between possessiveness over Luca, and almost indifference. She was restless. They played tennis – leaving Luca in Dr Mikilari's care – Antonia played a hard game and drew satisfaction from beating James – almost as if she was punishing him.

***

"Mikey, there's something you could do for me."

"Paintings to take to the Gallery?"

"Not exactly. Antonia needs a distraction. I wondered

– once term ends – whether you'd consider taking her to Munich for a weekend? It doesn't have to be Munich – it could be Paris or Amsterdam – just somewhere with concerts, restaurants, a quiet hotel...museums, canal walks...that sort of thing. Would you do that for me?"

"Sure you trust me with her?" Michael grinned at his brother.

"It would mean so much. Obviously I can't take her. A long weekend would be brilliant!"

"She might not want to…"

"I think she'd jump at the chance."

"I was planning a week in Vienna… The Philharmonic are on tour. Is a week too long?" Michael gave his brother a searching look. "Are things a bit difficult between you?" He did not wait for an answer. "Actually, I'm driving down to see Dad this weekend. I could take Antonia. Debs keeps asking when Antonia's coming to see them. You never took her to meet them when they still lived at Brascombe?"

"No, Antonia wasn't into commitment. Meeting the parents does suggest commitment."

***

"Good Evening!" The Range greeted the Witch courteously. "Coffee?" The Witch inclined her head and accepted a mug of coffee. She observed her two grandsons.

"What are you two hatching?" she enquired.

"Oh, Hello, Granny!" Michael gave her a warm smile.

"I was suggesting I might take Antonia to visit Dad and Debs on Sunday."

"Why?" asked the Witch tartly.

"It's good for Antonia to be out in the real world... and James is a bit limited in what he can do."

"How long is it since you've seen your father?"

"Well, I saw them briefly at Jake's Graduation."

"You'll find a change, then."

James looked keenly at his grandmother, divining her meaning. He said nothing.

Michael opted to stay the night. He would drive Antonia down on Sunday The Witch settled herself in the rocking chair (that wasn't there). She sipped her coffee.

"So, where is Antonia?" she asked James.

"Working in her study. She told me she has a deadline to meet." He did not add that he thought this was a ploy to avoid him. "I'll call her."

He stood up, stretched and strolled through to Antonia's study.

"Shall you give it a rest, Antoni-ni? Come and join us – wind down before bed. Michael's here. He wondered if you'd like to drive down with him to see Dad and Debs?"

Reluctantly Antonia switched off her laptop, turned off her desk lamp and stood up. James wrapped his arms around her, hoping she would return his kiss.

"Missed you!" he said.

"What's there to miss? You knew where I was."

However, she was pleasantly surprised to be offered a day with Michael, visiting his parents.

***

They set off after breakfast. James, with Luca on his hip, waved them off a little sadly.

"Dadadada!"

"What shall we do today, little man? Shall we go down to the beach and build sandcastles?"

"Da!"

***

Antonia relaxed. The drive took them through small villages snuggled into the countryside. Michael deliberately chose the smaller rural roads. The sun shone down warmly and they wound down their windows letting in birdsong and summer scents. An hour later they were on the outskirts of a large town.

"Not far now!" Michael turned to look at her. "Do you remember this from the last time we came?"

"I think so. Mike, they *do* know we're coming?"

"Absolutely. Huge waste if we came and they'd gone out! But I don't think they go out much."

He turned into the Retirement Complex and parked in the Visitors' car park. In the spacious foyer they signed in and took the lift to the fourth floor and Dr Gregory's apartment 425.

Debs answered their ring and welcomed them.

"Come in! Come in! Your father's looking forward to seeing you! Gavin, here's Michael!"

Dr Gregory made no move to get up. He was sitting in an armchair, glancing at a photograph album. Antonia thought he looked shrunken.

"Hello, Dad! How are you?"

"Not so bad. Come and talk to me, son."

Michael made a point of reminding them that Antonia had been James's special friend. Debs smiled at her warmly.

"Did Hugo give you the reprints of James as a little boy?"

Antonia wished she had thought to bring some photographs of Luca.

"He'll be a year old next month," she told Debs.

Dr Gregory glanced at Antonia without recognition.

"Do I know you?" he enquired.

"Dad, this is Antonia. I brought her to see you before. You don't remember?"

Dr Gregory looked at him imploringly. Life was becoming increasingly confusing.

"Will you have coffee?" enquired Debs, turning to Antonia.

"Can I help?"

"No, dear. It's all ready." She drew up a small trolley set out with pretty cups and a large insulated coffee pot.

Dr Gregory was struggling to remember something. Finally, his face cleared and he asked:

"How's Morton's?"

"Fine, Dad. I enjoy the teaching. You came down for Jake's Graduation. Remember?"

"Jake is James's son," Debs reminded him. "We were just looking at photos of the grandchildren."

She placed a cup of coffee beside him. Her eyes held his affectionately.

"James doesn't come anymore," his father said sadly. "I *would* like to see James. Shall you bring him next time you come?"

"He doesn't remember," added Debs sotto voce. There were tears in her eyes.

"Has Dad had a stroke?" Michael asked, turning to her. Debs looked away as if admiring the view from their window.

"It's his memory."

"He seems so frail?" Antonia murmured, remembering how fit he'd been the last time she'd seen him – playing golf… taking them on a tour of the extensive grounds…

She reached for a biscuit and nibbled it. Granny had tried to warn them '*You'll find him changed*'

They took the lift down to the restaurant. As before there was a choice of main meals and a sumptuous dessert trolley. Antonia watched Debs helping Dr Mikilari with his food. She glanced surreptitiously at Michael to see what he was making of all this, but his face gave nothing away.

"It's a lovely place here!" she said, to make conversation.

"Yes," Debs smiled at her. "We have everything we need. It was a good move. After all, we didn't need a six bedroomed house!"

"Lovely grounds!" said Dr Gregory unexpectedly. "And no mowing!"

Antonia smiled, thinking of James mowing the orchard. A day away from him and Luca was making her appreciate them more – and dear old Dr Mikilari!

"Would you like coffee before you go?" Debs

enquired. "Only Gavin usually sleeps in the afternoons. Have a wander round the grounds, if you like?"

The visit was coming to a natural conclusion.

"It's been such a pleasure to see you."

"You must come again soon –while Gavin still remembers who you are."

***

While Gavin dozed, Debs read a novel. She was grateful for the extensive, well stocked library. She had good friends here and was able to enjoy their company over Bridge Evenings after Gavin was tucked up in bed, asleep. How lonely it would have been if she had been trying to care for him on her own. They'd had good years. They'd been happy. And she loved him. He'd been a wonderful companion, kind, thoughtful and grateful to her for the life they'd shared after the lonely and difficult years after his wife had… She wouldn't think about that.

She took Gavin down for Sunday High Tea.

"Who was that Michael brought with him?"

"Antonia. She was a friend of James's, but now she seems to be Michael's friend."

"James doesn't come to see me!"

"No, dear. James died in a car crash, you remember?"

Gavin didn't remember. He shook his head sadly.

"But Michael came to see you today."

"Yes. Michael and his girlfriend."

Was she his girlfriend? In all the years she'd known him, Michael had never seemed interested in girls. His twin brother, Steve was openly gay, living in a stable relationship with Charlie. She'd liked James from the start…Poor James, he'd had so much sadness in his life!

"Michael came today?" Gavin interrupted her reverie.

"Yes, dear. Michael came to see us."

"Perhaps James will come next time?"

***

Michael was very quiet on their drive home.

"He's well looked after," Antonia offered. But Michael made no comment.

He took the faster A roads rather than dawdling along the country lanes.

"I'll drop you off and say Hello to James. Then I must head back to Morton's. Always a lot to do at the end of term."

"What're Jake's plans?"

"Oh… well, he's out in the States. Concert tour of some kind." He was brushing aside her enquiry. After several miles of silence, he said: "I've planned a week in Vienna the second week in August. James wondered if you'd like to come with me. The Philharmonic's playing. And if you don't know Vienna, it's an…interesting place."

"He hasn't said."

"Well you can talk about it. See what you think."

"He trusts you with me?" It was meant to be a joke.

"Presumably. Or he wouldn't have suggested it."

They drove the rest of the way without talking.

***

"Your father kept asking for you," Antonia told James after they'd put Luca to bed. "He doesn't remember." She had his full attention. "He's suddenly got so frail… didn't you notice the change in him at Jake's graduation?"

"They were very late. Margaret got lost. It was very crowded." He paused thoughtfully. "And, of course, none of them expected to see me…so they didn't."

"James, when your father dies, will he come here? Will he be able to find you?"

"I doubt it. You're thinking of the concept of Heaven where one finds the people they've loved waiting to welcome them. After Gran died, Mum tried to comfort us with this idea. But I'm not sure she believed it herself. And Dad was too devastated after Mum took her life. He made it clear that he has no belief in life after death."

"Good thing *we* do!"

"The Back Garden isn't Heaven, Ni-ni. It's a way of holding onto the things and people that matter, so that they go on existing for us while we need them."

"I need you to go on existing!"

"Of course you do!" He drew her into his arms and kissed her. "We missed you today! Was Michael good company?"

"He said you'd suggested I should go with him to Vienna?"

"I thought it might make a nice break. I would have loved to take you away if things were different. And next year won't be so easy – Dominic will be less than six months."

"I've only just got used to Luca."

"It will be so much easier with a second baby!"

"By the way, I think I offended Michael: I asked him if he thought you trusted him with me. I'm afraid he was not amused."

"It's a sore point. He'll survive. We need to let him know if you're happy to do Vienna. It's less than three weeks away!"

"I wish it was with you!"

"And I was beginning to think you didn't care for my company!"

"I wasn't too thrilled about being pregnant, no."

***

Antonia was pegging out the washing: Luca's sleep-suit and tiny vests, towels, muslin napkins, James's Boxer shorts, her own underwear and an assortment of cheerful tea-towels.

"*Gonna hang out the washing on the Seigfried Line!*
Have you any dirty washing, Mother Dear?"

"That's an old song, Granny!"

"The old were young once!"

"I suppose Grandad was too young for the trenches. Was he in the Second World War?"

The Witch shrugged.

"War is no concern of mine!"

"War is terrible! Think of…"

But the Witch had gone.

Antonia finished pegging out and sauntered through

to the Back Garden where Dr Mikilari sat on his customary bench deep in old news. He smiled warmly at her and folded his newspaper.

"Come and sit down, my dear!"

Antonia sat. A gentle breeze – which she hoped would dry her washing – caressed their faces and rustled the folded paper.

"Granny was singing one of those old First World War songs," she began. "Grandad were you in the War?"

"Which war would that be?"

"Well, obviously not the First World War! But I wondered if you were Called Up for the Second?"

Dr Mikilari thought.

"I think I was too young," he reflected.

"What about National Service? Did you get Called Up for that?"

"I seem to remember they deferred my Call Up until I'd completed my medical studies. They said a trained doctor would be more use to them. I told them I could never kill anyone – I'd work in a Field Hospital, Clearing Station or in the Ambulance Corps, but I would never shoot anyone." There was a long pause. "I think they failed me on medical grounds. Just as well, really!"

"I can't imagine James killing anyone, either. I think he'd have been a pacifist."

"James and I hold that all life is sacred."

"Even an enemy life? Wouldn't you have defended yourself?"

"Gavin, James's father, he reckoned there are worse things than war."

"But he'd have been too young, anyway."

"That is so," pronounced Dr Mikilari judiciously.

"Granny said that war is no concern of hers," persisted Antonia.

"Dear Ragwort!" Dr Mikilari's face broke into a tender smile.

"You really love her, don't you!"

"Oh yes! Adore her. Cherish her. She is the light of my life!" They were silent for a while. "She had a difficult childhood," he reminisced. "After she lost her mother, she had to fend for herself, living on leaves and roots and flowers... A wild child. She was so desperate for love," he mused, "that one day I found her fashioning a little pastry man – an effigy, in effect. She made a scar on the pastry man's cheek to copy the scar I have." He touched his cheek reminiscently. "She painted the scar with blackcurrant juice. She stole loose hairs from my brush. She even went delving into the bathroom bin for my nail clippings! It had to be as realistic as possible. Apparently."

"And what did she do with it, then?"

"She ate it. She said she was supposed to swallow it whole, but it was too big. She had to bite off my head first. She was so apologetic about that!" He smiled.

"What was the point of that?"

"Eating my likeness would ensure that I would fall in love with her! I told her it was unnecessary as I'd already fallen in love with her – but she couldn't believe she was worth loving."

"She knows that now."

"Oh yes, she's known that for a long, long time."

Antonia reached down and picked a daisy.

"At school, we used to pull off the petals one by one: *he loves me, he loves me not!*"

"He loves me," quoted Dr Mikilari. "He loves me not. He'll have me, he'll have me not. He would if he could, but he can't!" He smiled. "The man in question was already married!"

Antonia was intently pulling off the petals one, by one.

"We are both loved," continued Dr Mikilari. "James loves you with his heart, soul and mind. He has never loved anyone as he loves you."

"Except Luca."

"He has always loved his children… and broken his heart over them. But the love between a man and his wife is something else."

"You know we're expecting another baby?"

"I had noticed."

"We're calling him Dominic."

"A playmate for Luca."

"That's what everyone says!"

Dr Mikilari considered her shrewdly, well aware of the undercurrents which no one acknowledged in his presence.

"You'll enjoy him when he comes." He laid his wrinkled old hand on her arm. "Luca is a dear little boy. We have long conversations."

"Hardly! He only says a few words. The rest is just babble."

"Sometimes you don't need words. He understands more than you think."

"He's only a baby!"

"He's James's child. He will have special abilities."

"I just want a normal child!"

"You'll have Dominic." Dr Mikilari patted her arm reassuringly.

"You mean *he* won't have *special abilities*?"

"Time will tell." The conversation was clearly at and end.

Antonia considered her mutilated daisy There was one petal left, but she had lost track whether it was a 'He loves me!' petal, or not.

***

Several days later she was shopping in the village, having wheeled Luca down in his pram, to buy fresh vegetables, bread and brown rice. Luca was sitting up in his harness, alertly watching the shoppers, looking at the displays of fruit under the greengrocer's awning. Antonia consulted her list. She had everything that the Witch had asked for.

"I'll take you up to the park now," she told Luca. "You can have a ride on the swings."

There were usually other small children in the park with their mothers. She enjoyed chatting with them – mother-talk. Two years ago she would never have imagined the life she had now. She would have had nothing to say to these young women, no interest in their babies!

"Hiya, Antony!"

Shaz emerged from the supermarket, clutching a

half-eaten doughnut in her hand, her mouth sticky with powdered sugar.

"Hello, Shaz." She waited for the child to catch up. "No school?"

"It's holidays, Silly!"

"Of course."

"You takin' Luke up the park? I'll come too. Here, like a doughnut?" she dug the opened pack out of her pocket and offered it to Antonia who shook her head.

"Your Dad was very cross with you."

"Yeah! He walloped me when we got home."

"It's against the law to do that."

"Yeah? Like it's against the law to bunk off school? Get real, Antony!"

"I suppose he'd been so worried where you'd got to – whether you'd had an accident… and then he just lost his temper in relief at finding you. Grown-ups do that when they get upset."

"I know." Shaz gave her an old-fashioned look. "He's okay… mostly. Hey, can I push the pram?"

"Carefully, then!"

***

"So how was Vienna?" James welcomed her back home.

"Fabulous! I really enjoyed it. I had such a lovely time!"

"You look well!" He searched her face. "It's done you good."

Belatedly she said:

"Would have been nice if you'd been there."

He understood from her body language that she hadn't really missed him. He listened while she described sightseeing, concerts, restaurants, shopping. Yes, she was glad to be home, but it had been a wonderful week. Michael had been great company. She'd enjoyed being with him. She remembered that just occasionally there had been his hand on her shoulder, a brief touch. Michael did not do intimacy. He did not hold her hand. He would help her on with her coat, draw out her chair at the restaurant, converse animatedly over a glass of wine…but it was music that brought him alive, not her presence. She had sat beside him in the concert hall, watching his face, watching him drink in the music, utterly absorbed, seeing his face light up…

She remembered being taken to the opera by Phil. His enjoyment was palpable. He would watch and listen with the same intensity and pleasure. But he would also take her hand, turning to her, wanting her to share his pleasure…his eyes caressing her…

"How's Luca?" she asked, almost as an afterthought.

"Fast asleep. He's been his usual happy self. He knows you'll be home tomorrow."

"I don't suppose for one moment he understands the concept of tomorrow!"

"He understands a lot more than you think."

"Grandad said that." She gave James a small smile.

"So, how are you, Ni-ni? Are you tired after the flight? Would you like an early night?"

"No. I slept on the plane. The Hotel had amazingly comfortable beds! I slept really well. No early morning stuff! Leisurely breakfasts…"

James knelt in front of her and placed his hand on her rounded stomach. He yearned to take her to bed and make love. He had missed her *so* much!

"You can have breakfast in bed tomorrow, if you like." Antonia looked him straight in the eye.

"We had separate rooms. And we didn't… I might have, if he'd been in the least interested. But he wasn't."

"No, it's not his style." James looked at her thoughtfully. "Thank you for your honesty."

"Well, I knew you'd wonder!"

"Oh, my darling Antoni-ni! I've missed you so much! Come to bed! I want to make love to you all night!"

"I haven't even unpacked yet!" Teasing him.

"Sod the unpacking!"

***

The Witch had invited Antonia's father to celebrate Luca's first birthday. She had made a birthday cake with a dragon on top which breathed fire when the candle was lit. Luca, sitting on his father's knee, clapped his hands and crowed with delight.

"It's hard to believe he's only a year old," remarked Antonia's father. "I think he's going to be a very intelligent little boy."

"Going to be?" muttered the Witch, "He already is!" They sang Happy Birthday to Luca.

"Dadadada-Loooo!"

"Daddy and Luca," interpreted James. He offered Luca a sandwich which Luca grabbed enthusiastically, squashing it in his fist so that most of it fell into James's lap.

"Next year there'll be two," observed Dr Mikilari.

"He'll be two," agreed Antonia's father, not understanding.

"Two children! I'm expecting another baby."

"Oh, congratulations! A playmate for Luca!"

"That's what everyone says!" Antonia sounded exasperated.

"Two boys: twice as much mischief!" muttered the Witch.

"Antonia just had a week in Vienna with my brother," James mentioned.

He shared a sandwich with Luca, breaking it in half.

"Indeed?" Antonia's father gave her his full attention, inviting her to recount the highlights of her week.

"Dadadada-Loooo!" crowed Luca, interrupting his mother.

"More tea, Froggy?"

"Don't mind if I do!"

During a lull in the conversation Dr Mikilari caught the eye of their guest.

"Do you happen to play chess?" he enquired.

"Don't we all!" Mr Throgmorton was feeling expansive.

"Perhaps I could offer you a game after tea?"

"My pleasure!"

The Witch considered the empty plates lavishly covered in cake crumbs, the depleted teapot, the remaining sandwiches now curling their edges in the heat. It seemed that tea was over. Froggy was replete. She gathered the plates and cups onto a tray and carried it across to the kitchen. Antonia picked up the plate bearing the remaining segments of birthday cake and the defunct dragon. The Witch returned with an empty tray and cleared the table, sweeping cake crumbs onto the patio beneath. She placed a chessboard between the two men. As they set out the chessmen, Luca lunged forward to grab a bishop.

"Found his vocation!" said Antonia's father jovially.

James was wondering what the Witch might have added to the birthday cake, when she drifted past, placing two tall glasses of wine by the men.

"I don't think he's ready for bed," she observed, looking at Luca.

James picked up his son, deftly extracting the purloined bishop. They strolled out to the Back Garden where he put Luca down to crawl on the grass. Luca could walk, but often preferred his speedier crawl. His walking relied on grabbing a handy adult finger to maintain his balance. James sat down on the grass inviting Luca to crawl all over him with much chortling.

Antonia washed up, considering whether to join James in the garden or whether to take some time for herself.

"Thank you for going to all this trouble," she addressed the Witch. "That was an amazing cake!"

The Witch considered Antonia's rounded stomach. This pregnancy was far more pronounced. She had hardly showed with Luca – but then he'd barely weighed five and a half pounds. Domino was going to be a lusty baby.

"So, Vienna was a success?"

"I had a wonderful time!"

"He didn't come back with you, then?"

"Michael? He brought me home, but he didn't come in. He said he was driving up to see Steve and Charlie."

The Witch knew exactly what Michael was doing, as she knew so many things.

Seventeen

Then there were two

Dominic weighed in at eight and a half pounds, a big healthy baby. Luca looked at him in astonishment – this red faced squalling monster they said was his brother. He no longer slept in the cot beside his mother. He had been moved, several weeks before Dominic's arrival, into the nursery into a proper bed. He still had baths with Daddy and lots of Daddy-time. And there was Grandad – he loved Grandad. Mummy was very busy with the baby… she didn't seem to have much time for him.

Antonia, at James's insistence, had salt baths morning and evening which were soothing and healing. She was very sore after the birth. James brought her breakfast in bed and looked after her solicitously. The baby was noisy, demanding and always hungry. But he was not the tiny fragile scrap which had made her feel so inadequate. She bonded with her baby – her noisy, demanding, lovable baby. She was very comfortable with him, and happy to leave Luca to James's care. Proudly she pushed the pram down to the village to show off her new baby. She sang to him in the baby bath, talked to him while she nursed him. She discovered that Luca's tiny vests and babygros were too small for her big lusty baby! She was happy. Her family was complete. She asked the doctor for a contraceptive prescription despite James's assurances that another pregnancy was beyond the bounds of possibility.

Luca was clean and dry. His speech was articulate. He swam with his Daddy in the sea. He happily built towers with his blocks and knocked them down again. While James painted in his studio, Luca sat on the floor and explored colour and shape and daubed paint on his hands, his face, his clothes. Occasionally he held the pegs for his mother while she pegged out.

Hugo and Eleanor came for the weekend. Antonia liked Eleanor and was happy to let her share in Dominic's care. Hugo played with Luca and updated James on Margaret's 'tribe'. She was already pregnant with her third child – necessitating a move to a four bedroomed house with a large garden. Her grandfather had gifted a substantial proportion of the cost. Andy was up at Oxford. Stephen had two more years before he would sit the scholarship exam.

"Hear anything of Jake?" James asked casually – hiding his pain. Not even Mike had any news.

"He sends the odd postcard, but no real news. I think he's opted to stay in America for the time being, but he doesn't share his plans." Hugo changed the subject. "Eleanor's becoming broody! She's trying to negotiate a career break… Our flat's not big enough to accommodate a baby. I expect we'll have to move. We're talking about a holiday touring Scandinavia before settling down.

***

"I don't know if this will work," Michael said thoughtfully. "Dad keeps asking for you. Could I try driving them both over? I don't know if he'll be able to see you, but it's worth a try. What d'you think?"

The following weekend he drove the elderly couple over, ostensibly to see Antonia and her two little boys. Gavin now required a wheelchair which took up the whole boot of Michael's car and much of the back seat, leaving Debs squashed into the remaining space.

The Witch brought tea into the sitting room for Antonia and Debs, while Michael wheeled his father out to the Back Garden. Gavin stared as James strolled towards them, his unfocused gaze suddenly sharp.

"Hello, Dad!"

"James! James! My James!" Gavin struggled to stand as James caught him and held him close. "They said you were dead. I knew that couldn't be right! And here you are, my boy! My James!"

They sat in the garden and talked. James held his father's hand. Happiness suffused the frail old man's face.

The Witch brought out a tray of tea. James helped his father who could no longer hold a cup.

"Both my boys!" said the old man happily. "My James and Michael!" He clutched James's hand as if he would never let go.

***

"He was so happy!" Debs told them the following day. "He kept smiling all evening. When I helped him into bed, he grasped my hand and told me he'd had a perfect day!"

Gavin died peacefully in his sleep that night. The certifying doctor and the Home's manager expressed their opinion that the outing had been too much for him. But Debs, Michael and James who had witnessed his happiness knew otherwise.

***

James sat in the garden with Luca facing him. They were deep in a wordless conversation. Antonia wheeled Dominic across the grass.

"What are you doing?" she asked, frowning.

"Talking."

"No, you're not!"

"We don't need words. Luca understands what I'm thinking."

Antonia watched them. She felt it was somehow underhand. Why couldn't he behave normally! She positioned the pram so that Dominic wouldn't have the sun in his eyes and watched him kicking. He had

294

a powerful kick. He had kicked far more boisterously than Luca in the womb. Perhaps he was going to be a footballer like Steve. She noticed that there was a big soft ball lurking in the shrubbery. Retrieving it, she brought it over to the pram and lifted Dominic out He wasn't yet crawling. She supported him, holding him under his arms so that he was upright.

"Kick the ball, Dominic!"

Luca turned round on his father's knee and watched.

He wriggled free and ran to fetch the ball for his brother. They played together for as long as Antonia held her son.

"See!" she said to James. "He's going to be a footballer!"

"He's got a strong kick, certainly."

But his co-ordination gave James cause for concern. Dominic's hands were clumsy. He reached for objects but often failed to pick them up. He said nothing of this to Antonia.

***

Antonia's father visited. He came again for Luca's second birthday. Luca chattered away to him and Mr Throgmorton found himself quite taken with the little fellow. Dominic was now seven months old, a noisy, happy child. Antonia was surprised how heavy he was. She sat him in a high chair for meals, and fed him from a spoon. He had a huge appetite, but made no attempt to feed himself. Luca had progressed to using cutlery, but much preferred his father's lap to an independent chair.

He played with Dominic, fetching the balls that Dominic kicked.

***

"My Antoni-ni," James stood at the bedroom window which he had flung wide open, inhaling the freshness of the early morning. "Would you like a week away with me, tramping the Yorkshire moors? We haven't been away together since Luca was born. I yearn for wide open spaces, the air fresh and damp… the smell of heather."

Antonia sat up in bed.

"Who'd look after the boys?"

"I'm sure Granny would. And Luca adores Grandad. We'll be back for his birthday. What d'you think?"

"Yes please!" Antonia yawned. "Now can I go back to sleep?"

James turned from the window and smiled at her, but Antonia had already snuggled down under the covers. He slipped out of their bedroom and put his head around the nursery. Dominic lay sprawled on his back, sound asleep.

Glancing at Luca's bed, James saw that his small son was awake. Putting a finger to his lips, he picked Luca up and carried him downstairs.

"Good Morning! You're up early! I'm barely awake myself!" The Range yawned. "Coffee?"

James accepted a mug of coffee and poured a glass of cold milk for Luca.

"We'll have breakfast later," he suggested. "I thought we might go swimming."

He opened the back door and inhaled the morning air. Luca drank his milk. He studied the kitchen clock. His Grandfather had begun teaching him to tell the time. It was very early, but it was daylight.

"Half past four," he observed.

"I know!" James gave him a conspiratorial smile. "We'll have the morning to ourselves, just us two! Mummy's fast asleep."

"We're still in our 'jamas!"

"We don't need clothes to go swimming, do we!"

Barefoot across the courtyard, into the Back Garden, the grass dew-wet underfoot. In the orchard the hammock rocked gently. Luca pointed. He looked up questioningly at his father.

"Granny-Grandad sleeping!" he whispered.

James glanced at his grandparents snuggled up together. Although Dr Mikilari often drowsed during the day, he didn't think he'd ever seen his Grandmother asleep.

Hand in hand, barefoot, in the stillness of the early morning. James and Luca walked to the far end of the garden and out onto the sandy beach. James shed his pyjama trousers and waited while Luca unbuttoned his pyjama jacket and then pulled off his trousers. The sea lay calm and gentle before them. They watched the susurrating waves. Luca wriggled his toes in the wet sand.

"I expect the water will be cold." James held out his hand. "Shall we paddle a bit first?"

Luca squealed as they walked into the shallows.

"Too cold?"

"Tis a bit!"

They retreated. James got down on all fours, offering Luca a ride on his back, crawling along the shoreline.

"You're my horse!" Luca crowed. "And if we go in the sea, you can be my sea-horse!"

James crawled into the shallows with Luca perched on his back. The water was still horribly cold, but Luca tolerated it for the sake of the fun they were having. James crawled out further and began to swim with Luca still astride. The sky showed the first faint pink flush of morning sunrise. Luca moved his feet in the gentle waves that lifted them. After a while, James turned and began to swim back to shore. Luca was surprised by how far out the sea had taken them. James crawled out of the water towards a waiting towel and lay outstretched, tipping Luca off his back.

"I'm a bit cold, Daddy! And you're taking all the towel!"

"So I am!"

James rolled onto his back. Luca promptly climbed onto his tummy. Reaching out, James grabbed a second towel and began to rub Luca dry. They never brought towels to the beach, yet there were always towels awaiting them. Luca wriggled pleasurably, skin to skin, against his father, feeling himself wrapped in a towelling blanket. He lay still. His father's body warming him, secure and happy in his father's undivided attention. For a few minutes he drowsed...

After what might have been a short time, or a longer time, Luca became aware of James stroking his hair. He yawned and wriggled comfortably against his father.

"Breakfast?" suggested James. "I could eat a horse!"

"You are a horse! A sea-horse! We went riding in the sea!"

"You have to feed your horse if you want to go riding."

"What do horses eat?"

"Grass, hay, apples… Oats."

"Porrage is oats, isn't it?"

"Right."

"Grandad pours syrup on his porrage…"

James sat up and rolled Luca onto the sand, tickling him so that the little boy shrieked in delight.

"There! Let's go and see if Granny's preparing breakfast, shall we."

They got up and strolled towards the Back Garden.

"We didn't put our 'jamas back on," observed Luca, reaching for James's hand.

"I like the feel, of the early morning on my skin."

"Are we going to have breakfast with no clothes on?"

"Quite possibly."

"Mummy might be cross!"

"Mummy's fast asleep!"

"Will Granny mind?"

"I doubt it."

"She might put a fried mouse on your plate!"

"Horses don't eat mice."

"Not even sea-horses?"

The Witch glanced at them as they came in from the courtyard. She raised an eyebrow.

"Morning, Granny! We're wearing our birthday suits!" James grinned at her boyishly.

"Whose birthday is it, Daddy?"

"He means," put in Dr Mikilari who had already started his breakfast "Naked as the day you were born!"

The Witch piled a generous breakfast platter and put it in front of James as he sat down.

"Can I sit on your knee, Daddy, a'cause the seat's cold!"

James lifted him onto his knee.

"Shall we share, then?" He offered Luca a sausage.

Luca held the lovely warm sausage in his hand and began nibbling it.

"We went swimming in the sea," Luca reported. "Daddy was my sea-horse."

"Ragwort doesn't much care for the sea," Dr Mikilari mentioned.

Luca extracted a piece of crispy bacon from James's plate, crunching it with great enjoyment.

"Wouldn't mind a rasher myself." Dr Mikilari looked hopefully at the Witch.

"Are you, or are you not, Jewish!" asked the Witch with some asperity.

"I hoped it might be Tuesday," pleaded Dr Mikilari. "You sometimes let me have bacon on Tuesdays."

Luca found another piece of bacon on his father's plate and handed it to his Grandfather. A beatific smile crept over the old man's face.

The Witch hid a smile up her sleeve and offered Luca a piece of crispy fried bread. She watched James hungrily devouring fresh mushrooms, tomatoes and fried eggs. Finally, he took a slice of bread and wiped it around his plate.

"Clean plate!" observed Luca. "No need to wash up!" He grinned at his father. "Shall we get dressed now?" He scrambled off his father's knee and wrapped himself round the Witch. "Thank you for breakfast, Granny!"

"What are you? A piece of seaweed?" She shrugged him off, secretly warmed by his affection.

James stood up, stretched, and exchanged a slightly embarrassed look with the Witch.

"Propriety calls!"

He held, out his hand to Luca and together they climbed the stairs.

Dominic was awake. He lay on his back, contentedly chewing the ear of his toy rabbit.

"Hello, little man!" James laid a hand on his son's tummy.

"*I'm* your little man, Daddy!"

"Yes, you are," James acknowledged the reproach.

"And Mingo isn't *little*! Mummy calls him a whopper!"

"Hello, Little Whopper!" James smiled at the baby.

"We'll just get Luca dressed and then we'll see to you."

He turned and steadied Luca as he climbed into his pants. Luca pulled his vest over his head.

"Back to front!" James murmured. "Arms up to the ceiling!" He removed the vest and slipped it right way round over his son's head.

"I have to have my green tee-shirt," Luca announced. "Cause I'm a piece of seaweed. Granny said!"

James rummaged in the chest of drawers, finding the green tee-shirt and helped Luca on with it. He offered Luca his shorts. Luca pulled them on, balancing against his father. He beamed up at him.

"I dressed myself!"

"Well done! Why don't you run and tell Mummy!"

James picked Dominic up from his cot, carrying him to the bathroom to change his nappy. As they passed the airing cupboard he grabbed a pair of Boxer shorts for himself. Antonia didn't approve of him wandering around naked.

Dr Mikilari was still sitting at the kitchen table. He offered to take Dominic. The Witch put a bowl of warm oatmeal and a teaspoon in front of him.

"You may as well take some coffee up to Sleeping Beauty," she remarked, handing James a mug. "And one for yourself."

James carried the two mugs upstairs. The bedroom door was wide open. Luca was standing beside the bed, talking to his mother.

"…Seahorse, and after breakfast Granny called me a piece of seaweed!"

Antonia smiled at her son.

"D'you think it's time Mummy got up?" she asked him.

"Well, here's a mug of coffee to start the day!"

James placed the mug beside her and sat down on the edge of the bed. Luca came around the bed and stood leaning against James's knees.

"I explaining to Mummy that I'm wearing green 'acause I'm a piece of seaweed!"

James drank his coffee, looking thoughtfully at Antonia. She seemed in no hurry to get up. He stood up.

"We'll leave you to get dressed." He held out his hand to Luca.

"Granny, I'd like to take Antonia away for a week…"

"That's nice," observed the Witch neutrally.

"If you'd look after the boys?"

There was a considerable silence.

"I'll think about it."

The Witch began clearing the table. She looked meaningfully at the sink.

"Leave the washing-up! I'll do it. We'd be ever so grateful! We've not been away together since Luca was born. I know it's a lot to ask, but…"

"You're right there!" The Witch muttered less than graciously.

"Well, five days if a week seems too long?"

The Witch turned her back on him and seemed to fade through the back door. James ran water into the sink. He pulled up a chair for Luca to stand on beside him.

"Have you upset her?" enquired Dr Mikilari.

"What?" James glanced at his Grandfather – did he mean Granny or Antonia? Had he unwittingly upset either of them?

Dr Mikilari looked meaningfully at the back door through which Ragwort had vanished.

"I was asking if she'd look after the boys while I take Antonia away for a few days."

"I dare say she'll come round."

Dominic grabbed the teaspoon from the table and began banging it noisily. His Grandfather's hand closed around the little fist.

"Not so noisy, my friend!" he murmured.

Eighteen

Witches never keep promises

Luca was nearly three. Dominic was now eighteen months old, an energetic fast crawler, but not yet walking unaided. James and Antonia walked him between them, encouraging him to kick the big red ball which Luca would chase and bring back.

James explained to Luca that he and Antonia were going away for five days, but Granny and Grandad would look after them. He started bathing Luca and Dominic together in the big bath, encouraging them to play with bath toys. Luca practised dressing himself. He collected up all their toys at bedtime. He stood on his chair at the sink and carefully dried mugs and plates while James or Antonia washed up.

"I look after Mingo while you away," Luca promised. "I cuddle him if he cries."

"He won't understand that we'll only be away five days. I expect he will cry for Mummy. But Granny will be here."

"And Grandad!"

"Yes, and Grandad! You love your Grandad, don't you!"

***

Breakfast on the day of departure: The Witch presiding at the Range. James thanked her profusely for undertaking to look after the little boys. The Witch was non-commital. Antonia would drive as they would need the car to access the moors.

"A day to drive up, a day to drive home: it only gives us three days," she pointed out.

"Hardly worth going!" The Witch muttered to the Range.

"I know, darling, but at least it's a proper break."

James was doing justice to his fried breakfast. "If it goes well, we might plan a longer break next time."

"Pshaw!" spat the Witch into the frying pan.

"Perhaps Dominic will be walking by the time we get back," suggested Antonia hopefully.

"Children develop at different rates," James assured her. "Luca was 'furniture walking' before his first birthday, but our Dominic is a much heavier child. He'll walk when he's ready."

Dominic sat on his Grandfather's knee, dribbling oatmeal down his front and happily banging a spare spoon.

Luca, who spent hours sitting with his Grandfather, had begun recognizing capital letters in Dr Mikilari's newspaper. He also knew a range of simple words from his picture-Alphabet. Sometimes James covered the pictures up, but Luca knew that a Cat was a Cat, and a Dog was a Dog. James drew a picture of a dog in the bath, much to Luca's delight. Then he drew a picture of a cat in the bath.

"No, Daddy! Cats don't like it if you put them in the bath!"

"How do they tell you they don't like it?"

Luca gave a realistic imitation of a cat yowling. He reached out and scratched James's arm with sharp little nails.

"Ouch! That hurt!"

"Well, you asked, Daddy!"

***

The car was loaded. Dr Mikilari stood in the doorway with Dominic in his arms and Luca clutching his trouser leg. Neither child had seemed upset as James and Antonia kissed them goodbye. Dominic, who had no inkling that his mother was about to disappear for five days, smiled beatifically at her. They waved as Antonia reversed out into the lane. The sun was shining, it was going to be a glorious day. James relaxed, secure in the knowledge that they were leaving the children in Granny's capable hands.

Three days of tramping the moors! Feeling the air fresh and damp on his face. Returning to an evening meal, chatting to other guests, after which they would relax in comfortable chairs and investigate the selection of jigsaws and board games. James felt his heart lift. He hummed quietly. He let his hand rest on Antonia's knee as she drove. He was happy.

They were welcomed and shown to their room. Dinner would be at six.

"Isn't this nice!" Antonia smiled at him and reached for his hand.

She was tired after the long drive and they retired early.

"D'you want to shower first?" James asked.

"No, I showered before dinner. I really don't need another one!"

"You're quite sure? I could massage your shoulders? We could stand under the shower together…"

"And I know where that would lead!"

Their bed was comfortable. They lay companionably, pleasantly tired. Antonia stretched pleasurably.

"Just us! No patter of little feet to wake us!"

James rolled over and stroked her cheek with his thumb. She turned her face to look at him. His hands caressed her…

***

The open moorland. Heather underfoot. Sunshine tempered by a fresh breeze. James lifted his face to the soft moorland air. He sang under his breath. Antonia looked at his face, seeing that enraptured expression she had seen on Michael's face when he was caught up in music.

"Would you have liked to live up here?" she asked.

"It's part of who I am. The moors meant Dad…and then Sam and Phil." He smiled at her. "And now, you, my Antoni-ni."

"I don't really have a special place. I've lived all over – so many different countries." She was silent for a moment. "I guess 'home' is where you are!"

He caught her to him. He was happy, so happy! And Antonia was relaxed, free to be herself.

For those three precious days they walked. They walked in sunshine. They walked in persistent drizzle. They walked under cloudy skies.

"Do you remember wanting me to come and live with you?"

"And you refused."

"You cried!"

"Did I?"

"You absolutely did! I'd never seen a grown man cry before!"

"But you're happy to live with me now?"

He didn't wait for her answer, but pulled her into his arms and kissed her for a long time.

"Did I ever tell you I don't do kissing!"

"You didn't need to tell me. The first time I tried to kiss you, you flinched."

"M'm… Luca doesn't do kissing either."

James frowned. Luca was very ready with his kisses. He was an affectionate little boy, Antonia seemed to have forgotten how she had adored him…She had lavished him with her kisses. But it was true, Luca no longer kissed his mother and Antonia did not kiss him.

***

On their last day they set off after a leisurely breakfast, only regretting they could not stay longer.

"But we'll come again," James assured the proprietor.

"It's the first time we've left our little boys," Antonia explained. "Fortunately we are blessed with devoted Grandparents. It's made these five days possible."

They packed the car, paid the bill on Antonia's credit card and set off on the long journey home. As they turned into their drive, Antonia asked:

"Do you ever have a moment's anxiety in case the cottage isn't here?"

"Well, as you can see, no one has picked up the cottage and tossed it away!"

The front door opened wide. Dr Mikilari welcomed them home.

"Daddy!" Luca yelled, pushing past his Grandfather. James scooped him up:

"Have you had a nice time while we've been away?"

"I did reading with Grandad! I can read my byself now! We did painting and we did shopping and I helped wash up every day. And I can change Mingo's nappy! I do it better'n Grandad! And when Mingo and me sit in the bath Grandad sings us the same lullaby that you sing!"

"Well Grandad taught me!"

"Where's Dominic?" asked Antonia anxiety written across her face.

"He's in bed, Mummy! Grandad said I could stay up till you came home. And Mingo can walk, Mummy!"

"My baby boy is walking! What a lovely surprise!"

They carried their luggage in, dumping it in the hall, and congregated in the kitchen.

"I'm afraid the Range is out," apologised Dr Mikilari.

"Soon get it going," James reassured him. "Granny about?"

"No, 'fraid not."

"So, where is she?" demanded Antonia.

"Granny gone," said Luca helpfully.

"What d'you mean, gone?"

James looked at his Grandfather, nagged by a premonition that something was wrong.

"Grandad, she *has* been looking after the children?"

Dr Mikilari shook his head. He looked suddenly dispirited.

"Granny just went," Luca explained. "She said small children were not her thing. But it's alright! Grandad and me did everything. Only Grandad doesn't cook as well as Granny. He does breakfast and then mostly we have sandwiches and beans on toast. I like beans on toast! But I change Mingo's nappy real good!"

"She promised!" James shook his head in disbelief.

Dr Mikilari sighed.

"Witches never keep their promises," he said sadly. "As I learned to my cost."

"Grandad, I'm sorry!

"Not to worry. We did alright, didn't we, Luca?"

"We went to the beach!" Luca remembered. "Grandad helped me make sandcastles, and we let Mingo bash them down! I wanted to swim, but Grandad said only if you here."

Antonia took in the unwashed floor. It was sticky. Crumbs had been trodden underfoot.

"Grandad did washing!" Luca added.

"Couldn't remember how the machine functioned... Got there in the end."

"I held the pegs for him!"

"You were a big help to Grandad, weren't you!" James turned his attention to more pressing matters: "I'd better get the Range going and then we can all have coffee ... and this young man can have a bath!"

"Grandad had to drink his coffee cold this morning!"

"Grandad, can you spare me one of your old newspapers to get this thing alight?"

Almost begrudgingly Dr Mikilari parted with an old 'Telegraph'. James set about relighting the Range. He wondered for how many days there had been no hot water. Luca came over and leaned against him.

"I'm glad you're home, Daddy!"

"It's a good job Grandad had you to help him!"

"M'm! Grandad isn't much good at shopping. He says our money is all wrong."

Pre-Decimal, James realized. It was years since his Grandfather had handled money!

***

While Luca had coped really well, Dominic failed to recognize his mother. He howled and kicked when she went to pick him up. She put him on his feet and dragged him unceremoniously to the bathroom. His unremitting screeching brought James running. He looked at the distressed toddler's bright red face and knelt down, talking quietly to his son while sending Luca to fetch Dr Mikilari.

"I thought he'd be alright with Granny looking after him. Grandad's been the one safe adult in his little world. We'll have to ask Grandad to go on looking after him until he feels comfortable with us again."

Dr Mikilari, Antonia acknowledged, was good with her baby boy. Dominic allowed the old man to change his nappy and dress him. He sat on his Grandfather's lap and swallowed warm oatmeal. His eyes stared reproachfully at his mother. He did not bang his spoon. He had lost weight. He had been her happy, chunky, noisy baby, now he just sat on his Grandfather's knee, subdued, sad, withdrawn.

"It happens, Ni-ni. Babies cannot hold on to the concept of a mother who isn't there."

"Why didn't you tell me! Why did you insist on this holiday, knowing what it might do to my baby!"

She was angry. Angry with James for his selfishness in wanting a holiday to the detriment of her baby. Angry with the Witch for her dereliction of duty. Obscurely angry with Luca who had come off scot free! She stoked her resentment, picking quarrels, shouting at James, finding fault with Luca.

It was ten days before the Witch re-appeared. And then, one afternoon she was just there again, in the kitchen.

"Granny's back!" shouted Luca, running to find James. "Granny's back!"

"My Ragwort!" murmured Dr Mikilari. "I've missed you!"

"Well, you've taken your time!" James sounded less than gracious.

"Nice to see you too!" retorted the Witch.

"You promised!" James reproached her. "You promised to look after the boys!"

"I did no such thing. I said I would think about it."

"You let us believe you were going to be here for them!"

"Believe what you like!"

"Granny, "James made an effort. "You do so much for us. It was just such a shock to find Grandad had been left on his own to cope."

"Did alright, though, didn't he!"

"We'd hoped to go away again, but…"

"Teach you to make assumptions!"

The Witch muttered something unprintable to the Range, who coughed, and looked faintly embarrassed.

***

"Hugo? It's James."
"Hello, Dad! Great to hear your voice! How are things?"

"It would be so good to see you both. Any chance you and Eleanor might come down for a weekend?"

"Sure! Great! When are you thinking?"

"It's Luca's birthday…"

"Let me check with Eleanor. Hold on!" Hugo walked through to the bedroom where Eleanor was luxuriating in a lazy morning. "Hi, Dad," He returned to their kitchen where he had taken the call. "Yes, that's fine with Eleanor. We could come down on Friday after work, and stay till Sunday. I'm thinking Luca will be three?"

"Great! We'll be expecting you. I can't tell you how much we're looking forward to seeing you!"

"I wonder what's up?" Hugo mused, carrying a breakfast tray through to Eleanor.

"Oh! That's so sweet of you!" Eleanor sat up in bed. "Why should something be up?"

"Can you remember when we last saw them? And now Dad phones out of the blue, sounding so eager to see us! Ostensibly we're celebrating Luca's birthday, but I get the feeling there's more to it."

Eleanor crunched a piece of toast thoughtfully.

"Uncle Mike would know if anyone does. Why don't you give him a call, if you're worried."

"I'm not worried. I just wondered."

***

Antonia didn't feel like celebrating Luca's third birthday. She didn't want to invite her father down. She was put out that James had taken it upon himself to invite

Eleanor and Hugo. She was not on speaking terms with the Witch, so presumed there would be no birthday cake. In fact, she had been forced to take over planning and preparing the meals.

She couldn't even take Dominic to the shops, given the noisy rendering of his displeasure. Every time she tried to pick him up, he struggled and kicked and howled. Once he bit her and she slapped him.

***

As they drove down to Chervil, Hugo appeared preoccupied. Eleanor observed his hands tense on the wheel. She said nothing.

"I did phone Uncle Mike," Hugo said into the silence. They went away for a few days, just the two of them. Apparently they thought Granny was going to look after the little ones, but she absconded."

"So, what happened?"

"Grandad did his best. But Antonia was furious…still is!"

"I should think so!" Eleanor could well imagine the horror of their return to the chaos that must have ensued. "Mind you, Margie's house always looks as if a hurricane has hit it!"

"Yes!" Hugo smiled at her. "Margie loves being surrounded by small kids, but housework isn't a priority with her!"

"I couldn't live in such a mess!"

"Well you don't have three babies."

"And Pippa's not three till October!"

"I know!" He turned his head and smiled at her, teasingly. "I shan't expect three babies in three years… that's *if* we get married!"

"Were you thinking of getting married any time soon?"

"Could be… I have a very good prospect in mind: Oxford educated, brilliant cook… not bad in bed!"

Eleanor gave him a playful punch. "Hey! Don't do that while I'm driving!"

Eleanor folded her hands demurely in her lap.

"I'd forgotten it's such a pretty drive down! Would you like to swap London for this?"

"Actually, No. It would take nearly two hours to drive to work. Whereas now, we can both jump on the tube."

"I won't be jumping into the tube with three babies in tow!"

"I don't suppose you will!" He smiled at her.

"It's a pity they fell out with Margie when their children are all of an age."

"M'm…"

Eleanor watched woodland passing by. Here and there were small villages. Finally, they drove through Chervil and slowed down to turn through James's dilapidated gates. James was at the door to greet them, Luca wound round his trouser-leg.

"Hugo! Good to see you! Hello, Eleanor. Luca's been looking forward to seeing you, haven't you, old chap!"

But Luca uncharacteristically buried his face against his father's leg, unaccountably overcome with shyness.

James stooped and picked him up, sitting him astride his hip.

"He's not usually like this!" James apologised, as Luca buried his face into his father's sweater.

"Hello, Luca!" Eleanor addressed the back of Luca's head. "I've been really looking forward to seeing you! I hope you'll show me some of your toys later."

"She likes kids," Hugo murmured to James. "Perhaps we could come in?" he added.

"Of course!" James moved aside to let them in. "Luggage?"

"We'll get it later."

They moved into the sitting room. Antonia rose to greet them.

"Can I get you coffee?"

"That would be lovely. Weak for me, please."

She returned with a tray of coffee and a glass of squash for Luca.

"I've spent the week cleaning!" she said ruefully. "We went to Yorkshire for five days and came home to the house in a state you wouldn't believe!"

"Sounds like Margie! She's had three in three years! Not a lot of housework gets done!"

"We knew about Pippa. Tell us about the others."

There was a small commotion in the kitchen and a howl that could only be Dominic. James went to investigate. He returned with an unsteady Dominic holding tightly to his hand – but walking!

"Oh! Isn't he adorable!" Eleanor breathed. "I want one like him!"

"Hey! Hold your horses! Life will never be the same!" She could tell from Hugo's mock horror that he was teasing her.

"You could always practice on our two," James suggested. "Look after them for a weekend and see if you're still enamoured."

He sat down and lifted Dominic onto his knee, to Luca's visible upset. The outgoing, happy little boy had become dependent and clingy overnight. He now woke crying several times a night, stumbling into his parents' room, wanting his Daddy to comfort him – and incurring his mother's irritation.

"You were going to show me your toys," Eleanor reminded him, picking up on his unhappiness.

But Luca wouldn't look at her. He tried to burrow in beside his father. James cuddled him against him.

"They don't want me!" Antonia said over brightly. "They seem to have forgotten I'm their mother!"

***

"Could Mummy bath you tonight?" James asked Luca.

"Why?"

"Daddy would like to go for a walk with Hugo."

"I could come too?"

"It's nearly your bedtime. Nice splashy bath?"

"Don't want to!" Luca's lip trembled. He was close to tears.

"He's so clingy!" Antonia muttered, exasperated.

"Well, they all are at that age, aren't they! He'll outgrow it." Eleanor said comfortably.

"It's only since we went away. James knew it might upset them, but he was so keen to get away! And now look! Selfish bastard!"

"D'you want to show us where we're sleeping?" Eleanor said, to hide her embarrassment.

She followed Antonia upstairs and along the landing to the far end.

"This is where Michael sleeps when he stays over." Antonia pushed open the door of the single room. "And this is your room."

A double room opened on the right, a mirror image of the room she shared with James. It was a propitiation gift from the Witch – not that Antonia saw it that way. Looking up at the cottage from the gravel drive (that wasn't there) one could see that the cottage protruded on one side only: their bedroom above the sitting room and the bathroom over the kitchen; with the nursery to the right of the stairs. Over the years the Witch had created a studio for Dr Mikilari, and the study, both to the left of the hall where there had only been a blank exterior wall. Now the cottage had four bedrooms! James had told her how the reclusive old lady who'd lived there had gifted the cottage to Dr Mikilari in her will.

"I hope you'll be comfortable." Antonia indicated the spacious bedroom. "Shut the door at night because Luca keeps disturbing us." She turned into the bathroom and began running a shallow bath. "Could you bring the boys up, d'you think? Grandad had them bathing together."

Eleanor coaxed Dominic as far as the bathroom where he threw a tantrum, kicking and screaming.

"Luca wouldn't come," apologised Eleanor.

"I want my Daddy!" the little boy had sobbed.

Their walk abandoned. James picked up Luca and headed upstairs where an angry Antonia was trying to manhandle Dominic into the bath.

"Alright, Ni-ni. Go and calm down, I'll deal with this."

"Let's go down and have a coffee," suggested Eleanor, taking Antonia's arm.

James shut the bathroom door and gently undressed Luca, leaving Dominic sitting on the floor. Peace was restored. The silence after Dominic's outrage was blissful. James began singing nursery rhymes. After a moment Luca joined in. James lifted him into the bath and stood Dominic on his feet.

"Luca's having such fun in the bath, would you like to get in with him? Let's just get these clothes off, shall we?"

"Come on, Mingo!" Luca held out his arms in welcome. James knelt by the bath, gently splashing his sons, remembering bathing the twins all those years ago… Steve and Michael …telling them stories, tucking them up in their bunk beds. Singing the old Russian lullabies that his grandfather had sung to him.

"Daddy not go away again!" Luca besought him.

"Dadadada!" Dominic competed for attention.

Perhaps they could all go down to the beach tomorrow. They could build sandcastles, sprawl in the sun. Hugo and Eleanor might like to bathe…

"All quiet on the Western Front?" Hugo asked when James joined them downstairs.

"It was amazing!" Eleanor looked up. "It was as though you'd switched off all the noise!"

"Shall we say I've had a lot of practice," James said quietly.

***

The next morning before breakfast James took Hugo out across the courtyard and through the green gate into the Back Garden.

"I don't remember this at all!" Hugo stared about him.

"I remember that green gate – Jake used to pass through doors that I couldn't access. It made Mum so mad!"

Sitting across from them on his old garden bench, Dr Mikilari was engrossed in his ancient newspapers.

Hugo went across to greet him.

"Breakfast?" enquired the old man hopefully.

"Not quite yet, Grandad. Everyone else is asleep!"

"Not quite everyone!" Luca hitched himself up beside his Grandfather. "Grandad taught me chess!" he mentioned. James noted that Luca had dressed himself and seemed more contained than yesterday.

"I'm just going to show Hugo the beach," he told Luca. "Then we'll all go in and see about breakfast."

"I hear you play chess?" Hugo addressed Luca over the breakfast table. "D'you think you might give me a game?"

Eleanor said brightly to Antonia:

"You mentioned a little park with swings – why don't we take Dominic. I expect he enjoys swings!"

Hugo stood up and began clearing breakfast dishes to the sink. He and James washed up. Dominic, on his Grandfather's knee, had eaten his warm oatmeal and chewed a rusk. He stared at Eleanor as she held out her arms and said brightly:

"Let's go to the swings!"

To everyone's surprise he allowed her to scoop him, up and sit him in his pram.

"You are such a good boy!"

She leaned towards him, chuckling to him, and pushed the pram into the hall.

In the Sitting room Hugo was setting out chessmen on their board. He sat on the floor. Luca had wound himself around James's leg. He observed Hugo and the waiting board. James sat down on the sofa with Luca between his knees. After a moment Luca slid down to the floor and noticed that he had the white chessmen.

They began to play. Presently Luca pushed forward a pawn, exposing his rook.

"Oh dear! I might have to take that!" Hugo indicated his bishop strategically placed to sweep diagonally across the board to the undefended rook. Luca's bottom lip quivered, He looked up at Hugo:

"What should I do?"

"Well you could move that pawn to block me."

Luca picked up the pawn. He looked across at Hugo's bishop.

"But then you'll take my pawn!" He said sadly.

"But look what happens if I do!" Hugo slid his bishop across the board, removing Luca's pawn. "See who's protecting your pawn?"

"Oh!" Luca looked up at Hugo. "My Queen!"

His Queen charged forward and took Hugo's bishop. Luca grinned at Hugo, pleased with himself.

James marvelled how patiently Hugo played with Luca.

***

Things had not gone well in the park. Dominic liked the swing. He didn't mind who pushed him as long as they didn't stop. However, when Antonia decided it was time to let somebody else have a turn, and tried to lift Dominic off, a very public tantrum erupted. Dominic screamed. He kicked. He tried to hold onto the chains of his seat. Another toddler began to cry. Other mothers looked askance or simply ignored them. Antonia was embarrassed. She was furious with Dominic. Eleanor tried to distract him, but he kicked her. Antonia tried to wrench his hand from the chain and he bit her. She slapped his face, hearing the sharp intake of Eleanor's breath. Dominic howled. He was red in the face, crying so hard that she was afraid he would choke. Eventually they got him back into his pram and wheeled him away, still screaming.

"That's Mingo!"

Hugo and James looked up. Luca scrambled to his feet, knocking over the chessmen. As the pram entered the hall, James scooped up Dominic, soothing him as only he could.

"He's a monster! He bit me!" Antonia was furious. "He showed me up in front of all those mothers! Just look at him! It's so unfair! He screams and screams and then you take him and he stops!"

Hugo looked meaningfully at Eleanor.

"Shall we make some tea for everybody?" he said quietly. In the kitchen he found a rarely used electric kettle, filled it and turned to Eleanor, noticing that she seemed upset.

"She lost her temper with the baby!" whispered Eleanor. "She slapped his face!"

Hugo frowned. Antonia didn't seem to be herself at all. He wondered again why they'd been invited for the weekend – and then remembered it was Luca's birthday.

***

After breakfast Eleanor helped Antonia make sandwiches and iced buns for the special tea.

"I was going to make a birthday cake, but there's just been too much… I wonder if you'd mind going down to the village and see if there's something in the supermarket?"

"I could make one," offered Eleanor.

"I expect he'll think the supermarket one is more exciting."

She sounded sad and defeated. Eleanor felt sorry for her.

"Why don't we go down together?" she suggested. "We could even take Luca and let him choose! Tell him it's a secret cake!"

James and Hugo had taken Dominic into the Back Garden and supported him while he kicked his ball. Hugo mentioned what Eleanor had told him and then apologised in case he had spoken out of turn.

"She's been so volatile, irrational and upset since the holiday. It really threw her finding Granny gone, the kitchen in a mess, Dominic upset… And then finding that she had to prepare the meals and manage the housework. Granny had been doing all the cooking. I mean Antonia has always kept her study immaculate and polished…and I assumed she coped with the rest of the house. I didn't think the house was a mess, apart from the kitchen. She just wasn't prepared to find Dominic didn't recognize her. Five days is forever for a baby."

"But you'd have known that, wouldn't you?"

"Grandad was brilliant but I *thought* Granny had promised to look after them…If she'd made it clear she had no intention of doing that, I'd never have left them. Antonia blames me."

"She's blaming everyone, it seems!"

"I'm sorry you've had to put up with us."

"Let's hope Luca enjoys his birthday tea!"

***

Luca had been delighted to choose his surprise birthday cake. They sang him Happy Birthday, assisted by a noisy Dominic on James's knee. Hugo and Eleanor had bought him a garage with a set of toy cars. Antonia had bought him a large toy rabbit which he hugged and stroked and loved. James had bought a train set, remembering how much pleasure this had given Jake. Dr Mikilari, to their surprise, had acquired three early reading books for Luca. The little boy's delight in all this fuss especially for him was heart-warming.

"We will need to be getting back before long," Hugo observed as they cleared away the remains of the tea.

"Thank you so much for coming. It made a really special birthday for Luca!" Antonia sounded so much happier.

"You come again soon?" asked Luca hopefully. "But Daddy no go away again!" He turned to look at his father, worry lines etched on his small face.

James looked steadily at Luca with so much love in his eyes that there was no need of a spoken answer.

Nineteen

Introducing Dr Lyle

James woke early. Antonia was still deeply asleep as were both little boys. James padded downstairs to the kitchen.

"Good Morning!" The range greeted him. "Up with the lark? Coffee?"

James accepted a mug of coffee and stood at the open back door, inhaling the fresh, inviting morning air. Taking his coffee with him, he stepped into the courtyard and walked across to the Back Garden. The grass was dew-wet beneath his bare feet. Sleepy twitterings greeted him. There was a hint of early blossom in the apple trees – the Garden was in Spring mode. Springtime...his Persephone, his springtime baby. The old swing moved gently. He put down his mug and lifted his baby daughter from the pram that was no longer there. He kissed her forehead and strolled down through the orchard with the little daughter he had loved and lost cradled in his arms. From the far end of the garden he could glimpse the sea. Humming softly to his daughter, he stood gazing out at the ceaseless inviting motion of the waves. A swim would be good! But some sixth sense deterred him. He turned back through the orchard. Kissing his daughter, he laid her gently back in her pram and walked briskly to the green gate, glancing over his shoulder at the moving swing, noting that the pram was no longer there. The kitchen was quiet. The Range had gone back to sleep. He started up the stairs. Perhaps Antonia would like breakfast in bed? And then he would get the boys up – though Luca would probably have dressed himself.

Antonia was standing by the open window holding Dominic in her arms – but her arms were outstretched as though she was about to throw him out of the window.

"Antonia, give me the baby." James's voice was quietly authoritative. He moved swiftly across the bedroom, pulling her away from the window. His arms held both her and their baby son. "Give me the baby." he said again.

Antonia let him extract the baby from her hold without a struggle. James reached across her and shut the window.

"What were you doing?" he asked very gently, aware now that Dominic was ominously quiet.

Antonia did not reply. She seemed barely aware of him. James checked the baby. There were bruises on his neck, but he was breathing. He laid the baby on their bed and pulled Antonia towards him, taking her in his arms.

"Antoni-ni? What's the matter, darling?"

There was no response. He ran a gentle finger down her cheek. Nothing. Luca? Where was Luca? For a horrid, terrifying minute he envisaged Luca lying smashed on the concrete below the window. Antonia needed help – help he could not give her. He needed to phone. But he dared not leave Antonia with the baby… and where was Luca? He drew Antonia back towards the bed and sat her down. As he turned a small movement caught his eye. Luca was crouched under the dressing table, pressed up against the wall. He knelt down and tried to coax Luca out.

"Luca? Daddy's here! Come to Daddy."

But the little boy stared at him with terrified eyes and only pressed back harder against the wall. Suppose he hadn't sensed something was wrong! Suppose he had been too late! What had driven Antonia to breaking point? If only Granny was here!

Someone was coming up the stairs! The Witch breezed in.

"Time for breakfast!" she announced, picking up Dominic from the bed. She gave James a long look from under her snaggled brows. "Bring Luca down."

Antonia remained sitting exactly as he'd put her. He stood looking at her and passed his hand in front of her eyes. There was no reaction. He crawled back to the dressing table and tried coaxing Luca to come to him. Luca was too terrified to move.

"Mummy's gone to sleep sitting up. It's safe to come out. Daddy's here… I'll have to move the dressing table…"

In the end he had to lift and swivel the dressing table and grab Luca who was attempting to scuttle away. He carried his son downstairs to the study to phone the Emergency Services.

The police were mercifully quick, assessed the situation and took a statement from James. A paramedic arrived next and then an ambulance. Antonia was brought downstairs, still in her nightdress, seemingly unaware of her surroundings. She made no protest as she was taken away. The police also wanted to check the children. Dr Mikilari sat in his usual chair in the kitchen bottle-feeding Dominic who had regained consciousness, but seemed limp and unnaturally quiet. Luca was glued to his father's hip like a limpet. He buried his face into James's chest and refused to speak.

"She'll need you to pack some bits and pieces, your wife," said one of the police officers. "She'll be on a Secure Ward and probably no visiting for at least a week."

James carried Luca upstairs, hurriedly packing a bag for Antonia, hampered by Luca's refusal to be put down. He took the opportunity to throw some clothes on – he was still wearing only his pyjama trousers.

"You alright, sir?" asked the same police officer. "You want me to call someone?" James shook his head.

Luca peeped at the man talking to his Daddy. The man had a kind face. Luca's understanding of the police was very limited: they caught burglars and sorted out road accidents. They were taking Mummy away because Mummy had tried to throw them out of the window. '*I've had enough of you!*' she'd shouted…only she hadn't shouted…it had been more cold and chilling and scary.

James held it together until the police had driven

away. He was shaking so much that he had to sit down. The Witch put a mug of coffee at his elbow but his hands were trembling too much to pick it up. He was vividly remembering his mother being taken away... All those months in a psychiatric facility, recognizing neither her husband nor her children.

The Witch relieved Dr Mikilari of Dominic, placing him carefully in his pram which she wheeled into the courtyard.

"He'll sleep," she said quietly. "I added something to his bottle."

She put a bowl of oatmeal and a small spoon in front of Dr Mikilari.

"Come and sit of Grandad's knee and have some breakfast," she suggested to Luca. "Daddy's not going anywhere, but he's a bit upset."

Luca demurred. James reached for his coffee with shaking hands but spilled most of it on the table.

"Daddy needing a bottle too!" observed Luca.

"You come and sit on my knee," his Grandad invited him.

James attempted to smile at his Grandfather, mutely thanking him. He needed to check Dominic... Luca, secure on his Grandfather's knee, hungrily spooned his oatmeal. Picking up his father's anxiety, he said:

"Mummy shook Mingo. She shook him and shook him 'cause he wouldn't stop crying. And then he just went quiet. She was very cross."

"Was she cross with you too?" asked Dr Mikilari, reaching for the mug of coffee the Witch was offering him.

Luca had trotted in to see his mother, expecting that she would be pleased that he had dressed himself. He noticed that his father was not there.

"Where's Daddy?" he asked.

Antonia sat up in bed. Her voice sounded funny as she said:

"*Where's Daddy?* And here's Daddy's special little boy. He doesn't love his Mummy. He just wants his Daddy, Daddy's boy!"

Her voice was menacing. Luca backed away. Then Antonia was out of bed, grabbing him by the arm, hauling him across to the window.

"Let's see what Daddy makes of this, shall we?"

She picked up the terrified child and was about to throw him out of the window when a deep growl made her turn. A large heavy paw knocked her off her feet and for a moment a large stripey Tiger stood over her, allowing Luca a moment to escape and crawl under the dressing table. Antonia picked herself up, dazed. There was, of course, no tiger. She saw that Luca was crouched under the dressing table, out of reach.

"I'll deal with you later!" she muttered.

Then she'd taken Dominic from his cot and, as usual, he'd started grizzling. She had shaken him roughly.

"Shut up! Shut up! I've had enough of you!"

Luca waited for the big fierce Tiger to reappear…but Antonia kept shaking Dominic until he was quiet and then it was Daddy, not the Tiger who came to rescue Dominic.

Later he would tell Daddy all this… But Daddy was

just sitting there with his spilled coffee and tears running down his face.

***

That afternoon in the Back Garden James sat on a rug playing with a strangely quiet Dominic. He was building little towers of blocks for Dominic to knock down. Occasionally he was rewarded by a smile. Dr Mikilari sat on his bench with Luca on his knee. They were looking at one of the early reading books. Luca leaned back against his Grandfather's tweed jacket. He watched a bee buzzing inside a foxglove flower.

***

"They said I could phone in the morning," James said.

"Aye," The Witch observed his strained face. "You need some food inside you. You've not eaten anything today."

James shook his head. He could not tolerate the idea of food.

"Dandelion milkshake?" suggested Luca hopefully. The Witch smiled.

"He was a great one for the dandelion milkshakes when he was your age!"

"You could make him one, and if he won't drink it, I could finish it!"

James smiled at Luca. The smile made Luca feel warm inside.

"We'll keep Antonia sedated for the time being," said

the doctor on the end of the phone. "She may come out of this spontaneously. We would ask you not to visit at this time."

James noted the 'Royal We'. Antonia was in a secure facility under a twenty-eight day Order. James knew that it might be much longer than twenty-eight days before they would consider discharging her. He anticipated that Social Services would become involved. They would want to see the children.

The Witch had provided a picnic which could be eaten with fingers. He'd fed Dominic and watched Luca sharing a plate with his Grandfather. He felt obscurely that it was all his fault. If he had not wanted to go on holiday so badly… but Antonia had enjoyed their break. She had been relaxed and happy.

If only Granny…

Luca enjoyed a boiled egg and buttered soldiers for his tea. He was occupied with his toy cars, running them across the table, chattering to his Grandfather. James picked Dominic up and carried him upstairs. Although quiet, the little chap did not seem distressed. He enjoyed splashing in the bath. There were other bruises on his arms apart from the bruising to his neck. He had been wearing only a vest and his nappy when James had intervened to take him from Antonia. He did not remember dressing him…Perhaps Granny had dressed him? He stood Dominic up in the bath ready to lift him out, cuddling him in a big fluffy towel, singing nursery rhymes to him. He sat rocking him for quite a long time until little eyelids drooped. He was about to put a clean vest and nappy on him when the Witch appeared with a made-up bottle to which she had added a little something from her herb garden, comforting, sleep-inducing.

"Help him sleep," she mentioned.

James settled Dominic into his cot in the nursery. Luca was not keen to go to bed. James suggested that they bath together, encouraging Luca to talk to him about what had happened that morning, squeezing comforting hot water over his shoulders.

The thing that puzzled him was Luca's insistence that the big friendly Tiger had knocked Mummy down, thus enabling him to escape under the dressing table. Later, after Luca was tucked up in bed with a nice warm drink inside him, James went in search of his Grandfather.

"Luca insists that a big stripey Tiger knocked Antonia down so that he could crawl under the dressing table."

"Ah yes!" Dr Mikilari smiled reminiscently. "Don't you remember the old tiger skin which your Tricia wanted to consign to the bonfire?"

"If I did, I've forgotten."

"He that has eyes to see…"

But despite the *soothing* drink, Luca awoke crying several times in the night. He wet himself. James took him into his own bed and held him close, but everything in the room reminded Luca of his trauma and in the end James carried him downstairs, wrapped in a blanket and they slept in the rocking chair in front of the Range.

***

Some days later, when the news from the hospital had not changed, the Tiger appeared in the Back Garden sauntering through the orchard. Luca immediately ran over and stroked the stripey fur. The Tiger yawned hugely and lay down. Luca buried his face in the Tiger's neck, crooning to him. The Tiger wrapped his long stripey tail around the little boy. By the time James noticed them, the Tiger had rolled onto his back with Luca perched on his tummy.

"Look, Daddy! My Tiger!"

Delight was written all over his face. James saw more than an affectionate Tiger, he saw that the anxiety and fear had left Luca's face. The Tiger padded upstairs when he put Luca to bed and slept by his side on the floor.

***

Antonia opened her eyes and stared around the strange room. She was in an unfamiliar nightgown, in a narrow bed with an institutional bedcover. An anonymous wooden cabinet stood beside the bed. A framed print of a countryside scene hung on the wall opposite. There didn't appear to be a door to the room, the floor drifted out into the corridor under its layer of orange vinyl. A fixed window with no way of opening it looked out onto a lawn. A white washbasin was attached to the wall just inside the non-existent door. Was this a hospital? Why was she here? Had there been an accident? She seemed to be all in one piece. Cautiously she slid her feet out of bed and stood up, feeling faintly dizzy. She wondered what time it was

– her watch had been removed. At the basin she splashed cold water on her face and dried it on the neatly folded towel. She wondered where her clothes were. There was a pressing need to relieve herself. She stood in the doorway looking to right and to left, wondering where the toilets might be. She was making her way along to the left when a nurse came briskly along.

"What are you doing!" exclaimed the nurse.

"I need the lavatory."

"I'll show you. You're not supposed to be out of bed."

The nurse waited until Antonia emerged and escorted her back to her room past similar rooms, all unoccupied, but clearly in use. The beds were identical under their institutional cotton blankets, but the bedside cabinets held personal effects. Antonia wondered vaguely where these neighbours might be. She got back into bed.

Presently another nurse appeared carrying a tray.

"Lunch," she said firmly, placing the tray on a bed-table which had been standing at the foot of the bed.

Antonia picked up her cutlery and considered the plate of shepherd's pie. It was not as tasteless as it looked. There was also a small pot of trifle and a glass of water which the nurse had placed on the bedside cabinet.

There was a considerable bustling of trolleys on squeaky wheels past her doorway as lunch was taken up to the Day Room where the other patients were seated around small tables. Eventually Antonia's tray was removed and a cup of tea brought to her.

"Doctor will see you at two o'clock. So don't go wandering off!" admonished the nurse.

She dumped a magazine on the cabinet.

"How will I know when it's two? I don't seem to have my watch."

"You'll be fetched," said the nurse abruptly, and left.

Antonia was grateful for something to read. She picked up the magazine which had been well read. Someone had already completed the crossword at the back. Normally Antonia would not have given the magazine a second glance, but now she idly turned the pages: how to lose weight successfully…delicious menus…knitting patterns…clothes to flatter your figure…a serial…short romances. It seemed a long time until two o'clock.

Eventually the nurse reappeared, and escorted Antonia to the doctor's office, knocking on the door and ushering Antonia in. Carpet under her feet. Several pictures on the walls. Two armchairs facing each other. Beyond them, a large desk covered in files and papers. The doctor rose to welcome her.

"Come in, Antonia. I'm Dr Lyle. I'll be looking after you while you're here."

"Why am I here?" asked Antonia, staring at him confrontationally. Dr Lyle noted the hint of aggression in her voice.

"We need to look after you until you're well enough to go home. Do sit down."

He indicated one of the armchairs and sat down in the other.

"Am I ill?"

"You've had something of an upset," said Dr Lyle

smoothly. He smiled at her. "Now, tell me about home – your family."

"James," began Antonia, wondering if she'd had an accident. Where was James?

"Yes?" encouraged Dr Lyle. "Children?"

"Luca is just three. Dominic is eighteen months."

"You wanted children?" asked Dr Lyle casually.

Antonia frowned. There seemed to be huge gaps in her memory.

"Why am I here? Did I have an accident? Has something happened to James?" She felt a shiver of fear.

"James is fine," Dr Lyle assured her. "He's at home looking after the little boys. He's been talking to me on the phone."

"Yes, but *why* am I here?"

Dr Lyle looked at her over the steeple of his fingers.

"Antonia, you tried to throw your little boys out of the bedroom window. We need to help you understand why. We need to get to the bottom of whatever's troubling you."

Antonia stared at him horrified.

"I did that?"

"I'm afraid so." Dr Lyle let a significant pause fall before he said: "Your husband loves you. He is very supportive. We now have to help you find yourself."

"Will I be able to go home eventually?"

"That is what we will work towards." He smiled at her. There was kindness in his smile. "Now we need to get you some slippers and a dressing gown. I expect the floor's rather cold under bare feet."

"What about clothes? Do I have to stay in a nightdress while I'm here?"

He heard the distress in her voice.

"How about you can get dressed tomorrow and spend some time in the Day Room? Get to know the other patients? Can someone bring in some clothes for you?"

"I don't know." Antonia hesitated.

James could only visit places he'd been to previously. Would he have ever come here? Would he send Granny?

There was something about Granny she could not remember…

"We'll see what we can do." Dr Lyle's body language indicated that the interview was at an end. "I'll see you tomorrow at ten." He got to his feet.

"How will I know when it's ten?" asked Antonia crossly. "I don't have my watch and there's no clock in my room."

"Nurse will fetch you."

"And I want something to read – not the rubbishy magazines nurse brought me!" Her eye fell on Dr Lyle's copy of 'The Economist'. Could I borrow your Economist?"

"Yes, of course," he said surprising her. "And in the Day Room you'll find quite a decent library…" he paused. "Perhaps when someone brings your clothes, they could bring some of your books. I understand you read Russian literature." He ushered Antonia out. "You can find your way?"

The afternoon dragged interminably, punctuated by a cup of tea and a slice of cherry cake. She found she could not concentrate on the magazine. A tray arrived with her evening meal. Patients began drifting past her doorway on the way to their rooms. Some glanced in at Antonia, but she refused to acknowledge them. She wanted James. She thought fleetingly of the children. She had no memory of trying to throw them out of the window. She couldn't believe she would have done that.

The night seemed to last for ever. The overhead light was switched off at eight-thirty and replaced by a faint blue light which was impossible to read by. It stayed on all night which made it difficult to sleep. Footfall in the corridor ceased. Sleep was impossible. Antonia felt like banging her head against the wall in frustration. She needed James, and James was beyond her reach. She was not going to think about the boys. There was no way she would have thrown them out of the window! James adored his boys…Had he sent her here because he wanted to get rid of her?

Had what she'd done meant he didn't love her anymore?

At ten o'clock the Night Sister appeared and offered Antonia something to help her sleep.

"Dr Lyle prescribed this for you," she said, pouring a tumbler of water, watching as Antonia swallowed the two tablets. She also produced a box of tissues. "Here, wipe your face, dear. Everything will seem better in the morning."

Antonia was sound asleep when the Night Sister looked in half an hour later.

***

Breakfast on a tray: soggy cornflakes in milk, a slice of toast, a cup of tea. Antonia thought of the lavish fried breakfasts of home. She felt wave after wave of depression. A nurse came with a pair of slippers, a towelling dressing gown and some clothes.

"Didn't I have my own clothes when I came in?" asked Antonia.

"You came in wearing a nightdress," said the nurse shortly.

"Oh." Antonia considered the clothes: a vest, a long-sleeved sweatshirt, pants and a pair of joggers.

For Antonia who had always been a fairly fastidious dresser, the idea of wearing someone else's cast off clothes was humiliating. Nevertheless, she dressed.

Presently she was escorted to the Day Room. A dozen people sat around in armchairs or working at a jigsaw at one of the tables.

"This is Antonia," announced the nurse brightly. People looked up, some curiously, some blankly. "Now, what would you like to do?" asked the nurse: "Knitting? We have several knitters here!" Antonia could see three or four elderly ladies so engaged. "Jigsaw?" suggested the nurse. Antonia shook her head. "Plenty of magazines," coaxed the nurse.

"Library!" Antonia remembered Dr Lyle mentioning books.

The nurse indicated a bookcase across the room.

Antonia stared around her at the carpeted room. There were unexciting pictures on the walls. From where she stood the far wall was glass with what looked like French windows giving onto a manicured garden. Trolleys held a large number of boxed jigsaws, board games, a chess set, magazines. She walked over to the bookcase and ran her eyes along the titles: murder mysteries, romance, a battered copy of Sir Walter Scott's 'Guy Mannering'. She pulled it out. Someone had scribbled telephone numbers on the flyleaf. A forgotten bookmark had settled a third of the way through, where the previous reader had abandoned the book. Antonia took the book along to her room and settled down to read.

"Oh no, you don't!" an orderly, who was cleaning her room, accosted her. "You go back to the Day Room."

"Why?" Antonia sounded belligerent – this was only a cleaner after all.

"Rules," returned the orderly, scrubbing the basin.

"I have an appointment with Dr Lyle shortly," Antonia said firmly.

"Ten o'clock, is it?" The orderly ignored Antonia's manner. "He won't see you before ten o'clock. He's in a meeting."

"I'll wait."

"Not here, you won't. You're supposed to be in the Day Room."

"Tough!" Antonia noticed there was now a chair in her room and sat down on it purposefully. She opened her book.

Ten o'clock.

"Ah Antonia, come in!" Dr Lyle greeted her affably. He waited for her to sit down, nodded to the nurse to withdraw and sat down opposite Antonia. "I see they found you some clothes."

"I feel as if I'm in prison! I don't have my own clothes. I have no privacy. I'm supposed to spend the day with people I don't want to be with." She twisted her hands in her lap.

I'm offered jigsaws, knitting, rubbish magazines... there's no decent books – oh! here's your 'Economist' – at least that's an intelligent read. Don't they have any newspapers here? Or just the rubbish ones! I want to go home! I want James!"

"I'm afraid going home is not an option at present. You're here under an Order. So, if it feels like prison, I'm sorry. But you are not being punished, Antonia. You are here so that we can help you."

Dr Lyle had had several long phone conversations with James.

"What do I have to do to be allowed out?"

"It depends what you mean by 'out'? You can have access to the grounds – under supervision, of course. We don't want you absconding!"

"I mean when can I go home?"

"Shall we take it a day at a time? See how things go?"

"What *things*?"

"We need to review your childhood, Antonia. Your relationship with your parents. I understand your mother is dead? Are you in touch with your father? Perhaps he might come and visit you while you're here?" Dr Lyle was curious to meet Cyril Throgmorton. "Was he pleased to become a grandfather?"

"Like a cat with two tails!" Antonia remembered his visits, smiling when she thought how outrageously the Witch had flirted with her father.

"Yes?" prompted Dr Lyle.

"He was always inclined to be a bit pompous until Granny called him 'Froggy'!"

**

Cyril Throgmorton had also had several long phone conversations with Dr Lyle and readily agreed to visit the hospital. He arrived with half a dozen Russian Classics, a dozen red roses and an aura of culture that was sadly lacking among the Day Room clientèle. He walked with Antonia around the grounds, admiring the specimen trees and the thoughtful planting of flowers and shrubs in the borders.

His tweed jacket smelled comfortingly familiar.

It seemed to Cyril Throgmorton that as psychiatric institutions went, this was a cut above the rest. He had, of course, been appraised of the reason for Antonia's admission. If he was shocked, he concealed his feelings – he had, after all, spent his working life as a diplomat. He kept up a flow of conversation until Antonia stopped walking beside him and burst into tears, throwing herself against him in a totally unexpected and highly embarrassing, gesture of familiarity.

"Whatever's the matter?"

"Take me away from here!" Antonia sobbed.

"In time," he counselled. "These things can't be rushed."

A nurse appeared to take Antonia in for tea.

"Dr Lyle wondered if you would like a cup of tea

with him," she addressed Antonia's father, by which he understood this was less of an invitation and more of a demand.

A tray of sandwiches and scones awaited him as he was ushered in to tea with the Consultant.

"I would be grateful," said Dr Lyle, biting into a rather crumbly scone, "If you could tell me a bit about Antonia's childhood?"

"I suppose she may have been rather lonely," her father reflected. "Our days revolved around Embassy business. Antonia had a number of nannies as we were moved to different postings. We sent her to boarding school in England when she was eleven." He drank his tea, observing Dr Lyle over the rim.

"Would you describe your relationship with your daughter as affectionate?"

Cyril Throgmorton considered the question as he ate a couple of sandwiches. He was of a generation that did not readily express emotion.

"As a small child, did she sit on your knee? Did you read to her? Cuddle her?"

"No, I don't suppose we did. That would have been left to the nanny." He cleared his throat and took a sip of tea. "When she was older, I certainly found we had interesting conversations. She is highly intelligent. I don't suppose I told you that she speaks six or seven languages fluently? That was one of the benefits of the various postings..." He picked up his cup but it was already empty. "She stopped contact after graduating from the Sorbonne – never explained why. We understood she was translating Russian novels..."

"So, how many years were you out of contact, would you say?"

"My last posting was to Washington. We planned to remain in the States on retirement. Life was very comfortable. I only returned to England after my wife died. I was so pleased when Antonia contacted me and said she would like to meet. I have enjoyed her visits so much. And, of course, I'm delighted to be a grandfather!"

"Twice over."

"Yes." Cyril Throgmorton fidgeted. "I don't understand what's gone so wrong? She seemed so happy. And James is a wonderful husband and father."

"I should very much like to meet him. We talk on the phone, but I understand he is unable to travel?"

Cyril Throgmorton had not been aware of that. He concealed his surprise by adjusting his trouser crease.

Realizing that Antonia's father was not about to enlighten him, Dr Lyle observed that it would benefit Antonia to have visits from her family.

"Perhaps something can be arranged," suggested her father. "They live with James's grandparents, so there's always someone to look after the children."

"Except on the morning in question."

"Quite."

Dr Lyle made a note to ask Antonia if living with James's grandparents put a strain on their relationship while Cyril Throgmorton wondered if Antonia's tea had been as generous as his.

Twenty

Antonia and Dr Lyle...

In bed, under the dim blue light, Antonia wept. She wept for James…for his voice, his touch, his smile. He understood her as no one else did. She needed him so much! The Night Sister came and sat with her and held her hand. It seemed to Antonia that she was the only person who showed her any kindness. The nurses were abrupt, often curt with her, although they were noticeably kinder to other patients. They had been supporting a young mother whose toddler had been killed in a hit and run accident and had scant sympathy for this mother who had tried to throw *her* toddlers out of a window. The Night Sister sedated Antonia and reported her distress to Dr Lyle in the morning.

After morning coffee, a nurse brought a letter to Antonia in the Day Room. It was James's familiar writing:

Antoni-ni, my darling,

This letter is to tell you how much I love you and miss you.

I hope they are looking after you, and that you find you can talk to Dr Lyle – the talking is so important.

The boys are fine. Luca is reading confidently.

He had drawn you a picture of a daisy – it seems to be significant but he didn't tell me why.

As I cannot visit you, I wondered if you'd like Granny to come? She could bring you your own clothes.

I love you so much and yearn for you to be well enough to come home.

Your James

Antonia read and re-read the letter. She found a separate sheet with Luca's drawing. It was a recognisable daisy with one petal floating away. She remembered talking to Dr Mikilari about daisies: He loves me/he loves me not. How had Luca picked up on this?

James had written '*from Luca with love*' adding a row of kisses.

Antonia hid the letter under her pillow – having no pocket in the joggers she wore day in, day out.

Dr Lyle was not seeing her until two o'clock. He was holding a Case Conference this morning discussing the patients' progress. A new patient was to be admitted from the Courts for a psychiatric evaluation.

Shortly before two o'clock Antonia returned to her

room to fetch her letter. She reached under the pillow but the letter had gone! Throwing her pillow on the floor, she searched frantically dragging the bed away from the wall, tearing her sheets off the bed, pulling her mattress onto the floor, hunting through her bedside cabinet, shaking her books. Nothing. It was not there. Someone had taken her letter!

Her nurse came to fetch her for her appointment.

"You stole my letter!" Antonia shrieked. "I put it under my pillow and it isn't there! What have you done with it? Give me back my letter!"

She began hitting the nurse, shouting at her, sobbing. Staff appeared, restrained Antonia, rescued the nurse.

"Calm down, Antonia!"

"I won't calm down! She stole my letter!"

Dr Lyle stood in the doorway. Antonia struggled to reach him.

"That won't be necessary," he said to a staff nurse who was preparing a syringe.

"They stole my letter!" Antonia sobbed.

"Come and tell me." Dr Lyle's calm demeanour tilted the world back on its axis. Restraining hands released her and she followed him down the corridor to his Consulting Room. He sat her down, offering her a glass of water and his box of tissues.

"Was it a letter from James?" he enquired, taking in her dishevelled appearance.

"Yes!" Tears ran unchecked down her face.

"Tell me what he said. I'm sure you can remember it word for word."

She was with him for an hour. Shortly before he concluded the session, he rang for tea – tea in a proper cup and saucer. Antonia felt almost human at this touch of kindness.

"I expect the letter will turn up" he assured her as he showed her out.

Her bed had been remade. The overturned furniture replaced. Her books left in a neat pile. She reached under her pillow and there was the letter.

***

"You're having a visitor today," a nurse she hadn't seen before, told her.

Antonia scrutinised the stranger.

"Where's nurse Maureen?" she asked.

"It's her day off." The nurse smiled at Antonia. "Did you think you'd scared her off?"

"She stole my letter."

"I wouldn't know about that. But I'm here to tell you that your Granny's coming to visit you".

The Witch propped her broomstick in the front entrance. And, without ringing the bell to be admitted, strode in. She carried an ungainly parcel of clothes under her arm. Glancing in the empty bedrooms, she proceeded along the corridor to the Day Room and stood, taking it all in. A nurse, who was sitting talking to one of the patients, glanced up.

"Can I help you?"

"Quite possibly," said the Witch. "I have come to see Antonia."

Antonia, who had been bent over the jigsaw table, straightened up, rubbing her back. She felt like hugging the Witch, but contented herself with a broad smile.

"Granny!"

"Brought you some clothes!" The Witch observed the joggers and sweatshirt with something akin to disdain.

Antonia led her back to her room.

"James sends his love," remarked the Witch, dropping her parcel on the bed. "Shall we stroll around the garden?"

They walked in silence around the manicured garden, discreetly followed by an unobtrusive nurse. The Witch gently touched the tips of overhanging branches and twigs as though communicating with them. Her keen eye recognized a variety of flowers and shrubs in the borders. Antonia knew there was something about the Witch she needed to remember but gave up, defeated. There was such a lot she wanted to ask…but felt somehow inhibited.

"I miss him so much!" she admitted.

"I dare say you do." The Witch wiped her nose on her sleeve. She wondered whether she might bring Domino next time…

***

Over their early evening meal Antonia found herself sitting opposite a middle-aged shapeless woman whose grey hair hung loosely round her pallid face. The woman leaned forward:

"You 'ad a visitor today," she said conversationally.

"Yes." Antonia kept her eyes on her plate, her body

language discouraging further engagement.

"Nice to 'ave visitors," continued the woman, almost confrontationally. "Me, I don't get no one."

"Maise," a male patient on her left spoke sharply. "Can't you see Antonia don't want to talk to you. Leave her alone."

"Stuck up cow!" Maisie sniffed, glaring at the man and leaned over her meal muttering about people who thought they were a cut above the others. Antonia gave the man a small grateful smile.

They were not supposed to return to their rooms until seven-thirty which was their official bedtime. Antonia had intended bringing one of her Russian novels to pass the time, but had annoyingly left it in her room. She glanced despairingly at the 'library'...and noticed a new patient studying the shelves.

He was wearing a suit which made him stick out like a sore thumb. Thirtyish? Tall, dark hair falling over his forehead. Sharp featured. As if aware of her scrutiny, he turned round.

He smiled at her.

"Hello," he said. "I'm Max. I see it's murder mysteries or nothing!"

"Actually I found a battered Sir Walter Scott."

"I guess we're all feeling a bit battered! Have you been here long?"

"It feels like forever!"

"Apart from reading, what else do people do here?"

"Knitting, jigsaws, board games." She gave him a wry smile. "Chess?" She pointed out the trolley holding the assortment of board games. "Can't vouch that all the pieces will be there."

Max went over and rummaged, triumphantly extracting a chess set and board.

"You do play?" he asked almost shyly.

Antonia played to a high standard. She preferred to play with James, as Dr Mikilari often took an inordinately long time over his moves.

They sat at one of the tables which had already been cleared and wiped down, and set out the chessmen.

"We're in luck!" Max grinned at her. "We have a full complement."

He played a fast, incisive, strategic game, assessing Antonia's reactions, giving nothing away.

"Check!" Antonia's bishop attacked Max's king.

"Bugger!" shouted Max, seeing Antonia's advantage too late.

The room was suddenly quiet as everyone stared at Max. As Antonia took Max's queen, she gave him a small triumphant smile.

"That was one sneaky move!"

The room resumed its chatter.

A bell rang.

"Seven-thirty, ladies and gentlemen!" The duty nurse began ushering patients back to their rooms.

"Just finishing me row, Nurse" pleaded a knitter.

"Can we finish our game?" The game was Ludo.

Patients shuffled out. Max and Antonia were engrossed in their match. Max was no pushover. Despite the loss of his queen, Max was a fighter. The nurse passed by their table.

"You'll have to put that aside now. Finish it tomorrow," she said firmly.

"Bugger that!" muttered Max, ignoring her.

The knitter finished her row, rolled up her wool and stuck her needles into the ball. She levered herself out of her chair, smiled at the nurse and took herself off to bed.

"Five minutes!" the nurse said to the Ludo players.

"I don't suppose I could borrow Sir Walter Scott?" Max enquired, catching Antonia's eye.

"Seeing as I've just got some books from home, it would be my pleasure."

"Books from home?"

"Russian novels, I'm afraid. That's what I do, translate. I don't suppose you read Russian?"

"Actually, no." Max grinned at her. "I'll take Sir Walter Scott."

"Time!" called the Nurse.

Reluctantly, the Ludo players abandoned their game, leaving the nurse to pack up their counters, dice and board. She called across to Antonia and Max.

"Time's up. You can move your board to one of the far tables or you can pack up now."

"What happens if we refuse?" asked Max, amusement inflecting his voice.

"Rules are rules," said the nurse firmly. "I shall switch off the light and leave you no choice."

"Well, we could just sit here in the dark and talk."

"This is not a holiday camp, Mr Weiner. You are expected to co-operate."

Antonia looked at Max to see what he would do.

Giving her a rueful smile, he swept the chessmen into their box and folded the board.

"I concede," he murmured. "Until tomorrow!"

They stood up and strolled unhurriedly out into the corridor. Behind them the nurse switched off the light and shut the door. A key turned in the lock.

"You go that way, Mr Weiner. This is not your corridor."

"As I am well aware, but Antonia is lending me a book." He accompanied her to her room and waited while she brought him the book. "Do you really read Russian?"

"Yes."

"I'm impressed!" Max gave her a deferential bow. "Good night."

Antonia folded her nightdress over her arm and walked down to the bathroom suite. She took a quick shower and returned to her room, discarding the hospital underwear, sweatshirt and joggers on the floor. Tomorrow, she could wear her own clothes.

Another long night stretched ahead of her.

***

"Shall we take a stroll around the grounds?" Max suggested after breakfast. He glanced at her approvingly. "You're looking very chic, if I may say so."

"Thank you! It's good to be rid of those dreadful hospital clothes!" She smiled at him. "I'm afraid they keep the French windows locked."

"Then we'll use the front entrance."

They strolled down the corridor and out of the front door, turning onto the expanse of lawn that wrapped itself around the hospital. Max admired the specimen trees and commented on some of the rarer shrubs.

"What are you doing out here!" A nurse accosted them.

"Strolling round the grounds." Max sounded impatient. "What do you think we're doing!"

"You're not allowed out here unescorted." She glanced at Antonia: "*You* are only allowed out here if your Father is with you, or an approved visitor."

"We're escorting each other," suggested Max. He smiled winsomely at the nurse.

"I'm afraid that's not good enough."

"So, would you care to chaperone us?" he spoke good naturedly.

"I'll arrange for an orderly to escort you this afternoon, but you will have to come in now."

"I'm sorry," Max said, turning to Antonia.

"Rules are rules!" she shrugged.

"We'll have to content ourselves with chess, I suppose." The nurse glanced at her watch.

"Dr Lyle is expecting you, Mr Weiner."

Max gave Antonia an apologetic smile and followed the nurse in.

***

He didn't return to the Day Room until lunch was being served. Antonia had saved him a seat next to her and waved to him to join her, but he ignored her and went to sit at a table where two older men were already sitting. Antonia felt rebuffed. She had already had an altercation with Maisie for trying to reserve a place for Max:

"I'm saving this seat for Max."

"Oh, Miss Hoity-Toity, didn't they tell you reserving seats 'snot allowed!"

"You can't sit here! This seat's taken!"

"Try and stop me, Posh Cow!"

"Give over, Maisie! Come and sit with us!"

The nurse was serving the next table. She came over to Antonia:

"You don't want to sit by yourself. Go and join the next table."

"I'm waiting for Max."

It was at that moment that Max walked into the Day Room, ignoring her. The nurse compressed her lips in disapproval, but served Antonia. It seemed that Max did not want her company. He disappeared after lunch. Later she saw him in the grounds escorted by an orderly.

He appeared as tea and cake were being served and came over to join her. She stared at him reproachfully.

"Difficult session," he said, giving her a disarming smile. "After all, as I'm reminded, this is not a holiday camp."

"Will you have any visitors?" asked Antonia, thawing rapidly.

"Shouldn't think so, for a moment! No, I'm something of a black sheep, I'm afraid! Persona non grata, and all that!"

"Family?"

"Not that speak to me."

Over a game of chess, Antonia enquired:

"Well, you know what I do. I translate Russian novels. What do you do?"

"That's a good question." Max declined to answer.

***

"Max doesn't seem ...ill?" Antonia ventured at her next session with Dr Lyle.

"He seems an agreeable young man." Dr Lyle smiled at her. "I'm glad you enjoy his company, but I don't discuss my patients."

It was said gently, but Antonia sensed an unspoken reproof.

***

Two days later, glancing out of the Day Room window, Antonia recognized the Witch prowling purposefully around the garden. Without drawing attention to herself, Antonia slipped out of the Day Room, along the corridor, and, satisfying herself that no one was about, let herself out of the front door.

"Hello, Granny," she greeted the Witch who was kneeling at one of the flower beds, weeding.

"Hello yourself!" returned the Witch without looking. Antonia squatted down beside her.

"I didn't know you were coming."

The Witch sniffed, wiping her nose on her sleeve. She pulled up a weed.

"Invasive little bugger! Turn your back and he'll be all over the garden."

Antonia noticed that the Witch had brought a trug with her, into which she deposited the offensive weed.

"How's James?"

"Missing you," returned the Witch, keeping her attention on her weeding.

"I miss him so much!"

"I expect you do," said the Witch, not unkindly.

"I've no idea how long they'll keep me here."

The Witch sat back on her heels and observed Antonia.

"Do you miss the boys?" she enquired.

"Of course," said Antonia uncertainly.

"You don't sound very sure?"

"It's James I want! I want him so much!"

"You already said." The Witch continued weeding.

"It's very kind of you to come," Antonia tried.

"Yes," said the Witch shortly. "Well, someone has to keep an eye on you."

***

"I see your Grandmother came to visit you?" Dr Lyle opened the session. "I'd quite like a word with her. I did mention it to Nurse, but she'd already left." He waited for Antonia to comment.

It was observed that Antonia's Grandmother was

making regular visits. Never announcing herself, but quietly weeding until Antonia noticed her and joined her in the garden.

"The Granny brought Antonia's baby today," The Nurse reported.

"Did she!" Dr Lyle studied the nurse. "How did Antonia seem?"

Antonia had not expected that the Witch would bring Dominic. She saw him toddling across the grass towards her – her baby boy! He was so much bigger! Round and chubby and walking! She knelt down on the grass and held out her arms. Dominic toddled confidently towards her, beaming happily.

"Hello, Mingo!"

"Dadadadada!"

"It would be 'Daddy'!" Antonia smiled ruefully. "Can you say 'Mama'?"

"Dadadadada!"

He let her hold him, cuddling him to her... and then wriggled free, toddling towards the flower bed and pulling up a pansy.

"Dada," he said thoughtfully.

"How many words does he say?" she asked the Witch.

"He doesn't have language as such."

"Oh," Antonia was disappointed.

"All in good time."

Dominic, with a big beaming smile, offered her the flower.

"Thank you, darling. Oh, you are such a gorgeous boy!" She looked over at the Witch. "Shall you bring Luca next time?"

"That's a long row to hoe." The Witch gave her a look from under her snaggled brows.

"I don't understand?"

"See, this one doesn't remember. He'll come to you. But not that one."

"Why? What doesn't he remember?"

"Seems you don't remember either!"

***

"What don't I remember?" Antonia asked Dr Lyle.

He regarded her thoughtfully over the steeple of his fingers.

"Sometimes we choose not to remember things that are too painful to confront."

"But if I don't remember, how can I confront it?"

"All in good time. You'll remember when you're ready." He smiled at her encouragingly. "Tell me about Dominic."

"He's still my gorgeous roly-poly boy! He's walking now! He was pleased to see me too! He let me cuddle him. It feels as if my world's still intact out there. I want James so much! I want to be at home with him and my baby boy! I want to look after him again!"

"That's good." Dr Lyle smiled at her warmly. He let a little silence fall before asking "How do you feel about Luca?"

"Well, him too, of course," said Antonia, not looking at Dr Lyle.

"You find it harder to love Luca? Is he a difficult child, would you say?"

"Not difficult so much as different."

"Different how?"

"Well, Dominic is a proper baby, just how you'd expect a baby to be. Luca is just… different."

"I'm not sure I understand?"

"Well, he's too intelligent for one thing: he's three and he's already reading and telling the time and…well…lots of things… and he prefers James. He doesn't like me."

"How does that make you feel?" Dr Lyle waited… "Rejected?"

"James is such a lovely father. He plays with Luca. He gets down on the floor and plays with him. I don't remember anyone playing with me when I was little. I don't really know how to be around small children. James is just so special! He knows what's the matter if they cry. He only has to pick Dominic up and he stops crying. And he understands Luca. Sometimes they just sit and look at each other as if they know what each other is thinking. Sometimes I feel that Luca is James's child in a way that he'll never be mine."

"Does that make you feel some resentment towards him?"

"It just makes me feel inadequate…"

Dr Lyle observed her for some time in silence.

"There are centres for mothers and small children where specialized play therapists help you engage with your child – effectively showing you how to play. Do you think that might be helpful? Tell me, do you read stories to Luca?"

"James does it so much better! He sits in the bath with

Luca, sings nursery rhymes, tells him stories… They have a really happy time in the bath."

"Can you remember being a little girl in the bath? How was it for you?"

"We moved when I was three and left my lovely Spanish nanny behind. I screamed for weeks! I hated the new nanny! There was never any playtime in the bath…it was just a chore…part of going to bed… My mother told the nannies, '*I'm afraid Antonia is not an affectionate child*'. But I didn't dare make friends with any other nanny because we always moved on and left the nanny behind. But my Spanish nanny loved me… I think she was the only person who ever loved me! I never remember being cuddled. I watch James cuddling Luca, and it makes me feel…" Antonia began to cry.

Dr Lyle waited. Presently he pushed the box of tissues towards her.

"Until James, I didn't know what it was to be loved…"

"Your first husband?"

"Oh *him*! I just thought everything might be better – I mean, people my age just got married… and had babies. I didn't even want a baby. I hated babies! Anyway, it didn't last. We didn't even like each other very much."

Antonia gave a bitter little laugh: "One of the attractions of getting married was getting a new surname to replace Fortesque-Throgmorton!"

She looked at Dr Lyle through her tears, expecting a smile. There was no smile.

"You just said you hated babies. What made you change your mind?"

"James. I just wanted… I wanted to have his baby."

"And now you have two. Did you plan two?"

"No. Dominic was an accident. I actually thought I was starting the menopause!"

"You're a bit young for that!"

"Everyone said how lovely to have two so close together, and how they'd be playmates for each other. But actually, I enjoyed Dominic so much more – I was terrified with Luca! I'd never handled a baby before, and he was such a tiny baby! Dominic's so lovely, so roly-poly happy. He's everything a baby should be!"

"Did you enjoy breastfeeding? Sometimes it's when you feel most needed... and once the baby is weaned, it might feel as if they don't need you any more..." Dr Lyle was studying her. "And when your toddler starts getting more independent and doesn't seem to need you as much... when he develops a mind of his own and doesn't want to do what you want him to do... that can be difficult..."

Antonia sighed. She fiddled with a tissue.

"And you think play therapy will help me?"

"I think it will help both of you."

"And if I agree to do it, will you let me go home?"

"Not yet, Antonia. But you are making a lot of progress. We're beginning to understand how things went wrong."

"I miss James so much!" Tears streamed down her face.

"Is James the mother you never had?"

Antonia looked up sharply. She stared at Dr Lyle.

"James cuddles you and make you feel secure and loved.

He cuddles the three- year-old you. But James also cuddles and loves Luca. I think the attention he gives Luca makes you feel threatened… a little jealous… as if you have to compete with Luca for James's love. Perhaps that was why your three-year-old self wanted to get rid of Luca."

There was a long silence. Antonia blew her nose, wiped her face, composed herself.

"I shouldn't be jealous of my little boy," she muttered.

"Feelings don't always follow how we think we ought to be and behave. Understanding how you feel and why you feel like that…why you believe things that are not quite rational… will help you change your behaviour. And then we can begin to think about you going home. It's a long road, Antonia, but you are doing really well. We'll talk more about this tomorrow."

Antonia's head jerked up. Was that it? She wasn't ready to go! The session could not end while she was in the middle of such an emotional roller coaster. She shook her head.

"You need a bit of quiet time." Dr Lyle glanced at his watch. "I'm going to ask one of the nurses to take you out in the gardens. You can have some time to yourself before lunch. And as I said, you are making very good progress."

He stood up. Antonia fought the almost overwhelming urge to remain seated, refusing to let the session end. Reluctantly she stood up and made her way back to her room, her shoulders sagging, feeling utterly dispirited. A few minutes later a nurse she hadn't seen before, collected her and took her out into the garden. They sat on a bench under the trees, out of sight of the Day Room.

***

"Are you Jewish?" Antonia asked Max over a game of chess.

"Is that of any consequence?"

"I just thought with a surname like Weiner?" She waited. "Actually my husband is part Jewish."

"Really?" Max raised a sceptical eyebrow. "Gregory doesn't sound very Jewish!"

"His mother was Jewish. James said his great-great-great grandparents came from a little village in Russia. They were called Mikilarovitch... How do you know my surname?"

Max gave her a mischievous smile.

"I happened to be in the corridor as the trolley with all the case files was passing by. Your file was on top. At least, I assume it was yours. Antonia is not a common name among the clientèle in the Day Room."

"I don't suppose you had time to glance inside?"

"Would I do that?"

"Knowing you, quite possibly!"

"You do me an injustice!" He grinned at her. "So why *are* you here, exactly?"

"In a moment when I was not quite myself I tried to throw my little boy out of the window."

Max looked at her thoughtfully.

"Which one?" he asked.

"Both, actually."

"Oh dear!" He studied her face, saying nothing more.

"Max?"

367

"M'm?"

"Why are you here?"

"That's the million dollar question."

"What d'you mean?"

"It means… if you can guess, I pay you a million dollars."

"Can't you just tell me?"

"Nope. Now, shall we get on with the game?"

***

She was waiting to be called for her afternoon appointment with Dr Lyle when Max emerged. He did not see her – or if he did, he simply ignored her.

"Bugger! Bugger! Bugger! Damn!" He swore volubly as he headed off along the corridor.

A nurse went into Dr Lyle, shutting the door behind her. Antonia waited impatiently. The nurse came out, again shutting the door.

"Dr Lyle's having a cup of coffee" she said to Antonia. "D'you mind waiting in your room till he's ready to see you."

Dr Lyle was his usual composed self when she was admitted. To Antonia's surprise there was a tray with two cups on the coffee table between the armchairs.

"Tea?" enquired Dr Lyle, pouring her a cup, anyway. "Sorry to keep you waiting."

"Max was quite upset" Antonia mentioned pointedly.

"I can't discuss Max with you."

Dr Lyle glanced at her before pouring himself a cup of tea. He was reflecting that it had been necessary to confront Max with things that were difficult to hear.

Antonia replaced her empty cup on the tray. Dr Lyle sounded purposeful as he said:

"We were saying that you feel challenged by James's relationship with Luca."

He made a steeple of his hands, regarding Antonia over their point. He waited.

Antonia did not feel like re-opening what had been a painful discussion. She folded her hands in her lap and crossed her legs. She stared at the floor and then at Dr Lyle's brown laced-up shoes. They were in need of a polish. Dr Lyle noted her body language. After a longish silence, he said, "James tells me that when Luca was a baby, you adored him. He painted portraits of you cradling your baby, looking down at him with such love. Do you remember feeling like that?"

Antonia blushed, recalling the picture James had hung in their bedroom depicting her breastfeeding Luca.

"Can you remember loving Luca so tenderly?"

"He was so little and helpless, so dependent on me. The feeding time was the easy part – but I was terrified I'd drop him... or drown him in the bath... or dislocate a limb... he was such a fragile little thing! And when he cried, I didn't know what to do. When he yelled I just panicked!"

Why did he yell?"

"When I undressed him or tried to lift him out of the bath. He liked being in the bath but hated being taken out."

"Babies enjoy being immersed in warm water. They

spend their first nine months floating in the womb."

"That's what James said. He knows all about babies – after all. he had four before Luca."

Dr Lyle looked at her intently.

"Tell me about them."

"Well, he got married while he was still a medical student because Tricia got pregnant – that was Hugo. And then they had Jake. And when Hugo was five, Tricia admitted that Tom was Hugo's father and went to live with him. Tom is James's brother. And then James married Suki and they had Persephone who died and Delfina who was mentally handicapped." Antonia took a deep breath. "Hugo still looks on James as his father and comes to see us." She paused. "Jake has severed contact. But James…" She took a deep breath. "But James never quite let go of Persephone. He kept her pram in the garden and talked to her… In fact, he also kept his baby sister's pram in the garden too." Antonia twisted her hands. "He needed a real baby to love."

She could feel her heart hammering. She looked at Dr Lyle, wanting him to understand what she could not put into words.

"That must have been difficult for you" he said gently. "Have the prams gone now that you have *real* babies?" Antonia nodded. "So James lost his baby daughters as well as his baby sister. And he nearly lost his little boys too, didn't he? What would that have done to him?" He gave Antonia a penetrating glance. "You tried to throw his little boys out of the window, Antonia."

Antonia flinched as if he had struck her. She shook her head.

"I love James!"

"I know you love him. But you also need him to be your Mummy. Your three-year-old self wants him all to yourself. You felt that the love he shows his boys means he doesn't have as much love for you. It made you feel threatened. And when a three-year old feels threatened, they try to get rid of what's threatening them. That's what you were trying to do."

"And then there would have been four prams in the back garden!" She was crying now. "Is that why James put me here, to keep them safe? Doesn't he want me back?"

"James loves you, Antonia. He understands that you had a difficult childhood, a largely unloved childhood." Dr Lyle glanced momentarily at a tea stain on the coffee table. "James understands why you feel threatened by his love for Luca. He is very concerned for you. You are not here as a punishment. You are here so we can help you understand yourself and begin to build warm, loving relationships with your sons. This is going to take time. Luca is still very traumatised."

***

In one of his long phone calls, James had told Dr Lyle about Luca's persistent nightmares. The little boy refused to go into his parents' bedroom. He drew endless pictures of tigers, slept with an old tiger skin at the foot of his bed to protect him, and screamed if he found himself alone in a room.

In other respects he seemed a normal little boy: sitting with his Grandfather, reading; playing with Dominic; playing with his toy cars and his train set...and surprisingly, taking everywhere with him the beautiful toy rabbit Antonia had given him for his birthday. He had long conversations with the rabbit. "Almost a therapeutic toy" James said.

***

Antonia left the session in a thoughtful mood. She returned to the Day Room, looking for Max. There was no sign of him. However, she caught a glimpse of the Witch in the garden, kneeling at one of the borders, weeding. By the time she'd gained access to the garden herself, the Witch had disappeared. Antonia felt exasperated that the French windows of the Day Room were kept locked. Perhaps she would confront Dr Lyle with the unfairness of it.

***

Expecting to be collected for her ten o'clock session, Antonia saw a nurse approaching her.

"Your Granny is here to visit you," the nurse smiled.

"Aren't I seeing Dr Lyle?"

"Later. He'll see you this afternoon. You may go out in the garden with your Granny."

Antonia hurried out and was astonished to see the Witch with a pushchair.

"Granny?"

The Witch turned and gave her an amused smile. Dominic drowsed in the pushchair.

"You brought Dominic! But this isn't his pushchair!"

"It is now! It folds up, you see. Easier to transport."

"You drove? I didn't know you could drive!"

Antonia recalled shopping expeditions where she had always been the driver. The Witch said nothing. Driving was not one of her accomplishments. She remembered an evening where Dr Mikilari had suffered a heart attack while driving as the result of her ill-thought-out abduction of young Tom... The drive home had been decidedly hair raising!

Dominic woke, opened his eyes and stared at Antonia. His lower lip trembled. Antonia knelt down and smiled at him.

"It's Mummy! Mingo's come to see Mummy!" She looked up at the Witch. "Can I hold him?"

"Why not?" The Witch unfastened his harness. Dominic began whimpering. *"Hush, little baby! Don't you cry!"* sang the Witch in her gravelly voice.

Dominic's face broke into a smile. He beamed at Antonia and allowed her to pick him up.

"There's my beautiful boy! My roly-poly pudding of a boy!"

Antonia bounced him up and down on her lap. Dominic chortled. She picked him a clover leaf. He grabbed at it and missed.

"All gone!" he told her.

"You're talking!"

"Dadadada!"

Antonia felt overwhelmed with love for him, her baby

boy. She longed to be home, caring for him, bathing him, cuddling him.

"Granny brought Dominic to see me!" she reported to Dr Lyle.

"How did that make you feel?" he asked, looking at her glowing face.

"I just want to be home, looking after him!"

"And James?"

"Oh yes! And James!"

"And Luca?"

Antonia looked away. She did not reply.

"Would you like to see Luca?"

"I don't know."

Dr Lyle considered her over his fingertips.

"You understand that you came in here under a Section. That means that after the twenty-eight days are up, we could let you go home for a day visit to see how things go. It would give you and Luca the chance to see each other."

"Really go home for a day?" Her face was alight with hope.

Dr Lyle had observed Antonia's interaction with Dominic. He had also made an unscheduled Home Visit to meet James and, in particular, to observe Luca. He concluded that Luca was normally a confident, happy little boy, secure in his father's care. James had shown him the two portraits he had painted of Antonia – the one breastfeeding, her face focused on her baby, looking down at him with such love; the other, in which she sat cradling Luca while looking straight at James, her face alight with happiness. Dr Lyle had discussed with James the possibility of allowing Antonia a home visit. He had met old Dr Mikilari and watched Luca climbing confidently onto his knee to read aloud from his Early Reading books.

"She misses you" Dr Lyle said, not quite asking why James was unable to travel.

"I miss her too!" James's expression was wistful.

"She cries for you at night." Dr Lyle watched James's face. "I think it's important for her to see you. This seems to be the way forward."

"Can she stay overnight?" James tried to keep his voice neutral.

"A Day Visit doesn't usually include overnight."

James had to restrain himself from begging.

"It would mean so much to both of us" he said quietly.

"I can see that."

Dr Lyle concluded his visit and returned to the hospital.

***

"You went to see James?" Antonia had received a letter from James – he wrote three or four times a week.

She guarded his letters, re-reading them hungrily. At first she carried them round tucked into the waistband of her tailored slacks. Latterly she tucked them between her underwear in her bedside cabinet.

***

"You remember we talked about the possibility of a home visit" said Dr Lyle evenly. "I will be happy to arrange this. And I will see you the following day to hear how you feel it went."

"Oh yes!" Antonia clapped her hands together. "O yes!" She could have hugged Dr Lyle.

"Dr Lyle's letting me go home for a day visit!" she told Max.

"That's nice!" He smiled at her.

He was looking strained, but in her excitement this did not register. They strolled round the garden together. Antonia chattered. Max listened. He had less to say these days. But his wry sense of humour was clearly evident.

Antonia confronted Dr Lyle with the absurdity of keeping the Day Room's French windows locked, while turning a blind eye to egress through the front door of the hospital.

"Well, let's see" said Dr Lyle, staring at a point over Antonia's head. "Suppose, shall we say, there is a woman in the Day Room who is terrified that some unspecified monster might break into the Day Room and savage her. In that hypothetical scenario there is less need to keep patients locked inside, as helping them stay safe from imagined intruders."

"And you say you never discuss your patients!" observed Antonia provocatively.

"I was providing a rational explanation for what you find unreasonable."

"No, you were giving me *the* reason! Just protecting her identity."

"Did I say it was a 'her'?"

"Yes, you did!"

Dr Lyle smiled complicitly at Antonia. This was the feisty girl James had fallen in love with.

"And another thing! Your shoes need polishing!" – she'd wanted to say that for ages!

"Do they indeed?"

"You say one should treat the whole person with respect and then you neglect your shoes! Like telling me my body isn't just a suit of clothes I can shrug off after…" She caught herself. She was on dangerous ground! She would be blurting out things she did not want him to know.

"Did I say all that?" He wasn't smiling now.

"No. it was probably Phil."

"Well, perhaps we'll talk about Phil tomorrow." He stood up and showed her out.

Twenty-One

Home is where the heart is

The Witch collected Antonia after breakfast on the day designated for the home visit.

"Have a nice time!" Max waved her off.

Once out of sight of the hospital the Witch drew Antonia into a pentagram roughly scratched in the gravel of the hospital drive.

A moment later Antonia stepped into the courtyard. She was home! James enveloped her in a long hug.

"My Antoni-ni! I've missed you so, so much! How are you, darling?"

Antonia clung to him, her face buried in his sweater, her fingers clutching at him, breathing in his dear familiar smell. Finally, he lifted her tear wet face to his and kissed her for a long time. She felt as though she could never let him go.

In the kitchen Dr Mikilari sat at the table with Luca on his knee. They were making a jigsaw. Luca gave a quick covert glance at his mother and concentrated fiercely on his jigsaw.

"Coffee?" suggested the Range.

"That sounds splendid!" James said heartily.

"I have so missed the Range!" Antonia realized.

The Witch appeared holding Dominic's hand.

"Sit you down," she addressed Antonia, indicating the rocking chair. "Here's Mummy!" she said to Dominic, letting him toddle over to her. He climbed on her knee and patted her face.

"Dadadada!" he chortled. "All gone!"

Antonia smiled up at James.

"It's so good to be home!" Her eyes sought his. "How long do I have?"

James bent and dropped a kiss on her forehead.

"You're staying the night."

"Am I? Really? I thought… They didn't tell me!"

"I negotiated it." James laid a hand on her shoulder. Antonia breathed a deep sigh.

"Thank you!" she whispered.

***

"After I've put Luca to bed, would you like a long leisurely bath?" James enquired.

"That sounds nice!" Antonia was sitting in the rocking chair giving a sleepy Dominic his bedtime bottle.

James picked up Luca, sitting him astride his hip. Luca

turned his head and stared at Antonia over his father's shoulder. He had not spoken to her and she had done no more than smile at him across the room. James ran the bath and added bubbles. They both undressed and then James stepped into the bath and sat down, inviting Luca to scramble in with him.

"Is Mummy staying tonight?" Luca asked anxiously.

"That's right. And then she goes back to the hospital tomorrow."

"I don't want her here!" He rocked back and forth in the bath and began to cry.

"It's alright, little man. Mummy won't come into your room. You'll have Mingo and your rabbit and Tiger."

"No!"

"Daddy needs Mummy, darling. Daddy misses her and wants her. I only have her for tonight. Could you be a brave boy and let Mummy stay just one night?"

Luca was clearly not happy. He wouldn't sing nursery rhymes, or play any of the bath-time games they usually played. He sat on James's knee to be dried, but when James carried him to bed he began crying pitifully, clinging to James.

"Don't go, Daddy! Don't leave me! Daddy stay!"

There were steps on the stairs. The Witch appeared, carrying Dominic. She settled him into his cot. He sighed deeply, closed his eyes and fell asleep.

"And here's a nice drink, a sleepy-time drink for Luca!" The Witch crooned in a sing-song voice.

Luca looked at her doubtfully. He looked at his father.

"Daddy drink first," he insisted.

"Like the King's wine-taster!" James smiled. He obligingly swallowed a mouthful. "It's rather nice!" He coaxed Luca.

"Daddy stay!"

"Yes, Daddy's here."

James sat down on the end of Luca's bed. He hummed. He sang Luca the old Russian lullabies. He arranged the old tiger skin on the bed so that Luca could hold a paw. He went on sitting there, talking softly to Luca until the little boy's eyes closed and he slept. Then he ran Antonia a deep scented bath and pulled on a pair of pyjama trousers. While Antonia lay in the bath, he sat on the bath stool and talked to her.

"I've so missed a bath!"

"Do they not have baths?"

"Showers. And the doors don't lock. And you're expected to be quick. It's lovely not to be chivvied and hurried." She gave a deep sigh of contentment. "James, are we going to bed after?"

"Absolutely, we are!"

"It's very early! It seems almost indecent!"

"I think 'indecent' is what we want!"

"Oh James, I have missed you so, so much!"

"Did you think I haven't missed you!"

He helped her out of the bath and held her warm and wet against him while he dried her with a big fluffy bath towel.

His hands on her were gentle as they made love. She wept. He kissed her tears, held her, stroked her, hungered for her again. They lay together, holding each other. Their hands stroking each other.

"I cry for you every night."

"I know. Dr Lyle told me."

"Is that why he's allowed me to stay tonight – even when he said a Day Visit doesn't include overnight?"

"Might well have something to do with it!" James stroked her cheek. She could hear the smile in his voice.

In the early dawn they made love again. He brought her coffee in bed. And they held each other and spoke words of love. They heard the Witch come up, to dress Dominic and take him down for breakfast. They heard Luca scampering down. James looked at Antonia, brushed hair from her face.

"I love you, my Antoni-ni! I think it's time we got up."

"I don't want to get up! Ever! I want to stay here with you! I don't want to go back!"

She began to sob, deep heart-breaking sobs.

"I know, my Antoni-ni! I know!" He gathered her against him. "There'll be more home visits like this, while you and Luca learn to make friends again. And then you'll come home for good… and I'll hold you and make love to you night after night after night!"

"How long will I have to stay there?"

"Dr Lyle won't keep you there any longer than he feels is necessary."

"I need you!"

"I know you do."

"The nights are so long! They make us go to bed at half past seven!"

"It's not for ever."

"Will Granny go on bringing Dominic to see me?"

"I'm sure she will."

"How long do I have before I have to go back?"

"Granny will take you back in time for lunch. That's the deal. Now, let's get dressed and go down. Have some breakfast – I expect you've missed Granny's breakfasts! And you'll have time to play with Dominic."

Luca stared at his mother from the safety of his Grandfather's knee:

"Mummy's been crying!" he announced.

***

There was no sign of Max at lunch. Antonia had been looking forward to seeing him. She wondered if she might find him in the grounds later. After lunch she was taken to see Dr Lyle.

"How did it go?" he asked, smiling at her.

She saw that he had ordered coffee for them both.

"It was wonderful to be home! Thank you for letting me stay the night! Just to be with James! I've missed him so much!"

"Dominic?"

"Yes! I fed him and played with him and gave him his night-time bottle… All the things I've been missing! I can't wait to go home!"

"And Luca?"

Dr Lyle had already established in a telephone call with James that Antonia and Luca had largely ignored each other, that the relationship would have to proceed very slowly. That Luca was hostile.

"James said there would be more home visits while Luca and I learn to make friends."

"H'm" Dr Lyle observed Antonia's body language.

"There will be, won't there? More home visits?"

"Indeed there will. Meanwhile we have work to do."

***

Was Max on a home visit himself? There was no sign of him at the evening meal. He just wasn't there.

"No, He was only here for a month," the nurse told her.

"Has he gone home?"

"You'll have to ask Dr Lyle tomorrow."

***

"Where's Max?" asked Antonia as soon as she'd sat down in the Consulting Room.

"Max?" Dr Lyle looked at her keenly. "Max was here for Assessment only. The Courts sent him here for a psychiatric report before sentencing him. You knew that."

"But…What will happen to him now?"

"I'm afraid he will go down for a long time."

"Down? You mean prison?"

Dr Lyle inclined his head.

"But, what had he done? He wouldn't tell me."

"You know I can't tell you that."

"But why couldn't you tell the Court that he was a really nice man? You said yourself that he was very personable! He was my friend! I don't want him to go to prison! Why does he have to go to prison? Why?"

"Sometimes we have to protect vulnerable people from harm. Sometimes it's necessary to remove people like Max from situations where they may harm others. And that means depriving him of his liberty."

"But he wouldn't hurt anybody!" Antonia was angry now And then a thought struck her: "What you just said, about removing people from situations where they might hurt others? You removed me here because I tried to harm my boys. Might I have gone to prison?"

"If James hadn't been able to intervene. If you had actually killed your sons, yes, you probably would have gone to prison." The colour drained form Antonia's face. She stared at Dr Lyle. "The difference is that you didn't plan to harm them. What you did was very obviously a cry for help. You were, as they say, out of your mind." He paused. "But some people know that what they are doing is very wrong. They know, and they do it again and again. That is why we have to protect society from them."

"What did he do?" Antonia's voice shook.

"You don't want to know, Antonia. Believe me. You said yourself that he wouldn't tell you."

"Can I write to him? I mean none of his family visited him while he was here. I don't suppose they'll visit him in prison. I might be the only person who cares enough to write. He's my friend!"

"I don't even know where he'll be sent."

"But you could find out."

"Antonia, you formed a friendship which was important

to you both, but that was one month out of your whole life." He looked at her over his finger tips. "Your life is with James and your little boys."

"Are you telling me I can't write to him?"

"I can't stop you from writing, but I don't advise it."

"But you will find his address for me?"

"I really don't think it's in your best interests."

"That phrase 'In your best interests' it's what they say when they take your child away from you – 'in the best interests of the child'. You could decide it was in Luca's best interests to remove him from my care, couldn't you?"

"I could make a recommendation to that effect, yes. But I hope that wouldn't be necessary. That is why we're working on the difficulties in your relationship. It's why you're not ready to go home yet. We need to know that you can re-establish a loving relationship with him… and give him the time and space he needs to trust you again."

"But Dominic's alright with me."

"He's too young to remember. Luca, however, still has nightmares about being thrown out of the window."

"What would have happened if I actually had?"

"Almost certainly he'd have been killed and you would have been charged with manslaughter due to diminished responsibility. That would have meant a custodial sentence…"

"Like Max?"

Dr Lyle ignored her interruption.

"In a secure mental hospital." He paused. "Fortunately James was able to avert such a tragedy. Now, when we meet tomorrow, I would, like you to have thought about how you might begin to make friends with Luca."

He stood up, indicating the session was at an end. Antonia returned to her room and lay on her bed, crying into her pillow. Presently a nurse came and took her to walk in the grounds.

It was a long lonely night. Antonia ached for the loving security of James's arms, his touch, his lips on hers… his slow smile, his voice… his dear familiar smell. She was still awake when the Night Sister did her round.

"Something to help you sleep, dear?"

"No. I can't rely on pills forever!"

"See how it goes. If you feel you need something later, I'll be around."

***

The following night just as the Night Sister retired for her break, the Witch appeared at Antonia's bed.

"Half an hour with James," murmured the Witch. "While Night Sister's on her break. But you can only have half an hour. Yes or No?"

Antonia scrambled out of bed, and a moment later was back in the bedroom she shared with James. He was sitting up expecting her.

"Half an hour" said the Witch firmly.

Antonia flung herself into James's arms. He drew her under the duvet. His hands were gentle upon her.

"Is there time?" she asked, wanting him so badly.

"We always have time," he murmured, kissing her.

She lay quietly in his arms, her head on his shoulder, utterly relaxed.

"We fit together like jigsaw pieces. We belong together!"

"My Antoni-ni!"

"It feels so right! You make me feel I belong!"

"You do belong!"

"Time's up!" said the Witch, appearing at the foot of the bed.

Antonia clung to him, wanting so desperately to stay.

"Come on, Ni-ni. This will only work if you're back in your bed before Night Sister does her next round.

Acknowledging the truth of this, Antonia got reluctantly out of bed and pulled her nightdress back on. A moment later the Witch deposited her back in her hospital room. She got back into bed, savouring the memory… the feel, of his hands on her body…his dear familiar smell …their brief but exquisite love-making.

***

"You seem very bright, this morning!" Dr Lyle commented. He looked at her keenly. Antonia dropped her gaze. A flush stole over her cheeks.

"So…" Dr Lyle waited for Antonia to speak, and when she did not, he reminded her: "You were thinking how you might begin to make friends with Luca?"

Antonia glanced up at him and then, surprising

herself, said: "Well, if I had more time at home, so he could get used to me being there, it would be easier. Perhaps I could have a long weekend at home?"

Dr Lyle considered. "That might be possible." He made a steeple of his fingers and considered her over their tips. "Yes, we'll pencil it in for the weekend after next. Shall we say: Friday after breakfast until lunch time Monday. I will drive you down myself. I would like to observe your interaction with Luca."

"I'd like that very much."

They talked about Antonia's early childhood and her devastation when the nanny Juanita disappeared from her life.

"I cried and cried!"

"I expect you felt very angry?"

"Don't remember feeling angry. Just utterly abandoned"

"We don't always recognize our angry feelings. Sometimes they are so overwhelming that we feel, unable to cope. We may try to deny the anger, bury it, lock it deep inside. Can you tell me what the three- year-old Antonia felt like when she stopped crying for Juanita?"

Antonia closed her eyes. Her hands gripped the arms of her chair so tightly that her fingers turned white.

"I want to scream and scream!"

"Okay!" he said gently. "And if you could put your scream into words, what would you like to scream?"

"I hate you! I hate you! I hate you! You stole Juanita! You sent her away for ever and ever because she loved me! I won't let anyone love me again because you'll just make them go away. You're horrible, horrible, horrible…!"

Antonia opened her eyes and looked at Dr Lyle. She was trembling. Her face was wet with unbidden tears.

"I never let anyone near enough to love me!" She added.

"You got married" observed Dr Lyle quietly. "Did you believe he loved you? Did you think you loved him… in the beginning?"

"No."

Antonia rubbed her sleeve across her face.

"It just seemed a reasonable thing to do at the time. We got on quite well when he suggested it. But it didn't last long. We realised we didn't actually like each other very much, after all. Love didn't come into it."

"And then?"

"I moved to London and got on with life. I had my translating."

"How did that pay?"

"Not much to begin with. It took time to get established."

"Is that why you financed yourself with your *other work*?" Antonia flinched. "No one is judging you, Antonia. I'm just trying to understand. Do you think you were looking for love in a particularly proscribed way?"

"No! Love never came into it. I wanted to make them *pay* for the way I'd been used and hurt."

"Who used you?"

"One of the Embassy staff. And when I complained to my father, he told me not to make a fuss."

"So, I think what you're saying is that you allowed your clients to make use of your body so long as they paid you extortionately?"

Antonia's jaw stuck out defiantly.

"No one was ever going to hurt me again."

"It sounds to me as if there's a lot of unexpressed anger in there." He waited. "How did you feel about your body?"

"They couldn't touch me! My body was just like a coat I wore – not me!"

"Disassociating yourself like that is dangerous."

"I know. James told me."

"And what does James feel about that period of your life?"

"Well he was one of them."

"I don't quite understand?"

"Phil made me promise to be there for James if he ever needed me."

"Remind me who Phil is?"

"He was this posh doctor who sort of took me over. He paid off my mortgage, helped me buy the flat I have now, on condition that I stopped seeing clients – apart from him. He wanted exclusive rights, not that he wanted much in the way of sex. He wanted someone presentable whom he could take out to dinner in exclusive restaurants, and the opera...Culture and Haute Cuisine instead of sex!" Antonia gave a wry smile. "He made it very clear: no emotional entanglement, more of a business proposition, but he was very generous." She took a deep breath. "James was like the son he never had. And he knew that after he died, James would be very lonely... He *was* lonely! He came to see me and he cried and cried!

I'd never seen a grown man cry before. But he wasn't into business propositions and clear cut rules. He wanted a relationship and I didn't do relationships. He wanted love and commitment. I told him I didn't do commitment. It wasn't until, after he died that I realized how much I needed him…"

"Hold on! You just said *he died*? I don't quite follow." Antonia's body language betrayed her discomfort. Panicked, she struggled for a moment.

"It was Phil who died," she prevaricated. "I'd promised to be there for James, but he was too needy. He got under my skin. I didn't know I needed him until later." She was talking too quickly, trying to distance herself from her gaffe. "Anyway, you've talked to James on the phone. You couldn't have a phone conversation with someone who's dead! But, when he had that massive heart attack, I thought he had died. And I was so distraught and… and… and he came and gathered me up and took me home… and we've been together ever since. I'm afraid I sounded rather muddled back then!" She was gabbling and clearly defensive.

"It's alright, Antonia. You're not on trial! Calm down. We'll talk again tomorrow. Just one thing" he smiled at her, inviting her to confide in him. "You've told me about your former attitude to sex, distancing yourself from any emotional involvement, and so on. How is it with James?"

Antonia took a deep breath. She smiled. She relaxed. She radiated happiness. She looked, Dr Lyle thought, quite beautiful, as she replied:

"So, so different! You see, he loves me."

***

"I had a very strange conversation with Antonia" Dr Lyle observed later to James on the phone".

"Yes?"

"She was at great pains to assure me that you are not dead…" He left a delicate pause.

James chuckled.

"Well, you've met me. You're welcome to come again!"

"I intend to. However, official records confirm that a James Gregory, Consultant Psychiatrist at a certain well-regarded hospital did, in fact, suffer a fatal heart attack some six years ago."

"They say love is stronger than death."

"Meaning?"

"Exactly that. There are more things in heaven and earth than this world dreams of."

"You're a man of riddles."

"But not a ghost."

"Leaving that aside, Antonia is asking for a long weekend to give her the opportunity to bond with Luca. I suggested that I could drive her down so that I could observe their interaction."

There was a short silence. James considered the suggestion.

"We can see how it goes." He sounded doubtful.

"Friday week, then. I'll drive her down after breakfast.

She can have three days. Back here in time for lunch on the Monday."

***

That night as Antonia lay in James's arms for their illicit half hour while Night Sister took her break, James mentioned Dr Lyle's inference.

"It just slipped out!" confessed Antonia. "He was asking about the years before you and Phil, and how we met. And it was out before I could retract it. He asks an awful lot about sex!"

"M'm?"

"It's embarrassing, in a way – I mean suppose, after all this, I met him at a dinner party, it would feel as if he could see me naked!"

"Well, I don't think that's likely…"

"Your time is up!" announced the Witch.

"Bugger that!" whispered Antonia, thinking of Max.

"*What* did you say!" James stared at her.

"Half an hour is so short!"

"But we've got a long weekend ahead of us, darling. Half an hour is so much better than nothing."

Reluctantly Antonia started to get out of bed. She reached for her discarded nightie, and then she rebelled.

"No!" she said. "I'm not coming! Not yet. Come back in forty-five minutes and I'll be ready."

The Witch's lips twitched. An expression akin to mischief slipped across her face, and she was gone.

"Rebellious wench!" whispered James, pulling her down beside him.

"We were so busy talking, we used up our half hour and we haven't even made love!"

"How remiss!" She could hear the amusement in his voice.

"Why else am I here?"

"Why indeed?"

And then they did not speak again as he kissed and caressed her and they came together like two pieces of jigsaw.

***

"And where were you last night?" Dr Lyle enquired "Night Sister reported that you were not in your room when she came back from her break, and she could not find you."

"Perhaps I popped out for a little night air!" Antonia exuded an almost feline sexiness.

Dr Lyle observed her in silence. His expression was deliberately neutral.

"I'm looking forward to my weekend! I'm really excited!"

"How do you feel it will, go?"

Antonia grinned like a Cheshire cat.

"What are you thinking?" He stared at her intently.

"Three nights to make love without being hassled!"

Twenty-Two

Making friends with Luca

Antonia was allowed a long weekend once a fortnight, with a two-day weekend in between.

"I think you might go home for Christmas" Dr Lyle suggested. "Five days. We'll review how that goes, and then I'm thinking, if all goes well, I'll discharge you as an inpatient and see you Mondays, Wednesdays and Fridays as an outpatient. How does that sound?"

"It sounds pretty good!" Antonia smiled at him. "Have you told James?"

"I've discussed it with James, yes."

"Do you tell him everything I say?"

"Not everything, no."

"Some of the stuff I tell you is pretty embarrassing."

"Your James is a professional. He's fairly objective."

"I think you have a lot of respect for him."

Dr Lyle crossed his legs.

"So what would you like to tell me today?"

***

Luca sat on his Grandfather's knee in the garden. They were considering the headlines of an out-of-date newspaper. Luca traced his finger over the black capital letters.

"L" he said triumphantly, "L for Luca."

"Just so."

Luca searched for a D. Eventually he shook his head.

"No D for Daddy!"

"However, I can see a G for Grandad."

Dr Mikilari regretted that there was no Alphabet book in the cottage. There had always been plenty of children's books at Brascombe as the five children were growing up. And, of course, there'd been books for Hugo and Jake …which Tricia had removed when she took the boys. A bad business that! And then, the books which James had bought for Jake, had migrated when they'd gone to live with Mr Carew Robinson.

Now, Dr Mikilari taught Luca word recognition in his early reading books, but, he reflected, it was one thing to know that a cat was a cat, however, it didn't teach Luca how to read a sentence.

"Let's go in" he suggested. "I could do with a cuppa." They sat at the kitchen table and Dr Mikilari read some of his old newspaper to Luca. It was not very interesting and Luca began playing with stray breadcrumbs on the table.

The Witch placed a mug of tea in front of Dr Mikilari. Luca looked up.

"Where's Daddy?"

"He's out in the garden walking with your mother."

"Mingo?"

"I believe Domino is with them."

Luca sighed. He wished his mother would go back to that hospital so he could have his father's attention all to himself.

"You can help me make some chocolate brownies for tea," invited the Witch.

And so it was that Luca was standing on a chair at the table, industriously stirring chocolate into creamed butter and sugar…and a touch of aphrodisiac that usually found its way into the Witch's chocolate brownies.

"What a busy boy!" Antonia paused at the table and smiled at him. Luca glanced at her and quickly back to his stirring. Unobtrusively he edged further away from her.

"James, my boy, Luca needs more books. Are you able to access the bookshop in town?"

"We could get books from the Library," Antonia observed.

"No." Dr Mikilari frowned. "Children need their own books which inspire their imagination, books they grow up with and love into raggedness."

"I agree."

James wondered how it was that they hadn't provided books for Luca. Of course, he had been re-telling favourite stories to Luca as soon as he had the child's attention.

He'd created stories around Luca's toys... drawing him pictures out of which grew more stories...

"He recognizes letters and the words in his early reader" mentioned the Witch, supervising the stirring. "I think, Luca, the brownies are ready to go in the oven, now."

She greased a tray and began spooning the mixture into small mushroom shapes.

"Oh dear! You've got chocolate powder all down your jersey!" Antonia scolded.

"I don't think that really matters." Noticing Luca's flinch, James distracted Antonia. "I think Dominic needs changing." Antonia scooped Dominic up and took him up to the bathroom. He would be two in February and had not the least idea about toilet training. She changed his nappy, washed her hands and lifted him up for a cuddle, He had that delicious baby smell of crushed biscuits and baby powder.

"Who's my gorgeous boy! Mummy's roly-poly-dumpling!"

"Dadadada... all gone!" Dominic beamed at her.

She'd asked James what 'all gone' signified.

"When he's eaten his dinner and his plate's empty, we say 'All gone!' It's praising him... letting him know we're proud of him... positive reinforcement, if you like."

"Makes a change from, 'You'll sit there until you've cleared your plate!"

Downstairs in the kitchen, Luca wrapped himself around his father's leg.

"I found an L for Luca in Grandad's newspaper. And a G for Grandad. But there wasn't a D for Daddy."

James picked him up and sat him astride his hip.

"What else does D stand for?"

Luca thought.

"Dinner?" he suggested. "Dog?"

"Who's having his nappy changed?"

"Oh!" Luca's face lit up. "Dominic!"

"There's a clever sixpence!"

The Witch shut the oven door with a satisfactory bang.

"You're well, out of date, Daffyn! They don't use silver sixpences anymore… nor the old shiny threepenny pieces…not even a silver grote."

"Roubles…" suggested Dr Mikilari reflectively.

"*You* were born out of date!"

"May I suggest you get Antonia to drive you into town tomorrow and buy Luca some books. They'll be so much more fun than my old '*Telegraphs*'. I remember teaching Mlilka to read. She was as bright as a button."

"Daddy, why are buttons bright?"

"Some buttons are really shiny. In the Army you had to polish your buttons!" James reached a finger to brush Luca's hair out of his eyes. "You need a haircut, young man!"

Antonia returned to the kitchen with Dominic.

"We could invite my father for tea tomorrow," she suggested.

"Yes, of course," James agreed readily. "Why don't you phone him now?"

The Witch smiled to herself. She was quite taken with 'Froggy'.

It was early Saturday morning. Luca slid out of bed, grasping rabbit by one ear, he padded to his parent's bedroom door and very carefully inched it open. He had hoped his mother might have gone back to the hospital, but now he saw that his parents were cuddled up together, asleep. He gave a deep sigh and went back to the nursery to get dressed. Mingo was still fast asleep, sprawled on his back. Perhaps Granny would be in the kitchen getting breakfast. She might make him a frothy hot chocolate. He came downstairs, still clutching his rabbit. As he reached the bottom step, the Witch came in from the courtyard. She looked rather dishevelled, having spent the night in the hammock with Dr Mikilari who had been rather greedy with the chocolate brownies. The Witch wondered what effect they might have on Cyril Throgmorton.

"Hello, Luca! What would you like for breakfast?"

***

Cyril Throgmorton was pleasantly surprised to find his daughter out of hospital and inviting him for tea. He drove down in sunshine, humming to himself. She was obviously well on the road to recovery. That psychiatrist clearly had his head screwed on! The Witch welcomed him quite effusively.

"They're all out in the courtyard. Why don't you join them Shall I take your coat?"

He demurred, thinking it would be chilly out

there – it was only January! The Witch thought he was looking very smart, quite distinguished, in fact! She led him through the kitchen which was busy with tea preparations.

"I'm afraid you're going to a lot of trouble!"

"It's not every day I have such a handsome visitor to entertain!"

"Flirtatious old baggage!" muttered the Range provocatively.

The Witch ignored him and ushered her guest out to the courtyard where the family were sitting around the garden table under a sunshade. It might well have been June, Antonia's father reflected! He was rather discomforted by the sudden switch from a chilly winter's day to this unprecedented warmth. He allowed the Witch to take his coat, after all.

"How good to see you, sir!" Dr Mikilari stood up and offered his hand with old world courtesy.

"Hello, Father."

Antonia also stood up, and then, unsure of herself, sat down again beside James who had Luca on his knee.

"You're looking very well, my dear." His eyes rested on his daughter. He sat down on her left and smiled at Luca. "Hello, young man. Haven't seen you in quite a while. Let me see, how old are you now?"

"Mingo's nearly two; and I'm three and a half. How old are you?"

James smiled over his head at Antonia's father.

"Pretty old, come to think of it! Are you pleased to have your mother home?"

Luca looked at his grandfather for a long moment without saying anything. Finally:

"Mummy tried to push me out of the window."

Antonia flinched. James laid a comforting hand on her arm.

Dr Mikilari drew the older man into conversation.

"By the way, I don't see Dominic?"

"Oh, he had a bit of a tummy upset. He's sleeping."

"He was sick all down himself," Luca elaborated.

"Shall we draw a picture for Grandad?" James suggested to Luca.

He produced a sheet of notepaper and some crayons. Luca selected a green crayon and drew a recognisable frog.

"A frog for Froggy," he announced. "And I've put an L for Luca at the bottom, like Daddy puts his name at the bottom of his pictures."

"Hah!" exclaimed the Witch, setting down the tea tray on the table. "A frog for Froggy! Very good, Luca!"

"Did you see a picture of a frog?" asked James.

Luca shook his head.

"I found a frog in the back garden... with Granny."

"Perhaps Granny thought if she kissed the frog it would turn into a prince," suggested Dr Mikilari. Everyone laughed. "I remember Mlilka turning a little boy into a frog at nursery..."

"Really? I didn't know that!" James shook his head, amused.

"She had a lot of her mother in her."

Luca cast a sidelong glance at his mother. He slid down from his father's knee, walked right around the table, avoiding his mother and presented his drawing to his Grandfather.

"Thank you, Luca."

"You can put him in your bath," Luca said solemnly. "He might come alive."

"That would certainly put the cat among the pigeons!"

"What cat?" asked Luca, thoroughly confused.

Conversation eddied about him. He stood leaning against his Grandfather's knee, watching the adults eating and drinking.

He noticed how quiet his mother was. Presently he sidled behind his Grandfather's chair, positioning himself behind Antonia. He could sense her isolation in the midst of social chatter. Tentatively he reached out and surreptitiously touched her arm, withdrawing his hand before anyone might notice. Antonia turned her head and for a brief moment their eyes met. Luca retreated to his father's knee and accepted a scone.

"You should try one of Ragwort's brownies!" Dr Mikilari passed the plate to Antonia's father. "They're very fine indeed!"

***

James ran a bath and lifted Luca into the warm water. He undressed and climbed in after him, settling the little boy between his outstretched legs. Luca gave a great sigh of contentment as James squeezed a sponge over his shoulders. Antonia sat on the bath stool with a towel draped over her knees. She watched their interaction,

Luca happily splashing, patting his father's thighs, joining in the nursery rhymes which James was singing.

"Shall we let the bath water out now?" James suggested. "Get you dried and into your pyjies... and have a story in bed?"

He stood up, wrapping himself in a bath towel and lifted Luca out of the bath and onto Antonia's waiting lap. Luca gave a yelp of protest.

"It's alright, Luca! Daddy's here. Mummy's going to dry you tonight."

Antonia patted the rigid little body. Luca's anxious eyes never left James's face. Antonia also sought James's eyes. She felt as anxious as Luca! And yet...and yet...he had reached out and secretly touched her over tea. Luca allowed her to help him on with his pyjamas and then reached out for his father, relief flooding him as James gathered him up. Antonia glanced at James's bath towel.

"Aren't you going to get dressed?"

"Later." James smiled at her over Luca's head.

He settled Luca into his own bed.

Leaning over the cot, he felt Dominic's forehead. It was too warm, but the baby was peacefully sleeping, a smile on his small face.

***

As sleep enfolded her, James murmured:

"I thought you coped well today." He turned his head and gently kissed her. "Sleep well, my Antoni-ni."

***

Back at the hoispital, a nurse came to tell Antonia that her Granny was here with the baby. She ran across the grass and knelt down to hug her baby boy. He chortled to her happily.

"He's alright? No more sickness?:

The Witch shrugged. She continued weeding the border. Antonia bounced Dominic up and down to his great delight. When she released him, he toddled over to the flower bed and grabbed a handful of brightly coloured flowers.

"No! Dominic, no!"

Giving her his cherubic smile, he offered her the bouquet. Antonia accepted the flowers. She would put them in water later. She got to her feet and offered Dominic her hand. They walked slowly around the lawn…

"I nearly forgot!" The Witch handed her a paper bag. "Eleanor took this photo and posted it to you. But you'd gone back. James has found a frame for it." She watched while Antonia drew out the framed photograph of Dominic beaming at the camera. "Thought you'd like it!" The Witch looked rather pleased with herself.

"Dr Lyle will probably ask me where my photo of Luca is!"

"All in good time."

The Witch unfolded the pushchair, indicating that the visit was at an end. Antonia returned to her room, put the wilting flowers into a glass of water, arranged her photograph of Dominic on her bedside cabinet, and went in for Tea.

Without Max there was no one to play chess with, no one she could have a decent conversation with.

She returned to her room to fetch a book. At least she could read until it was time for the Evening meal. She had left her treasured photograph on her cabinet. She saw at once that it was lying face down on the floor, smashed.

"No! No! No!" Antonia screamed.

She was on the floor beating her hands into the shards of glass, screaming. A nurse came running and tried to pick her up. Antonia was incoherent in her distress.

"Look! You're bleeding! Let's get you to…"

Another nurse appeared. Between them they got Antonia out of her room and along the corridor. They began removing glass from her hands, debating if she would need stitches. Antonia struggled and cried. She was making so much noise in her distress that Dr Lyle left his Consulting Room to investigate.

"Alright, Antonia, calm down, Come with me."

He took her back to his room, sat her down, asked one of the nurses to bring tea and calmed her hysteria.

"Tell me what happened." He listened while she poured it out.

"It must be Nurse Maureen! She hates me! They all hate me! She stole my letter! Now, she's smashed my photo of Dominic! She did it deliberately!"

"Antonia, Nurse Maureen is on holiday. She's not even here. Tell me why you think the nurses hate you?"

"Because I tried to throw my little boys out of the

window. They have it in for me because they're all sorry for the young mother whose toddler got run over and killed."

"The nurses obviously know why you were admitted here. But they are trained to treat each patient as a person in need of help and support. None of them would deliberately smash your photograph. Now, let me look at your hands. You have gone to town on the glass, haven't you!"

Carefully he removed the splinters of glass, bandaged her hands, talked to her calmly and gently. She drank her tea.

Her hands hurt! She wondered how she would manage her cutlery for the evening meal.

"I want James! I want to go home!"

"You've been doing really well. It won't be long until we'll convert you into an outpatient, but we can't have these outbursts. What if this had happened at home?" He regarded her steadily.

"Don't *you* have a home to go to?"

"Indeed I do!" He smiled at her. "And I shall shortly be on my way. Night Sister will look after you. You may find some pain control helpful."

"I want to ask you something."

"Yes?"

"You said that the nurses know why I'm here. Do they know why all the patients are here?"

"Yes."

"So they knew why Max was here?"

Dr Lyle regarded her thoughtfully for a long moment.

"Why is it so important to you, Antonia?"

"He was my friend!"

"Sometimes there are things in our lives we would much prefer other people didn't know. You are very fortunate that with James you have someone who accepts you just as you are, knowing *everything* about you, and loving you more than you have ever been loved. Not many people have that." He stood up. "Now, I will see you tomorrow. Take care of those hands." He ushered her out and locked the door behind him.

***

"Do you have children?" Antonia enquired, as she sat down for her next session.

"I have two boys, both grown up. Why do you ask?"

"Well, in the beginning I just assumed you were here all the time. I didn't think of you as having a wife, a family, going home at the end of the day. You've sort of become a real person!"

"It sounds to me as if you're getting better." He smiled.

"James tells me that Luca allowed you to help bath him at the weekend?"

"He's very wary of me, but he is beginning to talk to me. We asked him if he'd like to move into another bedroom, and he told us he felt safer in the nursery because it has no windows. Do you think he'll ever forget?"

"Have you ever forgotten Juanita?"

"No."

"But he will move on, just as you have moved on.

James tells me that Luca has started at the local nursery school. Mornings only. Is there a reason you haven't mentioned it?"

"Sometimes I feel that you and James do so well telling each other everything about me, that you don't actually need me at all!"

Twenty-Three

From Monster Mummy to Music

Antonia was officially an outpatient now. At first she saw Dr Lyle on Mondays, Wednesdays and Fridays – transported by the Witch who spent the hour on her knees weeding the borders.

"Perhaps we should put your Granny on the payroll! The grounds have never been so well tended!"

"It gives her something to do while she waits for me."

"I see." Dr Lyle considered her over his fingertips. "So how have things gone over the weekend?"

"Luca got himself into a right state!"

"Tell me."

Sunday morning. Luca was half dressed when Antonia came in to see to Dominic.

"No!" protested Luca, backing away from her. "Go away!"

"It's alright, Luca." It clearly was not alright.

"No! No! You go! I want Daddy!"

"I've just come to get Mingo dressed."

"Daddy do! Daddy! Daddy!"

He started screaming, crouched into a little heap by his bed. Antonia retreated. Dominic stood up in his cot and began crying in sympathy. James emerged from the bathroom.

"I was only going to pick Dominic up!" Antonia defended herself.

"Let me pass" James said quietly. He pushed past Antonia and gathered Luca into his arms. "Alright, little man! It's alright. Daddy's here. We'll just finish getting you dressed and then Mummy can see to Mingo." He picked Dominic up and handed him to Antonia. "Clean nappy, I think!" He waited a moment until Antonia had taken Dominic to the bathroom, and then sat Luca down on his bed. "Mummy wasn't going to hurt you, treasure. Let's get your trousies on and then you can run down and tell Granny what you'd like for breakfast."

He helped Luca on with his shorts, gave him a reassuring cuddle and waited while Luca, rabbit in hand, started down the stairs. Then he went to reassure a rather shaken Antonia.

"He thinks I'm a monster!" Antonia said to Dr Lyle.

"I think he panicked. He just felt trapped because you were blocking his way of escape. It's quite scary when your child starts screaming like that." He gave Antonia a smile. "So what are you going to do differently next time?" Antonia shook her head. "You took him by surprise. Could you warn him you're there? Could you knock on his door and ask if you may come in to fetch Dominic? By the way, why is he called Mingo?"

"I don't think Luca could pronounce 'Dominic'... he calls Eleanor, Ellie."

"Remind me who Eleanor is?"

"She's Hugo's fiancée. Hugo is James's grown up son."

"How is Luca getting on at nursery?"

"Thriving! He comes home and chatters about what they've all been doing."

"That's good. I gather you and James play tennis in the afternoons and take Luca with you?"

"He fetches the stray balls. He seems to enjoy doing that."

"How is he sleeping? Is he still troubled by nightmares?"

"Yes. But not every night. James goes in to him and calms him down. Sometimes he takes him down to the kitchen and they have a warm drink..."

"I wonder how you would feel if we reduce your sessions to Mondays and Fridays?" Dr Lyle looked at her intently. "You are making such good progress."

"A lot of the time it doesn't feel like that."

"Well, shall we say, next Wednesday I'll do a home visit. Luca just does mornings at Nursery?"

Antonia nodded. "Right. I'll expect to be with you just after two.

***

Wednesday morning. They were gathered around the breakfast table. Luca, sitting next to Dr Mikilari watched as the old man drizzled syrup onto his porridge. Luca reached for the green tin.

" 'L' for Luca" he announced. " 'G' for Grandad, and 'S' for… sunshine!"

"Lyle's Golden Syrup," confirmed Dr Mikilari.

Luca traced the letters in spilled milk on the table top.

"Luca, please don't play with the spilled milk! Eat your cereal."

Luca stopped smiling. He glanced across the table at his mother, hearing the censure in her voice. He picked up his spoon. James noticed the droop in Luca's shoulders. Were table manners so important? The Witch raised an eyebrow and exchanged a meaningful look with James.

"Luca, d'you think Mingo might like to come to Nursery with us this morning?" Luca looked up. "We'll take him in his pushchair. If I push Mingo, would you hold Mummy's hand?"

"No! That's not fair! Mummy can push Mingo!"

"Mummy would like to hold your hand."

Luca scowled at Antonia. He pushed his cereal bowl away and hunched over the table sulking.

"Perhaps tomorrow?" suggested Antonia tentatively.

They set off for the nursery. Luca clutched James's hand, his small face looking like a thunder cloud. Antonia walked beside them, pushing Dominic. As they turned in at the gate, Luca tugged James's hand:

"You meeting me after?" he demanded, warily.

"Yes, Daddy'll be here." Antonia hid her disappointment. "Bye, Luca!"

But Luca scowled at her and said nothing.

James slipped an arm around Antonia's shoulders as they turned back.

"Would you like to go up to the park and let Dominic go on the swings?"

"What would happen, d'you suppose, if I went to meet him at lunch time on my own?"

"I'm rather afraid he'd throw a tantrum. I'll go. We've got Dr Lyle coming this afternoon. I'd prefer it if Luca's not upset."

***

There was a scrunching of tyres on the gravel as Dr Lyle pulled up. He sat for a moment observing the front of the cottage and the tangle of shrubs hemming in the small front garden. The cottage exuded an air of respectable neglect. James's Granny obviously did not regard the area as worth her gardening skills.

In the normal course of things, there was no gravelled drive – a dilapidated gate hung off its hinges under a tangled overhang of trees and unkempt shrubs, almost obscuring the cottage. A cottage which had ostensibly stood uninhabited and neglected for years. Today, however, it looked bright and cheerful because he was expected. Dr Lyle emerged from his car, locked it, and rang the doorbell. He waited. The door was opened by the Grandmother whom he had tried unsuccessfully to interview on several occasions.

"I'm very pleased to meet you, at last!" he said, offering his hand. The Witch observed his hand without taking it.

"Good afternoon," she said crisply. "You are expected. I'll take you through."

James and Antonia sat side by side on a sofa in the sitting room. Dominic had been put down for his rest. Luca had been building something with coloured wooden blocks. He looked up as Dr Lyle entered and took an armchair.

"Dr Lyle," announced the Witch unnecessarily.

"Dr Lyle Syrup! Luca exclaimed gleefully.

"Luca is learning to read," explained James. "He identified 'Lyle' on the syrup tin at breakfast."

Luca abandoned his blocks. He came and stood by the doctor's knee.

"You making Mummy better?"

"That's the idea." Dr Lyle studied the little boy. "How are you finding it, having Mummy home?"

"You know she tried to push me out of the window?" Luca said relentlessly.

"So I understand." Dr Lyle gave Luca his full attention. "How do you feel about that, now?"

Luca considered his reply. He looked the doctor straight in the eye.

"Tiger saved me."

"Tell me about your Tiger."

"He jumped on Mummy and knocked her down."

"Yes?"

"So I could crawl under the dressing table."

Dr Lyle looked at Antonia who was pretending to

be absorbed by a hair on her skirt. She radiated tension. James had placed a comforting hand on her arm. Dr Lyle turned his attention back to Luca.

"What have you been doing this morning?"

"I drew letters in the spilled milk and made Mummy cross. And then we went to nursery. Mummy wanted to hold my hand, but I didn't want to!"

"Luca, would you like to ask Granny if she'd make us some coffee – or would you prefer tea?" James glanced at Dr Lyle. "I'm afraid we're rather inveterate coffee drinkers!" Luca scampered off. Dr Lyle looked across at Antonia.

"How do you feel it's going?" he asked gently.

Antonia glanced at him and then, quickly, away. Her restless hands plucked at her skirt.

"It's not easy," she admitted.

"We try and do things together," James offered. "Luca's quite happy being our ball boy while we play tennis. At least he expresses what he's feeling very clearly, but he does panic very easily…"

"He told me he wished I'd go back to the hospital!"

Whatever Dr Lyle was about to reply was lost as the Witch breezed in with a tray of coffee, handing a cup to Dr Lyle.

"Biscuit?"

"No, thank you."

"I could have your biscuit?" suggested Luca, who had been entrusted with the plate of biscuits.

"That sounds an eminently sensible idea."

James lifted Luca onto his knee. The Witch offered Luca a mug of hot chocolate.

"Careful!" she admonished him. "You don't want to spill it on Daddy!"

Luca held the mug with both hands.

"Sprinkles!" he exclaimed. "You put sprinkles on my chocolate! Thank you, Granny!" He beamed up at her. The Witch acknowledged his evident delight. She handed James the plate of biscuits.

"Daffyn?"

James took a biscuit, breaking it in half. He and Luca always shared their biscuits. Beside him Antonia reached for her coffee and took a biscuit.

They made small talk. James gave Luca half another biscuit. They exchanged a small conspiratorial smile. Dr Lyle observed them. Their close bond did tend to exclude Antonia, he could see that very clearly.

"The more you can involve Antonia, the more progress you'll make." Dr Lyle engaged James who had put Luca down to draw a picture. He spoke quietly to Antonia for some time and then, replacing his coffee cup on the tray, he stood up.

"I'll see you on Friday as usual."

"I'll show you out." James stood up too.

They spoke for several minutes on the doorstep, by which time Luca had followed them out. Dr Lyle stooped to say goodbye to the child.

"This is for you!" Luca handed him the drawing he'd just completed.

"Ah yes!" Dr Lyle recognized himself in the little boy's portrait – his habitual pose as he regarded the onlooker over the steeple of his fingertips. "This is very good!"

They watched Dr Lyle reverse out of the drive and then returned to the sitting room.

"D'you think that went alright?" Antonia looked at James for reassurance.

"It will take time, Antoni-ni. There's no quick fix. But it'll get easier. Now, I expect Dominic's ready to join us. Why don't you change him and bring him down. Shall we take the boys down to the beach?"

James built sandcastles which Dominic took great delight in smashing. Antonia took Dominic to the edge of the sea and let him splash. She jumped him up and down in the waves, just as Luca was doing. Then Luca pulled all his clothes off and waded out.

"Hold on, Luca. I'll come in with you." James undressed and waded out after Luca.

Antonia watched them. Luca was a confident little swimmer. His co-ordination was good. James had suggested that they might begin teaching him to play tennis. He had also tentatively suggested to Antonia that she might invite Luca to start playing the clarinet. He already played chess with Dr Mikilari, but had not been willing to play with her. He liked to win, James explained. She watched James and Luca, thinking it was time they turned and swam back. She wished James would wear swimming trunks – she was uncomfortable with his nudity. They returned, splashing through the shallows. Luca was laughing, happy. James greeted her, grabbed a beach towel and began drying Luca who had begun shivering.

"Come on! We'll run! Warm you up! Race you to the ice cream kiosk!"

"James! Antonia shouted. "For goodness sake put a towel on, or something!"

James glanced at her in surprise. He fastened the towel around his waist and ran after Luca who was already some way ahead. Dominic toddled unsteadily after them. Antonia stood up, offering Dominic her hand and together they straggled along the beach and the promise of ice cream!

Headed paper in the waste paper basket, with the hospital's address, caught Antonia's eye. She pulled it out. It was a rather large bill, apparently paid. She frowned.

"James, do you have to pay for my sessions with Dr Lyle?"

"Actually, yes." He saw the paper in her hands. "We felt it would be helpful to have these extra sessions. The NHS only goes so far. But I don't want you to worry about it."

"I wasn't worried, I just didn't know. Can we afford it?"

"Mikey will take some more paintings to the Gallery. The important thing is that Dr Lyle is really helping you."

"I'm sorry."

"Why sorry?"

"Putting you to all this expense and trouble."

"I love you, Antoni-ni. Beside that, nothing is too much trouble!" He gathered her into his arms and kissed her. "I do love you!"

***

Luca was in the garden sitting beside his Grandfather on the bench. In the distance they could hear the sweet treble notes of Mlilka's flute.

"I like it when Uncle Mike plays his violin," Luca observed. "I would like to learn to play the violin."

Dr Mikilari seemed lost in thought. Luca looked up at him, wondering.

"Once upon a time I used to play," reflected Dr Mikilari. "My Grandfather taught me. I gave Michael my violin when he was ten. Didn't think I'd play again… Next time he comes, we'll ask him to bring you a small violin."

Luca absorbed the rudiments of playing with astonishing ease. He learned his scales. He learned to play 'Pieces for Beginners'. He listened carefully to the old Russian lullabies until, he could pick out the melodies for himself. Sometimes he seemed to listen to the wind in the tree tops and tentatively play music which no one had written.

Mlilka danced out of nowhere and accompanied him on her flute. Antonia helped him with his scales, encouraged him and began offering an accompaniment on her clarinet. They began bonding over their shared music. Michael came as many Sundays as he was free and taught Luca. He was an exacting teacher and set high standards.

"Luca has a real gift," he told James. "If he perseveres, Morton's will accept him and hone his playing."

"Just don't push him too hard," James cautioned. "He's not four until August."

He made sure that Luca had time to play as a child should. He also began teaching him to play tennis. Luca had a good eye and his co-ordination was exceptional. He clearly enjoyed playing – largely because there was no pressure. Now he not only acted as ball boy for his parents, but keenly observed their form. In the garden he played 'kick-about' football with Dominic who had a strong kick but was noticeably clumsy.

"Is his clumsiness because I shook him… back then…?" asked Antonia anxiously. Had she caused irreparable harm to her cheerful, chubby, affectionate boy?

"He doesn't have Luca's co-ordination, but I'd noticed that from well before your…breakdown. When you handed him something, he would grab and miss – much as he does now. He'll probably always be on the clumsy side, but that is not your fault, darling. I know you compare him with Luca, but Luca is exceptionally gifted. However, on the plus side, Dominic is happy and stable, and very affectionate.

Luca had blossomed. He was confident and self-assured. He was more than ready for school. He practised diligently and was making enormous strides under Michael's tuition. He had now happily moved into a bedroom of his own, leaving Dominic sole possession of the nursery. There were no more tantrums. He was no longer afraid of his mother. In her sharing of his music. she had, seemingly, become human!

Dr Lyle discharged her from his care.

Twenty-Four

To be or not to be?

September. Luca was now at school full time and had been moved up a year in recognition of his abilities. He quickly made friends and enjoyed the challenge of new subjects. Antonia had time and energy for her translating. James entertained Dominic and worked on his motor skills. They tried taking him up to the tennis courts to be their ball boy, but he was more of a hindrance than a help.

Late one sunny afternoon, Luca was sitting with his Grandfather, absorbed in a game of chess. Dominic lay spread-eagled on a rug, drowsing after an energetic play time with his father who had retreated to his studio to paint. Antonia had been to the doctor.

If the front door had not been so stiff and unyielding, she would have slammed it. She was so angry, she was tempted to start smashing crockery in the unoccupied kitchen. The Range, sensing this, kept quiet. Antonia badly needed to shout at someone. Where was James? He was going to bear the full brunt of her anger. She made her way to her study. Luca had obviously been sitting at her desk, drawing. A half completed picture of two people playing tennis had been abandoned, his crayons scattered on her desk top. She pushed open the dividing door to James's studio, almost incoherent with rage. He looked up, welcome stillborn on his lips.

"I hate you!" shouted Antonia, approaching him, intending to knock over his easel, smash his painting…

"What's wrong?" James carefully lowered his brush into a jar of turpentine, his deliberate calm infuriating her.

"You are! I hate you!"

He tried to draw her into his arms, but her flailing fists would not be gathered.

"What is it, Ni-ni? What's happened?"

"You promised!" she shouted. "You promised, and it's all your fault! I hate you!"

She kicked out at the easel which toppled over with a satisfying crash, taking the painting with it. Glad that she had disrupted and ruined his work, she threw him a malevolent glance. She had half a mind to kick the stack of completed canvasses.

"You'd better tell me what's the matter." James's voice was controlled but there was a definite edge to it. "Come through, and stop wrecking my work." He manoeuvred her through the door which led directly into the kitchen. The door closed behind them. The wall recomposed itself. There was no door. "Would a coffee help?"

"I'd probably throw it in your face, you bastard!"

"Sit down, Antonia, Take a deep breath." His voice was authoritative.

"Deep breath, my foot! Anyone would think this is an antenatal clinic!"

"Is it?" James's voice was very quiet. "Is that what this temper tantrum is about? You're pregnant?"

Antonia half rose from the chair he had pushed her onto.

"You promised there would only be two children! You knew I didn't want any more babies! You knew! It's all your fault! You promised! Well, I'll just take matters into my own hands! I'll get rid of it! It's my body and I don't want another incubus, thank you very much!"

James sat down. Very Quietly, Very controlled.

"I cannot allow you to do that"

"It isn't up to you! It's my body!"

"It's our child. I cannot allow you to murder my child."

"Should have thought of that before, shouldn't you!" She glared at him.

"You told me you were on the pill. Did you forget to take it?"

"I stopped taking it when you incarcerated me in that hospital. I hardly needed it there!" Her sarcasm was biting.

"But then you were fitted with a coil?" he remembered.

"It gave me the most horrible tummy ache. I got them to remove it."

"I see."

"I'm not having this baby, James!"

His voice was firm, but quiet.

"You've loved Dominic. You'll find you'll love this baby too. I would like us to have this baby. When does the doctor say it's due?"

"February. But I'm not having it! I told you!"

"And I hope you will."

"It's alright for you! You just use my body and expect me to bear the consequences!"

"That's not fair. I have never *used* you."

"Why are you so reasonable! Why don't you shout at me!"

"It wouldn't help. I understand how angry you are…"

"Bullshit! You do this to me and then you '*understand*' how angry I am! Too right, you bastard!" She was working herself into a tantrum.

"Would it help to talk to Dr Lyle?"

"I never want to see him again! You just collude and connive with him! You'll just tell him to make me change my mind!"

"You would need a psychiatrist's report."

"Oh, I would, would I? Don't you think I've done this before? I know my way around, James! And you won't be holding my hand at the abortion clinic, you can be sure of that!" Antonia glared at him. "Well, what have you got to say for yourself?"

"Antonia, if you do this, there will be no home for you here. You will lose the children and you will never see me again. Think very carefully."

He stood up and walked out into the courtyard.

"Two can play at that game!" Antonia yelled after him. "It's just empty threats. You'd never leave me!"

"He might" observed the Range, giving an apologetic cough. "Why not have a coffee and just sit quietly for a bit."

Antonia's throat was sore from all the shouting. She saw that there was already a mug of coffee awaiting her. She accepted the mug and began slowly sipping at it. The Range had thoughtfully added a spoonful of syrup which soothed her raw throat. Rather to her surprise she felt herself calming down. James wouldn't leave her. She was sure of that. But he was angry with her in his quietly controlled way, his anger cold and unforgiving. She would have preferred him to shout back, even to hit her...a proper fight. She thought about going back to his studio and wrecking that stack of finished canvasses – but when she sauntered back later, the connecting door was firmly shut.

Presently she walked across the courtyard into the Back Garden. There was Dominic, her cuddly, affectionate, bouncy boy. She sat down on the rug with him, noticing that he was eating daisies. He gave her a wide grin.

"Mummy!" he chortled.

On his usual bench, Dr Mikilari sat with Luca, engrossed in a game of chess. Of James there was no sign. Dr Mikilari observed Antonia over Luca's bent head. There had been a row of some sort. James had stormed across the garden, angrier than Dr Mikilari thought he had ever seen him. Antonia was wondering whether it was down to her to prepare their high tea, when the

Witch blew into the garden, announcing that tea was ready. Antonia picked Dominic up and sat him astride her hip. She looked across at Dr Mikilari.

"Are you coming?"

"Most certainly we are! Tea sounds most excellent! Shall we leave the game there, Luca?"

They sat around the kitchen table. Luca smiled at his mother.

"Did you have a nice time, Mummy?" he asked, aware that she had been out.

"Did I hell!" Antonia's face was a thundercloud.

She passed Dr Mikilari's mug of tea to him with shaking hands.

"Are you going to have tea?" she asked Luca. "Or d'you want juice?"

For a moment Luca considered what was the right answer – the answer his mother wanted. He appealed to the Witch who planted a beaker of orange juice in front of him.

"Where's Daddy?" he asked as Antonia knew he would.

"Sulking" Antonia answered him.

"But where is he?"

"I have no idea."

Luca looked at his mother. She was angry about something. He remembered that he had sat at her desk to draw a picture. She always kept her desk so tidy. Was she angry because he had left the picture and his crayons on her desk.

"Sorry, Mummy." He said.

"What have you got to be sorry about?" she snapped. Luca quailed.

"I left my crayons on your desk instead of tidying them away. I'm sorry, Mummy!"

"I don't think your mother's upset about your crayons, Luca" Dr Mikilari said comfortingly.

But Antonia glared stonily at her penitent son who was such a Daddy's boy. Luca inched closer to his Grandfather.

"Mummy! Mummy! Mummy!" chortled Dominic, grabbing at his food. He beamed at her. Luca watched, knowing that if *he* had grabbed his food like that, his mother would have scolded him. He hunched over his plate, eating tidily, casting anxious glances at her. The meal continued in silence.

Dr Mikilari sat back and smiled at the Witch.

"That was very welcome!" he said.

The Witch began gathering the plates, clearing the table.

"What about Daddy? Won't he want his tea when he comes back?"

"He's had sour grapes" the Witch remarked. "Very sour!" She exchanged a look with Antonia. "You can help me wash up, Luca. Bring a chair up to the sink. Be useful!"

Luca quite often helped wash up. Today he was relieved that for the time it would take him to help Granny, he could avoid his mother in the mood she was in.

"And then you can do your practice" Antonia directed him, scooping up Dominic and taking him up for his bath.

Luca waited until she was out of earshot.

"I don't want Mummy bathing me!" he implored his Granny.

"No surprise there!" she murmured.

***

Leaving his clothes on the beach, James had swum far out, allowing strenuous exercise to dissipate his anger. The tide was going out and he relished the roughness of the waves as they tossed him up and flung him down. The huge expanse of living water gave him a sense of proportion. He swam until he was exhausted and finally turned for the shore. There was no sign of the shore… just a huge expanse of sea which tugged at him as he tried to fight his way back against the tide. If he allowed himself to drift, the tide would remorselessly take him further and further out. He no longer had the strength to swim strongly enough to battle the tide. Well, he reflected wryly, he was already dead, so he could hardly drown! Or could he?

I need a boat. I need rescuing. I'm not going to make it…He gave up and let himself drift. Antonia had won. But then he thought of Luca, the little son he loved more than life.

"Foolish boy, Daffyn!" He heard his Grandmother's voice in his ear.

"Granny!" he whispered. "Help me!"

He came to, lying sprawled on the beach, utterly exhausted, but safe. He turned his head, looking for his

Grandmother, but the beach was deserted. His clothes lay where he'd left them, the beach towel neatly folded beside them. It had been late afternoon… It was now night. A bright moon illuminated the beach. He lay, too exhausted to move.

A small pyjama-clad figure approached and sat down beside him. Luca should have been in bed, fast asleep.

"You went out too far, Daddy."

"I did."

"Were you scared?"

"A bit. The tide was taking me further and further out."

"Shall you get dressed now?"

"In a bit. I'm so, so tired."

"Mummy was very upset about something!"

"I know."

"I thought I must have upset her: I left my crayons all over her desk. But Grandad said it wasn't anything I'd done."

"No. Mummy went to see the doctor. What he told her made her angry."

Luca waited for his father to explain, but James seemed disinclined to say more.

"I think you should get dressed and come home." Luca tried.

"I expect you're right." James sat up, reaching for his clothes.

They walked very slowly through the orchard, James stumbling in his weariness. The hammock offered its emptiness invitingly. James sank gratefully into it.

"That's Grandad's hammock" Luca mentioned, doubtfully.

"He doesn't need it right now."

"Are you going to sleep?"

There was no reply as James fell into a deep, dreamless slumber. Luca stood watching him. Eventually he walked back to the kitchen and found his Grandfather asleep in the rocking chair (that wasn't there)

"Daddy's sleeping in your hammock."

"Quite so" murmured Dr Mikilari, rousing. He patted his knee. "Do you want to sleep with me tonight…what's left of tonight?"

***

"Good morning!" The Range greeted the world. "Coffee for sleepy-heads?"

Luca sat up. He had slept on Grandad's knee. Daddy was out in the garden, asleep in the hammock.

"I could take coffee out to Daddy?" he suggested.

James roused, surprised to find himself in the hammock. He needed a bath! He needed coffee! Walking carefully across the grass Luca carried a mug of coffee, trying not to spill any.

"Coffee, Daddy! Did you sleep alright? Grandad and I slept in the rocking chair."

James sat up and swung his legs over the side of the hammock. He took the mug from Luca and drank gratefully.

"Shall you come in, now, Daddy?"

"I need a bath. What time is it?"

"Early. I guess you could have a bath. Granny hasn't started breakfast."

They went in and crept silently up the stairs. James ran a bath and sank gratefully into the warm water. Luca waited to be invited to join him. But James's eyes closed.

"Daddy! Are you falling asleep again?"

James sat up and shook his head. All he wanted to do was sleep. He lay back down, sinking into a profound sleep. After watching him for a while, Luca slipped out and went to dress for school.

Antonia was surprised to find James asleep in the bath when she came to change Dominic's nappy. At two and a half, he showed no sign of continence – however often she sat him on his potty.

"Daddy! Daddy!" Dominic greeted his father with a happy shout. James did not stir. Antonia left him in the bath. She dressed Dominic and took him down for breakfast.

With Dominic in his pushchair, she walked Luca to school. He was very quiet. She left him at the school gate. He said Goodbye to her and went in happily enough. Antonia did not feel inclined to go home and face James. She took Dominic up to the park and played with him. Presently they were joined by other mothers who had dropped off an older child at school. They sat and chatted.

An uneasy truce existed between James and Antonia for several days. They were polite to each other but kept their distance. It was tacitly agreed that Antonia would take Luca to school and James would collect him. James spent the day in his studio, painting. The door between his studio and her study remained firmly shut. Antonia made it clear that she did not want to share her bed with James. He moved into the double room that Hugo and Eleanor used when they visited. Luca took advantage of his father's proximity and slipped into bed with him. No one explained to him what the disagreement was about. James took him up to the tennis court. Antonia did not come. Luca practised his violin reluctantly. He was miserable.

"Don't you love Mummy anymore?" he asked sadly.

"I'm not sure" James answered honestly.

"How can you not be sure?"

"I can't explain."

"Grandad?" Luca lacked concentration for their game of chess. "Do you think Daddy and Mummy will ever be friends again?"

"That's something they'll have to sort out between them."

Luca helped his Grandmother wash up. She noticed that he was crying quietly into the washing up bowl.

"They'll sort it out, one way or another" she said briskly. "Your mother has a decision to make. She has only a couple of weeks if she's going to act."

Luca was aware how tense his father had become. He didn't smile. And while he was never impatient with Luca, there was none of the easy camaraderie and fun. And sometimes when he held his mug, his hands shook. Michael stayed away.

On Monday, after a fraught weekend, Antonia announced at breakfast.

"I'm going up to London to see my father."

James studied her face in silence. Was this visit to escape the painful impasse at home? Or was this the pre-arranged visit to the abortion clinic?

There was a certain hostility in her expression as she added.

"I might stay over at the flat."

James said nothing. Whatever he might say was likely to inflame the situation. Antonia glanced at him, knowing what he was thinking and deriving perverse pleasure from his silent anguish.

"You can take Luca to school."

Silently James acknowledged her decision. The colour had drained from his face. He did not offer to accompany her. He watched her as she picked up Dominic, kissed his chubby little face and then wiped his slobbery oatmeal kiss from her cheek. He was such an easy child. He didn't cry when she left him, but always greeted her exuberantly on her return. For a brief moment James laid his hand on her arm.

"Take care" he murmured, his eyes searching her face. Then he turned away and held out his hand to Luca. "Let's be going, little man!" he said huskily.

"Will you watch Dominic until James comes back?" Antonia asked the Witch.

"Possibly" The Witch sounded disinterested.

James did not wave her off, expressing the hope that she would have a nice time with her father. He simply set off for school with Luca.

***

The morning stretched interminably. James worked on Dominic's motor skills and then played ball with him. Dominic thoroughly enjoyed kicking his ball, but he could never catch a ball thrown to him. When he tired, James sat with his Grandfather and watched Dominic happily eating flowers. However, he did not care for the dandelion sap.

"You are such a nasty little flower!" he said, in exact imitation of Antonia scolding Luca. It was the first time he had managed a whole sentence! James sat up alertly. Presently he went into the house to find Luca's word recognition picture books. He sat on the grass with his younger son, aware that Dominic knew what the pictures represented.

He tried coaxing him to repeat the words after him.

It occurred to him that Antonia was reinforcing his baby behaviour rather than encouraging him to develop to his full potential. She was very comfortable with her affectionate, cuddly baby. Leaving Dominic with the books, He walked down through the orchard torturing himself with his anxiety over the day's outcome. He could not eat lunch. Dominic ate hungrily, joyfully, messily.

"Nice!" he pronounced. He looked at his father for approval. "Mingo good boy!"

"Grandad, I'm off to fetch Luca from school. We might be a while. Would you keep an eye on Mingo for me?"

It was not an onerous task. Dominic was perfectly happy, kicking his ball and then running after it.

James collected Luca. They walked a little way up the lane and stepped aside into a pentagram scratched into the roadside dirt. Brascombe Woods. They walked in silence, listening to the wind in the tree tops, noticing woodland flowers, recognizing bird calls, pausing to stroke the bark of favourite trees. Luca watched his father and waited. They came to the great fallen oak and sat down. James took a chocolate biscuit from his pocket, unwrapped it, broke it in half and offered half to Luca. He had not spoken a word. Luca munched his biscuit thoughtfully.

"Are you sad, Daddy?" he asked breaking the silence.

"M'm."

Luca waited for his father to tell him why he was so sad, but James simply sat there, staring into the distance.

"Can I hug you better?" There was no response. After a long silence Luca asked. "Is it about the baby?"

"What baby?" James jerked up, startled by the question His voice unnaturally sharp.

"The baby Mummy doesn't want." Luca looked up at his father. "He's called Fox."

"How did you know?"

"Just did."

"Nobody told you?"

"No."

"Luca, I don't know if we're going to have this baby. I think Mummy is…I think that's why she's gone to London." His fists were clenched and his face drawn. Luca digested what he heard.

"Is Mummy going to throw the baby out of the window?"

"Something like that!" James voice was so bitter!

"You'll have to send her back to the hospital."

As if he had not heard, James continued:

"You see, Grandad and I believe all life is precious and no one has the right to kill – especially an unborn baby who hasn't had the chance to love and be loved, to grow, to enjoy life…to see and touch, to feel, and hear…and experience all the wonder and joy of living. It's why we don't kill any of the little creatures in the garden."

"But we eat them!"

"You mean meat? But Granny doesn't kill them – they're already dead. She goes out in the mornings looking for animals that have been run over and killed in the night."

"So, didn't you tell Mummy it's wrong to kill the baby?"

"Of course I did. But she was too angry to listen!"

"Is Mummy coming home?"

"I expect so."

"Will you still love her?"

"I don't know, Luca. I really don't know!"

Luca thought of all the times he had overheard his father say, 'I love you, my Antoni-ni'… the way he looked at her with so much love in his face… the way he held her close and kissed her…and how sometimes he took her hand and dropped a kiss in her palm. He knew his Daddy loved her. It would break his heart. Tears ran down his cheeks. James picked him up, and sat him on his knee, cradling him. It was appalling that he had unburdened himself to Luca, like this. He laid his face against Luca's head, breathing in his sweet familiar smell. He was making Luca's hair wet with his tears, but Luca stoically forbore to mention it.

Antonia met her father at his club. He thought she looked strained.

"Is everything alright, my dear?" he enquired over coffee.

Antonia studied her father's face.

"Remind me why you didn't have any more children?"

"Your mother didn't want any more."

"Did you?"

"I'd hoped for a son. Most men want a son."

"So…did you try for a son?"

Cyril Throgmorton's fingers played with his teaspoon. Shadows moved across his face.

"Your mother did get pregnant. I rather hoped it would be a boy. But she arranged a termination…" His hands clenched and unclenched. "It would have been a boy."

"That's sad."

"Well, it's a long time ago."

"And after that" pursued Antonia. "Was everything alright between you?"

Her father looked at her for a long time, sensing that the conversation was somehow important to her.

"It was the end of an… intimate relationship" he said carefully. "I moved into a separate room. Your mother" he paused delicately, "Your mother had a number of liaisons. She was discreet."

"And you? Did you have other…liaisons?"

"One or two. As I said, It's a long time ago."

"So, would you say you had a happy marriage, all in all?"

"As happy as most. But nothing like the relationship you have with James. You are blessed with so much love."

"But perhaps not for much longer."

"What?"

Antonia sat up straight and looked her father in the eye.

"We have two boys. James understood very clearly that I didn't want any more. He promised."

In fact, James had never made such a promise. But she had persuaded herself that he had -

"And now I find I'm pregnant and I really, really don't want another baby. I've told James that I've made an appointment to have an abortion."

Long years in the Diplomatic Service enabled Cyril Throgmorton to keep his feelings to himself.

"And what did James say?" he asked carefully.

"He's threatened to leave me. He said I would never see him again, and he would take the boys."

"Oh dear!" said Mr Throgmorton inadequately. "And what are you going to do?"

"On a practical level, I have my flat. I have my translating. I can support myself. But I don't want to lose Dominic! He's such a happy, cuddly baby. I don't think I can bear to lose him!" Angrily, she brushed unwanted tears away.

"Do you still love James?"

"I love him and I hate him!"

Antonia accepted her father's starched white handkerchief as her tears overwhelmed her.

"To put it in a nutshell, abortion will cost you your marriage. If you go through with the pregnancy, you will have James's love and support – and he does love you, my dear. Make no mistake about that. You will have your home and your boys. To lose all that is a terrible price to pay."

"And having a baby I don't want is a terrible price to pay in order to keep James and my boys! And that child will grow up knowing I resent him. Mother never really wanted me. No, don't argue! She told me so, herself."

"James isn't Catholic, is he?"

"No. His grandfather is Jewish. Why?"

"Well Catholics are brought up to believe abortion is wrong. Is that what James thinks?"

"He said I'd be murdering his child. I don't see that.

I mean, it's just a collection of cells – not a human being."

"James is a doctor. Maybe he views all life as sacred."

"You're probably right." Antonia sounded defeated.

"Well, I can't pretend to advise you, my dear. It's a drastic step…"

"Not that drastic! People do it all the time. I should just have gone ahead and done it, without telling James!"

Her father said nothing.

"I was just so angry when I found out! I went home and shouted at James and we had the most acrimonious row. We both said things we really didn't mean. And then James took himself off and nearly drowned himself."

"That would have been such a tragedy."

"Perhaps" Antonia gave a hollow laugh. "It would have solved this problem!"

"Antonia, my dear…" Mr Throgmorton seemed at a loss for words. "As I see it, you are pregnant. You don't want the baby. James does want the baby. And although he loves you, he is threatening to break up your marriage if you go through with the abortion. Of course, he may not. I expect you have considered whether this was a threat in the heat of the moment? The question you have to consider is whether it is worth risking everything – and it is a very real risk. Or whether, if James means as much to you as I think he does, you could go through with the pregnancy."

"It might all break up, whatever I do."

"Yes, there is that."

"It's my body! Don't I have the right to…"

"Yes, you have the right. But making that choice will have consequences you may regret for the rest of your life." He cleared his throat to indicate that the conversation was at an end. "Now, let's go and have a nice meal and you can tell me about the boys."

***

The family were having a late tea in the kitchen. Dr Mikilari enquired whether they were expecting Antonia.

"She may be staying at her flat" James said wretchedly.

"In that case we won't wait."

The Witch served up plates of toast heaped with baked beans. She looked at James.

"You haven't eaten anything for two days." She chided him.

"I can't." James reached for Luca's plate and cut up his toast for him. Luca adored baked beans.

Dominic had eschewed his cutlery and was grabbing handfuls of beans. He had tomato paste smeared all over his face and down his jersey.

"Good thing your mother's not here to see how much you're enjoying yourself!" remarked the Witch.

"Daddy and I went for a walk in Brascombe Woods" Luca mentioned.

"I wondered where you'd got to." Dr Mikilari looked at his older grandson. "I was expecting a game of chess."

James let the conversation wash over him. He felt utterly drained. He drank the mug of tea which the Witch had placed in front of him. The worst was simply not knowing whether Antonia was coming home…and what her decision – and the fate of their baby – and whether their relationship would survive…could survive. He did not even register the crunch of tyres on the gravel.

Antonia came in. She looked tired and strained. Luca looked up expectantly. James hardly dared look. Dominic gave a roar of delight and held out his arms in excited welcome. Antonia glanced at him with a lurch of mother-love. He was going to need a bath!

"Tea?" The Witch filled a mug.

"Yes. Thank you."

Across the table she met James's eyes. He sat very still. There was not a flicker of emotion on his face. He looked ill. Antonia took a deep breath:

"We're going to have a baby."

"We're calling him Fox" added Luca.

"I was thinking Toby would be a good name!" Dr Mikilari remarked, wiping a slice of bread and butter around his plate.

"Where did that come from!"

Dr Mikilari looked at Antonia mischievously.

"To be, or not to be! Isn't that what this week has been about?"

James pushed back his chair and stood up. He came shakily around the table and drew Antonia into his arms. He was trembling.

"I was so afraid you wouldn't come home!" he whispered brokenly.

"Let the girl sit down, Daffyn! She's had a long day and she's tired. But nothing that a pot of tea won't cure!"

James pulled out a chair for her and stood behind her, a hand resting on her shoulder. Stooping he pressed his face into her hair. Tears ran down his face. Luca thought about telling him that he was making her hair all wet, but, it seemed, his mother didn't mind. Dominic banged the spoon he wasn't using on his high chair. He threw his plate on the floor. Dr Mikilari raised a tolerant eye and smiled fondly at the Witch.

"Alright, Mingo! I know you want Mummy all to yourself. Just let me have my tea and then we'll get you into the bath"

"I'll help Granny wash up" offered Luca. "And then I'll do my practice."

Antonia drained her mug. She pushed back her chair, gave James a small smile and picked up her messy son. James made to follow her, then changed his mind. She probably wanted to lavish love and cuddles over bath-time. He could wait. He went through to the sitting room and collapsed onto the sofa. When Luca peeped in he saw that his father had fallen into an exhausted slumber.

Luca finished his practice. He brought his violin into the sitting room and played the Russian lullabies he had perfected. James opened his eyes and smiled at him with great tenderness.

"That's beautiful! Did you play that specially for me?"

Luca nodded. He looked at his father. The little sleep had done him good. He no longer looked so haggard.

"Would you like to bath with me?" he enquired, trying to sound casual.

"Let's do just that" James smiled at him.

They went upstairs hand in hand. James ran a bath. He undressed. He seemed to have been wearing the same clothes for …how long? Luca waited for him to get into the bath first and then climbed in, settling himself between his father's legs. He gave a deep sigh of contentment.

"This is so nice, Daddy! Just you and me!" James sponged warm water over Luca's shoulders. "You and Mummy going to be alright now?" And when his father did not answer. "When's Fox coming?"

"February."

"How old will I be then?"

"How many birthdays do you have in a year?"

"Just one?"

"And how old were you on your last birthday?"

"Four."

"So, in February you'll be four and a half."

"Okay."

"And Mingo will be three."

"And will you still love me best?"

"What makes you think I do?"

"Well, Mummy loves Mingo. She sort of lights up when she sees him. So, I thought it would be only fair if you loved me best."

"I see."

James sounded very serious, but he was smiling. Luca swivelled round to search his father's face. After a moment he said thoughtfully:

"Perhaps you love Mummy best?"

"Love is love, Luca. I don't love you less if I love Mummy. And I won't love you less if I also love Fox."

"I just hoped you might love me best." Luca sounded hurt.

"I don't measure 'best'. The question is, do I love you enough?"

Luca wriggled pleasurably against his father, savouring his father's hands on his torso and shoulders.

"Guess so! And" – as an afterthought – "You love Mingo too."

"Indisputably."

As James towelled him dry, Luca enquired, "Are you sleeping with Mummy tonight?"

"If she'll have me!"

***

For a long time they simply held each other. It was enough. His arms were round her. His fingers gently caressing her cheek. He loved her. She was home! Finally, he kissed her and began to talk.

"My Antoni-ni, you are loved, honoured and so precious to me."

"Honoured?"

"You took a very difficult decision today. I am so proud of you."

"I didn't want to lose you. I couldn't imagine living without you. But I still don't want the baby."

"That's why it was such a courageous decision."

He kissed her again. He wanted to make love. The trauma of the last week slid away. Nothing had changed, she thought. She still did not want another baby, but James loved her…and February was a long way off. There was, however, something she needed to say:

"I did tell you I'd done it before" she said hesitantly.

"I don't need to know" James said quietly. "It was long before I met you. It isn't relevant."

He kissed her and for a while they lay quietly.

"You know" said Antonia a while later. "I did wonder why my parents were so remote with each other. My father told me today that my mother didn't want another baby after me, but she got pregnant, and he hoped it would be a boy. He wanted a son. She went ahead and had a termination. It would have been a boy."

"That was hard."

"He said, after that, he moved into a separate bedroom. It was the end of their sex life, but they stayed together.

I guess divorce wasn't the done thing then."

"So, you decided to go through with this pregnancy rather than sacrifice our love life?"

"I didn't want to end up with the sort of marriage my parents had. And I didn't know whether you were serious about telling me I would never see you again. I didn't dare risk it. Would you have done that? Would you have taken the boys and gone? Would you have done that to me?"

"I don't know. I asked myself if I would ever be able to forgive you if you killed my son before he could even taste life. I love you, Antoni-ni. But could I love you enough to live with that?"

Antonia reached out and stroked his face. She had seen what the week had done to him.

"Perhaps" she said lightly. "You'd have been the one needing Dr Lyle Syrup!"

Twenty-Five

"Tramping in the rain on muddy moors"

Luca sat beside Dr Mikilari, his reading book open on his lap:

> *"Heckledy, Speckledy, my black hen,*
> *She lays eggs for gentlemen.*
> *Sometimes nine and sometimes ten*
> *Heckledy, Speckledy, my black hen."*

Luca looked up at his Grandfather and smiled.

"She sounds a nice hen!"

"Oh, hens have personalities. One can get very fond of hens."

"Where do hens come from?"

"Well, you can buy them as chicks, or you can offer a home to old Battery hens that have stopped laying…and let them live out their days in peace."

"Could we do that?"

"You'd have to ask your father."

Over tea, Luca enquired.

"Why hens, Luca? Most little boys would ask for a rabbit or a guinea pig or a kitten?"

"We already have a cat. No, I'd like to offer a home for old Battery hens who need to be loved!"

"Hens are messy" objected Antonia.

"Not free-range hens" Dr Mikilari mentioned.

Antonia looked at James.

"Who's going to look after them?"

"I will" Luca told her. "I'm going to love my hens. They might lay eggs for me when they feel better."

"I remember how caring for a pet turned Jake around. His class had pet hamsters which the children took turns looking after. We bought him two pet rabbits of his own. He loved his rabbits… I don't see why Luca shouldn't have pet hens, if that's what he's set his heart on."

"Be sensible, James! Luca's only four. How d'you expect him to look after hens?"

"I daresay I could help" suggested Dr Mikilari.

"How many hens are you thinking of, Luca?"

"Five."

"And one for the pot!" added the Witch.

"No, Granny! They're not for eating!"

A couple of weeks later when Luca was still asking about his hens, Hugo and Eleanor drove down with five bedraggled hens in a crate. Hugo carried the crate through to the Back Garden and released them.

"This one's black" he pointed out to Luca. "Is this Heckledy Speckledy?"

"And that one's called Raggle-Taggle."

"Yes, she is a bit bedraggled! She will grow her feathers back. I don't think they're very kind to Battery hens. What's that one called?"

"Henny-Penny."

"You do give your hens nice names! What about that one?"

"That's Toby."

"Uh, Toby is normally a boy's name. We've got lady hens here."

"Maybe she's called Tabitha? And the last one is Eleanor."

"Brilliant! I think Eleanor will be chuffed to have a chicken named after her!"

"What do we do with them now?"

"Just love them and let them be. They'll explore the garden and scratch up some earth. It's probably the first time they've ever been out of a cage. Later we'll feed them. We brought some chicken feed with us."

Hugo went to join the rest of the family and acquainted Eleanor with the honour of having a chicken named after her. Luca stayed in the garden, wandering round after his hens, talking to them...

Presently Eleanor came out to be introduced to her hen.

She had Dominic astride her hip. Luca glanced at his younger brother disparagingly.

"He'll go to anyone. He not very discriminating."

"Wow" That's a long word for a little fellow!"

"I like long words!"

In the Sitting Room Hugo was suggesting to James and Antonia that he and Eleanor would love to look after the little boys for a week.

"We thought you might like to have a break before the baby arrives…and obviously you want to be home over Christmas. I know it was something of a disaster when you thought Granny was going to look after the boys, that time… What d'you think?"

"I think it's a very generous offer. The boys know you and are always excited when you come." James glanced at Antonia. "What d'you think, Ni-ni?" His eyes held hers. She could see how much the idea appealed to him.

"Tramping in the rain on muddy moors?"

"The weather can be beautiful in late October!"

"There's always plenty to do in York, even if it does rain. It's a beautiful city."

Antonia looked at Hugo.

"Et tu, Brute?"

"Would you rather just stay home?" James asked, his voice tinged with disappointment. "I thought it was a wonderful opportunity…"

"The things I do for you!"

"Shall I leave you to think about it?" Hugo diplomatically withdrew. "I don't think Antonia's very keen" he said to Eleanor.

***

After lunch Luca and James washed up.

"What would you think if Hugo and Eleanor looked after you two while Mummy and I had a little holiday?"

Luca turned round from the sink and considered his father.

"When?"

"Soon. Before winter."

"Before Fox comes?"

"That's the idea."

"You promise to come back?"

"Absolutely! It's only for a week. And Grandad will be around."

"Okay." Luca bent over the washing up bowl. He was clearly not enthralled with the prospect. "Uncle Mike come on Sunday?" he asked wistfully.

"I'm sure he will if we ask him." James scooped Luca into his arms, hugging him. "What is it? What's bothering you, my little man?"

Luca swallowed. He wound his wet arms around his father's neck and held him tightly.

"Last time you went away..." He left the sentence unfinished.

"That's why Hugo and Eleanor will look after you and Mingo. It won't be like last time."

"I was so, so frightened!"

"I know! I think it's important for Mummy to have this little holiday. I want her to feel happy about the baby." James cast about for a distraction. "Hugo would take you up to the tennis courts... Why don't we lend him Mummy's racquet and go up this afternoon?"

"Okay." Luca unwound his arms from James's neck and slid down. "We'll finish washing up and go."
He brightened, clambered back up onto his chair and attacked a messy saucepan with gusto.

Hugo gave James a good match while Luca acted as their ball boy and observed how hard and fast the two men played. When it was his turn he told Hugo:

"I don't want you slamming those balls at me, like you did to Daddy!"

"Why don't I watch you play with Daddy first?"

***

It appeared that Hugo and Eleanor were expecting to stay the weekend. Antonia and Eleanor took Dominic in his pushchair down to the little supermarket for extra provisions. And then up to the little park so Dominic could play on the swings and in the sandpit.

"He's such an easy child" Antonia mentioned.

"He's gorgeous! I can't wait to have one of my own!"

"Well, you can practice on the pair of them, if we go away."

"Don't you want to go?"

"I really didn't want another baby."

"Maybe Hugo and I could adopt it!"

Antonia smiled at Eleanor. It was the first time she'd smiled since they'd arrived.

"Thanks! But James would never agree. He really wants this baby – as if two's not enough!"

***

For the first four days the weather was sunny, although chilly round the edges. James and Antonia enjoyed a leisurely breakfast before driving up to the moors. She watched the transformation in his very being. He was happy. He strode out, drinking in the fresh, crisp air. She was glad, for his sake, that they had come. He was considerate of her, gentle, tender and companionable. The late October days were shorter. They had not so long to be out before dusk gave way to dark. But they returned to a warm welcome, tea and buns…and a cooked evening meal. They were the only guests and the landlady made a fuss of Antonia. After their meal they relaxed in front of a log fire and read or investigated the plentiful supply of board games and jigsaws.

"This is new!" James exclaimed, pulling out a yellow board and associated box. "It's called 'Touring England'. Why don't we try this?"

Antonia extracted the leaflet detailing the rules. James opened the board, set up the shaker and dice, picked up the pile of small purple cards and dealt seven purple cards each.

Antonia delighted over the miniature antique cars which were their counters. She chose her car and waited while James organized his cards. She looked at the towns she had to visit and planned her route.

"Oh dear! Look what I've given myself." James shook his head. "I've got Newcastle, up north. Then Penzance and Llandudno … Brighton, Dover and Nottingham. What have you got?"

"Guess what! I've got York!"

James planned his route, shook the dice and set off. Antonia sailed through her towns and appeared to be winning while James was stuck at a ferry for which he had to throw a six. He had only achieved four of his seven destinations when Antonia was en route for her final city. To enter a town or city the exact number had to be thrown. Antonia's final destination was Coventry. She was within five squares. James secured Brighton and shortly after, Dover, while Antonia moved forward two squares. She needed a three. James set off for Newcastle. Antonia threw a six. James headed up the board. Antonia threw a four. James threw a six and a five. Antonia threw a one and inched forward. James was making progress. Antonia threw fours and fives. She needed a two.

"This is so frustrating!" she complained. "I should have won!"

"I expect you will. You only have two squares and you're home and dry."

"I know! But I can't throw a two, or even a one!"

In the end, James won. Much to Antonia's chagrin.

"I'm sorry, Antoni-ni!" He squeezed her hand. "Perhaps we'll play chess tomorrow. No dice, just strategy and cunning."

"You're out of luck: there isn't a chess set. I looked."

"Perhaps Luca would enjoy 'Touring England' – it would certainly help his geography."

"I hope they're alright."

"I'm sure they are. With Hugo and Eleanor, they'll be absolutely fine."

"D'you know what Eleanor told me? She'd picked up

Dominic and Luca said that he'd go to anyone, he's not very discriminating!"

James chuckled appreciatively.

"Perhaps he'll be a writer, like you."

They had an early night. Antonia lay, encircled in James's arm. The bed was very comfortable. James kissed her very gently. She felt like telling him she wouldn't break.

"May we make love, my Antoni-ni? Permission to enter Coventry?"

"Only if you throw a six!"

James reached under the pillow and found a stray sock.

"Not a six, but a sock! Will that do?"

Antonia laughed.

***

The following day was wet. They spent the day in York: the museum, York Minster, the bookshop, lingering in a coffee shop. They bought toys for the children, presents for Hugo and Eleanor…and a boxed set of 'Touring England'…and after lunch they went to the cinema.

It was still raining the next day. Steady, unremitting rain. They sat over breakfast, hoping the rain would ease. It was their last day. Antonia knew how much James wanted to be out there on the moors.

"I'm afraid it's set in for the day!" the landlady said as she cleared their table. "You're welcome to stay in."

"You actually want to be out there in the rain, don't you?" Antonia recognized.

James didn't reply. She could see the yearning in his face. It was the last day for who knew how long. The baby would be barely six months by next summer. Too little to be left.

"I guess we'll stay in…" James said. "Unless you want to go home a day early?"

"Let's go out on the moors. Goodness knows when we'll be able to come again. Does it matter if we get wet? We can have a hot shower when we come back."

"Are you sure?" He lit up.

If it meant so much to him, she could put up with getting wet through.

The rain was relentless. Antonia clenched her fists inside her pockets and trudged along beside him. James had his face raised to the rain, soaking up the very essence of the day, emanating happiness. Antonia hunched into her waterproof which was fiendishly allowing rain to penetrate the seams. Her boots squelched. Her legs ached. She was determined not to complain. Finally, after two hours, James stopped.

"My poor darling! You're hating this! Shall we turn back?"

"Yes please!"

"My Antoni-ni, you should have said!" He pulled her into his arms and kissed her wet face. "I'm sorry! What a brute!!"

"No, you needed to come. If we'd gone home early, like you suggested, you'd have regretted it. You'd have been so disappointed."

He touched gentle fingers to her face.

"I love you, my Antoni-ni. I love you so much! Thank you for giving me this holiday. Thank you for Fox. Tomorrow we'll go home and I'll take care of you and look after you… We'll be fine."

"Well, there's no one else I'd rather live with, even if you do expect me to tramp across wet, squelchy moors in the pouring rain, and carry a baby I didn't want, and… and…"

"Not forgetting Coventry!"

"You're impossible!"

"But you love me?"

"Would I be here, if I didn't!"

***

The boys were glad to see them, full of chatter, obviously happy and well cared for. Dominic seemed much more independent. He ate with a spoon rather than his hands. He was clean and dry – though Eleanor had still been putting a nappy on him at night. He was speaking clearly.

He had become a little boy rather than Antonia's baby. But he was still his happy, affectionate self, accepting kisses and cuddles.

"You've achieved wonders" James said to Hugo. "It's high time Antonia allowed Dominic to grow up before she has the new baby to care for."

They were sauntering down through the orchard, observing the rescued hens scratching and pecking. They already looked happier. Presently Luca came running after them, grabbing his father's hand, wanting to be included.

"Uncle Mike came last Sunday," Hugo mentioned. "He was very pleased with Luca's progress."

"And he's coming tomorrow! It is Sunday tomorrow, isn't it?"

"That's right, Luca. How's the tennis?"

"We've been going up every afternoon after school. He's coming along brilliantly." Hugo smiled. "It's been a real pleasure looking after them."

"I'm so glad. It was very kind of you to offer."

"So, now I've got Eleanor on my back wanting a baby of her own!"

"Any plans for the wedding?"

"I've been holding fire – the parents will want the whole shindig like they did for Margaret."

"And you don't?"

"We'd much prefer a quiet wedding... "

***

Hugo and Eleanor intended driving back after Sunday lunch They were both expected back at their respective jobs the following day. They were up early. While Hugo stowed their luggage in the car, Eleanor was chatting to the Witch and laying the breakfast table.

"I'd love a baby of my own" she said wistfully. "But Hugo keeps prevaricating – he's reluctant to upset his parents. They want this huge wedding!"

The Witch sniffed. She passed her sleeve across her nose.

"When you're dealing with people of impossibly high

moral standards" she mentioned, "Sometimes you just have to take matters into your own hands. Present him with a *fait accompli!*"

"Isn't that rather dishonest?"

"Accidents will happen" murmured the Witch, "when you least expect them..." Her frying pan sizzled as she added several rashers of bacon. "How long have you been together?"

"Well, in the time we've been an item, his sister's had four babies and plans another two!"

"Quite the broody hen!" observed the Witch, piling the fried bacon onto a warmed plate and adding mushrooms, tomatoes and sliced potatoes to her pan.

"That smells good!" Hugo joined them. "Can I expect such splendid breakfasts once we get home?"

He slipped his arms around Eleanor and imprinted a kiss on the nape of her neck.

"Only if I'm eating for two!"

Hugo stepped back. He looked from Eleanor's nonchalant back to the Witch, intent on her frying pan.

"High time we went home! Looking after the little boys is giving you ideas."

"I already nurtured the ideas. I guess you can inscribe my gravestone with '*She spent her life yearning for a baby!*' "

"Hey! Hey! Don't cry, Ellie! You're still very young. There's plenty of time."

"Meanwhile your sister's expecting her fifth!"

"And Mummy's going to have her third!"

They hadn't heard Luca coming downstairs.

"Exactly!"

"Actually, Mummy's very tired and she wants her breakfast in bed. Daddy's getting Mingo dressed."

"He's been dressing himself."

"Yes, but he gets everything on the wrong way round! It's quicker if someone helps."

The back door pushed open, admitting Dr Mikilari.

"Is it Tuesday?" he asked hopefully.

"Granny only lets him have bacon on Tuesdays" Luca explained.

"Really?" Hugo was amused.

"On account of he's Jewish. He's not supposed to eat bacon."

"Poor Grandad!"

Dr Mikilari took his place at the head of the table. Luca sat beside him. Eleanor brought the highchair up to the table. She and Hugo took their places. The Witch began serving breakfast. James came downstairs, holding Dominic's hand. Progress was slow as Dominic only managed one step at a time. The Witch placed a generous plate on the highchair as James lifted his son into the seat. Dominic grabbed a sausage with one hand and a rasher of crispy bacon in the other. He beamed. Across the table, Luca was also eating with his fingers.

"That's what your cutlery's for!" prompted Hugo.

Luca grinned.

"Saves washing up!"

Twenty-Six

Five hens and a birthday

Fox arrived on the seventh of February weighing just five pounds. He lay in the palm of James's hand, a tiny scrap of humanity, fragile but healthy. If James had been anxious that Antonia might reject the baby, all such worries were dispelled as he laid the baby in her arms and watched the tenderness in her face.

Later, James brought Luca up to be introduced to his baby brother.

"My Fox!" Luca's face was alight with wonder. "He's so tiny!"

"You were that small once!"

Luca looked up at his father.

"Can I hold him?"

Carefully James placed the tiny bundle in Luca's arms. Luca gently rocked him and began singing one of the old Russian lullabies. It was a very special moment.

Dominic was not impressed. Here was his mother holding this intruder when she should have been cuddling him! James gave him extra attention, taking him down to the supermarket and letting him stand in the trolley while they scoured the isles for groceries: oats for Dr Mikilari's porrage and another tin of syrup; milk, orange juice, bread, potatoes and root vegetables, baby powder, detergent…James made finding the items on his list fun. He took Dominic up to the park. He played with him in the back garden, and discussed with Antonia whether they might start him at the Nursery.

Antonia treated Fox as if he were a precious object to be handled with extreme care. He was the price she had paid for holding James's love and her boys. She did not explain this to James, but it did not escape his attention that she displayed something akin to reverence as she cared for her baby. She was also extremely tired – far more tired than after Dominic was born. James brought her breakfast in bed.

He took it upon himself to prepare night feeds for the baby, carrying his tiny son down to the kitchen where he sat in the rocking chair in front of the Range, bonding with Fox over his bottle… and sipping the mug of coffee which the Range thoughtfully provided.

After the first two or three nights he was joined by Luca who had padded down to keep watch over his baby brother.

"I could give him his bottle" he suggested. "I did give Mingo his bottle when you and Mummy went away."

He stood leaning against his father's knee stroking the baby with a gentle finger.

"When he's had his feed, we'll go into the sitting room and you can hold him...and sing to him" James suggested. The following night Luca was already in possession of the rocking chair when James came down with Fox. James placed the baby gently into Luca's waiting arms while he prepared the bottle. Fox needed feeding at least every four hours. James did not enlighten Luca about the four a.m. feed. He allowed Luca to carry his baby brother upstairs.

"He could come and sleep in my room" Luca suggested. "I'll look after him."

"You need your sleep too" James murmured. "It's school tomorrow."

"It's school every day! And he's my brother every day!"

James took the sleeping baby from Luca and placed him in his cot, trying not to disturb Antonia.

"Would you sleep better if we move Fox into the nursery?" James suggested to Antonia.

"I don't think Dominic will be very happy about that." Dominic threw an uncharacteristic temper tantrum. There was no way he was going to share his room with the baby that now monopolised his mother. Nor was he disposed to move in with Luca. The nursery was his domain. He would fight tooth and nail – not to mention bruising kicks – to keep possession.

Luca, however, was overjoyed to have Fox's cot moved into his room.

He wanted to help bathe his baby brother, but Antonia, while allowing him to watch, insisted that Fox's bath-time was her sole prerogative. The early weeks served to deepen the bond between Luca and his father. James noticed that just as he often addressed Antonia as 'My Antoni-ni', so Luca called the baby '*My* Fox'. He adored his baby brother.

Preparations were now under way for Dominic's third birthday. Antonia's father had been invited, along with Hugo and Eleanor. Michael would come, but might be late – he had a masterclass that morning.

Luca was helping the Witch prepare the birthday tea. He sifted and stirred. He beat eggs. He sprinkled 'hundreds and thousands' over the iced cake.

"You made me a dragon that breathed fire!" he reminded the Witch. "Is Mingo having a dragon?"

"You'll have to wait and see!"

The pram was parked beside Dr Mikilari in the back garden. James was playing with Dominic. Antonia was making sandwiches for lunch.

"It's an Alfresco lunch" she told her father.

He had sent money ahead for the purchase of a pair of football boots for his grandson who was determined to wear them all day.

Hugo and Eleanor arrived shortly after and made their way through to the back garden. James glanced at Eleanor, surprise followed by a slow smile.

"Congratulations!" he murmured.

Eleanor looked radiant. Hugo looked proud. From her bag Eleanor drew out the three-month scan.

"Meet our baby!"

"Let me see!" suddenly Luca was there, tugging on Eleanor's arm. "I want to see the baby!"

"Of course you do!" she bent down to show him.

"That's a baby?" He looked disappointed.

"Baby's tucked up in Ellie's tummy" explained Hugo. "It's a bit blurry. Now, are you going to show us Fox!"

Over tea, which was spread on the table in the courtyard, Luca asked:

"What will you call your baby?"

"Faye" answered Hugo.

"After *Fait Accompli*" Eleanor grinned impishly at him. The Witch hid a smile in her sleeve.

"When's she due? I take it that Faye is a girl's name?"

"August."

"Yes!" Eleanor bounced on her chair. "Since Dominic's had a baby brother for his birthday, we thought it only fair that Luca should have a baby to celebrate his fifth birthday."

Hugo and Eleanor had brought a starter trike for Dominic. It had no pedals, but could be scooted along. It was an instant success. He particularly enjoyed scooting along the lane to the park and, once he had started at Nursery, he insisted on riding there and back.

Michael arrived just as Cyril Thogmorton was leaving. He scooped Luca up for a violin lesson in Antonia's study. Hugo played football with Dominic. Eleanor came upstairs with Antonia and watched her bathing Fox.

"Isn't he a little treasure!"

"I'm just so bloody tired!"

"But James helps?"

"Oh yes, James is wonderful. But I didn't really want another baby."

"The offer to adopt him still stands!"

"You'd have a fight on your hands! Luca adores him."

"What about Dominic?"

"His nose is really out of joint! James spends a lot of time with him, but as far as Mingo's concerned, I'm a horrid Mummy!"

"Was Luca jealous when Dominic was born?"

"No, he's always been a Daddy's boy!"

After his lesson, Luca took Michael out to be introduced to his hens. They were not yet laying but looked much happier and less bedraggled than when they'd first arrived.

James had built them a spacious hen house which the hens had investigated but were not yet using.

"You see, there's no foxes, so they're quite safe" Luca said earnestly. He looked up at his uncle. "Are you staying tonight?"

"I thought I might … unless Hugo and Eleanor…?"

Hugo and Eleanor had expected to stay the weekend but realised that there were not enough beds.

"No, we're driving back tonight!" Hugo decided.

"No!" Dominic stamped his foot. "I want you stay!"

"We came for your birthday, Mingo. We've had a lovely time, haven't we. We'll come again soon. I expect you'll be a real whizz on your trike!"

Antonia declared herself too tired to bath Dominic, rather to Eleanor's delight. She bathed him – once they'd resolved the vexed question that football boots do not go in the bath! Dr Mikilari declared that he'd had enough excitement for one day and retired to his hammock.

James and Hugo sat nibbling cheese and biscuits in an absent-minded way until Michael and Luca came in from the garden. Eventually Eleanor came downstairs looking decidedly rumpled after Dominic's enthusiastic and prolonged goodnight kisses.

"We need to be making tracks" Hugo told her.

"And feel free to come back and practise on our boys any weekend!" James saw them off and then picked up Luca. "Alright, little man? Time for bed, I think." – One day Luca would bath himself, James reflected. He was tired too. "If you have a quick bath, you can give Fox his bottle."

Luca was disappointed that his father didn't appear to have time for their usual companionable bath-time. He accepted the compromise. However, Antonia decided that she wanted to feed Fox herself. She assumed that the reason Luca was crying was because he was overtired It had certainly been a full day! James brought Antonia up a cup of tea and then went to comfort Luca. The little boy cried brokenly into his father's shoulder unable to cope with what felt like betrayal.

"Luca, my little man, Daddy needs to go down and make supper for Uncle Mike and Mummy. Let's just sing one of Grandad's lullabies and then you need to try and go to sleep. I'll bring Fox in later. I know you'll watch over him all night."

"And I give him his midnight bottle?"

"Of course you can!" – But James hoped Luca would be sleeping soundly.

***

469

Although Michael had always declared that he was married to his music, he was keenly aware of James's happy family and Luca's phenomenal promise. He had seen Tom's family growing up and Margaret's brood. And now Hugo and Eleanor were expecting a baby. Over the weekend he watched Luca cradling his baby brother, singing to him, loving him.

Was there a void in *his* life?

Would he one day grow old and lonely?

What would it be like to have a wife whom he loved with all his heart and who, presumably, loved him? But he had no time for a relationship. He had no time to court anyone. In fact, did he even know anyone who might be a suitable prospect? He didn't think so.

"Brooding?" enquired James as they sat over a late night coffee.

"I was remembering one of my former students, Charlotte. She had a very bright future ahead of her. She used to write me long letters… Funny thing was, Jake had this idea that I should marry her! She was barely eighteen at the time, but she'd looked after him when he first came to Morton's. I suppose he had something of a crush on her…"

"Did you keep in touch? Did you answer her letters?"

"Yes, at first. I wrote to encourage her. I thought she'd stop writing once she was established, but she seemed to want to keep telling me about the places she visited, the orchestras she played with… . She wrote long descriptive letters… I began to feel she ought to move on, to make new friendships. Much as I enjoyed her letters, I wanted her to move on with her life. I began to discourage her…Just sent the odd postcard… finally stopped writing. I thought it was for the best. The tragedy is that she gave up her career to tuck herself away in the wilds of Scotland to look after her sister's child – I suppose he'd be about Luca's age. Her sister died. She seems to have made her home up there. I believe she does some teaching. It must be six or seven years since I last heard."

"Have you thought about writing?"

"What would be the point? I expect she's forgotten about me by now."

"Mike, to have someone come to mind that you've had no contact with in years, has to be significant. If you still have her address, I think you should write – just a casual, friendly letter: wondering how she is."

"She may be married by now."

"Yes, she may be. In which case she'll write and tell you. No harm done."

"I'll think about it."

"You do that! Now, I ought to see if Fox needs a feed and, I expect, you're ready for bed. You're in the double room. Luca is in the small single."

They stood up. James bent to place the fire guard in front of the glowing logs. A small pyjama clad figure came in from the kitchen, carrying the baby.

"He's ready for a feed" Luca stated. "Can I feed him? You said I could, earlier."

"It's still nice and warm in here. Sit yourself down and I'll warm his bottle."

Luca sat down carefully, gently rocking Fox. Michael prepared to leave.

"Oh, you don't have to go!" Luca told him. "You can watch me feeding Fox, if you like."

"Shouldn't you be in bed, asleep? We've got another lesson tomorrow. You want to be fresh for that!"

"I'll be fresh! Don't worry. I change Fox's nappy and take him in to Mummy. Then I help Mingo get dressed.

He's pretty rubbish if you leave him to it! Then I go down and feed my hens and talk to them... and by then Granny's getting breakfast."

"Everyone should have a Luca, don't you think!" James returned with the baby's bottle.

They watched Luca intent on his baby brother. After a moment, Luca began to sing to him.

"He reminds me so much of myself" James murmured. "Hurrying home from school, to look after you and Steve: playing with you, bathing you, reading..."

"And you use to sing to us. I remember you singing!"

"Grandad sang it to Daddy" said Luca, removing the teat from Fox's flaccid mouth. "And Daddy sang it to me...and now I sing it to Fox!" He propped the baby against his shoulder and gently patted the little back as his father had shown him.

***

Michael and Luca decided they would hold the violin lesson in the garden. James came to sit with Dr Mikilari and listen. Michael had been barely ten when he had started lessons, and had made phenomenal progress. Luca was not yet five, James reflected. He showed the same promise that little Jake, at three, had shown. Music was in their very genes. Michael was a demanding teacher, James hoped he wouldn't push Luca too hard. He expected Luca to practise for forty-five minutes every day… and Luca did.

As the lesson drew to a close, the Witch appeared with a tray of coffee for the men and a dandelion milkshake for Luca.

"My arms do ache a bit!"

Luca climbed onto James's knee and smiled gratefully at his Granny as she handed him the milkshake.

"I expect they do" James massaged Luca's right arm. "We won't expect you to play tennis this afternoon."

"Oh, they'll be better by then!"

Luca thoroughly enjoyed tennis with his father. It had become part of the special time they shared together.

***

Antonia wheeled the pram into the back garden. She smiled at her menfolk.

"Where's Dominic?" James asked, suddenly alert.

"Riding his trike."

"Where?" James had a sudden vision of his son unsupervised out in the lane.

"Along the landing and round the bedrooms."

"I don't suppose you thought to fix the stairgate in place? We don't want him hurtling downstairs." James shifted Luca off his lap. "I'd better check."

Antonia felt crushed. She bent over the pram to hide her feelings. A hand on her shoulder told her that James instinctively knew and understood. Then he was gone. Antonia drank his coffee and asked Luca how his lesson had gone. She wondered if he minded that Dominic had a trike and he didn't. Michael was chatting to his Grandfather. He seemed more relaxed than yesterday. Presently James and Dominic came out into the courtyard which was paved and therefore accessible to the trike.

***

Early evening. Michael had returned to Morton's. Antonia allowed Luca to 'help' her bathe baby Fox. He seemed much more confident in her company and chattered away to her. Giving him responsibility and treating him as if he were almost an adult seemed to work. He took everything in his stride – his music, tennis, reading… She was proud of him, but slightly overwhelmed, feeling much more comfortable with her bouncy, affectionate Dominic. She had hoped that Dominic might like to cuddle up with her while she fed Fox, but he clearly resented the attention she gave to her baby.

"Daddy's playing with Mingo" Luca informed her, following her into the bedroom.

"Perhaps you'd like to go down and ask him if he wants to bath Dominic. Actually you could both share a bath."

Thus dismissed, Luca dawdled downstairs and out to

the back garden. Dominic was kicking his ball. His aim was improving.

Luca watched for a while.

"Mummy said to ask you if you wanted to bath us."

James heard the lack of enthusiasm. Luca clearly didn't want to share a bath with his brother. He wanted his Daddy all to himself.

"Why don't you talk to the hens while I bath Mingo" he suggested.

This would give Antonia time to settle Fox into his cot and be ready to offer Dominic some much needed Mummy-time, while He and Luca shared a bath.

"Yes please" Luca murmured just as if James had spoken aloud.

Twenty-Seven

I'd let my golden chances pass me by

"Did you write to Charlotte?" enquired James casually, a couple of weekends later.

"Thought about it." – in fact, Michael had made several attempts which had been discarded, scrumpled up and thrown into his waste paper basket.

"Even a postcard would be a start."

"Stop, hassling me!" Michael was irritated.

Luca wandered in from the study where he had been practising.

"Procrastination is the thief of time" he announced with panache.

"For goodness sake, Luca! Do you even know what that means?"

Luca observed his uncle with surprise.

"It's letting your golden chances escape."

"What?"

"It's something Mummy sings: like" and in a sweet treble he sang:

"Longing to tell you, but afraid and shy,
I'd let my golden chances pass me by!"

Michael looked considerably startled. James concealed a smile.

"It comes from a Musical called *South Pacific*" he told his brother. Rather apt in the circumstances."

"Where does Luca get these long words from!"

"It must be inherited from Antonia. She's the one with words."

"Might you like a game of chess?" Luca addressed his father.

"It's nearly your bedtime" James observed. "Have you said goodnight to the hens?"

Luca sighed. He trailed off… running back excitedly:

"Daddy! One of my hens laid an egg! Look!"

"Why don't you ask Granny to cook it for your breakfast!"

***

"What's the name of the place where your Charlotte lives?"

"She isn't *my* Charlotte!"

"Okay. I'm sorry."

"It's just a little nowhere place. D'you have an A – Z?" James produced a book of road maps and observed his brother locating the village with an ease that belied his feigned indifference.

"Right on the coast…heck of a long drive! You'd need more than a weekend."

"Well, I couldn't attempt a visit in term time. Obviously. Perhaps in the summer holidays…" He sounded uncertain.

"May I suggest that if you sent that postcard, you'd know long before the summer holidays whether a visit is appropriate."

"Or, maybe not." Michael shrugged.

"Well, you'll never know unless you explore the possibility."

"It's alright for you! You never had to go looking for a wife! They just fell into your lap."

"Actually, Antonia didn't even want to marry me. She didn't do commitment."

"So, what changed her mind?".

"I died!" James gave a rueful smile. "And Antonia discovered that she couldn't live without me!"

"Bit drastic!"

"The boys are a real miracle. I didn't think we'd be able to have children."

"I wouldn't mind a son like Luca."

"Just get that letter written. You never know, things might just fall into place."

The spring term at Morton's became busy. Pressures piled up. For long stretches of time Michael did not entertain further thoughts about Charlotte. He was involved in preparing students for their exams and graduations. There were concerts, testimonials to write, advice and guidance to offer…He tried to come over to give Luca a lesson on Sunday afternoons, but rarely stayed beyond tea. The all-important letter was not written. The possibility not pursued.

***

Luca was given a bicycle for his fifth birthday. Initially he rode in the garden on grass, so that he would not hurt himself too much when he fell off. He progressed to riding up the lane to the tennis courts, with a steadying hand from James. Inevitably, there came a day when he picked up speed, hit a rut in the road and flew over the handlebars, skinning his knees, spraining his wrist and suffering a nasty abrasion to his forehead. James bathed his cuts and bandaged his wrist.

"You won't be able to play your violin for a few weeks" he observed.

"Will Uncle Mike be cross?"

"It was an accident. He'll understand."

Michael, however, was extremely put out. He scolded Luca, reducing him to tears. Luca hid in the hen house and cried.

"You're driving yourself too hard" James said gently.

"I know you're under a lot of pressure. Give yourself a break. Just come and spend time with us, without feeling you've got to concentrate on Luca."

He refrained from enquiring if Michael had written *that* letter. Dominic invited Michael to play football with him – an invitation which was politely declined.

"Go and see if Luca will play with you" suggested Antonia. "But remember he's got a hurt wrist!"

Dominic set off to look for his brother, eventually discovering him in the hen house. He came running back to the adults, covered in wisps of straw, flapping his arms and giving a fair imitation of a cockerel.

"I'm a hen!" he shouted gleefully, forgetting his football.

***

Antonia's father suggested that she might bring Luca up to see him. They would have a day out in London. Perhaps they would go to the zoo. Did Antonia think Luca would be interested in the Tower of London? Maybe a ride down the Thames to Greenwich?

Dominic kicked up a fuss, sensing that he was missing out.

"He might fancy a ride on my broomstick?" suggested the Witch.

"I remember when you took Tom off riding and crashed into a tree. Dad was furious!"

"Mikil was pretty upset with me too!" agreed the Witch unrepentantly.

Antonia drove up to her flat and initiated Luca into the joy of Underground trains. They met her father at Regents Park Zoo. Luca was enthralled by seeing a real tiger.

"He's so big!" he exclaimed, awed.

"You certainly wouldn't want him sleeping on your bed!"

Antonia was hoping that Luca would soon outgrow the moth-eaten old tiger skin he insisted on sharing his bed. Luca stood for a long time in front of the Tiger enclosure and had almost to be prised away to see the other animals. Clearly the zoo was a huge success.

Cyril Throgmorton was impressed by Luca's table manners as they ate lunch at the outdoor café. Luca chattered away to his Grandfather.

"Of course, I can't play my violin at present" he mentioned. "And I can't play tennis or go swimming with Daddy, but we go for walks in the woods where Daddy was a little boy…and we play chess and board games after Mingo's in bed. Everything gets knocked about if *he* plays!"

"And you make jigsaws too, don't you!" – Luca was good at jigsaws.

They decided to leave the Tower of London for another day and took the boat trip down the Thames to Greenwich.

Luca was fascinated as they explored the Cutty Sark.

"Did you do this when you were little?" Luca asked his mother.

"We didn't live in England when I was five."

"Why not?"

"Your Grandad worked in different countries: Spain, France, Germany, Russia… and later America. When we go home I'll show you where all these places are on the map."

"Which country did you like best, Grandad?"

"Well, we had a good life out in America, but I'm glad I came back to England."

"Why?"

"Well, I wouldn't get to see you very often if I'd stayed out there!"

After a high tea, Antonia decided it was time to go home. Luca thanked his Grandfather and politely offered to shake hands. Mr Throgmorton saw them off at the Underground and telephoned James to advise him they were on their way home.

"What a delightful boy your son is! So interested in everything, talks so sensibly – you'd never think he's only five! And beautiful table manners! He's a real credit to you both!"

"I'm so glad you had a nice day!"

"Oh, and before I forget! A message from Luca to ask if you'd put his hens to bed because it might be after his bedtime when he gets home."

"Of course I will. Luca loves his hens."

***

"You know, Daddy, there's such a lot of unnecessary words in the dictionary!"

"Are there?"

"I think I'll make my own dictionary with only useful words."

"That'll be quite a big project. You know so many long words."

"But I'll make it a lot easier! I thought I'd make a new language. All the important words like night and day; sun, moon and stars; home, kitchen, breakfast, shopping, school…all the important words will begin with A. Then all the 'doing' words like swimming, riding, playing, sleeping, eating…they can all begin with B."

"Go on."

"Next the 'how' words like big and small, hungry, messy (like Mingo!) wet, slippery, hot and cold…they can all begin with C."

"What about 'Love'?"

"Oh, Love is such a big word! It needs a letter all to itself! I think we'll have a letter just for Love and kindness and…hope and joy… and forgiveness…"

James watched Luca silently tracing a word on the kitchen table. There was a palpable tension in the air.

"Who might you want to forgive?" he asked very quietly.

"Mummy." Luca gave a deep sigh. "I would like to love Mummy."

"That would make Mummy very happy. It makes me happy too."

"But I'll always love you best!" He looked up and smiled at his father.

"I rather thought you might!" James smiled back.

***

A year passed. Fox was now eighteen months old. Like Luca he was an early developer and already walking. Luca was now allowed to bath his little brother. He walked down the garden with Fox and they talked to the hens. Antonia spent time with Luca: they looked at a map of the world, identifying the countries where her father had been posted. She played 'Touring England' with him as a way of teaching him England's towns and cities. As his musical talent developed, she sometimes accompanied his practice on her clarinet. They had become friends. Michael came over most weekends, ostensibly to teach Luca, but James was aware of an aura of wistfulness… and still, he could not bring himself to write that all-important letter.

Sunday morning. The family roused to the aroma of frying bacon. Luca dressed Fox and together they came down to the kitchen. Dr Mikilari sat at the head of the table chatting to Michael. James came down ahead of Antonia who had gone to wake Dominic. Her bouncy, affectionate boy was something of a sleepyhead.

"I'd prefer Fox to be in his highchair" she addressed James who had his small son on his knee and was spooning cereal into him.

Luca exchanged a rueful smile with his father. They had this conversation every morning.

The Witch was busy serving everyone. Luca noticed that Grandad had been allowed bacon – much to his delight.

"It must be Tuesday!" he mentioned, exchanging a smile.

"Watch it! Or Granny might serve you a fried mouse!" James whispered.

Michael listened to their banter, saw how happy they all were... wondered, not for the first time, if he would ever... He looked up and saw the Witch watching him. As she placed a pile of toast on the table, she gave him a penetrating look. Conversation spilled around him. Hands reached for toast, for butter and marmalade. Luca decided he wanted some Dr Lyle Syrup on his toast and everyone laughed. Michael pushed back his chair and stood up. Unobserved, he quietly followed the Witch across the kitchen, out into the courtyard. Conversation around the kitchen table hardly paused. Only James noticed Michael's departure.

Twenty-Eight

Finding Charlotte

Michael looked about him. The Witch had deposited
him in the town square of a remote Scottish village. He
could detect a faint sea breeze. This must be the village
where Charlotte lived. It was still chilly, the sun was only
just skimming the rooftops. He was not sure he could
remember the address – not having expected to be so
peremptorily dumped in the town square. How was he to
find her? He had not written to tell her he was coming – if
indeed that had ever been his intention. Would he even
recognize her? It must be fifteen – maybe eighteen years
– since he'd seen her. In that time a girl could change
dramatically… He noticed that somehow his violin case
was lying at his feet. Perhaps if he began to play, someone
might come by, and he could ask them where Charlotte
lived. This was the sort of small village where everyone

knew each other. He picked up his violin, adjusted his bow and began to play. At first, he played to the empty square. Gradually, in twos and threes, people drifted into the square and stopped to listen.

One or two came forward and dropped coins into his violin case, as if he were busking.

The square began to fill up. Michael forgot himself, lost in his music. It was only the resounding applause that brought him back to himself. A small boy, about Luca's age, pushed forward and approached him.

"Are you Michael?"

"Yes. Yes, I am!" Michael stared at the boy, dumbfounded.

"Thought so!" The boy gave him an insouciant smile. "See Charlotte's got a photograph of you on her piano. She talks to it. Have you come to see her?"

"Yes!" Michael whispered.

"I'll fetch her. Does she know you're coming?"

Michael shook his head. For a wild moment he thought about stepping back into the Witch's pentagram, and fleeing.

But, for better or for worse, he was here now. He must play something for Charlotte... The Bruch had always been her favourite. He remembered her as an eager twelve year old, telling him it was her ambition to play the Bruch *like he did!*

He adjusted his violin and began to play. A sigh of pleasure ran through his impromptu audience.

Pushing through the crowd came the boy, his auburn hair falling over his forehead. Excitedly he dragged a young woman after him. If this was Charlotte, was this her son? Was she married? It was madness to have come expecting she would be unchanged. He broke off, unable to continue, stooping to replace his violin in the case. As he straightened up, she drew level. Her hand covered her mouth. Her face registered shock.

"Michael? Michael, is it…? Can it really be you?"

"Charlotte?" He reached out his hands, suddenly unsteady on his feet.

Charlotte caught his hands and held them as if she would never let go. Neither spoke. The crowd watched as the violinist pulled Charlotte hard against him, his eyes searching her face.

"Why are you here?" she whispered.

"To ask you to marry me." – he hadn't meant to say that! That was not why he was here. It was too late to retract his words – and, in any case, she might be married! Charlotte stared at him, astonished, unable to form a coherent reply. The boy arranged the violin and bow and fastened the case. Picking it up, he held it to his chest.

"You staying here all day?" he demanded.

"Oh Robbie! I'm sorry!" Charlotte pulled away. "Robbie, this is Michael…"

"Told you, didn't I!" Robbie was clearly pleased with himself.

"Michael, this is Robbie. My sister's son. She…"

"She got cancer and died" said Robbie matter of factly.

"So Robbie lives with me" Charlotte added.

The crowd began to disperse.

Charlotte pulled herself together. She invited Michael

back to her cottage. He reached out and gently touched her wet cheek.

"I'm sorry" he said, thinking the tears were for her late sister.

"No, they're happy tears! Oh Michael, it's so wonderful that you're here! I can hardly believe it!"

"I can hardly believe it either!"

"Shall we go? We've so much to catch up… and you must be freezing! You haven't even got a coat!"

"Actually," he smiled into her eyes. "Neither have you!"

They followed Robbie across the square into a narrow lane, turning out of that into a terraced street. Robbie stopped outside one of the cottages and pushed open the front door into a low-ceilinged room where a log fire burned under an old-fashioned mantle. Across the room stood Charlotte's piano and a music stand. A large framed photograph of a younger Michael stood prominently on the piano. Robbie indicated the photograph.

"Told you!" he addressed Michael. "Said she kept you on her piano and talks to you every day!"

Charlotte blushed, deeply embarrassed.

"Reckon she's sweet on you!" mentioned Robbie.

"Robbie, could you fill the kettle and put it on. I think we could all do with a hot drink."

"I didn't know if you'd still…want to see me?"
Michael sat down in a saggy chintz-covered armchair.

"Of course I did! Why d'you think I kept on writing!"

"You write such beautiful letters! I loved getting them… but I felt I was holding you back. You needed to move on with your life…"

"I didn't want to 'move on'. I wanted you!"

"That was what I was afraid of! You were eighteen – going on nineteen. You needed to grow up and forget about me."

"I didn't want to forget about you! I used to tell anyone who looked at your photograph 'That's the man I'm going to marry!' And you did write for quite a long time." Charlotte knelt at his feet. "I came back for Jake's graduation. I wanted so much to see you – but you were engulfed in your family…and in the end I realised you didn't have time for me."

"I looked for you when I could get away, but you'd gone."

He didn't tell her how disappointed he'd felt.

She took his hands in hers.

"I hoped" she said. "For years I hoped…Well, I realised that your letters were becoming more infrequent – I thought it was just that you were so busy…and then the odd postcard…and then everything sort of stopped. Did stop. And I told myself that you were never coming back for me, that you weren't interested…that…" Her head drooped. "Well, I'd come up here to take care of Robbie… I figured it made sense to stay here, away from everyone…away from you!"

"But your sister was up here. Is Robbie's father Scottish?"

"I've no idea!" she smiled up at him impishly. "See, when Rachel, found out she was pregnant, our parents were horrified. They more or less threw her out. She only came up here because we'd once been here on holiday –

and it was about as far away as she could go! I've been so lonely, Michael! All these years waiting and hoping…"

"Didn't you ever have a boyfriend in all this time?"

"I wanted you! No one else would do."

"I'm nothing special. I'm old enough to be your father!"

"You'd have had to start very young!" – that impish smile again.

Robbie appeared, carefully balancing a tray with three mugs.

"Made tea" he informed them. "Wasn't sure if you wanted sugar?" He looked at Michael.

"It's fine as it comes."

"You getting up? Or you want your tea on the floor?" he addressed Charlotte. As she made no move, he placed her mug beside her. They drank their tea.

Robbie put down his mug. With remarkable diplomacy he stood up and shrugged unto an anorak.

"Going out" he announced, "Going round Jackson's. See ya later."

"Jackson's his friend. They're almost inseparable!" Charlotte put her hand on his knee. "Where are you staying?"

"I'll probably head back this evening." – It would be Monday tomorrow.

"You can't! It must have taken you hours and hours to drive up here – or did you fly? You can't possibly go back tonight! I won't allow it! I…I need you!"

"You may well want me, but I don't think you need me." Charlotte shook her head, impatiently.

"I remember when I first came to Morton's. You were

newly appointed and they told us you'd graduated from Morton's and started out on a brilliant career. And then, the orchestra you played with…the plane crashed…and you were the only survivor. They said you'd been paralysed and no one thought you would ever walk again. They told us how brave you were, how you'd fought to be able to play again – even from a wheelchair. They told us you were a hero! And they explained that you were often in a lot of pain and might need to take classes sitting down. And I was so sorry for you and wanted to do my very best for you…I worshipped you! But, of course, I couldn't let it show!"

"A hero with feet of clay."

Charlotte looked up at him, questioningly.

"Why didn't you ever get married?" she asked. "I was so afraid you would!" Again that impish smile.

"The short answer is that I was married to my music."

"Wouldn't have stopped you having someone to love."

"Oh Charlotte! Who'd have wanted me, a crippled old has-been?"

"A wonderful, good looking, talented musician. An amazing, inspirational teacher. And, apart from a limp, as good as new!"

"Not quite, I'm afraid."

"I'd love you and take care of you…and make you happy!"

"I have to go back to Morton's. That's my work. It's what I do. And you're here, raising Robbie and…and, I think you said you teach in the local school?"

"We could move. You said you came to ask me to marry you."

"I shouldn't have said that! I'm not the right man for you, Charlotte. It was selfish of me to come. You need someone to love who will love you. I'm not that someone. I've never felt able to love – I loved the friends who died in that plane crash. Part of me died with them. I couldn't give you what you need and want. I couldn't give you children. It just wouldn't work. You'd be hurt. I'd make you unhappy. I should never have come!"

"You seem very sure how I feel!" Charlotte said bitterly. "How I'd feel hurt and unhappy. How you couldn't love me. How you're too old and knackered." She stood up, and for a moment he thought she was dismissing him. "Well, here's the thing: *you came*! You came, which means you wanted to see me. You're scared of commitment because you might get hurt – though you turn it inside out and say you're afraid of hurting me! You think it's not enough that I love you and waited all these years for you. *You've* decided that there's no room to manoeuvre, that it has to be your decision entirely. *I love you, Michael.* I want to be with you. I don't care that you're a bit crippled. I don't care that you feel unable to express love. I don't care that you're so bloody scared of relationships that you're prepared to run away from what you really want! Why else are you here?" She drew breath. "Well, since you are here, since for one unguarded moment you asked me to marry you – which you have no intention of honouring – I'm offering you a challenge: you are going to stay here overnight and just experience how it might be, with no strings, no expectation, no penalty. And if in the morning you decide that you never want to see me again, you can walk out of here a free man, and I will never bother you again."

Michael closed his eyes. She was talking about sharing her bed with him, showing him how much she loved and wanted him. And he had shrunk from telling her the real reason why he could never be the husband she longed for… And in the morning he would go back to Morton's and she would never know how much he wanted her! She was watching him, watching the emotions chasing across his face, recognizing the pain she saw there. Her anger dispersed as the morning mist.

"Michael, you're not feeling well" she said gently. And when he did not reply, "I'll make some soup. It's probably hours since you had anything to eat. I should have realised."

He let her make the soup. She was right, he did feel better with the hot soup inside him, and a thick slice of corn bread.

"That was so good!" He put down his bowl decisively, his knuckles clenched white. "There's something I ought to tell you."

"Yes?"

"Charlotte, the accident…I was paralysed for a long time, and …some things have never worked properly since…" He bit his lip. "What I'm trying to say is that I can't…I wouldn't be able to…I couldn't make love to you."

There. It was said. He hadn't even admitted this to James.

He was less of a man. He could never inflict this on Charlotte.

"Is that all?" asked Charlotte. "Do you think I wouldn't want you? Do you think I would love you any less?...Well, thank you for telling me – it must have been difficult – but it makes not a scrap of difference to how I feel about you. The challenge still stands!"

He looked at her unhappily.

"What about Robbie?"

"What about him?"

"What will he think about my staying here? Or do you sometimes have other men in your bed?"

"All the time!" She gave him that impish grin. "No, there's never been anyone but you. And Robbie knows how I feel about you. Don't worry. He's a sound sleeper. He won't know you've stayed the night until he sees you at breakfast. I know you have to go back to Morton's. I won't try to stop you. If you never come back, you'll have given me one night of being held and loved. And I shall cherish that until I'm an old lady ...but I hope you might want more."

Her voice shook a little. She turned her head impatiently, shaking away stray tears.

He stayed. He held her in his arms. He let her stroke and caress him and tell him how much she loved him. He felt he could have held her all night, close in his embrace. Perhaps he did? She was still enfolded in his arms when he awoke. He wanted to keep her there, belonging to him, wanted, cherished. She opened her eyes and smiled at him, kissed him very gently and sighed with pleasure.

"Thank you, Michael! Thank you for giving me so much happiness. It may be one night rather than a thousand, but I will never forget the joy of being held in your arms all night long."

"How long is a thousand nights?"

"Um, three hundred and sixty five is a year. So I suppose it's a trifle over three years."

"And you'd settle for a trifle over three years?"

"Oh yes! Yes!" She was all over him, laughing, crying, caressing him.

***

"You stayed the night" Robbie observed over breakfast. "Charlotte hoped you would."

"Robbie!" Charlotte reproved him.

"You don't have to kiss his photograph this morning, now he's here in person!" He watched her blush.

"But he has to go back this morning. Like I teach at the school, Michael teaches music at Morton's where I studied. We'll come and see you off. Did you fly up?"

"In a manner of speaking." He looked at her for a long time. "Might it be possible to do this again…sometime… soon?"

"I'll think about it!" Again that impish grin which he was growing to love.

"Well, if you ask me" said Robbie, addressing the marmalade jar. "You could come up on Friday evenings and stay over until Sunday evenings. Get you in practice for when you get married…if you're getting married, that is?" He watched Michael reach for her hand, and her face light up with happiness. "I told you he would come!

Now, I'm off to my mate's. I hope you come again soon!"

"Thank you, Robbie," Michael turned to Charlotte.

"I have a nephew the same age as Robbie. Perhaps they might…?"

"I have no doubt they will!" Charlotte smiled at him. She buttered a slice of toast. "I threw down a challenge last night!" Her eyes held his, "Do I win?"

His eyes teased her:

"I'll think about it!"

***

Monday evening. Michael was about to wind up his Master Class and finish for the day. His phone began ringing importunately. He picked it up impatiently.

"Michael Gregory" he said curtly.

"Mike?" – it was James.

"Give me a moment!" James could hear him dismissing a pupil. "Hello, James."

"So how did it go?"

"How did what go?" Michael's mind was still on his Master Class.

"Scotland? Charlotte? I presume that's where Granny whisked you off to?"

"Uh huh."

"So, you found Charlotte?" There was a pause. The pause went on a long time. "Mikey? Speak to me! Didn't it go as well as you hoped?"

"I need to talk to you."

"I'm listening."

"No, I mean…I need you here."

"Okay, Mikey. I'll be right over. I'll just tell Antonia I'm coming."

He would come through the pentagram. Michael picked up his violin, switched off the light, and shutting the door to the music room, limped back to his bungalow. Anxiety gnawed at him. James was the only person he could talk to about this… Filling his kettle, he set out two mugs. Meanwhile James went in search of Antonia. She had the two little ones in the bath, happily splashing each other.

"Daddy!" crowed Fox, catching sight of him.

Antonia swivelled round and looked questioningly at James.

"I have to go out for a bit. I think Mike has a problem. I'll be back in less than an hour."

"Promise?"

Hearing the insecurity in her voice, James gave her a quick hug.

"Absolutely I promise. Were you afraid I'd disappear?"

"Well, Mike was having breakfast with us, and he did exactly that – disappeared!"

"I think that's what he wants to talk about. I'll see you in an hour."

"Daddy gone" said Fox sadly. "Love Daddy."

"And Daddy loves you" Antonia reassured him.

***

"Mikey?" James stepped through the pentagram into Michael's sitting room.

"Thanks for coming. Coffee?"

James accepted a mug of coffee and sat down, waiting for Michael to tell him what was bothering him.

"Granny just dumped me in the market square of this little village. I didn't even have Charlotte's address with me..."

"Awkward! What did you do?"

"I played my violin. I thought someone would come by and I could ask. Eventually I had quite an audience – at a distance. Then, this boy, about Luca's age, came up and asked me if I was Michael!"

"Go on."

"He asked me if I'd come to see Charlotte. He'd recognized me from a photo Charlotte keeps on her piano...I never gave her a photograph. She'd cut it out of Morton's brochure and framed it. And then, he ran off to fetch her.

"That's amazing!"

"She took me back to her cottage and we talked and talked. I told her all the reasons why she should forget about me and lead her own life. Move on. She got quite angry with me and asked what right I had to decide her life for her."

He paused and drank his coffee, his hands tightening anxiously around his mug.

James waited. When it seemed that Michael could not, or would not, say more, he drank his coffee before prompting his brother to continue.

"In the end she threw down a challenge: she demanded

that I stay the night. She said that if, in the morning, I wanted to wash my hands of her, she would accept that and leave me alone…"

He was becoming distressed.

"She wanted you to sleep with her?" James suggested.

"She wanted me to hold her, to let her sleep in my arms all night long. She told me that if I had no interest in developing a relationship, she would just treasure this one night in her life when she had been held and loved."

James studied his brother, quietly waiting. Michael began wringing his hands in distress.

"Did you find you wanted her? Or did it go badly wrong?"

Michael looked up at him, haunted, distressed, wretched.

"It didn't matter before …all the years when I never made a relationship – it didn't matter that I couldn't. After the accident when I was paralysed…fighting to recover what might be possible… It didn't matter then, that I couldn't. James, I can't! I can't make love! Charlotte will want it, expect it – she'll think I don't want her. I know she said it doesn't matter, but it does! She'll want children and I won't be able to give her a child. I won't be enough for her! James, I've never loved anyone like that. I've never even seen a woman undressed. Never touched a woman. It didn't matter before, but it does now! I want to marry Charlotte and spend my life with her – I know I'm too old for her. I know I've got this gammy leg…I know all the reasons why not, but I love her!

I want her! And I can't! I can't! What kind of marriage would it be if I can't make love to my wife!"

He was crying now. James moved across to sit beside him and put an arm round his shoulders,

"Listen, Mikey. Let's just unpack this. After the accident no one thought you would ever walk again. I saw the x-rays. As a doctor, I knew it was impossible. But you were determined to do your utmost. Remember clinging to your walking frame, saying 'I *will* stand alone! I *will* stand!'. You never gave up. We put everything we had into getting you walking again. And more importantly, teaching your hands to play again, to fight for your future. You were so positive! You didn't slump in your wheelchair and say 'I can't! It's no use!' Don't condemn yourself, Mikey. Think positive. Charlotte loves you. She wants you. She understands. She's one remarkable girl! She just wanted you to hold her, make her feel loved – and if you'd simply walked away in the morning, she loves you enough to let you go. That's quite something! That girl has kept your photograph on her piano for what... eight years? Doesn't that tell you anything!" He offered Michael his handkerchief. "And this lad? Tell me about him."

"Robbie. He's her late sister's son. They're very comfortable with each other. He's about Luca's age."

"Okay, so if you never manage to have a child with Charlotte, she'd still have Robbie. However, I'm confident that if you and Charlotte are patient, don't try to *make* it happen, just let things take their course, eventually, I think, it will begin to happen as it's meant to."

"What makes you think that? I can't even masturbate!" He hunched over, his face turned away from James, deeply mortified.

"Mikey, Mikey, listen: do you remember when we brought you home – to Caroo's – and you couldn't do anything for yourself? No one thought you'd be able to do very much at all. And then Suki…" He left the sentence unfinished.

"Course I remember!" Michael said gruffly.

"We never asked what Suki did, and you didn't tell us. But you *knew* from that moment that there was life in your body." He took one of Michael's hands in his, gently massaging it with his thumb. "I'm guessing Suki seduced you?" Michael swallowed. He kept his face averted. James let a short silence elapse. "It's okay" he said softly. "I guessed a long time ago."

"She was a bloody nuisance sometimes!"

"She felt *safe* with you."

"What d'you mean?" Michael's head came up sharply.

"Your helplessness made her feel safe. Suki didn't actually like making love. She believed it was her duty as a wife. I think Tom hurt her. He wanted fireworks – the sort of response he got from Tricia. I think he deliberately hurt her. Hugo said something along those lines. I was always very gentle with her. I thought she responded to that, but eventually she told me she didn't actually like sex and wanted to have a separate bedroom…and, as you know, after Caroo died, she chose to leave me. So, you see, you being helpless meant you were no threat. She was always in control of whatever happened." He paused.

"I know she enjoyed looking after you. Actually, I rather thought you quite enjoyed her ministrations?"

"I don't remember!" Michael pulled his hand away, embarrassed and irritated. "It was Granny who made the real difference."

"Taking you to play your violin in the Back Garden?"

"Yes. That was when I began to believe I had a life, a future! She made me walk! She gave me Grandad's Stradivarius which had been lost in the crash…"

He had brightened up, seemed more himself. He sat up straight and considered his empty coffee mug. "Yes" he said reflectively. "Suki enjoyed nursing me and looking after me. It was nice that she wanted to, but she did overstep the mark a bit."

"So, Mikey, I think that given the right circumstances and a lot of patience, things will happen as they're meant to. You have explained all this to Charlotte?"

"I think I did. I was marshalling all the reasons why she wouldn't want to marry me, and I finally threw that into the mix!" He smiled ruefully. "She said it didn't matter… but it might later…when it's too late to pull out."

"Pessimist! What are you!" James sat back and stretched out his legs. "Tell you what, let's have another coffee and then I must be getting back to Antonia."

"Of course, you know this is all your fault!"

"How so?" James realised that Michael was teasing him.

"It was, one morning in particular, seeing how you are with Antonia, how much you love her…how much she loves you. And how happy you are as a family. The kitchen is alive with love and happiness – even when Granny is scolding Grandad! And it sort of hit me that I was just a lonely old has-been. I'd not only never had a proper relationship. I hadn't even noticed that I was missing out!"

"And I'll tell you something amazing! I'd actually met Antonia when she was fourteen and I was in Med School! I was out on an early morning run in Hyde Park and she was just dancing in and out of the trees like a woodland sprite. The morning you were talking about, she danced into my dreams – and I remembered her! And we had to go into the back garden and find each other again…and dance among the trees…" His face was alight with the memory.

Michael sat watching him… Finally, he remembered he was supposed to be making coffee.

"When are you seeing Charlotte again?"

"Robbie suggested I should turn up on Friday evening and stay the weekend. I think he sees himself a chief matchmaker!"

"Good for him!"

***

"Michael alright?" Antonia asked ungraciously. Cross because James had taken more than the agreed hour.

James smiled and drew Antonia into a resentful hug.

"He's going to be very alright!"

"Well, that's good." She sounded anything but pleased.

"I love you, my Antoni-ni!"

"And you think that makes everything alright! Promising me you'd be back within the hour…And when you waltz in an hour and a half later, you think you can just tell me you love me!"

"Oh Ni-ni, I'm sorry! I know I'm later than I said. But it's such good news! Michael's found someone he wants to marry!"

Antonia pulled out of his embrace, frowning.

"But he's scared of intimacy. He's either impotent or he's gay…"

"He's found someone who loves him as he is!"

"*Is* he gay?"

"No, not at all."

James wondered where she had dug that up from. Antonia shrugged. She did not hold out much belief that such a marriage would last beyond the honeymoon.

"I suppose you've invited him to bring his fiancée to meet us?"

"Not in the short term. She lives way up in Scotland. Antonia, are we having any supper?"

Antonia thought about telling him he could get his own bloody supper.

***

"Do you think he will come?" Robbie asked Charlotte as they ate tea.

"I hope so. I haven't heard from him. We'll have to wait and see."

She sounded resigned. Robbie studied her face.

"I really liked him" he offered.

"You didn't see very much of him actually."

"Well, it was *you* he came to see." He helped himself to a second slice of cake. "Have you got any pupils coming tomorrow?"

"No. I cancelled them. I was keeping the day clear for…if he came."

They sat in silence remembering the breakfast they'd shared with Michael. Six-thirty became seven-thirty… eight o'clock… Charlotte got up decisively and switched off the outside light. She busied herself in the kitchen, clearing away, washing up. Finally, at eight-thirty she sent Robbie to bed.

"He might still come tomorrow!" Robbie suggested as he hugged her good night.

Charlotte sat in one of the saggy chintz-covered armchairs and allowed herself to be overwhelmed with disappointment. She had so hoped he would come! She stood up and fetched his photograph from the piano.

"I love you so much!" she told the photograph. "I waited for you for eight long years. Is one night all the happiness I'll ever know? Please, please come back!"

Tears ran down her face. She made no effort to control them. The log burned down to glowing embers. She remained sitting in her chair, reluctant to go to bed…

It would only emphasize the emptiness of the bed-space beside her – a bed without Michael. Perhaps, in the cold light of day, he'd thought better of his proposal – if indeed, it had amounted to a proposal. She had so hoped he would come! The fire she had lit to welcome him had gone out. The scented candles she had lit in such happy anticipation had burned down. She pulled herself together and stood up to switch off the light and go to bed, when she heard a footstep outside…then a knock on the door. It wouldn't be him. Not at this hour. Without the least vestige of hope, she went to open the door.

"Michael!" she threw herself into his arms, sobbing with relief.

"Hey!" He enfolded her in an embrace. "Did you think I wasn't coming?"

She raised a tear-wet face to his. He kissed her… kissed the tears away. It was the first time he had kissed her, she realised.

"You're all wet!"

"It's pouring out there!"

"Is it? I hadn't noticed!"

"Might you offer me some tea, and I'll get these wet things off." He unwound her arms. "Is there anything to eat?"

"Bannock?"

"Sounds good."

He was hungry. She watched him devouring bannock and cheese, and downing a large mug of tea while she devoured his dear face.

"I'm afraid I let the fire go out. I could have dried your wet things on the clothes-horse."

"Please don't apologise. They'll be dry by morning." He watched her arranging his shirt, sweater and socks over an old wooden clothes-horse.

"And your trousers." She held out her hand.

"Uh…"

"You weren't planning on wearing your trousers to bed?"

"I just feel rather undressed without…"

"I'd hate for you to feel embarrassed!" That impish grin he adored. "I'll go on up, and you can remove your trousers in privacy! Don't forget to hang them on the clothes-horse!"

She was waiting for him in bed, discreetly night-gowned, the bedside light turned low. He slid in beside her pulling her warm body against his chilliness.

"Night two of my thousand nights!" she murmured.

"You've no idea how much I've longed to hold you in my arms, like this!"

"Really? You wanted me as much as I wanted you!"

"I was so afraid you'd have changed your mind… about me!" he admitted.

"Well, of course I have!!"

"What?"

"I want you always and forever! I might not let you go back to Morton's on Monday!"

"And you're alright with…that I can't…that I…?"

"Shut up, Michael! Just hold me!"

***

He held her. Weariness overwhelmed him, and he fell asleep long before sleep came to her. It did not matter that he was asleep. It was enough to hold him. She lay breathing in the faint scent of that morning's aftershave, loving him, wanting to keep him with her for always.

He woke as dawn reached cold fingers into the room and lay quietly, savouring the peace and tranquillity of early morning. Charlotte's body was warm against his, one arm flung possessively over him. She stirred and snuggled into him, her head on his shoulder, her breathing soft and regular. Would it always be like this, he wondered? There was just enough light to make out her features. He wanted to stroke her cheek... She woke abruptly, opened her eyes and smiled at him, breathing his name.

"Dear Charlotte!" he whispered, brushing his lips against hers in the lightest of butterfly kisses.

His fingers tentatively stroked her cheek. She waited.

At the village barn dances there were often wandering hands, invitations which she had always refused. Always? Well, mostly always... She waited now for Michael's hands to begin exploring her body, wanting him. But apart from stroking her cheek, he did nothing. Charlotte took his hand and pressed it to her lips, She placed his hand on her breast. Michael flinched.

"Don't you want me?" she whispered, close to tears.

"Of course I want you...but I can't..." He removed his hand and cupped her cheek. His thumb caressed her. "Just let me hold you."

Did he think it was wrong? Had someone long ago shouted at him, smacked him? Other people had become paralysed, but they hadn't lost their libido. Last weekend he had seemed so much more relaxed with her – was that because she hadn't expected anything of him, other than that he share her bed and hold her?

There was a knock at the bedroom door, startling them. The door opened.

"I brought your clothes" Robbie announced. "Your sweater's still rather damp, but your trousers are dry – they're the important thing! Can't have you coming down to breakfast with no trousers!" He placed the pile of clothes at the end of the bed, without looking at them. "I'll start the porrage. I expect you'll be down soon."

He withdrew. Michael raised himself on an elbow and smiled down at her.

"How fortunate that you don't have to come downstairs without your trousers!" She gave him that impudent grin "I love you, Michael. And don't worry, we have a thousand more nights to practise! It will come right eventually"

"Actually, it's only nine hundred and ninety eight nights! We used up two already!" His eyes teased hers. "Right now I need to use your bathroom."

The porrage was burnt. It had that distinctive taste which even a large dollop of syrup could not disguise…

"At least the toast's not burnt!" Robbie caught Charlotte's eye. "I was thinking" he said carefully. "If you could spare five pounds, I could nip down to the charity shop and find a dry sweater for Michael until his is properly dry."

Michael reached into his pocket and extracted a five pound note.

"I'd offer to come with you, but it's a bit nippy for just shirt-sleeves."

"But shirt-sleeves are ideal for washing up!" Charlotte wrinkled her nose at him, her eyes dancing with mischief.

After Robbie had scampered off, Michael pulled Charlotte into his arms and held her for a long time…

Robbie returned triumphantly with a Fair-isle sweater which looked new.

"Mrs Cameron said it's seven pounds fifty, but I can bring the rest later."

"It looks new!" exclaimed Michael, stroking the soft wool.

"It'll be Mr Davidson's – he died just a few weeks back. I expect Fiona has been sorting out his clothes."

Michael pulled the sweater over his head and stroked the sleeves.

"It's beautiful! I'd have paid a lot more for it. Are you sure that's all they want?"

"Tell you what" Charlotte gave him that impudent smile he loved, "After breakfast, why don't we introduce you to the village, and you can show Mrs Cameron how well you suit the sweater…and offer her a donation!"

Everyone was keen to be introduced to Michael. Robbie, it seemed, had told everyone who would listen about the romance. Charlotte was a much loved teacher at the local school, and popular in the village.

"We hope ye'll not be spiriting her away!" was said more than once.

They strolled down to the quayside, drawing in deep lungfuls of sea air.

"We could take the ferry over?" suggested Robbie hopefully.

"Where's it going?" asked Michael, seeing only grey sea under murky cloud.

"It goes over to the island" Charlotte told him, noticing that a light drizzle was starting. "Better leave it for another day."

"I did want to go!" Robbie's disappointment was evident.

"Do we have time to go back for anoraks?" asked Michael.

"You haven't got one!" Charlotte reminded him. "That was why you got so wet" And there's no shelter on the island."

"Does the ferry run tomorrow?"

"Probably. Let's see if the weather's better tomorrow." Robbie sighed. Michael laid a friendly hand on the boy's shoulder:

"I'm really looking forward to the ferry trip. Tell me about your island – can we explore?"

***

Sunday morning. Michael raised himself on an elbow and studied Charlotte's sleeping face. She opened her eyes and smiled at him.

"Can I bring you a morning cup of coffee?" he asked.

"I'd rather you cuddled me!"

"I can still do that, but I wanted to make you a morning drink."

"Why thank you, kind sir!"

Michael padded barefoot down to the kitchen, He

found a tray and placed two mugs on it, unhooking them from the shelf where they hung. He saw a row of three canisters variously labelled: Tea, Coffee, Sugar. He spooned coffee into the mugs and found a jug of milk in the fridge. Kettle? Where did Charlotte keep her kettle? He searched the worktop. No kettle.

Would he have to boil water in a saucepan?

"Good morning!" Robbie joined him. "Are you making coffee?"

"I would if I could find the kettle!"

"Here!" Robbie pointed to the solid old kettle sitting on the range. "Charlotte fills it before she goes to bed, and then it comes to the boil quite quickly." He picked up a tool and removed the lid on the range, sliding the heavy kettle across. "You'll need a glove to lift it!"

"I was expecting an electric kettle."

"No. This is what we use."

Observing the two mugs on the tray, Michael asked:

"Shall I make one for you?"

"I don't like coffee much. Drop a teabag into my mug. Okay?"

"Does Charlotte take sugar?"

"Not in tea, but she does in coffee. You'll get to know all this stuff." Robbie observed Michael's legs. He had good legs but not very hairy. Jackson's Dad had very hairy legs.

"You could bring your pyjamas next weekend" he mentioned, noticing that Michael was still wearing Friday's vest and underpants. "Actually you could bring a change of clothes and leave them here, now that you'll be coming every weekend…"

"Am I?" Michael had not thought that far ahead.

"Charlotte will be really disappointed if you don't come. You *are* going to marry her, aren't you?"

"We haven't actually talked about it…"

"I think you should buy her a ring. Then she'll know you want to marry her… Kettle's boiling! D'you want me to do it?" They filled the mugs. "I could start breakfast, if you're not going to be too long – or are you spending the morning making love?"

"You know a lot about it!" Michael felt distinctly embarrassed. Robbie gave him Charlotte's insouciant grin, picked up his mug and sauntered through to the living room.

"I'll be reading" he mentioned. "Don't feel you have to hurry down."

Michael carried the tray up to the bedroom, offered Charlotte a mug and relayed the conversation.

"He's very protective of you."

"He's a good kid."

"He thinks I should buy you a ring."

"He's nothing if not direct."

"Where would we go?"

"I could drive you into West… No! Why don't I give you my grandmother's ring which fits me perfectly, and you could choose a ring for me. Yes, I'd like that!"

It was not that she shrank from choosing a ring, but Jewellers tended not to display their prices. She would have been devastated if she'd selected a ring that was out of his price range. They sipped their coffee. Michael was sitting on the edge of the bed, seemingly not inclined to resume any intimacy. Charlotte repressed a wave of disappointment and smiled brightly at him.

"Robbie wanted a trip to the island" she mentioned. "Would you like a bath while I start breakfast?"

He reached across her, relieving her of her mug.

"I need you to understand that I can't be here every weekend. Some weekends I have a concert. Some weekends I'm on call – as you would remember. And I've been giving Luca violin lessons on Sundays – I'll have to arrange for him to attend Morton's on Saturdays, if they'll take him. He's certainly developing into a gifted player – but he's not yet seven. I'll come as often as I can – it's not that I don't want to be with you! You do understand?"

"Of course." Charlotte looked away, struggling with disappointment. "I know you can't be here all the time. I know Morton's has first call on your life. I understand. Now, go and have your bath."

Twenty-Nine

The long Engagement

"James," Michael sat at the kitchen table with a coffee. His hands were restless, betraying his tension. "This long distance thing isn't going to work. Charlotte wants me there every weekend and I just don't have every weekend. Besides that, I haven't been here for Luca for two weekends. I'll have to see if he can attend Morton's on a Saturday morning like Jake did."

"Jake was quite a bit older when he started going."

"I'd come over in the evenings for him, but it would be past his bedtime – he'd be too tired. What d'you reckon?"

"Could you just go up on Sundays?"

"I thought of that, but…"

James waited for the objection, but Michael just shook his head.

"You'll just have to take it more slowly. You've

established the connection…finally!" He smiled at his brother affectionately. "But Morton's is your work, your calling. You have to give that your priority. As you said, you don't have every weekend free. And there are your concerts. But there are the holidays and half-term breaks. You could take Charlotte away on holiday…"

"There's Robbie."

"Well, for that matter, you could leave Robbie with us. He's Luca's age, you said? He'll fit in."

"He's a really nice kid."

"It's early days yet. You don't have to wear yourself out rushing up all the time. One step at a time, Mikey."

"I told her I couldn't come up this weekend."

"Right. And we'd miss you if you were never here. We've got used to having you most Sundays at least." He looked up sharply, hearing footsteps on the stairs. "Luca? You should be asleep!"

"I was. I woke up. Is Uncle Mike giving me a lesson?"

"I'm sorry I haven't been here the last two weekends, Luca. We'll have a lesson after breakfast tomorrow."

"Thank you." Luca looked at his father, "Can I have a drink, Daddy?"

He waited while James made him a hot chocolate and then climbed on his knee with a contented sigh, just as Antonia came in from her study.

"Luca! What are you doing out of bed!"

"I woke up."

"He's alright. Leave him be." James made an effort. "How's your work? Have you done enough for today? Come and get a drink and sit with us."

Antonia noticed Michael. She helped herself to a coffee.

"Are you spending the weekend with us?" she asked.

Although she would not admit it, even to herself, she much preferred Michael single – not entangled with this Charlotte person. Michael was almost the brother she'd never had. She liked him being part of their weekend. And, knowing her as well as he did, all this was not lost on James.

***

Michael carried Charlotte's ring, wrapped in his handkerchief for four weeks before he discovered it lurking in his pocket. For a long moment he could not remember its significance. He had been supposed to buy her an engagement ring to seal their relationship! After some anxious nights, he prevailed upon Antonia to drive him into town and help him choose a suitable ring. Antonia was both annoyed and flattered – not least, because James had never bought her a ring.

***

"Another Gregory prodigy?" Morton's principal found his interest piqued. He agreed that the child could be assessed. The boy Jake had showed remarkable promise at a very young age… and had not disappointed.

James brought Luca over on the appointed day and sat at the back of the room while Luca performed confidently, faultlessly.

He was utterly caught up in his music. His violin sang. The principal recognized that he was in the presence of extraordinary talent. As Luca finished there was absolute silence. The men exchanged glances.

"Thank you for coming to play for us, Luca. Dr Gregory, your uncle, says that you would like to come to us on Saturdays for tuition?"

"Well, Uncle Mike's been teaching me, but now he has…other commitments at the weekends. So he isn't always free. He's going to be married."

There was a sharp intake of breath from Michael and raised eyebrows from the Principal.

"Congratulations, Michael" he said drily.

"Early days yet" Michael sounded defensive.

The Principal turned his attention back to Luca.

"You played very well, Luca. We wouldn't normally offer a place to someone your age…" He glanced at his colleagues. "How long do you practise each day?"

"An hour proper practise and then I explore."

"Tell me about 'exploring'?"

"Out in the garden, playing what the wind sings to me. It's not written down. It's just…free."

"If I asked, could you play one of these Wind-songs?" Luca looked at his uncle. Michael had discouraged his improvising, preferring him to work with the music he'd been given.

"I could" he replied cautiously. "But it sounds better outside." He hesitated. "Or I could play you one of Grandad's Russian lullabies."

Without waiting for permission, he picked up his

violin and began playing softly, almost sensuously. He played with his eyes closed, a smile on his face, playing tenderly as he often played Fox to sleep.

"Thank you, Luca. Is there anything else you would like to play to us?"

Luca thought for a moment and then he began to play something he had heard just once on Antonia's car radio. It was inexpressibly haunting. Watching him, Michael saw that Luca was listening, hearing the music as a memory. With every fibre of his being he wanted to nurture and help Luca develop his extraordinary gifting. He began to feel very torn: wanting Charlotte, but remembering how *he* had felt as a ten year old, starting out on his own musical debut when music had been the most important thing in his life.

***

"It's so long since you came, I was beginning to think you had no room in your life for me" Charlotte reproached him.

"I'm sorry! It's so difficult… Sometimes music takes over one's life and…"

"I had this stupid idea that you wanted to marry me."

"I do. I want that more than anything!"

Belatedly, he pulled out the jeweller's box from his pocket and offered it to her. It wasn't how she'd envisaged it – it seemed more as if he was paying his dues than asking her to marry him. She waited for him to take out the ring and put it on her finger. I've somehow got this all wrong, Michael thought.

"James never gave Antonia a ring at all" he said lamely.

"Bully for James!!"

"I don't know what you want me to do? Do I get down on my knees? Is that what you want?"

Charlotte pushed the box away, irritably.

"Robbie's gone to the cinema" she said inconsequentially.

"That was thoughtful of him.".

"Hardly! He didn't know you were coming."

"Well, I'm here now...I hoped you'd be pleased to see me."

Charlotte sighed. She pushed back her chair and stood up.

"I don't suppose you've eaten?" She glanced at him. "Why don't you play me something while I speak to the kitchen."

"I'm not a radio to be switched on and off!"

He was tired. This was not going well. He began to wish he hadn't come.

"We could take Robbie over to the island tomorrow.

I think it's going to be a nice day" suggested Charlotte from the kitchen. "You *are* staying?" She left the question dangling between them.

They ate. He helped her wash up. They sat across from one another by the fire, supposedly chatting. Neither comfortable with the other.

"I could go, if you'd rather?" He offered.

"And then I wouldn't see you for months!"

"Perhaps I should just come up at half term and the holidays."

"Perhaps you should." Charlotte was close to tears.

The latch lifted on the door and Robbie erupted into the cottage. His face broke into a huge grin as he saw Michael.

"Hey! I didn't know you were coming! You here for the weekend?"

"Good film?" Charlotte asked.

"Smashing!"

"Hungry?"

"No. Jackson's Dad bought us a huge bag of popcorn! I'm stuffed!"

"We thought we might take the ferry over to the island tomorrow. Would you like to ask Jackson to come too?"

"Brilliant!"

"Time you were in bed, then."

Robbie looked from Charlotte to Michael, sensing something was not quite right. Perhaps he'd interrupted something?

"Right!" He came over to hug Charlotte. "I'm so pleased Michael's here!" He beamed at Michael and scampered off up the stairs.

"Shall we have some coffee?" Charlotte suggested, sounding more like herself.

"That would be nice."

They continued sitting by the fire while they drank their coffee, watching the logs shift and settle, gradually feeling more comfortable with each other.

***

They lay side by side in Charlotte's bed, neither feeling quite able to make the first move.

"It's been too long." Michael muttered.

"It's not something you can just switch on…and off."

"Shall we just go to sleep and see how we feel in the morning?"

He was tired. It had been a long week. He sank gratefully into sleep. Charlotte lay awake, a mass of conflicting emotions. Here was the man she loved, the man she wanted to marry – and yet he was also a stranger. The last time he came, she'd lain in his arms all night, knowing herself loved and wanted. Did he not want to marry her after all? Was this more of a duty visit? Or were they back to day one when he'd been almost afraid to touch her? She lay still, waiting for sleep that did not come.

He woke abruptly in the early hours, disorientated, not knowing where he was.

"It's alright! You're here with me, Michael. You were dreaming."

She stroked his face. Still half asleep he pulled her into his arms, held her tightly, murmuring something she could not catch, and moments later had fallen asleep again.

***

Daylight filtered through the curtains. Michael opened his eyes. Charlotte was sleeping soundly. He dressed silently and crept downstairs before putting on his shoes.

Robbie was sitting at the table, shovelling cornflakes into his mouth, while engrossed in a borrowed comic. He looked up:

"Want me to make you a coffee? Porrage?" When Michael did not reply, he tried again."Are you taking Charlotte up a mug of tea?"

"She's still asleep" Michael said curtly.

He couldn't do this. Why had he ever thought it was possible? He glanced aound the room, feeling obscurely trapped.

Robbie watched him.

"You're not leaving, are you? Are you?"

Michael shook his shoulders irritably.

Robbie abandoned his cereal and his comic.

"You've only just come!" he protested. "We were going over to the island…You can't just go!" He was out of his chair, distress emanating from him. "Michael!"

He tried to block Michael's way to the door. "At least wrtite a note for Charlotte!"

He had Michael's attention.

"What would I say?"

"Tell her you love her! Tell her you'll be back very soon. Tell her you want her to be happy… You're getting married… Don't just go!"

Michael moved insistently towards the door.

"What will I tell Charlotte? I mean, you are coming back…You are coming back, aren't you? Aren't you?"

"What do you think?"

He moved seamlessly through the door. He was gone. Robbie stared after him. And then he noticed that Michael's violin had also vanished. He never went anywhere without his precious Stradivarius. He had gone. He had gone. Why had he gone? Was he coming back?

What do *you* think?